SHARPE'S DEVIL

Bernard Cornwell was born in London, raised in Essex, and now lives mainly in the USA with his wife. In addition to the hugely successful Sharpe novels, Bernard Cornwell is the author of the Starbuck Chronicles, the Warlord trilogy, the Grail Quest series and the Alfred series.

For more information about Bernard Cornwell and his books, please visit his website www.bernardcornwell.net or go to www.AuthorTracker.co.uk for exclusive updates.

D0550083

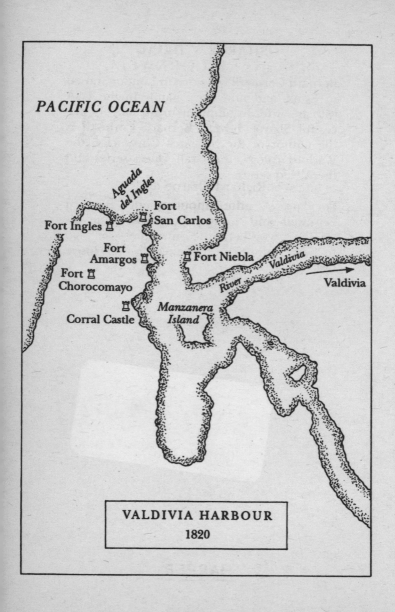

PACIFIC OCEAN

Aguada del Ingles

Fort Ingles

Fort San Carlos

Fort Amargos

Fort Niebla

Fort Chorocomayo

Valdivia

River

Valdivia

Corral Castle

Manzanera Island

VALDIVIA HARBOUR
1820

BERNARD CORNWELL

Sharpe's Devil

Richard Sharpe and
the Emperor,
1820–21

HARPER

Sharpe's Devil is for
Toby and Isabel Eady

This novel is entirely a work of fiction.
The names, characters and incidents portrayed in it are
the work of the author's imagination. Any resemblance to
actual persons, living or dead, events or localities is
entirely coincidental.

Harper
An imprint of HarperCollins*Publishers*
77–85 Fulham Palace Road,
Hammersmith, London w6 8jb

www.harpercollins.co.uk

This paperback edition 2006
1

First published in Great Britain by
HarperCollins*Publishers* 1992

A catalogue record for this book is
available from the British Library

ISBN 978-0-00-785512-4

Set in Postscript Linotype Baskerville with Meridien display by
Rowland Phototypesetting Ltd, Bury St Edmunds, Suffolk

Printed and bound in Great Britain by
Clays Ltd, St Ives plc

FOREWORD

On the night of 6 March 1815 a man escaped from the King's Bench prison in London. He did it by climbing from his cell window onto the roof, from where, with a rope made from short lengths of cord that had been smuggled into the prison, he lassooed the iron spikes topping the prison's outer wall. He tied off the other end of his rope then went, hand over hand, to the top of the wall where, balancing between the spikes, he dropped a second rope down to the street below. That second rope parted as he climbed down, leaving him stunned, but not badly injured. He vanished into the darkness. Next day wanted posters were pasted on London's walls, describing the fugitive as 'about five feet eleven inches in height, thin and narrow chested, with sandy hair and full eyes, red whiskers and eyebrows'. A reward of three hundred guineas was put on the escaped man's head.

The narrow-chested, sandy-haired man was one of the greatest heroes of the Napoleonic wars, a man who inspired both Horatio Hornblower and Captain Jack Aubrey. He was Admiral Lord Thomas Cochrane, Earl of Dundonald, and the devil of this novel's title. The bare facts of his life are sketched in the novel, so I shall not describe them here except to say his imprisonment was to do with a stock market scandal and was almost certainly prompted by his political enemies, of which he had many. He lived to see his name cleared, indeed he lived to be 85 and there is a photograph of him taken in his extreme old age and he still looks a formidable beast; he is dressed in his uniform and hung with decorations, but the face, surrounded by a mane of wild white hair, is bluntly forceful. It is very odd to look at a photograph and realise that it is the face of a man who once boarded enemy frigates. The photograph is reproduced on page 74 of Philip Haythornthwaite's *Who Was Who in the Napoleonic Wars.*

He was a great sailor and an awesome fighter, but he was never a prudent man. After the Napoleonic wars he sought out other battles and so became involved in the fights for Chilean, Brazilian and Greek independence, and this story tells of his victories in the first of those struggles. Yet, even as he was fighting against the Spanish imperialists, he was plotting to betray his Chilean employers with an improbable scheme to set up a United States of South America. Such an entity needed a ruler, and Cochrane reckoned he knew just the man. Not himself, but none other than Napoleon who was languishing on St Helena.

The year was 1821. Napoleon had been on St Helena for six years, yet he was only fifty years old. He had spent those six years laying the foundation of his legend, rewriting history to cast opportunism as glory. There were a number of wildly impractical schemes to rescue him, but none so wild as Cochrane's, yet it came nearest to fruition. Why would Cochrane even want to rescue his erstwhile enemy? I suppose because they were both adventurers and, after Waterloo, adventures were harder to come by in Europe. Thousands of men, like Cochrane, were now surplus to requirements and they were bored, yearning after the excitements of the long French wars.

Sharpe, though, is settled in Normandy. I suspect he has had enough excitement for one life, and I like to think he dies of old age in his chosen exile. No doubt, if he had been photographed in his last years, he would have looked as formidable as Cochrane. There were many like him, old soldiers and sailors who carried their memories of Waterloo and Trafalgar, Salamanca and Badajoz into the Victorian age, where, unseen by us, Sharpe must fade away.

PROLOGUE

There were sixteen men and only twelve mules. None of the men was willing to abandon the journey, so tempers were edgy and not made any better by the day's oppressive and steamy heat. The sixteen men were waiting by the shore, where the black basalt cliffs edged the small port and where there was no wind to relieve the humidity. Somewhere in the hills there sounded a grumble of thunder.

All but one of the sixteen men were uniformed. They stood sweltering and impatient in the shade of heavily branched evergreen trees while the twelve mules, attended by black slaves, drooped beside a briar hedge that was brilliant with small white roses. The sun, climbing towards noon, shimmered in an atmosphere that smelt of roses, pomegranates, seaweed, myrtle and sewage.

Two warships, their square-cut sails turned dirty grey by the long usage of wind and rain, patrolled far offshore. Closer, in the anchorage itself, a large Spanish frigate lay to twin anchors. It was not a good anchorage, for the ocean's swells were scarcely vitiated by the embracing shore, nor was the water at the quayside deep enough to allow a great ship to moor alongside, and so the sixteen men had come ashore in the Spanish frigate's longboats. Now they waited in the oppressive windless heat. In one of the houses just beyond the rose-bright hedge a baby cried.

'More mules are being fetched. If you gentlemen will do us the honour of patience? And accept our sincerest apologies.' The speaker, a very young red-coated British

Lieutenant whose face was running with sweat, displayed too much contrition. 'We didn't expect sixteen gentlemen, you understand, only fourteen, though of course there would still have been insufficient transport, but I have spoken with the adjutant, and he assures me that extra mules are being saddled, and we do apologize for the confusion.' The Lieutenant had spoken in a rush of words, but now abruptly stopped as it dawned on him that most of the sixteen travellers would not have understood a word he had spoken. The Lieutenant blushed, then turned to a tall, scarred and dark-haired man who wore a faded uniform jacket of the British 95th Rifles. 'Can you translate for me, sir?'

'More mules are coming,' the Rifleman said in laconic, but fluent Spanish. It had been nearly six years since the Rifleman had last used the language regularly, yet thirty-eight days on a Spanish ship had made him fluent again. He turned again to the Lieutenant. 'Why can't we walk to the house?'

'It's all of five miles, sir, uphill, and very steep.' The Lieutenant pointed to the hillside above the trees where a narrow road could just be seen zig-zagging perilously up the flax-covered slope. 'You really are best advised to wait for the mules, sir.'

The tall Rifle officer made a grunting noise, which the young Lieutenant took for acceptance of his wise advice. 'Sir?' The Lieutenant, emboldened by the grunting noise, took a step closer to the Rifleman.

'What?'

'I just wondered.' The Lieutenant, overwhelmed by the Rifleman's scowl, stepped back. 'Nothing, sir. It doesn't signify.'

'For God's sake, boy, speak up! I won't bite you.'

'It was my father, sir. He often spoke of you and I wondered if you might recall him? He was at Salamanca, sir. Hardacre? Captain Roland Hardacre?'

'No.'

'He died at San Sebastian?' Lieutenant Hardacre added pathetically, as though that last detail might revive his father's image in the Rifleman's memory.

The scarred Rifleman made another grunting noise that might have been translated as sympathy, but was in fact the inadequate sound of a man who never knew how to react properly to such revelations. So many men had died, so many widows still wept and so many children would be for ever fatherless that the Rifleman doubted there would ever be sufficient pity for all the war's doings. 'I didn't know him, Lieutenant, I'm sorry.'

'It was truly an honour to meet you anyway, sir,' Lieutenant Hardacre said, then stepped gingerly backwards as though he might yet be attacked by the tall man whose black hair bore a badger streak of white and whose dark face was slashed by a jagged scar. The Rifleman, who was wishing he could respond more easily and sympathetically to such appeals to his memory, was called Richard Sharpe. His uniform, that might have looked shabby on a beggar's back, bore the faded insignia of a Major, though at the war's end, when he had fought at the greatest widow-making field of all, he had been a Lieutenant Colonel. Now, despite his uniform and the sword which hung at his side, he was just plain mister and a farmer.

Sharpe turned away from the embarrassed Lieutenant to stare morosely across the sun-glinting sea at the far ships which guarded this lonely, godforsaken coast. Sharpe's scar gave him a sardonic and mocking look. His companion, on the other hand, had a cheerful and genial face. He was a very tall man, even taller than Sharpe himself, and was the only man among the sixteen travellers not wearing a uniform. Instead he was dressed in a brown wool coat and black breeches that were far too thick for this tropical heat and, in consequence, the tall man, who was also hugely fat, was sweating profusely. The discomfort had evidently not affected his cheerfulness, for he gazed happily about himself at the dark cliffs, at the banyan trees, at the slave huts, at the rain clouds swelling above the black volcanic peaks, at the sea, at the small town, and at last delivered himself of his considered verdict. 'A rare old shitheap of a place, wouldn't you say?' The fat man, who was called Mister Patrick Harper and was Sharpe's companion on this voyage, had expressed the exact same sentiment at dawn when, as their ship crept on a small wind to the island's anchorage, the first light had revealed the unappealing landscape.

'It's more than the bastard deserves,' Sharpe replied, but without much conviction; merely in the tone of a man making conversation to pass the time.

'It's still a shitheap. How in Christ's name did they ever find the place? That's what I want to know. God in his heaven, but we're a million miles from anywhere on earth, so we are!'

'I suppose a ship was off course and bumped into the bloody place.'

Harper fanned his face with the brim of his broad hat. 'I wish they'd bring the bloody mules. I'm dying of the bloody heat, so I am. It must be a fair bit cooler up in them hills.'

'If you weren't so fat,' Sharpe said mildly, 'we could walk.'

'Fat! I'm just well made, so I am.' The response, immediate and indignant, was well practised, so that if any man had been listening he would have instantly realized that this was an old and oft-repeated altercation between the two men. 'And what's wrong with being properly made?' Harper continued. 'Mother of Christ, just because a man lives well there's no need to make remarks about the evidence of his health! And look at yourself! The Holy Ghost has more beef on its bones than you do. If I boiled you down I wouldn't get so much as a pound of lard for my trouble. You should eat like I do!' Patrick Harper proudly thumped his chest, thus setting off a seismic quiver of his belly.

'It isn't the eating,' Sharpe said. 'It's the beer.'

'Stout can't make you fat!' Patrick Harper was deeply offended. He had been Sharpe's sergeant for most of the French wars and now, as then, Sharpe could think of no one he would rather have beside him in a fight. But in the years since the wars the Irishman had run a hostelry in Dublin. 'And a man has to be seen drinking his own wares,' Harper would explain defensively, 'because it gives folks a confidence in the quality of what a man sells, so it does. Besides, Isabella likes me to have a bit of flesh on my bones. It shows I'm healthy, she says.'

'That must make you the healthiest bugger in Dublin!' Sharpe said, but without malice. He had not seen his friend for over three years and had been shocked when Harper had arrived in France with a belly wobbling like a sack of live eels, a face as round as the full moon and legs as thick as howitzer barrels. Sharpe himself, five years after the battle of Waterloo, could still wear his old uniform. Indeed, this very morning, taking the uniform from his sea chest, he had been forced to stab a new hole in the belt of his trousers to save them from collapsing round his ankles. He wore another belt over his jacket, but this one merely to support his sword. It felt very strange to have the weapon hanging at his side again. He had spent most of his life as a soldier, from the age of sixteen until he was thirty-eight, but in the last few years he had become accustomed to a farmer's life. From time to time he might carry a gun to scare the rooks out of Lucille's orchard or to take a hare for the pot, but he had long abandoned the big sword to its decorative place over the fireplace in the château's hall, where Sharpe had hoped it would stay forever.

Except now he was wearing the sword again, and the

uniform, and he was once more in the company of soldiers. And also of sixteen mules because four more animals had at last been found and led to the waiting men who, trying to keep their dignity, clumsily straddled the mangy beasts. The black slaves tried not to show their amusement as Patrick Harper clambered onto an animal that looked only half his own size, yet which somehow sustained his weight.

An English Major, a choleric-looking man mounted on a black mare, led the way out of the small town and onto the narrow road which made its tortuous way up the towering mountainside towards the island's interior. The slopes on either side of the road were green with tall flax plants. A lizard, iridescent in the sunlight, darted across Sharpe's path and one of the slaves, who was following close behind the mounted men, darted after the animal.

'I thought slavery had been abolished?' commented Harper, who had evidently forgiven Sharpe for the remarks about his fatness.

'In Britain, yes,' Sharpe said, 'but this isn't British territory.'

'It isn't? What the hell is it then?' Harper asked indignantly, and indeed, if the island did not belong to Britain then it seemed ridiculous for it to be so thickly inhabited with British troops. Off to their left was a barracks where three companies of redcoats were being drilled on the parade ground, to their right a group of scarlet-coated officers were exercising their horses on a hill slope, while ahead, where the valley climbed out of the thick flax into the bare uplands, a guardpost straddled the road beside an idle semaphore station. The flag above the guardpost was the British Union flag. 'Are you telling me this might be Irish land?' Harper asked with heavy sarcasm.

'It belongs to the East India Company,' Sharpe explained patiently. 'It's a place where they can supply their ships.'

'It looks bloody English to me, so it does. Except for them black fellows. You remember that darkie we had in the grenadier company? Big fellow? Died at Toulouse?'

Sharpe nodded. The black fellow had been one of the battalion's few casualties at Toulouse; killed a week after the peace treaty had been signed, only no one at the time knew of it.

'I remember he got drunk at Burgos,' Harper said. 'We put him on a charge and he still couldn't stand up straight when we marched him in for punishment next morning. What the hell was his name? Tall fellow, he was. You must remember him. He married Corporal Roe's widow, and she got pregnant and Sergeant Finlayson was taking bets on whether the nipper would be white or black. What was his name, for Christ's sake?' Harper frowned in frustration. Ever since he had met Sharpe in France they had held conversations like this, trying to flesh out the ghosts of a past that was fast becoming attenuated.

'Bastable.' The name suddenly shot into Sharpe's head. 'Thomas Bastable.'

'Bastable! That was him, right enough. He used to close his eyes whenever he fired a musket, and I never could get him out of the habit. He probably put more bullets into more angels than any soldier in history, God rest his soul. But he was a terror with the bayonet. Jesus, but he could be a terror with a spike!'

'What colour was the baby?' Sharpe asked.

'Bit of both, as far as I remember. Like milky tea. Finlayson wouldn't pay out till we had a quiet word with him behind the lines, but he was always a slippery bugger, Finlayson. Never did understand why you gave him the stripes.' Harper fell silent as the small group of uniformed men approached a shuttered house that was surrounded with a neatly-trimmed hedge. Bright flowers grew in a border either side of a pathway made from crushed sea-shells. A gardener, who looked Chinese, was digging in the vegetable patch beside the house, while a young woman, fair-haired and white-dressed, sat reading under a gazebo close to the front hedge. She looked up, smiled a familiar greeting at the red-faced Major who led the convoy of mules, then stared with frank curiosity at the strangers. The Spanish officers bowed their heads gravely, Sharpe tipped his old-fashioned brown tricorne hat, while Harper offered her a cheerful smile. 'It's a fine morning, miss!'

'Too hot, I think.' Her accent was English, her voice gentle. 'We're going to have rain this afternoon.'

'Better rain than cold. It's freezing back home, so it is.'

The girl smiled, but did not respond again. She looked down at her book and slowly turned a page. Somewhere in the house a clock struck the tinkling chimes of midday. A cat slept on a windowsill.

The mules climbed slowly on towards the guardpost. They left the flax and the banyan trees and the myrtles behind, emerging onto a plateau where the grass was sparse and brown and the few trees stunted and wind-bent. Beyond the barren grassland were sudden saw-edged peaks, black and menacing, and on one of those rocky crags was a white-walled house which had the gaunt gallows of a semaphore station built on its roof. The semaphore house stood on the skyline and, because they were backed by the turbulent dark rainclouds, its white painted walls looked unnaturally bright. The semaphore machine beside the guardhouse on the road suddenly clattered into life, its twin black arms creaking as they jerked up and down.

'They'll be telling everyone that we're coming,' said Harper happily. He was finding every mundane event of this hot day exciting.

'Like as not,' Sharpe said.

The redcoats on duty at the guardpost saluted as the Spanish officers rode past. Some smiled at the sight of the monstrous Harper overlapping the struggling mule, but their faces turned to stone when Sharpe glowered at them. Christ, Sharpe thought, but these men must be bored. Stuck four thousand miles from home with nothing to do but watch the sea and the mountains and to wonder about the small house five miles from the anchorage. 'You do realize,' Sharpe said to Harper suddenly, and with a sour expression, 'that we're almost certainly wasting our time.'

'Aye, maybe we are,' Harper, accustomed to Sharpe's sudden dark moods, replied with great equanimity, 'but we still thought it worth trying, didn't we? Or would you come all this way and stay locked up in your cabin? You can always turn back.'

Sharpe rode on without answering. Dust drifted back from his mule's hooves. Behind him the telegraph gave a last clatter and was still. In a shallow valley to Sharpe's left was another English encampment, while to his right, a mile away, a group of uniformed men exercised their horses. When they saw the approaching party of Spaniards they spurred away towards a house that lay isolated at the centre of the plateau and within a protective wall and a cordon of red-coated guards.

The horsemen, who were escorted by a single British officer, were not wearing the ubiquitous red coats of the island's garrison, but instead wore dark blue uniforms. It had been five years since Sharpe had seen such uniform jackets worn openly. The men who wore that blue had once ruled Europe from Moscow to Madrid, but now their bright star had fallen and their sovereignty was confined to the yellow stucco walls of the lonely house which lay at this road's end.

The yellow house was low and sprawling, and surrounded by dark, glossy-leaved trees and a rank garden. There was nothing cheerful about the place. It had been built as a cow shed, extended to become a summer cottage for the island's Lieutenant Governor, but now, in the dying days of 1820, the house was home to fifty prisoners, ten horses and countless numbers of rats. The house was called Longwood, it lay in the very middle of the island of St Helena, and its most important prisoner had once been the Emperor of France.

Called Bonaparte.

*   *   *

They were not, after all, wasting their time.

It seemed that General Bonaparte had an avid appetite for visitors who could bring him news of the world beyond St Helena's seventy square miles. He received such visitors after luncheon, and as his luncheon was always at eleven in the morning, and it was now twenty minutes after noon, the Spanish officers were told that if they cared to walk in the gardens for a few moments, his Majesty would receive them when he was ready.

Not General Bonaparte, which was the greatest dignity his British jailers would allow him, but his Majesty, the Emperor, would receive the visitors, and any visitor unwilling to address his Majesty as *Votre Majesté* was invited to straddle his mule and take the winding hill road back to the port of Jamestown.

The Captain of the Spanish frigate, a reclusive man called Ardiles, had bridled at the instruction, but had restrained his protest, while the other Spaniards, all of them army officers, had equably agreed to address his Majesty as majestically as he demanded. Now, as his Majesty finished luncheon, his compliant visitors walked in the gardens where toadstools grew thick on the lawn. Clouds, building up in the west, were reflected in the murky surfaces of newly-dug ponds. The English Major who had led the procession up to the plateau, and who evidently had no intention of paying any respects to General Bonaparte, had stepped in the deep mud of one of the pond banks, and now tried to scrape the dirt off his boots with his riding crop. There was a grumble of thunder from the heavy clouds above the white-walled semaphore station.

'It's hard to believe, isn't it?' Harper was as excited as a child taken to a country fair. 'You remember when we first saw him? Jesus! It was raining that day, so it was.' That first glimpse had been at the battlefield of Quatre Bras, two days before Waterloo, when Sharpe and Harper had seen the Emperor, surrounded by lancers, in the watery distance. Two days later, before the worst of the bloodletting began, they had watched Bonaparte ride a white horse along the French ranks. Now they had come to his prison and it was, as Harper had said, hard to believe that they were so close to the ogre, the tyrant, the scourge of Europe. And even stranger that Bonaparte was willing to receive them so that, for a few heart-stopping moments on this humid day, two old soldiers of Britain's army would stand in the same stuffy room as Bonaparte and would hear his voice and see his eyes and go away to tell their children and their grandchildren that they had met Europe's bogeyman face to face. They would be able to boast that they had not just fought against him for year after bitter year, but that they had stood, nervous as schoolboys, on a carpet in his prison house on an island in the middle of the South Atlantic.

Sharpe, even as he waited, found it hard to believe that Bonaparte would receive them. He had ridden all the way from Jamestown in the belief that this expedition would be met with a scornful refusal, but had consoled himself that it would be sufficient just to see the lair of the man who had once terrified all of Europe, and who was still used by women to frighten their children into obedience. But the uniformed men who opened Longwood's gates had welcomed them and a servant now brought them a tray of weak lemonade. The servant apologized for such pale refreshment, explaining that his Majesty would have liked to serve his distinguished visitors with wine, but that his British jailers were too mean to grant him a decent supply, and so the lemonade would have to be sufficient. The Spanish officers turned dark reproving glances on Sharpe, who shrugged. Above the hills the thunder growled. The English Major, disdaining to mingle with the Spanish visitors, slashed with his riding crop at a glossy-leaved hedge.

After a half hour the sixteen visitors were ushered into the house itself. It smelt dank and musty. The wallpaper of the hallway and of the billiard room beyond was stained with damp. The pictures on the wall were black and white etchings, stained and fly-blown. The house reminded Sharpe of a poor country rectory that desperately pretended to a higher gentility than it could properly afford. It was certainly a pathetically far cry from the great marble floors and mirrored halls of Paris where Sharpe and Harper, after the French surrender in 1815, had joined the soldiers of all Europe to explore the palaces of a defeated and humiliated Empire. Then, in echoing halls of glory, Sharpe had climbed massive staircases where glittering throngs had once courted the ruler of France. Now Sharpe waited to see the same man in an anteroom where three buckets betrayed the fact that the house roof leaked, and where the green baize surface of a billiard table was as scuffed and faded as the Rifleman's jacket that Sharpe had worn in special honour of this occasion.

They waited another twenty minutes. A clock ticked loudly, then wheezed as it gathered its strength to strike the half hour. Just as the clock's bell chimed, two officers wearing French uniforms with badly tarnished gold braid came into the billiard room. One gave swift instructions in French which the other man translated into bad Spanish.

The visitors were welcome to meet the Emperor, but must remember to present themselves bareheaded to his Imperial Majesty.

The visitors must stand. The Emperor would sit, but

no one else was allowed to sit in his Imperial Majesty's presence.

No man must speak unless invited to do so by his Imperial Majesty.

And, the visitors were told once again, if a man was invited to speak with his Imperial Majesty then he must address the Emperor as *votre Majesté*. Failure to do so would lead to an immediate termination of the interview. Ardiles, the dark-faced Captain of the frigate, scowled at the reiterated command, but again made no protest at it.

Sharpe was fascinated by the tall, whip-thin Ardiles who took extraordinary precautions to avoid meeting his own passengers. Ardiles ate his meals alone, and was said to appear on deck only when the weather was appalling or during the darkest night watches when his passengers could be relied on to be either sick or asleep. Sharpe had met the Captain briefly when he had embarked on the *Espiritu Santo* in Cadiz, but to some of the Spanish army officers this visit to Longwood gave them their first glimpse of their frigate's mysterious Captain.

The French officer who had translated the etiquette instructions into clumsy Spanish now looked superciliously at Sharpe and Harper. 'Did you understand anything at all?' he asked in a bad English accent.

'We understood perfectly, thank you, and are happy to accept your instructions,' Sharpe answered in colloquial French. The officer seemed startled, then gave the smallest nod of acknowledgement.

'His Majesty will be ready soon,' the first French officer said, and then the whole group waited in an awkward silence. The Spanish army officers, gorgeous in their uniforms, had taken off their bicorne hats in readiness for the imperial audience. Their boots creaked as they shifted their weight from foot to foot. A sword scabbard rapped against the bulbous leg of the billiard table. The sour Captain Ardiles, looking as malignant as a bishop caught unawares in a whorehouse, stared sourly out of the window at the black mountains, about which cannoned an ominous rumble of thunder. Harper rolled a billiard ball slowly down the table's length. It bounced off the far cushion and slowed to a stop.

Then the double doors at the far end of the room were snatched open and a servant dressed in green and gold livery stood in the entrance. 'The Emperor will receive you now,' he said, then stood aside.

And Sharpe, his heart beating as fearfully as if he again walked into battle, went to meet an old enemy.

* * *

It was all so utterly different from everything Sharpe had anticipated. Later, trying to reconcile reality with expectation, Sharpe wondered just what he had thought to find inside the yellow-walled house. An ogre? A small toad-like man with smoke coming from his nostrils? A horned devil with bloody claws? But instead, standing on a hearth rug in front of an empty fireplace, Sharpe saw a short, stout man wearing a plain green riding coat with a velvet collar, black knee breeches and coarse white stockings. In the velvet lapel of the coat was a miniature medallion of the *Légion d'Honneur*.

All those details Sharpe noticed later, as the interview progressed, but his very first impression as he went through the door and shuffled awkwardly into line, was the shock of familiarity. This was the most famous face in the world, a face repeated on a million pictures, a million etchings, a million plates, a million coins. This was a face so familiar to Sharpe that it was truly astonishing to see it in reality. He involuntarily checked and gasped, causing Harper to push him onwards. The Emperor, recognizing Sharpe's reaction, seemed to smile.

Sharpe's second impression was of the Emperor's eyes. They seemed full of amusement as though Bonaparte, alone of all the men in the room, understood that a jest was being played. The eyes belied the rest of Bonaparte's face which was plump and oddly petulant. That petulance surprised Sharpe, as did the Emperor's hair which alone was unlike his portraits. The hair was as fine and wispy as a child's hair. There was something feminine and unsettling about that silky hair and Sharpe perversely wished that Bonaparte would cover it with the cocked hat he carried under his arm.

'You are welcome, gentlemen,' the Emperor greeted the Spanish officers, a pleasantry which was translated into Spanish by a bored-looking aide. The greeting prompted, from all but the disdainful Ardiles, a chorus of polite responses.

When all sixteen visitors had found somewhere to stand the Emperor sat in a delicate gilt chair. The room was evidently a drawing room, and was full of pretty furniture, but it was also as damp as the hallway and billiard room outside. The skirting boards, beneath the water-stained wallpaper, were disfigured by tin plates that had been nailed over rat holes and, in the silence that followed the Emperor's greeting, Sharpe could hear the dry scratching of rats' feet in the cavities behind the patched wall. The house was evidently infested as badly as any ship.

'Tell me your business,' the Emperor invited the senior Spanish officer present. That worthy, an artillery Colonel named Ruiz, explained in hushed tones how their vessel, the Spanish frigate *Espiritu Santo*, was on passage from Cadiz, carrying passengers to the Spanish garrison at the Chilean port of Valdivia. Ruiz then presented the *Espiritu Santo*'s Captain, Ardiles, who, with scarcely concealed hostility, offered the Emperor a stiffly reluctant bow. The Emperor's aides, sensitive to the smallest sign of disrespect, shifted uneasily, but Bonaparte seemed not to notice or, if he did, not to care. Ardiles, asked by the

Emperor how long he had been a seaman, answered as curtly as possible. Clearly the lure of seeing the exiled tyrant had overcome Ardiles's distaste for the company of his passengers, but he was at pains not to show any sense of being honoured by the reception.

Bonaparte, never much interested in sailors, turned his attention back to Colonel Ruiz who formally presented the officers of his regiment of artillery who, in turn, bowed elegantly to the small man in the gilded chair. Bonaparte had a kindly word for each man, then turned his attention back to Ruiz. He wanted to know what impulse had brought Ruiz to St Helena. The Colonel explained that the *Espiritu Santo*, thanks to the superior skills of the Spanish Navy, had made excellent time on its southward journey and, being within a few days' sailing of St Helena, the officers on board the *Espiritu Santo* had thought it only proper to pay their respects to his Majesty the Emperor.

In other words they could not resist making a detour to stare at the defanged beast chained to its rock, but Bonaparte took Ruiz's flowery compliment at its face value. 'Then I trust you will also pay your respects to Sir Hudson Lowe,' he said drily. 'Sir Hudson is my jailer. He, with five thousand men, seven ships, eight batteries of artillery, and the ocean which you gentlemen have crossed to do me this great honour.'

While the Spanish-speaking Frenchman translated the Emperor's mixture of scorn for his jailers and insincere flattery for his visitors, Bonaparte's eyes turned towards Sharpe and Harper who, alone in the room, had not been introduced. For a second Rifleman and Emperor stared into each other's eyes, then Bonaparte looked back to Colonel Ruiz. 'So you are reinforcements for the Spanish army in Chile?'

'Indeed, your Majesty,' the Colonel replied.

'So your ship is also carrying your guns? And your gunners?' Bonaparte asked.

'Just the regiment's officers,' Ruiz replied. 'Captain Ardiles's vessel has been especially adapted to carry passengers, but alas she cannot accommodate a whole regiment. Especially of artillery.'

'So the rest of your men are where?' the Emperor asked.

'They're following on two transport ships,' Ruiz said airily, 'with their guns.'

'Ah!' The Emperor's response was apparently a polite acknowledgement of the trivial answer, yet the silence which followed, and the fixity of his smile, were a sudden reproof to these Spaniards who had chosen the comfort of Ardiles's fast frigate while leaving their men to the stinking hulks that would take at least a month longer than the *Espiritu Santo* to make the long, savage voyage around South America to where Spanish troops tried to reconquer Chile from the rebel government. 'Let us hope the rest of your regiment doesn't decide to pay me their respects.' Bonaparte broke the slightly uncomfortable air that his unspoken criticism had caused. 'Or else Sir Hudson will fear they have come to rescue me!'

Ruiz laughed, the other army officers smiled and Ardiles, perhaps hearing in the Emperor's voice an edge of longing that the other Spaniards had missed, scowled.

'So tell me,' Bonaparte still spoke to Ruiz, 'what are your expectations in Chile?'

Colonel Ruiz bristled with confidence as he expressed his eager conviction that the rebel Chilean forces and government would soon collapse, as would all the other insurgents in the Spanish colonies of South America, and that the rightful government of His Majesty King Ferdinand VII would thus be restored throughout Spain's American dominions. The coming of his own regiment, the Colonel asserted, could only hasten that royal victory.

'Indeed,' the Emperor agreed politely, then moved the conversation to the subject of Europe, and specifically to the troubles of Spain. Bonaparte politely affected to believe the Colonel's assurance that the liberals would not dare to revolt openly against the King, and his denial that the army, sickened by the waste of blood in South America, was close to mutiny. Indeed, Colonel Ruiz expressed himself full of hope for Spain's future, relishing a monarchy growing ever more powerful, and fed ever more riches by its colonial possessions. The other artillery officers, keen to please their bombastic Colonel, nodded sycophantic agreement, though Captain Ardiles looked disgusted at Ruiz's bland optimism and showed his scepticism by pointedly staring out of the window as he fanned himself with a mildewed cocked hat.

Sharpe, like all the other visitors, was sweating foully. The room was steamy and close, and none of its windows was open. The rain had at last begun to fall and a zinc bucket, placed close to the Emperor's chair, suddenly rang as a drip fell from the leaking ceiling. The Emperor frowned at the noise, then returned his polite attention to Colonel Ruiz who had reverted to his favourite subject of how the rebels in Chile, Peru and Venezuela had overextended themselves and must inevitably collapse.

Sharpe, who had spent too many shipboard hours listening to the Colonel's boasting, studied the Emperor instead of paying any attention to Ruiz's long-winded bragging. By now Sharpe had recovered his presence of mind, no longer feeling dizzy just to be in the same small room as Bonaparte, and so he made himself examine the seated figure as though he could commit the man to memory for ever. Bonaparte was far fatter than Sharpe had expected. He was not as fat as Harper, who was fat like a bull or a prize boar is fat, but instead the Emperor was unhealthily bloated like a dead beast that was swollen with noxious vapours. His monstrous pot belly, waistcoated in white, rested on his spread thighs. His face was sallow and his fine hair was lank. Sweat pricked at his forehead. His nose was thin and straight, his chin dimpled, his mouth firm and his eyes extraordinary. Sharpe knew Bonaparte was fifty years old, yet the Emperor's face looked much younger than fifty. His body, though, was that of an old sick man. It had to be the climate, Sharpe supposed, for surely no white man could keep healthy in such a steamy and oppressive heat. The rain was falling harder now, pattering on the yellow stucco wall and on the window, and dripping annoyingly into the zinc bucket. It would be a wet ride back to the harbour where the longboats waited to row the sixteen men back to Ardiles's ship.

Sharpe gazed attentively about the room, knowing that when he was back home Lucille would demand to hear a thousand details. He noted how low the ceiling was, and how the plaster of the ceiling was yellowed and sagging, as if, at any moment, the roof might fall in. He heard the scrabble of rats again, and marked other signs of decay like the mildew on the green velvet curtains, the tarnish in the silvering of a looking glass, and the flaking of the gilt on its frame. Under the mirror a pack of worn playing cards lay carelessly strewn on a small round table beside a silver-framed portrait of a child dressed in an elaborate uniform. A torn cloak, lined with a check pattern, hung from a hook on the door. 'And you, *monsieur*, you are no Spaniard, what is your business here?'

The Emperor's question, in French, had been addressed to Sharpe who, taken aback and not concentrating, said nothing. The interpreter, assuming that Sharpe had misunderstood the Emperor's accent, began to translate, but then Sharpe, suddenly dry-mouthed and horribly nervous, found his tongue. 'I am a passenger on the *Espiritu Santo*, your Majesty. Travelling to Chile with my friend from Ireland, Mister Patrick Harper.'

The Emperor smiled. 'Your very substantial friend?'

'When he was my Regimental Sergeant Major he was somewhat less substantial, but just as impressive.' Sharpe could feel his right leg twitching with fear. Why, for God's sake? Bonaparte was just another man, and a defeated one at that. Moreover, the Emperor was a man, Sharpe tried to convince himself, of no account any more. The prefect of a small French *département* had more power than Bonaparte now, yet still Sharpe felt dreadfully nervous.

'You are passengers?' the Emperor asked in wonderment. 'Going to Chile?'

'We are travelling to Chile in the interests of an old friend. We go to search for her husband, who is missing in battle. It is a debt of honour, your Majesty.'

'And you, *monsieur*?' The question, in French, was addressed to Harper. 'You travel for the same reason?'

Sharpe translated both the question and Harper's answer. 'He says that he found life after the war tedious, your Majesty, and thus welcomed this chance to accompany me.'

'Ah! How well I understand tedium. Nothing to do but put on weight, eh?' The Emperor lightly patted his belly, then looked back to Sharpe. 'You speak French well, for an Englishman.'

'I have the honour to live in France, your Majesty.'

'You do?' The Emperor sounded hurt and, for the first time since the visitors had come into the room, an expression of genuine feeling crossed Bonaparte's face. Then he managed to cover his envy by a friendly smile. 'You are accorded a privilege denied to me. Where in France?'

'In Normandy, your Majesty.'

'Why?'

Sharpe hesitated, then shrugged. '*Une femme.*'

The Emperor laughed so naturally that it seemed as though a great tension had snapped in the room. Even Bonaparte's supercilious aides smiled. 'A good reason,' the Emperor said, 'an excellent reason! Indeed, the only reason, for a man usually has no control over women. Your name, *monsieur*.'

'Sharpe, your Majesty.' Sharpe paused, then decided to try his luck at a more intimate appeal to Bonaparte. 'I was a friend of General Calvet, of your Majesty's army. I did General Calvet some small service in Naples before . . .' Sharpe could not bring himself to say Waterloo, or even to refer to the Emperor's doomed escape from Elba which, by route of fifty thousand deaths, had led to this damp, rat-infested room in the middle of oblivion. 'I did the service,' Sharpe continued awkwardly, 'in the summer of '14.'

Bonaparte rested his chin on his right hand and stared for a long time at the Rifleman. The Spaniards, resenting that Sharpe had taken over their audience with the exiled tyrant, scowled. No one spoke. A rat scampered behind the wainscot, rain splashed in the bucket, and the trade wind gusted sudden and loud in the chimney.

'You will stay here, *monsieur*,' Bonaparte said abruptly to Sharpe, 'and we will talk.'

The Emperor, conscious of the Spaniards' disgruntlement, turned back to Ruiz and complimented his officers on their martial appearance, then commiserated with their Chilean enemies for the defeat they would suffer when Ruiz's guns finally arrived. The Spaniards, all except for the scowling Ardiles, bristled with gratified pride. Bonaparte thanked them all for visiting him, wished them well on their further voyage, then dismissed them. When they were gone, and when only Sharpe, Harper, an aide-de-camp and the liveried servant remained in the room, the Emperor pointed Sharpe towards a chair. 'Sit. We shall talk.'

Sharpe sat. Beyond the windows the rain smashed malevolently across the uplands and drowned the newly-dug ponds in the garden. The Spanish officers waited in the billiard room, a servant brought wine to the audience room, and Bonaparte talked with a Rifleman.

* * *

29

The Emperor had nothing but scorn for Colonel Ruiz and his hopes of victory in Chile. 'They've already lost that war, just as they've lost every other colony in South America, and the sooner they pull their troops out, the better. That man –' this was accompanied by a dismissive wave of the hand towards the door through which Colonel Ruiz had disappeared '– is like a man whose house is on fire, but who is saving his piss to extinguish his pipe tobacco. From what I hear there'll be a revolution in Spain within the year.' Bonaparte made another scornful gesture at the billiard room door, then turned his dark eyes on Sharpe. 'But who cares about Spain. Talk to me of France.'

Sharpe, as best he could, described the nervous weariness of France; how the royalists hated the liberals, who in turn distrusted the republicans, who detested the ultra-royalists, who feared the remaining Bonapartistes, who despised the clergy, who preached against the Orleanists. In short, it was a *cocotte*, a stew pot.

The Emperor liked Sharpe's diagnosis. 'Or perhaps it is a powder keg? Waiting for a spark?'

'The powder's damp,' Sharpe said bluntly.

Napoleon shrugged. 'The spark is feeble, too. I feel old. I am not old! But I feel old. You like the wine?'

'Indeed, sir.' Sharpe had forgotten to call Bonaparte *votre Majesté*, but His Imperial Majesty did not seem to mind.

'It is South African,' the Emperor said in wonderment. 'I would prefer French wine, but of course the bastards in London won't allow me any, and if my friends do send wine from France then that hog's turd down the hill confiscates it. But this African wine is surprisingly drinkable, is it not? It is called Vin de Constance. I suppose they give it a French name to suggest that it has superb quality.' He turned the stemmed glass in his hand, then offered Sharpe a wry smile. 'But I sometimes dream of drinking a glass of my Chambertin again. You know I made my armies salute those grapes when they marched past the vineyards?'

'So I have heard, sir.'

Bonaparte quizzed Sharpe. Where was he born? What had been his regiments? His service? His promotions? The Emperor professed surprise that Sharpe had been promoted from the ranks, and seemed reluctant to credit the Rifleman's claim that one in every twenty British officers had been similarly promoted. 'But in my army,' Bonaparte said passionately, 'you would have become a General! You know that?'

But your army lost, Sharpe thought, but was too polite to say as much, so instead he just smiled and thanked the Emperor for the implied compliment.

'Not that you'd have been a Rifleman in my army,' the Emperor provoked Sharpe. 'I never had time for rifles. Too delicate a weapon, too fussy, too temperamental. Just like a woman!'

'But soldiers like women, sir, don't they?'

The Emperor laughed. The aide-de-camp, disapproving that Sharpe so often forgot to use the royal honorific, scowled, but the Emperor seemed relaxed. He teased Harper about his belly, ordered another bottle of the South African wine, then asked Sharpe just who it was that he sought in South America.

'His name is Blas Vivar, sir. He is a Spanish officer, and a good one, but he has disappeared. I fought alongside him once, many years ago, and we became friends. His wife asked me to search for him.' Sharpe paused, then shrugged. 'She is paying me to search for him. She has received no help from her own government, and no news from the Spanish army.'

'It was always a bad army. Too many officers, but good troops, if you could make them fight.' The Emperor stood and walked stiffly to the window from where he stared glumly at the pelting rain. Sharpe stood as well, out of politeness, but Bonaparte waved him down. 'So you know Calvet?' The Emperor turned at last from the rain.

'Yes, sir.'

'Do you know his Christian name?'

Sharpe supposed the question was a test to determine if he was telling the truth. He nodded. 'Jean.'

'Jean!' The Emperor laughed. 'He tells people his name is Jean, but in truth he was christened Jean-Baptiste! Ha! The belligerent Calvet is named for the original head-wetter!' Bonaparte gave a brief chuckle at the thought as he returned to his chair. 'He's living in Louisiana now.'

'Louisiana?' Sharpe could not imagine Calvet in America.

'Many of my soldiers live there.' Bonaparte sounded wistful. 'They cannot stomach that fat man who calls himself the King of France, so they live in the New World instead.' The Emperor shivered suddenly, though the room was far from cold, then turned his eyes back to Sharpe. 'Think of all the soldiers scattered throughout the world! Like embers kicked from a camp fire. The lawyers and their panders who now rule Europe would like those embers to die down, but such fire is not so easily doused. The embers are men like our friend Calvet, and perhaps like you and your stout Irishman here. They are adventurers and combatants! They do not want peace; they crave excitement, and what the filthy lawyers fear, *monsieur*, is that one day a man might sweep those embers into a pile, for then their heat would feed on each other and they would burn so fiercely that they would scorch the whole world!' Bonaparte's voice had become suddenly fierce, but now it dropped again into weariness. 'I do so hate lawyers. I do not think there was a single achievement of mine that a lawyer did not try to desiccate. Lawyers are not men. I know men, and I tell you I never met a lawyer who had real courage, a soldier's courage, a man's courage.' The Emperor closed his eyes momentarily and, when he opened them, his expression was kindly again and his voice relaxed. 'So you're going to Chile?'

'Yes, sir.'

'Chile.' He spoke the name tentatively, as though seeking a memory on the edge of consciousness. 'I well recall the service you did me in Naples,' the Emperor went on after a pause. 'Calvet told me of it. Will you do me another service now?'

'Of course, sir.' Sharpe would later be amazed that he had so readily agreed without even knowing what the favour was, but by that moment he was under the spell of a Corsican magician who had once bewitched whole continents; a magician, moreover, who loved soldiers better than he loved anything else in all the world, and the Emperor had known what Sharpe was the instant the British Rifleman had walked into the room. Sharpe was a soldier, one of the Emperor's beloved mongrels, a man able to march through shit and sleet and cold and hunger only to fight like a devil at the end of the day, then fight again the next day and the next, and the Emperor could twist such soldiers about his little finger with the ease of a master.

'A man wrote to me. A settler in Chile. He is one of your countrymen, and was an officer in your army, but in the years since the wars he has come to hold some small admiration for myself.' The Emperor smiled as though apologizing for such immodesty. 'He asked that I would send him a keepsake, and I am minded to agree to his request. Would you deliver the gift for me?'

'Of course, sir.' Sharpe felt a small relief that the favour was of such a trifling nature, though another part of him was so much under the thrall of the Emperor's genius that he might have agreed to hack a bloody path down St Helena's hillside to the sea and freedom. Harper, sitting beside Sharpe, had the same look of adoration on his face.

'I understand that this man, I can't recall his name, is presently living in the rebel part of the country,' the Emperor elaborated on the favour he was asking, 'but he tells me that packages given to the American consul in Valdivia always reach him. I gather they were friends. No one else in Valdivia, just the American consul. You do not mind helping me?'

'Of course not, sir.'

The Emperor smiled his thanks. 'The gift will take some time to choose, and to prepare, but if you can wait two hours, *monsieur*?' Sharpe said he could wait and there was a flurry of orders as an aide was despatched to find the right gift. Then Napoleon turned to Sharpe again. 'No doubt, *monsieur*, you were at Waterloo?'

'Yes, sir. I was.'

'So tell me,' the Emperor began, and thus they talked, while the Spaniards waited and the rain fell and the sun sank and the redcoat guards tightened their night-time ring about the walls of Longwood, while inside those walls, as old soldiers do, old soldiers talked.

* * *

It was almost full dark as Sharpe and Harper, soaked to the skin, reached the quayside in Jamestown where the *Espiritu Santo*'s longboats waited to take the passengers back to Ardiles's ship.

At the quayside a British officer waited in the rain. 'Mister Sharpe?' He stepped up to Sharpe as soon as the Rifleman dismounted from his mule.

'Lieutenant Colonel Sharpe.' Sharpe had been irritated by the man's tone.

'Of course, sir. And a moment of your time, if you would be so very kind?' The man, a tall and thin Major, smiled and guided Sharpe a few paces away from the curious Spanish officers. 'Is it true, sir, that General Bonaparte favoured you with a gift?'

'He favoured each of us with a gift.' Each of the Spaniards, except for Ardiles who had received nothing, had been given a silver teaspoon engraved with Napoleon's cipher, while Harper had received a silver thimble inscribed with Napoleon's symbol of a honey bee.

Sharpe, having struck an evident note of affection in the Emperor, had been privileged with a silver locket which contained a curl of the Emperor's hair.

'But you, sir, forgive me, have a particular gift?' the Major insisted.

'Do I?' Sharpe challenged the Major, and wondered which of the Emperor's servants was the spy.

'Sir Hudson Lowe, sir, would appreciate it mightily if you were to allow him to see the gift.' Behind the Major stood an impassive file of redcoats.

Sharpe took the locket from out of his pocket and pressed the button that snapped open the silver lid. He showed the Major the lock of hair. 'Tell Sir Hudson Lowe, with my compliments, that his dog, his wife or his barber can provide him with an infinite supply of such gifts.'

The Major glanced at the Spanish officers who, in turn, glowered back. Their displeasure was caused simply by the fact that the Major's presence delayed their departure, and every second's delay kept them from the comforts of the *Espiritu Santo*'s saloon, but the tall Major translated their enmity as something which might lead to an international incident. 'You're carrying no other gifts from the General?' he asked Sharpe.

'No others,' Sharpe lied. In his pocket he had a framed portrait of Bonaparte, which the Emperor had inscribed to his admirer, whose name was Lieutenant Colonel Charles, but that portrait, Sharpe decided, was none of Sir Hudson Lowe's business.

The Major bowed to Sharpe. 'If you insist, sir.'

'I do insist, Major.'

The Major clearly did not believe Sharpe, but could do

nothing about his disbelief. He stepped stiffly backwards. 'Then good day to you, sir.'

The *Espiritu Santo* weighed anchor in the next day's dawn and, under a watery sun, headed southwards. By midday the island of St Helena with its ring of warships was left far behind, as was the Emperor, chained to his rock.

And Sharpe, carrying Bonaparte's gift, sailed to a distant war.

Part One

BAUTISTA

CHAPTER 1

Captain-General Blas Vivar's wife, the Countess of Mouro-morto, had been born and raised in England, but Sharpe had first met Miss Louisa Parker when, in 1809 and with thousands of other refugees, she had been fleeing from Napoleon's invasion of northern Spain. The Parker family, oblivious to the chaos that was engulfing a continent, could grieve only for their lost Protestant Bibles with which they had forlornly hoped to convert Papist Spain. Somehow, in the weltering chaos, Miss Louisa Parker had met Don Blas Vivar who, later that same year, became the Count of Mouromorto. Miss Parker had meanwhile become a Papist, and thereafter Blas Vivar's wife. Sharpe saw neither of them again till, in the late summer of 1819, Doña Louisa Vivar, Countess of Mouromorto, arrived unannounced and unexpected in the Normandy village where Sharpe farmed.

At first Sharpe did not recognize the tall, black-dressed woman whose carriage, attended by postilions and out-riders, drew up under the château's crumbling arch. He had supposed the lavish carriage to belong to some rich person who, travelling about Normandy, had become lost in the region's green tangle of lanes and, it being late on a hot summer's afternoon, had sought out the largest farmhouse of the village for directions and, doubtless, refreshments as well. Sharpe, his face sour and unwelcom-ing, had been prepared to turn the visitors away by directing them to the inn at Seleglise, but then a dignified woman had stepped down from the carriage and pushed a veil back from her face. 'Mister Sharpe?' she had said after a few awkward seconds, and suddenly Sharpe had recognized her, but even then he found it hard to reconcile this woman's reserved and stately appearance with his memories of an adventurous English girl who had impulsively abandoned both her Protestant religion and the approval of her family to marry Don Blas Vivar, Count of Mouromorto, devout Catholic and soldier of Spain.

Who, Doña Louisa now informed Sharpe, had disappeared. Blas Vivar had vanished.

Sharpe, overwhelmed by the suddenness of the information and by Louisa's arrival, gaped like a village idiot. Lucille insisted that Doña Louisa must stay for supper, which meant staying for the night, and Sharpe was peremptorily sent about making preparations. There was no spare stabling for Doña Louisa's valuable carriage horses, so Sharpe ordered a boy to unstall the plough horses and take them to a meadow while Lucille organized beds for Doña Louisa and her maids, and rugs for Doña Louisa's coachmen. Luggage had to be unstrapped from the varnished carriage and carried upstairs where the château's two maids laid new sheets on the beds. Wine was brought up from the damp cellar, and a fine cheese, which Lucille would otherwise have sent to the market in Caen, was taken from its nettle-leaf wrapping and pronounced fit for the visitor's supper. That supper would not be much different from any of the other peasant meals being eaten in the village for the château was pretentious only in its name. The building had once been a nobleman's fortified manor, but was now little more than an overgrown and moated farmhouse.

Doña Louisa, her mind too full of her troubles to notice the fuss her arrival had prompted, explained to Sharpe the immediate cause of her unexpected visit. 'I have been in England and I insisted the Horse Guards told me where I might find you. I am sorry not to have sent you warning

of my coming here, but I need help.' She spoke peremptorily, her voice that of a woman who was not used to
deferring the gratification of her wishes.

She was nevertheless forced to wait while Sharpe's two
children were introduced to her. Patrick, aged five, offered
her ladyship a sturdy bow while Dominique, aged three,
was more interested in the ducklings which splashed at
the moat's edge. 'Dominique looks like your wife,' Louisa
said.

Sharpe merely grunted a noncommittal reply, for he
had no wish to explain that he and Lucille were not married, nor that he already had a bitch of a wife in London
whom he could not afford to divorce and who would not
decently crawl away and die. Nor did Lucille, coming to
join Sharpe and their guest at the table in the courtyard,
bother to correct Louisa's misapprehension, for Lucille
claimed to take more pleasure in being mistaken for
Madame Richard Sharpe than in using her ancient title.
However Sharpe, much to Lucille's amusement, now
insisted on introducing her to Louisa as the Vicomtesse
de Seleglise; an honour which duly impressed the Countess
of Mouromorto. Lucille, as ever, tried to disown the title
by saying that such nonsenses had been abolished in the
revolution and, besides, anyone connected to an ancient
French family could drag out a title from somewhere. 'Half
the ploughmen in France are viscounts,' the Viscountess
Seleglise said with inaccurate self-deprecation, then
politely asked whether the Countess of Mouromorto had
any children.

'Three,' Louisa had replied, and had then gone on to
explain how a further two children had died in infancy.
Sharpe, supposing that the two women would get down to
the interminable and tedious feminine business of making
mutual compliments about their respective children, had
let the conversation become a meaningless drone, but
Louisa had suprisingly brushed the subject of children

aside, only wanting to talk of her missing husband. 'He's somewhere in Chile,' she said.

Sharpe had to think for a few seconds before he could place Chile, then he remembered a few scraps of information from the newspapers that he read in the inn beside Caen Abbey where he went for dinner on market days. 'There's a war of independence going on in Chile, isn't there?'

'A rebellion!' Louisa had corrected him sharply. Indeed, she went on, her husband had been sent to suppress the rebellion, though when Don Blas had reached Chile he had discovered a demoralized Spanish army, a defeated squadron of naval ships, and a treasury bled white by corruption. Yet within six months he had been full of hope and had even been promising Louisa that she and the children would soon join him in Valdivia's citadel which served as Chile's official residence for its Captain-General.

'I thought Santiago was the capital of Chile?' Lucille, who had brought some sewing from the house, enquired gently.

'It was,' Louisa admitted reluctantly, then added indignantly, 'till the rebels captured it. They now call it the capital of the Chilean Republic. As if there could be such a thing!' And, Louisa claimed, if Don Blas had been given a chance, there would be no Chilean Republic, for her husband had begun to turn the tide of Royalist defeat. He had won a series of small victories over the rebels; such victories were nothing much to boast of, he had written to his wife, but they were the first in many years and they had been sufficient to persuade his soldiers that the rebels were not invincible fiends. Then, suddenly, there were no more letters from Don Blas, only an official despatch which said that His Excellency Don Blas, Count of Mouromorto and Captain-General of the Spanish Forces in His Majesty's dominion of Chile, had disappeared.

Don Blas, Louisa said, had ridden to inspect the fortifications at the harbour town of Puerto Crucero, the southernmost garrison in Spanish Chile. He had ridden with a cavalry escort, and had been ambushed somewhere north of Puerto Crucero, in a region of steep hills and deep woods. At the time of the ambush Don Blas had been riding ahead of his escort, and he was last seen spurring forward to escape the closing jaws of the rebel trap. The escort, driven away by the fierceness of the ambushers, had not been able to search the valley where the trap had been sprung for another six hours, by which time Don Blas and his ambushers had long disappeared.

'He must have been captured by the rebels,' Sharpe had suggested mildly.

'If you were a rebel commander,' Louisa observed icily, 'and succeeded in capturing or killing the Spanish Captain-General, would you keep silent about your victory?'

'No,' Sharpe admitted, for such a feat would encourage every rebel in South America and concomitantly depress all their Royalist opponents. He frowned. 'Surely Don Blas had aides with him?'

'Three.'

'Yet he was riding alone? In rebel country?' Sharpe's soldiering instincts, rusty as they were, recoiled at such a thought.

Louisa, who had rehearsed these questions and answers for weeks, shrugged. 'They tell me that no rebels had been seen in those parts for many months. That Don Blas often rode ahead. He was impatient, you surely remember that?'

'But he wasn't foolhardy.' A wasp crawled on the table and Sharpe slapped down hard. 'The rebels have made no proclamations about Don Blas?'

'None!' There was despair in Louisa's voice. 'And when I ask for information from our own army, I am told there is no information to be had. It seems that a Captain-General can disappear in Chile without trace! I do not even know if I am a widow.' She looked at Lucille. 'I wanted to travel to Chile, but it would have meant leaving my children. Besides, what can a woman do against the intransigence of soldiers?'

Lucille shot an amused glance at Sharpe, then looked down again at her sewing.

'The army has told you nothing?' Sharpe asked in astonishment.

'They tell me Don Blas is dead. They cannot prove it, for they have never found his body, but they assure me he must be dead.' Louisa said that the King had even paid for a Requiem Mass to be sung in Santiago de Compostela's great cathedral, though Louisa had shocked the royal authorities by refusing to attend such a Mass, claiming it to be indecently premature. Don Blas, Louisa insisted, was alive. Her instinct told her so. 'He might be a prisoner. I am told there are tribes of heathen savages who are reputed to keep white men as slaves in the forest. And Chile is a terrible country,' she explained to Lucille. 'There are pygmies and giants in the mountains, while the rebel ranks are filled by rogues from Europe. Who knows what might have happened?'

Lucille made a sympathetic noise, but the mention of white slaves, pygmies, giants and rogues had made Sharpe suspect that his visitor's hopes were mere fantasies. In the four years since Waterloo Sharpe had met scores of women who were convinced that a missing son or a lost husband or a vanished lover still lived. Many such women had received notification that their missing man had been killed, but they clung stubbornly to their beliefs; supposing that their loved one was trapped in Russia, or kept prisoner in some remote Spanish town, or perhaps had been carried abroad to some far raw colony. Invariably, Sharpe knew, such men had either settled with different women or, more likely, were long dead and buried, but it was impossible to convince their womenfolk of either harsh truth. Nor did he try to persuade Louisa now, but instead

44

asked her whether Don Blas had been popular in Chile.

'He was too honest to be popular,' Louisa said. 'Of course he had his supporters, but he was constantly fighting corruption. Indeed, that was why he was travelling to Puerto Crucero. The governor of the southern province was an enemy of Don Blas. They hated each other, and I heard that Don Blas had proof of the governor's corruption and was travelling to confront him!'

Which meant, Sharpe wearily thought, that his friend Don Blas had been fighting two enemies: the entrenched Spanish interest as well as the rebels who had captured Santiago and driven the Royalists into the southern half of the country. Don Blas had doubtless been a good enough commander to beat the rebels, but was he a clever enough politician to beat his own side? Sharpe, who knew what an honest man Don Blas was, doubted it, and that doubt convinced him still further that his old friend must be dead. It took a cunning fox to cheat the hunt, while the brave beast that turned to fight the dogs always ended up torn into scraps. 'So isn't it likely,' Sharpe spoke as gently as he could, 'that Don Blas was ambushed by his own side?'

'Indeed it's possible!' Louisa said. 'In fact I believe that is precisely what happened. But I would like to be certain.'

Sharpe sighed. 'If Don Blas was ambushed by his own side, then they are not going to reveal what happened.' Sharpe hated delivering such a hopeless opinion, but he knew it was true. 'I'm sorry, Doña Louisa, but you're never going to know what happened.' But Louisa could not accept so bleak a verdict. Her instinct had convinced her that Don Blas was alive, and that conviction had brought her into the deep, private valley where Sharpe farmed Lucille's land. Sharpe wondered how he was going to rid himself of her. He suspected it would not be easy for Doña Louisa was clearly obsessed by her husband's fate. 'Do you want me to write to the Spanish authorities?'

he offered. 'Or perhaps ask the Duke of Wellington to use his influence?'

'What good will that do?' Louisa challenged. 'I've used every influence I can, till the authorities are sick of my influence! I don't need influence, I need the truth.' Louisa paused, then took the plunge. 'I want you to go to Chile and find me that truth,' she said to Sharpe.

Lucille's grey eyes widened in surprise, while Sharpe, equally astonished at the effrontery of Louisa's request, said nothing. Beyond the moat, in the elms that grew beside the orchard, rooks cawed loudly and a house martin sliced on sabre wings between the dairy and the horse chestnut tree. 'There must be men in South America who are in a better position to search for your husband?' Lucille remarked very mildly.

'How do I trust them? Those officers who were friends of my husband have either been sent home or posted to remote garrisons. I sent money to other officers who claimed to be friends of Don Blas, but all I received in return were the same lies. They merely wish me to send more money, and thus they encourage me with hope but not with facts. Besides, such men cannot speak to the rebels.'

'And I can?' Sharpe asked.

'You can find out whether they ambushed Don Blas, or whether someone else set the trap.'

Sharpe, from all he had heard, doubted whether any rebels had been involved. 'By someone else,' he said diplomatically, 'I assume you mean the man Don Blas was riding to confront? The governor of, where was it?'

'Puerto Crucero,' Louisa said, 'and the governor's name was Miguel Bautista.' Louisa spoke the name with utter loathing. 'And Miguel Bautista is Chile's new Captain-General. That snake has replaced Don Blas! He writes me flowery letters of condolence, but the truth is that he hated Don Blas and has done nothing to help me.'

'Why did he hate Don Blas?' Sharpe asked.

'Because Don Blas was honest, and Bautista is corrupt. Why else?'

'Corrupt enough to murder Don Blas?' Sharpe asked.

'My husband is not dead!' Louisa insisted in a voice full of pain, so much pain that Sharpe, who till now had been trying to pierce her armour of certainty, suddenly realized just what anguish lay behind that self-delusion. 'He is hiding,' Louisa insisted unrealistically, 'or perhaps he is wounded. Perhaps he is with the savages. Who knows? I only know, in my heart, that he is not dead. You will understand!' This passionate appeal was directed at Lucille, who smiled with sympathy, but said nothing. 'Women know when their men die,' Louisa went on. 'They feel it. I know a woman who woke in her sleep, crying, and later we discovered that her husband's ship had sunk that very same night! I tell you, Don Blas is alive!' The cry was pathetic, yet full of vigour, tragic.

Sharpe turned to watch his son who, with little Dominique, was searching inside the open barn door for newly-laid eggs. He did not want to go to Chile. These days he even resented having to travel much beyond Caen. Sharpe was a happy man, his only worries the usual concerns of a farmer, money and weather, and he wished Louisa had not come to the valley with her talk of cavalry and ambush and savages and corruption. Sharpe's more immediate concerns were the pike that decimated the millstream trout and the crumbling sill of the weir that threatened to collapse and inundate Lucille's water meadows, and he did not want to think of far-off countries and corrupt governments and missing soldiers.

Doña Louisa, seeing Sharpe stare at his children, must have understood what he was thinking. 'I have asked for help everywhere.' She made the appeal to Lucille as much as to Sharpe. 'The Spanish authorities wouldn't help me, which is why I went to London.' Louisa, who perhaps had more faith in her English roots than she would have liked to admit, explained that she had sought the help of the British government because British interests were important in Chile. Merchants from London and Liverpool, in anticipation of new trading opportunities, were suspected of funding the rebel government, while the Royal Navy kept a squadron off the Chilean coast and Louisa believed that if the British authorities, thus well-connected with both sides of the fighting parties, demanded news of Don Blas then neither the rebels nor the Royalists would dare refuse them. 'Yet the British say they cannot help!' Louisa complained indignantly. 'They say Don Blas's disappearance is a military matter of concern only to the Spanish authorities!' So, in desperation, and while returning overland to Spain, Louisa had called on Sharpe. Her husband had once done Sharpe a great service, she tellingly reminded him, and now she wanted that favour returned.

Lucille spoke English excellently, but not quite well enough to have kept up with Louisa's indignant loquacity. Sharpe translated, and added a few facts of his own; how he did indeed owe Blas Vivar a great debt. 'He helped me once, years ago.' Sharpe was deliberately vague, for Lucille never much liked to hear of Sharpe's exploits in fighting against her own people. 'And he is a good man,' Sharpe added, knowing the compliment was inadequate, for Don Blas was more than just a good man. He was, or had been, a generous man of rigorous honesty; a man of religion, of charity, and of ability.

'I do not like asking this of you,' Louisa said in an unnaturally timid voice, 'but I know that whoever seeks Don Blas must deal with soldiers, and your name is respected everywhere among soldiers.'

'Not here, it isn't,' Lucille said robustly, though not without an affectionate smile at Sharpe, for she knew how proud he would be of the compliment just paid him.

'And, of course, I shall pay you for your trouble in going to Chile,' Louisa added.

'I couldn't possibly . . .' Sharpe began, then realized just how decrepit the farm roof was, and how much a new weir would cost, and so, helplessly, he glanced at Lucille.

'Of course Richard will go,' Lucille said calmly.

'Though not for the money,' Sharpe said gallantly.

'Don't be a fool,' Lucille intervened in English so that Louisa would understand. Lucille had already estimated the worth of Doña Louisa's black dress, and of her carriage, and of her postilions and outriders and horses and luggage, and Lucille knew only too well how desperately her château needed repairs and how badly her estate needed the investment of money. Lucille paused to bite through a thread. 'But I don't want you to go alone. You need company. You've been wanting to see Patrick, so you should write to Dublin tonight, Richard.'

'Patrick won't want to come,' Sharpe said, not because he thought his friend would truly refuse such an invitation, but rather because he did not want to raise his own hopes that his oldest friend, Patrick Harper, would give up his comfortable existence as landlord of a Dublin tavern and instead travel to one of the remotest and evidently most troubled countries on earth.

'It would be better if you did take a companion,' Louisa said firmly. 'Chile is horribly corrupt. Don Blas believed that men like Bautista were simply extracting every last scrap of profit before the war was lost, and that they did not care about victory, but only money. But money will open doors for you, so I plan to give you a sum of coin to use as bribes, and it might be sensible to have a strong man to help you protect such a fortune.'

'And Patrick is certainly strong,' Lucille said affectionately.

Thus the two women had made their decisions. Sharpe, with Harper, if his old friend agreed, would sail to Chile.

Doña Louisa would provide Sharpe with two thousand gold English guineas, a coinage acceptable anywhere in the world, and a sum sufficient to buy Sharpe whatever information he needed, then she would wait for his news in her Palace of Mouromorto in Orense. Lucille, meanwhile, would hire an engineer from Caen to construct a new weir downstream of the old; the first repair to be done with the generous fee Louisa insisted on paying Sharpe.

Who, believing that he sailed to find a dead man, was now in mid-Atlantic, on a Spanish frigate, sailing to a corrupt colony, and bearing an Emperor's gift.

*   *   *

The talk on board the *Espiritu Santo* was of victories to come and of the vengeance that would be taken against the rebels once Colonel Ruiz's guns reached the battlefields. It was artillery, Ruiz declared, that won wars. 'Napoleon understood that!' Ruiz informed Sharpe.

'But Napoleon lost his wars,' Sharpe interjected.

Ruiz flicked that objection aside. The advance in the science of artillery, he claimed, had made cavalry and infantry vulnerable to the massive destructive power of guns. There was no future, he said, in pursuing rebels around the Chilean wilderness, instead they must be lured under the massed guns of a fortress and there pulverized. Ruiz modestly disclaimed authorship of this strategy, instead praising the new Captain-General, Bautista, for the idea. 'We'll take care of Cochrane in exactly the same way,' Ruiz promised. 'We'll lure him and his ships under the guns of Valdivia, then turn the so-called rebel navy into firewood. Guns will mean the end of Cochrane!'

Cochrane. That was the name that haunted every Spaniard's fears. Sharpe heard the name a score of times each day. Whenever two Spanish officers were talking, they spoke of Cochrane. They disliked Bernardo O'Higgins, the rebel Irish general and now Supreme Director of the independent Chilean Republic, but they hated Cochrane. Cochrane's victories were too flamboyant, too unlikely. They believed he was a devil, for there could be no other explanation of his success.

In truth, Lord Thomas Cochrane was a Scotsman, a sailor, a jailbird, a politician and a rebel. He was also lucky. 'He has the devil's own luck,' Lieutenant Otero, the *Espiritu Santo*'s First Lieutenant, solemnly told Sharpe, 'and when Cochrane is lucky, the rebellion thrives.' Otero explained that it was Cochrane's naval victories that had made most of the rebellion's successes possible. 'Chile is not a country in which armies can easily march, so the Generals need ships to transport their troops. That's what that devil Cochrane has given them, mobility!' Otero stared gloomily at the wild seas ahead, then shook his head sadly. 'But in truth he is nothing but a pirate.'

'A lucky pirate, it seems,' Sharpe observed drily.

'I sometimes wonder if what we call luck is merely the will of God,' Otero observed sadly, 'and that therefore Cochrane has been sent to scourge Spain for a reason. But God will surely relent.' Otero piously crossed himself and Sharpe reflected that if God did indeed want to punish Spain, then in Lord Cochrane he had found Himself a most lethal instrument. Cochrane, when master of a small Royal Naval sloop, and at the very beginning of the French wars when Spain had still been allied with France, had captured a Spanish frigate that outgunned and outmanned him six to one. From that moment he had become a scourge of the seas; defying every Spanish or French attempt to thwart him. In the end his defeat had come, not at the hands of Britain's enemies, but at the hands of Britain's courts that had imprisoned him for fraud. He had fled the country in disgrace, to become the Admiral of the Chilean Republic's navy and such was Cochrane's reputation that, as even the *Espiritu Santo*'s officers were forced to admit, no Spanish ship dared sail alone north of

Valdivia, and those ships that sailed the waters south of Valdivia, like the *Espiritu Santo* herself, had better be well-armed.

'And we are well-armed!' the frigate's officers liked to boast. Captain Ardiles exercised the *Espiritu Santo*'s gun crews incessantly so that the passengers became sick of the heavy guns' concussion that shook the very frame of the big ship. Ardiles, perhaps enjoying the passengers' discomfort, demanded ever faster service of the guns, and was willing to expend powder barrel after powder barrel and roundshot after roundshot in his search for the perfection that would let him destroy Cochrane in battle. The frigate's officers, enthused by their reclusive Captain's search for efficiency, boasted that they would beat Cochrane's ships to pulp, capture Cochrane himself, then parade the devil through Madrid to expose him to the jeers of the citizens before he was garrotted in slow agony.

Sharpe listened, smiled, and made no attempt to mention that Lord Cochrane had fought scores of shipborne battles, while Ardiles, for all his gun practices, had never faced a real warship in a fight. Ardiles had merely skirmished with coastal brigs and pinnaces that were a fraction of the *Espiritu Santo*'s size. Captain Ardiles's dreams of victory were therefore wild, but not nearly so fantastic as the other stories that began to flourish among the *Espiritu Santo*'s nervous passengers as the ship sailed ever closer to the tip of South America. Neither Colonel Ruiz nor any of his officers had been posted to Chile before, yet they knew it to be a place of giants, of one-legged men who could run faster than racehorses, of birds larger than elephants, of serpents that could swallow a whole herd of cattle, of fish that could tear the flesh from a man's bones in seconds, and of forests which were home to tribes of savages who could kill with a glance. In the mountains, so it was reliably said, were tribes of cannibals who used women of an unearthly beauty to lure men to their feasting-pots. There were lakes of fire and rivers of blood. It was a land of winged demons and daylight vampires. There were deserts and glaciers, scorpions and unicorns, fanged whales and poisonous sea serpents. Ruiz's regimental priest, a fat syphilitic drunkard, wept when he thought of the terrors awaiting him, and knelt before the crucifix nailed to the *Espiritu Santo*'s mainmast and swore he would reform and be good if only the mother of Christ would spare him from the devils of Chile. No wonder Cochrane was so successful, the priest told Harper, when he had such devilish magic on his side.

The weather became as wild as the stories. It was supposed to be summer in these southern latitudes, yet more than one dawn brought hissing sleet showers and a thick frost which clung like icy mildew in the sheltered nooks of the *Espiritu Santo*'s upper decks. Huge seas, taller than the lanterns on the poop, thundered from astern. The tops of such waves were maelstroms of churning white water which seethed madly as they crashed and foamed under the frigate's stern.

Most of the Spanish artillery officers succumbed to seasickness. Few of the sick men had the energy to climb on deck and, in front of the scornful sailors, lower their breeches to perch on the beakhead, so instead the passengers voided their bellies and bowels into buckets that slopped and spilt until the passenger accommodations stank like a cesspit. The food did not help the ship's wellbeing. At St Helena the *Espiritu Santo* had stocked up with yams which had liquefied into rancid bags, while most of the ship's meat, inadequately salted in Spain, was wriggling with maggots. The drinking water was fouled. There were weevils in the bread. Even the wine was sour.

Sharpe and Harper, crammed together in a tiny cabin scarce big enough for a dog, were luckier than most passengers, for neither man was seasick, and both were so accustomed to soldiers' food that a return to half-rotted

53

seamen's rations gave no offence. They ate what they could, which was not much, and Harper even lost weight so that, by the time the *Espiritu Santo* hammered into a sleety wind near Cape Horn, the Irishman could almost walk through the cabin door without touching the frame on either side. 'I'm shrivelling away, so I am,' he complained as the frigate quivered from the blow of a great sea. 'I'll be glad when we reach land, devils or no devils, and there'll be some proper food to eat. Christ, but it's cold up there!'

'No mermaids in sight?'

'Only a three-horned sea serpent.' The grotesque stories of the fearful Spanish army officers had become a joke between the two men. 'It's bad up there,' Harper warned more seriously. 'Filthy bad.'

Sharpe went on deck a few moments later to find that conditions were indeed bad. The ocean was a white shambles, blown ragged by a freezing wind that came slicing off the icesheets which lay to the south. The *Espiritu Santo*, its sails furled down to mere dark scraps, laboured and thumped and staggered against the weather's malevolence. Sharpe, tired of being cooped up in the stinking 'tweendecks, and wanting some fresh air, steadied himself against the quarterdeck's starboard carronade. There were few other people on deck, merely a handful of sailors who crouched in the lee scuppers, two men who were draped in tarpaulin capes by the wheel, and a solitary cloaked figure who clung to a shroud on the weather side of the poop.

The cloaked man, seeing Sharpe, carefully negotiated a passage across the wet and heaving deck, and Sharpe, to his astonishment, saw that it was the reclusive Captain Ardiles who had not been seen by any of the passengers since the *Espiritu Santo* had left St Helena.

'Cape Horn!' Ardiles shouted, pointing off to starboard.

Sharpe stared. For a long time he could see nothing,

then an explosion of shredded water betrayed where a black scrap of rock resisted the pounding waves.

'That's the last scrap of good earth that many a sailorman saw before he drowned!' Ardiles spoke with a gloomy relish, then clutched at the tarred rigging as the *Espiritu Santo* fell sideways into the green heart of a wave's trough. He waited till the frigate had recovered and was labouring up a great slope of savaged white sea. 'So what did you think of Napoleon?' Ardiles asked Sharpe.

Sharpe hesitated, wanting his answer to be precise. 'He put me in mind of a man who has played a hugely successful joke on people he despises.'

Ardiles, who had flat, watchful eyes in a hungry, cadaverous face, thought about Sharpe's answer, then shrugged. 'Maybe. But I think he should have been executed for his joke.'

Sharpe said nothing. He could see the waves breaking on Cape Horn more clearly now, and could just make out the loom of a black cliff beyond the battered water. God, he thought, but this is a fearful place.

'They made me sick!' Ardiles said suddenly.

'Sick?' Sharpe had only half heard Ardiles's scathing words and had assumed that the frigate's Captain was talking about the seasickness which afflicted most of the army officers.

'Ruiz and the others! Fawning over that man! Jesus! But Bonaparte was our enemy. He did enough damage to Spain! If it were not for Bonaparte you think there'd be any rebellion in South America? He encouraged it! And how many more Spaniards will die for that man's evil? Yet these bastards bowed and scraped to him. Given half a chance they'd have licked his bum cleaner than a nun's finger!'

Sharpe staggered as the ship rolled. A rattle of sleet and foam shot down the deck and slammed into the poop. 'I can't say I wasn't impressed by meeting Bonaparte!' he shouted in defence of the Spanish army officers. 'He's been my enemy long enough, but I felt privileged to be there. I even liked him!'

'That's because you're English! Your women weren't raped by those French bastards, and your children weren't killed by them!' Ardiles stared balefully into the trough of a scummy wave that roared under the *Espiritu Santo*'s counter. 'So what did you talk about when you were alone with him?'

'Waterloo.'

'Just Waterloo?' Ardiles seemed remarkably suspicious.

'Just that,' Sharpe said, with an air of irritation, for it was none of Ardiles's business what he and a stricken Emperor had discussed.

Ardiles, sensing he had offended Sharpe, changed the subject by waving a hand towards the cabins where Ruiz's artillery officers sheltered from the storm in their vomit-rinsed misery. 'What do you think of officers who don't share their men's discomforts?'

Sharpe believed that officers who abandoned their men were officers on their way to defeat, but tact kept him from saying as much to the sardonic Ardiles, so instead he made some harmless comment about being no expert on Spanish shipping arrangements.

'I think such officers are bastards!' Ardiles had to shout to be heard over the numbing sound of the huge seas. 'The only reason they sailed on this ship is because the voyage will be six or eight weeks shorter! Which means they can reach the whorehouses of Valdivia ahead of their sergeants.' Ardiles spat into the scuppers. 'They're good whorehouses, too. Too good for these bastards.'

'You know Chile well?' Sharpe asked.

'Well enough! I've visited twice a year for three years. They use my ship as a passenger barge! Instead of letting me look for Cochrane and beating the shit out of him, they insist that I sail back and forth between Spain and

Valdivia! Back and forth! Back and forth! It's a waste of a good ship! This is the largest and best frigate in the Spanish navy and they waste it on ferrying shit like Ruiz!' Ardiles scowled down into the frigate's waist where the green water surged and broke ragged about the lashed guns, then he turned his saturnine gaze back to Sharpe. 'You're looking for Captain-General Vivar, yes?'

'I am, yes.' Sharpe was not surprised that Ardiles knew his business, for he had made no secret of his quest, yet he was taken aback by the abrupt and jeering manner of the Colonel's asking and Sharpe's reply had consequently been guarded, almost hostile.

Ardiles leaned closer to Sharpe. 'I knew Vivar! I even liked him! But he was not a tactful man. Most of the army officers in Chile thought he was too clever. They had their own ideas on how the war should be lost, but Vivar was proving them wrong, and they didn't like him for that.'

'Are you saying that his own side killed him?'

Ardiles shook his head. 'I think he was killed by the rebels. He was probably wounded in the ambush, his horse galloped into deep timber, and he fell off. His body's still out there; ripped apart by animals and chewed by birds. The oddest part of the whole thing, to my mind, is why he was out there with such a small escort. There were only fifteen men with him!'

'He was always a brave man.' Sharpe, who had not heard just how small the escort had been, hid his surprise. Why would a Captain-General travel with such a tiny detachment? Even in country he thought safe?

'Maybe more foolish than brave?' Ardiles suggested. 'My own belief is that he had an arrangement to meet the rebels, and that they double-crossed him.'

Sharpe, who had convinced himself that Don Blas had been murdered by his own people, found this new idea grotesque. 'Are you saying he was a traitor?'

'He was a patriot, but he was playing with fire.' Ardiles

paused, as though debating whether to say more, then he must have decided that his revelation could do no harm. 'I tell you a strange thing, Englishman. Two months after Vivar arrived in Chile he ordered me to take him to Talcahuana. That means nothing to you, so I shall explain. It is a peninsula, close to Concepción, and inside rebel territory. His Excellency's staff told Don Blas it was not safe to go there, but he scoffed at such timidity. I thought it was my chance to fight against Cochrane, so I went gladly. But two days north of Valdivia we struck bad weather. It was awful! We could not go anywhere near land; instead we rode out the storm at sea for four days. After that Don Blas still insisted on going to Talcahuana. We anchored off Punta Tombes and Don Blas went ashore on his own. On his own! He refused an escort. He just took a fowling-piece! He said he wanted to prove that a nobleman of Spain could hunt freely wherever His Spanish Majesty ruled in this world. Six hours later he returned with two brace of duck, and ordered me back to Valdivia. So what? you are asking. I will tell you what! I myself thought it was merely bravado. After all, he had made me sail for a week through waters patrolled by the rebel navy, but later I heard rumours that Don Blas had gone ashore to meet those rebels. To talk with them. I don't know if that is true, but on my voyage home with the news of Don Blas's disappearance, we captured a rebel pinnace with a dozen men aboard and two of them told me that the devil Cochrane himself had been waiting to meet Don Blas, but that after two days they decided he was not coming, and so Cochrane went away.'

'You believed them?'

Ardiles shrugged. 'Do dying men tell lies or truth? My belief, Englishman, is that they were telling the truth, and I think Don Blas died when he tried to resurrect the meeting with the rebels. But you believe Don Blas to be alive, yes?'

Sharpe hesitated, but Ardiles had favoured him with a revelation, and Sharpe's truth was nowhere near so dangerous, so he told it. 'No.'

'So why are you here?'

'Because I've been paid to look for him. Maybe I shall find his dead body?' Because even that, Sharpe had decided, would give Louisa some small comfort. It would, at the very least, offer her certainty and if Sharpe could arrange to have the body carried home to Spain then Louisa could bury Don Blas in his family's vault in the great cathedral in Santiago de Compostela.

Ardiles scoffed at Sharpe's mild hopes. He waved northwards through the spitting sleet and the spume and the wild waves' turmoil. 'That's a whole continent up there! Not an English farmyard! You won't find a single body in a continent, Englishman, not if someone else has decided to hide it.'

'Why would they do that?'

'Because if my tale of carrying Don Blas to meet the rebels is right, then Don Blas was not just a soldier, but a soldier playing politics, and that's a more dangerous pastime than fighting. Besides, if the Spanish high command decides not to help you, how will you achieve anything?'

'By bribes?' Sharpe suggested.

Ardiles laughed. 'I wish you luck, Englishman, but if you're offering money they'll just tell you what you want to hear until you've no money left, then they'll clean their knife blades in your guts. Take my advice! Vivar's dead! Go home!'

Sharpe crouched against a sudden attack of wind-slathered foam that shrieked down the deck and smashed white against the helmsman and his companion. 'What I don't understand,' Sharpe shouted when the sea had sucked itself out of the scuppers, 'is why the rebels haven't boasted about Don Blas's death! If you're a rebel and you kill or capture your enemy's commander, why keep it a secret? Why not trumpet your success?'

'You expect sense out of Chile?' Ardiles asked cynically.

Sharpe ducked again as the wind flailed more salt foam across the quarterdeck. 'Don Blas's widow doesn't believe it was the rebels who attacked her husband. She thinks it was Captain-General Bautista.'

Ardiles looked grimmer than ever. 'Then Don Blas's widow had best keep her thoughts to herself. Bautista is not a man to antagonize. He has pride, a memory, and a taste for cruelty.'

'And for corruption?' Sharpe asked.

Ardiles paused, as though weighing the good sense of continuing this conversation, then he shrugged. 'Miguel Bautista is the prince of thieves, but that doesn't mean he won't one day be the ruler of Spain. How else do men become great, except by extortion and fear? I will give you some advice, Englishman.' Ardiles's voice had become fierce with intensity. 'Don't make an enemy of Bautista. You hear me?'

'Of course.' The warning seemed extraordinary to Sharpe; a testimony to the real fear that Miguel Bautista, Vivar's erstwhile enemy, inspired.

Ardiles suddenly grinned, as though he wanted to erase the grimness of his last words. 'The trouble with Don Blas, Englishman, was that he was very close to being a saint. He was an honourable man, and you know what happens to honourable men – they prove to be an embarrassment. This world isn't governed by honourable men, but by lawyers and politicians, and whenever such scum come across an honest man they have to kill him.' The ship shuddered as a huge wave smashed ragged down the port gunwale. Ardiles laughed at the weather's malevolence, then looked again at Sharpe. 'Take my advice, Englishman! Go home! I'll be sailing back to Spain in a week's time, which gives you just long enough to visit the *chingana* behind the church in Valdivia, after which you should sail home to your wife.'

'The *chingana*?' Sharpe asked.

'A *chingana* is where you go for a *chingada*,' Ardiles said unhelpfully. 'A *chingana* is either a tavern that sells whores, or a whorehouse that sells liquor, and the *chingana* behind the church in Valdivia has half-breed girls who give *chingadas* that leave men gasping for life. It's the best whorehouse for miles. You know how you can tell which is the best whorehouse in a Spanish town?'

'Tell me.'

'It's the one where all the priests go, and this one is where the bishop goes! So visit the *mestiza* whores, then go home and tell Vivar's wife that her husband's body was eaten by wild pigs!'

But Sharpe had not been paid to go home and tell stories. He had taken Doña Louisa's money, and he was far from home, and he would not go back defeated. He would find Don Blas, no matter how deep the forest or high the hill. If Don Blas still had form, then Sharpe would find it.

He had sworn as much, and he would keep his promise. He would find Don Blas.

*   *   *

Albatrosses ghosted alongside the *Espiritu Santo*'s rigging. The frigate, Cape Horn left far behind her, was sailing before a friendly wind on a swirling current of icy water. Dolphins followed the frigate, while whales surfaced and rolled on either flank.

'Christ, but there's some meat on those bloody fish!' Harper said in admiration as a great whale plunged past the *Espiritu Santo*. The ship was sailing north along the Chilean coast, out of sight of land, though the proximity of the shore was marked by the towering white clouds which heaped above the Andes. Inshore, the sailors said, were yet stranger creatures: penguins and sea lions, mermaids and turtles, but the frigate was staying well clear of the uncharted Chilean coastline so that Harper, to his regret, was denied a chance of glimpsing such strange monsters. Ardiles, still hoping to capture his own monster, Lord Cochrane, continued to exercise his guns even though his men were already as well-trained as any gunners Sharpe had ever seen.

Yet it seemed there was to be no victory over the devil Cochrane on this voyage, for the *Espiritu Santo*'s lookouts saw no other ships till the frigate at last closed on the land. Then the lookouts glimpsed a harmless fleet of small fishing vessels that dragged their nets through the cold offshore rollers. The men aboard the fishing boats claimed not to have seen any rebel warships. 'Though God only knows if they're telling the truth,' Lieutenant Otero told Sharpe. Land was still out of sight, but everyone on board knew that the voyage was ending. Seamen were repairing their clothes, sewing up huge rents in breeches and darning their shirts in readiness to meet the girls of Valdivia. 'One day more, just one day more,' Lieutenant Otero told Sharpe after the noon sight, and sure enough, next dawn, Sharpe woke to see the dark streak of land filling the eastern horizon.

That afternoon, under a faltering wind, a friendly tide helped the *Espiritu Santo* into Valdivia's harbour. Sharpe and Harper stood on deck and stared at the massive fortifications that guarded this last Spanish stronghold on the Chilean coast. The headland which protected the harbour was crowned by the English fort, which in turn could lock its cannon fire with the guns of Fort San Carlos. Both forts lay under the protection of the artillery in the Chorocomayo Fort which had been built on the headland's highest point. Beyond San Carlos, and still on the headland which formed the harbour's western side, lay Fort Amargos and Corral Castle. The *Espiritu Santo*'s First Lieutenant proudly pointed out each succeeding strongpoint as the frigate edged her way around the headland. 'In Chile,' Otero explained yet again, 'armies move by sea because the roads are so bad, but no army could ever take Valdivia unless they first capture this harbour, and I just wish Cochrane would try to capture it! We'd destroy him!'

Sharpe believed him, for there were yet more defences to add their guns to the five forts of the western shore. Across the harbour mouth, where the huge Pacific swells shattered white on dark rocks, was the biggest fort of all, Fort Niebla, while in the harbour's centre, head on to any attacking ships, lay the guns and ramparts of Manzanera Island. The harbour would be a trap, sucking an attacker inside to where he would be ringed with high guns hammering heated shot down onto his wooden decks.

Only two of the forts, Corral Castle and Fort Niebla, were modern stone-walled forts. The other forts were little more than glorified gun emplacements protected by ditches and timber walls, yet their cannon could make the harbour into a killing ground of overlapping gunnery zones. 'If we were an enemy ship,' Otero boasted of the ring of artillery, 'we would be in hell by now.'

'Where's the town?' Sharpe asked. Valdivia was supposed to be the major remaining Spanish garrison in Chile, yet, to Sharpe's surprise, the great array of forts seemed to be protecting nothing but a stone quay, some tarred sheds and a row of fishermen's hovels.

'The town's upstream.' Otero pointed to what Sharpe had taken for a bay just beside Fort Niebla. 'That's the river mouth and the town's fifteen miles inland. You'll be dropped at the North Quay where you find a boatman to take you upstream. They're dishonest people, and they'll try to charge you five dollars. You shouldn't pay more than one.'

'The *Espiritu Santo* won't go upstream?'

'The river's too shallow.' Lieutenant Otero, who had

charge of the frigate, paused to listen to the leadsman who was calling the depth. 'Sometimes the boatmen will take you halfway and then threaten to put you ashore in the wilderness if you won't pay more money. If that happens the best thing to do is to shoot one of the Indian crew members. No one objects to the killing of a savage, and you'll find the death has a remarkably salutary effect on the other boatmen.'

Otero turned away to tend to the ship. The Niebla Fort was firing a salute which one of the long nine-pounders at the frigate's bows returned. The gunfire echoed flatly from the steep hills where a few stunted trees were permanently windbent towards the north. Seamen were streaming aloft to furl the sails after their long passage. There was a crash as the starboard anchor was struck loose, then a grating rumble as fathoms of chain clattered through the hawse. The fragrant scents of the land vainly tried to defeat the noxious carapace of the *Espiritu Santo*'s cesspit-laced-with-powder stench. The frigate, her salute fired, checked as the anchor bit into the harbour's bottom, then turned as the tide pulled the fouled hull slowly round. The smoke of the gun salute writhed and drifted across the bay. 'Welcome to Chile,' Otero said.

'Can you believe it?' Harper said with amazement. 'We're in the New World!'

An hour later, their seabags and money chest under the guard of two burly seamen, Sharpe and Harper stepped ashore onto the New World. They had reached their voyage's end in the quaking land of giants and pygmies, of unicorns and ghouls; in the rebellious land which lay under the volcanoes' fire and the devil's flail. They were in Chile.

CHAPTER 2

George Blair, British Consul in Valdivia, blinked short-sightedly at Richard Sharpe. 'Why the hell should I tell you lies? Of course he's dead!' Blair laughed mirthlessly. 'He'd better bloody be dead. He's been buried long enough! The poor bugger must be in a bloody bad state if he's still alive; he's been underground these last three months. Are you sure you don't have any gin in your baggage?'

'I'm sure.'

'People usually bring me gin from London.' Blair was a plump, middle-aged man, wearing a stained white shirt and frayed breeches. He had greeted his visitors wearing a formal black tailcoat, but had long discarded the coat as too cumbersome in the day's warmth. 'It's rather a common courtesy,' he grumbled, 'to bring gin from London.'

Sharpe was in no state to notice either the Consul's clothes or his unhappiness, instead his thoughts were a whirlpool of disbelief and shock. Don Blas was not missing at all, but was dead and buried, which meant Sharpe's whole voyage was for nothing. At least, that was what Blair reckoned. 'He's under the paving slabs in the garrison church at Puerto Crucero,' George Blair repeated in his hard, clipped accent. 'Jesus Christ! I know a score of people who were at the damned funeral. I wasn't invited, and a good thing too. I have to put up with enough nonsense in this goddamn place without watching a pack of pox-ridden priests mumbling bloody Latin in double-quick time so they can get back to their native whores.'

'God in his heaven,' Sharpe blasphemed, then paused to gather his scattered wits, 'but Vivar's wife doesn't know! They can't bury a man without telling his wife!'

'They can do whatever they damn well like! But don't ask me to explain. I'm trying to run a business and a consulate, not explain the remnants of the Spanish bloody empire.'

Blair was a Liverpool merchant who dealt in hides, tallow, copper and timber. He was a bad-tempered, over-worked and harassed man, yet, as Consul, he had little option but to welcome Sharpe and Harper into his house that stood in the main square of Valdivia, hard between the church and the outer ditch of the town's main fort that was known simply as the Citadel. Blair had placed Louisa's bribe money, all eighteen hundred golden guineas, in his strongroom that was protected by a massive iron door and by walls of dressed stone blocks a foot and a half thick. Louisa had given Sharpe two thousand guineas, but the customs officials at the wharf in Valdivia had insisted on a levy of ten per cent. 'Bastards,' Blair had commented when he heard of the impost. 'It's supposed to be just three per cent.'

'Should I complain?' Sharpe had already made an unholy fuss at the customs post, though it had done no good.

'To Captain-General Bautista?' Blair gave another mirthless laugh. 'He's the bastard that pegs up the percentage. You were lucky it wasn't fifteen per cent!' Then, over a plate of sugar cakes and glasses of wine brought by his Indian servants, Blair had welcomed Sharpe to Valdivia with the unwelcome news that Vivar's death was no mystery at all. 'The bugger was riding way ahead of his escort, was probably ambushed by rebels, and his horse bolted with him when the trap was sprung. Then three months later they found his body in a ravine. Not that there was much left of the poor bugger, but they knew it was him, right enough, because of his uniform. Mind you, it took them a hell of a long time to find his body, but the dagoes are bloody inefficient at everything except levying customs duties, and they can do that faster than anyone in history.'

'Who buried him?' Sharpe asked.

The Consul frowned in irritated puzzlement. 'A pack of bloody priests! I told you!'

'But who arranged it? The army?'

'Captain-General Bautista, of course. Nothing happens here without Bautista giving the nod.'

Sharpe turned and stared through Blair's parlour window which looked onto the Citadel's outer ditch where two dogs were squabbling over what appeared to be a child's discarded doll, but then, as the doll's arm ripped away, Sharpe saw that the dogs' plaything was the body of an Indian toddler that must have been dumped in the ditch.

'Why the hell weren't you invited to the funeral, Blair?' Sharpe turned back from the window. 'You're an important man here, aren't you? Or doesn't the British Consul carry any weight in these parts?'

Blair shrugged. 'The Spanish in Valdivia don't much like the British, Colonel. They're losing this fight, and they're blaming us. They reckon most of the rebellion's money comes from London, and they aren't far wrong in thinking that. But it's their own damned fault if they're losing. They're too bloody fond of lining their own pockets, and if it comes to a choice between fighting and profiteering, they'll take the money every time. Things were better when Vivar was in charge, but that's exactly why they couldn't stomach him. The bugger was too honest, you see, which is why I didn't see too many tears shed when they heard he'd been killed.'

'The bugger,' Sharpe said coldly, 'was a friend of mine.' He turned to stare again at the ditch where a flock of carrion birds edged close to the two dogs, hoping for a share of the child's corpse.

'Vivar was a friend of yours?' Blair sounded shocked. 'Yes.'

The confirmation checked Blair, who suddenly had to reassess the importance of his visitors, or at least Sharpe's importance. Blair had already dismissed Harper as a genial Irishman who carried no political weight, but Sharpe, despite his rustic clothes and weathered face, was suddenly proving a much more difficult man to place. Sharpe had introduced himself as Lieutenant-Colonel Sharpe, but the war had left as many Colonels as it had bastards, so the rank hardly impressed Consul Blair, but if Lieutenant-Colonel Sharpe had been a friend of Don Blas Vivar, who had been Count of Mouromorto and Captain-General of Spain's Chilean dominion, then such a friendship could also imply that Sharpe was a friend of the high London lords who, ultimately, gave Blair the privileges and honours that eased his existence in Valdivia. 'A bad business,' Blair muttered, vainly trying to make amends for his flippancy.

'Where was the body found?' Sharpe asked.

'Some miles north-east of Puerto Crucero. It's a wild area, nothing but woods and rocks.' Blair was speaking in a much more respectful tone now. 'The place isn't a usual haunt of the rebels, but once in a while they'll appear that far south. Government troops searched the valley after the ambush, of course, but no one thought to look in the actual ravine till a hunting party of Indians brought news that a white god was lying there. That's one of their names for us, you see. The white god, of course, turned out to be Don Blas. They reckon that he and his horse must have fallen into the ravine while fleeing from his attackers.'

'You're sure it was rebels?' Sharpe turned from the window to ask the question. 'I've heard it might have been Bautista's doing.'

Blair shook his head. 'I've not heard those rumours. I'm not saying Bautista's not capable of murder, because he is. He's a cruel son of a whore, that one, but I never heard any tales of his having killed Captain-General Vivar, and, believe me, Chile breeds rumour the way a nunnery breeds the pox.'

Sharpe was unwilling to let the theory slip. 'I heard Vivar had found out about Bautista's corruption, and was going to arrest him.'

Blair mocked Sharpe's naïvety. 'Everyone's corrupt here! You don't arrest a man for breathing, do you? If Vivar was going to arrest Bautista then it would have been for something far more serious than corruption. No, Colonel, that dog won't hunt.'

Sharpe thumped a fist in angry protest. 'But to be buried three months ago! That's long enough for someone to tell the authorities in Europe! Why the hell did no one think to tell his wife?'

It was hardly Blair's responsibility, though he tried to answer as best he could. 'Maybe the ship carrying the news was captured? Or shipwrecked? Sometimes ships do take a God-horrible time to make the voyage. The last time I went home we spent over three weeks just trying to get round Ushant! Sick as a dog, I was!'

'Goddamn it.' Sharpe turned back to the window. Was it all a misunderstanding? Was this whole benighted expedition merely the result of the time it sometimes took for news to cross between the old and new worlds? Had Don Blas been decently buried all this time? It was more than possible, of course. A ship could easily take two or three months to sail from Chile to Spain, and if Louisa had been in England when the news arrived in Galicia then it was no wonder that Sharpe and Harper had come on a fool's errand. 'Don't you bury the dead in this town?' he asked bad-temperedly.

Blair was understandably bemused by the sudden question, but then saw Sharpe was staring at the dead child in the Citadel's ditch. 'We don't bury that sort of rubbish. Lord, no. It's probably just the bastard of some Indian girl who works in the fortress. Indians count for nothing here!' Blair chuckled. 'A couple of Indian families won't fetch the price of a decent hunting dog, let alone the cost of a burial!'

Sharpe sipped the wine, which was surprisingly good. He had been astonished, while on the boat coming from the harbour to the town, to see lavish vineyards terraced across the riverside hills. Somehow, after the grotesque shipboard tales, he had expected a country full of mystery and horror, so the sight of placid vineyards and lavish villas had been unexpected, rather like finding everyday comforts in the pits of hell. 'I'll need to go to Puerto Crucero,' he now told Blair.

'That could be difficult.' Blair sounded guarded. 'Very difficult.'

'Why?' Sharpe bristled.

'Because it's a military area, and because Bautista doesn't like visitors going there, and because it's a port town, and the Spaniards have lost too many good harbours on this coast to let another one go, and because they think all Englishmen are spies. Besides, the citadel at Puerto Crucero is the place where the Spanish ship their gold home.'

'Gold?' Harper's interest sparked.

'There're one or two mines left; not many and they don't produce much, and most of what they do produce Bautista is probably thieving, but what little does go back to Madrid leaves through the wharf of Puerto Crucero's citadel. It's the nearest harbour to the mines, you see, which is why the dagoes are touchy about it. If you ask to visit

Puerto Crucero they might think you're spying for Cochrane. You know who Cochrane is?'

'I know,' Sharpe said.

'He's a devil, that one,' Blair, unable to resist admiration for a fellow Briton, chuckled, 'and they're all scared to hell of him. You want to see a dago piss in his breeches? Just mention Cochrane. They think he's got horns and a tail.'

Sharpe dragged the conversation back to his purpose. 'So how do I get permission to visit Puerto Crucero?'

'You have to get a travel permit from army headquarters.'

'Which is where?'

'In the Citadel, of course.' Blair nodded at the great fort which lay on the river's bend at the very heart of Valdivia.

'Who do I see there?'

'A young fellow called Captain Marquinez.'

'Will Marquinez pay more attention to you than to me?' Sharpe asked.

'Oh, Christ, no! Marquinez is just an over-groomed puppy. He doesn't make the decision. Bautista's the one who'll say yea or nay.' Blair jerked a thumb towards his padlocked strongroom. 'I hope there's plenty of money in that box you fetched here, or else you'll be wasting your time in Chile.'

'My time is my own,' Sharpe said acidly, 'which is why I don't want to waste it.' He frowned at Harper who was happily devouring Blair's sugar cakes. 'If you can stop feeding yourself, Patrick, we might start work.'

'Work?' Harper sounded alarmed, but hurriedly swilled down the last of his wine and snatched a final sugar cake before following Sharpe out of Blair's house. 'So what work are we doing?' the Irishman asked.

'We're going to dig up Don Blas's body, of course,' Sharpe said, 'and arrange to have it shipped back to Spain.' Sharpe's confident voice seemed to rouse

Valdivia's town square from the torpor of siesta. A man who had been dozing on the church steps looked irritably towards the two tall strangers who strode so noisily towards the Citadel. A dozen Indians, their squat faces blank as carvings, sat in the shade of a mounted statue which stood in the very centre of the square. The Indians, who were shackled together by a length of heavy chain manacled to their ankles, pretended not to notice Sharpe, but could not hide their astonishment at the sight of Harper; doubtless thinking that the tall Irishman was a giant. 'They're admiring me, so they are!' Harper boasted happily.

'They're working out how many families they could feed off your carcass. If they boiled you down and salted the flesh there probably wouldn't be famine in this country for a century.'

'You're just jealous.' Harper, seeing new sights, was a happy man. The French wars had given him a taste for travel, and that taste was being well fed by Chile. His only disappointment so far was the paucity of one-legged giants, unicorns or any other mythical beasts. 'Look at that! Handsome, aren't they, now?' He nodded admiringly towards a group of women who, standing in the shade of the striped awnings which protected the shop fronts, returned Harper's curiosity and admiration. Harper and Sharpe were new faces in a small town, and thus a cause for excited speculation. The wind swirled dust devils across the square and flapped the ornate Spanish ensign which flew over the Citadel's gatehouse. A legless beggar, swinging along on his hands, followed Sharpe and pleaded for money. Another, who looked like a leper, made a meaningless noise and held out the stump of a wrist towards the two strangers. A Dominican monk, his white robes stained with the red dust that blew everywhere, was arguing with a carter who had evidently failed to deliver a shipment of wine.

'We're going to need a carter,' Sharpe was thinking aloud as he led Harper towards the Citadel's sentries, 'or at least a cart. We're also going to want two riding horses, plus saddlery, and supplies for as long as it takes to get to Puerto Crucero and back. Unless we can sail home from Puerto Crucero? Or maybe we can sail down there! That'll be cheaper than buying a cart.'

'What the hell do we want a cart for?' Harper was panting at the brisk pace set by Sharpe.

'We need a cart to carry the coffin to Puerto Crucero, unless, of course, we can go there by ship.'

'Why the hell don't we have a coffin made in Puerto Crucero?' Harper asked. 'The world's not so short of carpenters that you can't find a man to knock up a bloody box!'

'Because a box won't do the trick!' Sharpe said. 'The thing has to be watertight, Patrick, not to keep the rain out but to keep the decay in. We're going to need a tinsmith, and I don't suppose Puerto Crucero has too many of those! So we'll have a watertight box made here before we go south.'

'We could plop him in a vat of brandy,' Harper suggested helpfully. 'There's a fellow who drinks in my place that was a gunner's mate on the *Victory* at Trafalgar, and he says that after the battle they brought Nelson back in a barrel of brandy. My fellow had a look at the body when they unstowed it, and he says the Admiral was as fresh as the day he died, so he was, with flesh soft as a baby, and the only change was that all the man's hair and nails had grown wild. He tasted the brandy too, so he did. He says it was a bit salty.'

'I don't want to put Don Blas in brandy,' Sharpe said irritably. 'He'll be half rotted out as it is, and if we put him in a cask of bloody liquor he'll like as not dissolve altogether, and instead of burying the poor man in Spain we'll just be pouring him away. So we'll put him in a tin box, solder him up tight, and take him back that way.'

'Whatever you say,' Harper said grimly, the tone provoked by the unfriendly faces of the sentries at the fort's gate. The Citadel reminded Sharpe of the Spanish fortresses he had assaulted in the French wars. It had low walls over which the muzzles of the defenders' guns showed grimly, and a wide, dry moat designed to be a killing ground for any attackers who succeeded in crossing the earthen glacis which was banked to ricochet assaulting cannonfire safely up and over the defenders' heads. The only incongruity about Valdivia's formidable Citadel was an ancient-looking tower that stood like a mediaeval castle turret in the very centre of the fortifications.

A sergeant accosted Sharpe and Harper on the bridge, then reluctantly allowed them into the fort itself. They walked through the entrance tunnel, across a wide parade ground, then through a second gateway into a cramped and shadowed inner courtyard. One wall of the yard was made by the ancient limewashed tower that was pockmarked by bullet holes. There were smears of dried blood near some of the bullet marks, suggesting that this cheerless place was where Valdivia's prisoners met their firing squads.

They enquired at the inner guardroom for Captain Marquinez who, arriving five minutes later, proved to be a tall, strikingly handsome and extraordinarily fashionable young man. His uniform seemed more appropriate for the jewelled halls of Madrid than for this far, squalid colony. He wore a Hussar jacket so frogged with gold braid that it was impossible to see the cloth beneath, a white kidskin pelisse edged with black fur, and skintight sky blue cavalry breeches decorated with gold embroidery and silver side buttons. His epaulette chains, sword sling, spurs and scabbard furnishings were all of shining gold. His manners matched his uniform's tailoring. He apologized for having kept his visitors waiting, welcomed them to Chile on behalf of Captain-General Bautista, then invited Sharpe and Harper to his quarters where, in a wide, comfortable room, his servant brought cups of steaming chocolate, small gold beakers of a clear Chilean brandy, and a plate of sugared grapes. Marquinez paused in front of a gilt-framed mirror to check that his wavy black hair was in place, then crossed to his wide-arched window to show off the view. 'It really is a most beautiful country,' the Captain spoke wistfully, as though he knew it was being lost.

The view was indeed spectacular. The window looked eastwards across the town's thatched roofs, then beyond the shadowy foothills to the far snow-topped mountains. One of those distant peaks was pluming a stream of brown smoke to the south wind. 'A volcano,' Marquinez explained. 'Chile has a number of them. It's a tumultuous place, I fear, with frequent earthquakes, but fascinating despite its dangers.' Marquinez's servant brought cigars, and Marquinez hospitably offered a burning spill to Harper. 'So you're staying with Mister Blair?' he asked when the cigars were well lit. 'Poor Blair! His wife refused to travel here, thinking the place too full of dangers! Still, if you keep Blair filled with gin or brandy he's a happy enough man. Your Spanish is excellent, permit me to congratulate you. So few of your countrymen speak our language.'

'We both served in Spain,' Sharpe explained.

'You did! Then our debt to you is incalculable. Please, seat yourselves. You said you had a letter of introduction?'

Marquinez took and read Doña Louisa's letter which did not specifically describe Sharpe's errand, but merely asked any Spanish official to offer whatever help was possible. 'Which of course we will offer gladly!' Marquinez spoke with what seemed to be a genuine warmth. 'I never had the pleasure of meeting Don Blas's wife. He died, of course, before she could join him here. So very tragic, and such a waste. He was a good man, even perhaps a great man! There was something saintly about him, I always thought.' The last compliment, uttered in a very bland voice, somehow suggested what an infernal nuisance saints could be. Marquinez carefully folded the letter's pendant seal into the paper then handed it back to Sharpe with a courtly flourish. 'And how, sir, might we help you?'

'We need a permit to visit Puerto Crucero where we want to exhume Don Blas's body, then ship it home.' Sharpe, encouraged by Marquinez's friendliness, saw no need to be delicate about his needs.

Marquinez smiled, revealing teeth as white and regular as a small child's. 'I see no extraordinary difficulties there. You will, of course, need a permit to travel to Puerto Crucero.' He went to his table and riffled through his papers. 'Did you sail out here on the *Espiritu Santo*?'

'Yes.'

'She's due to sail back to Spain in a few days and I see that she's ordered to call at Puerto Crucero on her way. There's a gold shipment ready, and Ardiles's ship is the safest transport we have. I see no reason why you shouldn't travel down the coast in the *Espiritu Santo* and, if we're fortunate, you might even take the body back to Europe in her hold!'

Sharpe, who had been prepared by Blair for every kind of official obstructiveness, dared not believe his good fortune. The *Espiritu Santo* could indeed solve all his problems, but Marquinez had qualified his optimism with one cautious word that Sharpe now echoed as a tentative query. 'Fortunate?'

'Besides the permit to travel to Puerto Crucero,' Marquinez explained, 'you will need a permit to exhume Don Blas's body. That permit is issued by the church, of course, but I'm sure the Bishop will be eager to satisfy the Dowager Countess of Mouromorto. However, you should understand that sometimes the church is, how shall I say? Dilatory?'

'We came prepared for such difficulties,' Sharpe said.

'How so?' The question was swift.

'The church must have charities dear to its heart?'

'How very thoughtful of you.' Marquinez, relieved that Sharpe had so swiftly understood the obstacle, offered his guests a dazzling smile and Sharpe wondered how a man kept his teeth so white. Marquinez then held up a warning hand. 'We mustn't forget the necessary licence to export a body. There is a disease risk, you understand, and we have to satisfy ourselves that every precaution has been taken.'

'We came well prepared,' Sharpe said dourly. The requirements, so far as he could see, were two massive bribes. One to the church which, in Sharpe's experience, was always greedy for cash, and the other to the army authorities to secure the travel permit and for the licence to export a body, which licence, Sharpe suspected, had just been dreamed up by the inventive Marquinez. Doña Louisa, Sharpe thought, had understood Chile perfectly when she had insisted on sending him with the big chest of coins. Sharpe smiled at the charming Marquinez. 'So when, *señor*, may we expect a travel permit? Today?'

'Oh, dear me, no!' Marquinez frowned, as though Sharpe's suggestion of such haste was somehow unseemly.

'Soon?' Sharpe pressed.

'The decision is not mine,' Marquinez said happily.

'Our affairs will surely not be of interest to Captain-General Bautista?' Sharpe said with what he hoped was a convincing innocence.

'The Captain-General is interested in all our visitors, especially those who have been notable soldiers.' Marquinez bowed to Sharpe, whose fame had been described in Louisa's letter of introduction. 'Tell me,' Marquinez went on, 'were you at Waterloo?'

'Yes.'

'Then I am sure the Captain-General will want to meet

you. General Bautista is an aficionado of the Emperor. He would, I think, be delighted to hear of your experiences.' Marquinez beamed delightedly, as if a mutual treat awaited his master and Sharpe. 'Such a pleasure to meet you both!' Marquinez said, then ushered them back to the guardroom. 'Such a pleasure,' he said again.

'So how did it go?' Blair asked when they returned.

'Very well,' Sharpe said. 'All things considered it couldn't have gone much better.'

'That means you're in trouble,' Blair said happily, 'that means you're in trouble.'

*   *   *

That night it rained so heavily that the town ditch flooded with earth-reddened water which, in the moonlight, looked like blood. Blair became drunk. He bemoaned that his wife was still in Liverpool and commiserated with Sharpe and Harper that their wives were, respectively, in France and Ireland. 'You live in bloody France?' Blair kept asking the question as though to dilute the astonishment he evidently felt for Sharpe's choice of a home. 'Bloody funny place to live, I mean if you've been fighting the buggers. It must be like a fox moving in with the rabbits!'

Sharpe tried to talk of more immediate matters, like Captain-General Bautista and his fascination for Napoleon, but Blair did not want to talk about the Spanish commander. 'He's a bastard. A son of a whore bastard, and that's all there is to say about him.' It was clear that Blair, despite his privileged status as a diplomat, feared the Spanish commander.

'Are you saying he's illegitimate?' Sharpe asked disingenuously.

'Oh, Christ, no.' Blair glanced at the servants as though fearing they had suddenly learned English and would report this conversation to Bautista's spies. 'Bautista's a younger son, so he needs to make his own fortune. He got his posting here because his father is a minister in Ferdinand VII's government, and he greased his son a commission in the artillery and an appointment in Chile, because this is where the money is. But the rest Bautista did for himself. He's capable! He's efficient and a hard worker. He's probably no soldier, but he's no weakling. And he's making himself rich.'

'So he's corrupt?'

'Corrupt!' Blair mocked the word. 'Of course he's corrupt. They're all corrupt. I'm corrupt! Everyone here knows the bloody war is lost. It's only a question of time before the Spaniards go and the Chileans can bugger up their own country instead of having someone else to do it for them, so what Bautista and his people are doing is making themselves rich before someone takes away the tray of baubles.' Blair paused, sipped, then leaned closer to Sharpe. 'Your friend Vivar wasn't corrupt, which is why he made enemies, but Bautista, he's a coming man! He'll make his money then go home and use that money to buy himself office in Madrid. Mark my words, he'll be the power in Spain before he's fifty.'

'How old is he now?'

'He's a youngster! Thirty, no more.' Blair, clearly deciding he had said enough about the feared Bautista, pushed his glass to the end of the table for a servant girl to fill with a mixture of rum and wine. 'If you want a whore, Colonel,' Blair went on, 'there's a *chingana* behind the church. Ask for the girl they call La Monja!' Blair rolled his eyes heavenwards to indicate what exquisite joys awaited Sharpe and Harper if they followed his advice. 'She's a *mestiza*.'

'What's a *mestiza*?' Harper asked.

'Half-breed, and that one's half a woman and half a wildcat.'

'I'd rather hear about Bautista,' Sharpe said.

'I've told you, there's nothing to tell. Man's a bastard. Cross him and you get butchered. He's judge, jury and executioner here. He's also horribly efficient. You want some more rum?'

Sharpe glanced at the two Indian girls who, holding their jugs of wine and rum, stood expressionless at the edge of the room. 'No.'

'You can have them, too,' Blair said hospitably. 'Help yourselves, both of you! I know they look like cows, but they know their way up and down a bed. No point in employing them otherwise. They can't cook and their idea of cleaning a room is to rearrange the dirt, so what else are they good for? And in the dark you don't know they're savages, do you?'

Sharpe again tried to turn the conversation back to his own business. 'I need to find the American Consul. Does he live close?'

'What the hell do you want Fielding for?' Blair sounded offended, as though Sharpe's question suggested that Fielding was a better Consul than Blair.

Sharpe had no intention of revealing that he possessed a signed portrait of Napoleon which the American Consul was supposed to smuggle to a British Colonel now living in the rebel part of the country, so instead he made up a story about doing business for an American expatriate living in Normandy.

'Well, you're out of luck,' Blair said with evident satisfaction. 'Fielding's away from Valdivia this week. One of his precious whaling boats was impounded by the Spanish navy, so he's on Chiloe, trying to have the bribe reduced to something under a king's ransom.'

'Chiloe?' Sharpe asked.

'Island down south. Long way away. But Fielding will be back in a week or so.'

Sharpe hid his disappointment. He had been hoping to deliver the portrait quickly, then forget about the

Emperor's gift, but now, if he was to keep his promise to Bonaparte, he would have to find some other way of reaching Fielding. 'Have you ever heard of a Lieutenant-Colonel Charles?' he asked Blair, as casually as he could.

'Charles? Of course I've heard of Charles. He's one of O'Higgins's military advisers.'

'So he's a rebel?'

'Of course he's a bloody rebel! Why else would he have come to Chile? He likes to fight, and Europe isn't providing any proper wars these days, so all the rascals come over here and complicate my life instead. What do you want with Charles?'

'Nothing,' Sharpe said, then let the subject drop.

An hour later he and Harper went to their beds and lay listening to the water sluice off the tiles. The mattresses were full of fleas. 'Like old times,' Harper grumbled when they woke early.

Blair was also up at first light. The rain in the night had been so heavy that part of the misted square was flooded, and the inundation had turned the rubbish-choked ditch into a moat in which foul things floated. 'A horrid day to travel,' Blair complained when he met them in his parlour where coffee waited on the table. 'It'll be raining again within the hour, mark my words.'

'Where are you going?'

'Down river. To the port.' Blair groaned and rubbed his temples with his fingertips. 'I've got to supervise some cargo loading, and probably see the Captain of the *Charybdis*.'

'What's the *Charybdis*?' Harper asked.

'Royal Navy frigate. We keep a squadron on the coast just to make sure the bloody dagoes don't shoot any of our people. They know that if they upset me I'll arrange to have their toy boats blown out of the water.' Blair shivered, then groaned with pain. 'Breakfast!' he shouted towards the kitchens, then flinched as a muffled rattle of musketry sounded from the Citadel. 'That's another rebel gone,' Blair said thickly. There was a second ragged volley. 'Business is good this morning.'

'Rebels?' Sharpe asked.

'Or some poor bugger caught with a gun and no money to bribe the patrol. They shove them up against the Angel Tower, say a quick Hail Mary, then send the buggers into eternity.'

'The Angel Tower?' Sharpe asked.

'It's that ancient lump of stone in the middle of the fort. The Spaniards built it when they first came here, way back in the dark ages. Bloody thing has survived earthquake, fire, and rebellion. It used to be a prison, but it's empty now.'

'Why is it called the Angel Tower?' Harper asked.

'Christ knows, but you know what the dagoes are like. Some drunken Spanish whore probably saw an angel on its top and the next thing you know they're all weeping and praying and the priests are carrying round the collection plate. Where's my goddamned bloody breakfast?' he shouted towards the kitchen.

Blair, well-breakfasted at last, left for the harbour an hour later. 'Don't expect anything from Marquinez!' he warned Sharpe. 'They'll promise you anything, but deliver nothing. You'll not hear a word from that macaroni until you offer him a fat bribe.'

Yet, no sooner had Blair gone, than a message arrived from the Citadel asking Colonel Sharpe and Mister Harper to do the honour of attending on Captain Marquinez at their earliest opportunity. So, moments later, Sharpe and Harper crossed the bridge, walked through the tunnel that pierced the glacis, crossed the outer parade courtyard and so into the inner yard where two bodies lay like heaps of soiled rags under the bloodstained wall of the Angel Tower. Marquinez, greeting Sharpe in the courtyard, was embarrassed by the bodies. 'A wagon is coming to take them to the cemetery. They were rebels, of course.'

'Why don't you just dump them in the ditch like the Indian babies?' Sharpe asked Marquinez sourly.

'Because the rebels are Christians, of course.' Marquinez was bemused that the question had even been asked.

'None of the Indians are Christian?'

'Some of them are, I suppose,' Marquinez said airily, 'though personally I don't know why the missionaries bother. One might as well offer the sacrament to a jabbering pack of monkeys. And they're treacherous creatures. Turn your back and they'll stab you. They've been rebelling against us for hundreds of years, and they never seem to learn that we always win in the end.' Marquinez ushered Sharpe and Harper into a room with a high arched ceiling. 'Will you be happy to wait here? The Captain-General would like to greet you.'

'Bautista?' Sharpe was taken aback.

'Of course! We only have one Captain-General!' Marquinez was suddenly all charm. 'The Captain-General would like to welcome you to Chile himself. Captain Ardiles told him how you had a private audience with Bonaparte and, as I mentioned, the Captain-General has a fascination with the Emperor. So, do you mind waiting? I'll have some coffee sent. Or would you prefer wine?'

'I'd prefer our travel permits,' Sharpe said truculently.

'The matter is being considered, I do assure you. We must do whatever we can to look after the happiness of the Countess of Mouromorto. Now, if you will excuse me?' Marquinez, with a confiding and dazzling smile, left them in the room which was furnished with a table, four chairs, and a crucifix hanging from a bent horseshoe nail. A broken saddle tree was discarded in one corner, while a lizard watched Sharpe from the curved ceiling. The room's one window looked onto the execution yard. After an hour, during which no one came to fetch Sharpe and Harper, a wagon creaked into the yard and a detail of soldiers swung the two dead rebels onto the wagon's bed.

Another hour passed, noted by the chiming of a clock somewhere deep in the fort. Neither wine, coffee, nor a summons from the Captain-General arrived. Captain Marquinez had disappeared, and the only clerk in the office behind the guardroom did not know where the Captain might be found. The rain fell miserably, slowly diluting the bloodstains on the limewashed wall of the Angel Tower.

The rain fell. Still no one came and, as the clock chimed another half hour, Sharpe's patience finally snapped. 'Let's get the hell out of here.'

'What about Bautista?'

'Bugger Bautista.' It seemed that Blair was right about the myriad of delays that the Spanish imposed on even the simplest bureaucratic procedure, but Sharpe did not have the patience to be the victim of such nonsense. 'Let's go.'

It was raining much harder now. Sharpe ran across the Citadel's bridge, while Harper lumbered after. They splashed across the square's cobbles, past the statue where the group of chained Indians still sat vacant under the cloudburst, to where a heavy wagon, loaded with untanned hides, was standing in front of Blair's house. The untreated leather stank foully. A uniformed soldier was lounging under the Consul's arched porch, beside the drooping British flag, apparently guarding the wagon's stinking cargo. The day-dreaming soldier straightened as Sharpe approached. 'You can't go in there, *señor!*' He moved to block Sharpe's path. '*Señor!*'

'Shut up! Get out of my bloody way!' Sharpe, disgusted with all things Spanish, rammed his forearm into the soldier's chest, piling him backwards. Sharpe expected Blair's door to be locked, but unexpectedly it yielded to his thrust. He pushed it wide open as Harper ran into the porch's shelter. The dazed sentry took one look at the tall Irishman's size and decided not to make an issue of the confrontation. Sharpe stamped inside. 'Damn Marquinez! Damn Bautista! Damn the bloody Spaniards!' He took off his wet greatcoat and shook the rain off it. 'Bloody, bloody Spaniards! They never bloody change! You remember when we liberated their goddamned bloody country and they wanted to charge customs duty on the powder and shot we used to do it? Goddamned bloody Spaniards!'

Harper, who was married to a Spaniard, smiled soothingly. 'We need a cup of tea, that's what we need. That and some decent food, but I'll settle for dry clothes first.' He started climbing the stairs, but halfway to the landing he suddenly checked, then swore. 'Jesus!'

'What?'

'Thieves!' Harper was charging up to the landing. Sharpe followed.

'Get down!' Harper screamed, then threw himself sideways through an open doorway. Sharpe had a glimpse of two men in a second doorway, then the landing was filled with smoke as one of the men fired a gun. The noise was huge, echoing round the house. Bitter-smelling smoke churned in the corridor. Sharpe did not see where the bullet went. He only knew it had not hit him.

He scrambled to his feet and ran past the doorway where Harper had sheltered. He could hear the thieves running ahead of him. 'We've got the buggers trapped!' He shouted the encouragement for Harper, then he saw that there was another staircase at the back of the house, presumably a stair for servants, and the two thieves were jumping its steps three at a time.

'Stop!' Sharpe bellowed. He had visited the Citadel in civilian clothes, not bothering to wear any weapons. 'Stop!' He shouted again, but the two men were already scrambling out into the stableyard. The *mestiza* cook was screaming.

Sharpe reached the kitchen door as the thieves tugged open the stableyard gate. Sharpe ran into the rain, still shouting at the men to stop. Both thieves were carrying sacks of plunder, and both were armed with short-barrelled cavalry carbines. One carbine had been fired, but now the second man, fearing Sharpe's pursuit, turned and aimed his gun. The man had black hair, a bushy moustache and a scar on his cheek, then Sharpe realized the carbine was at point-blank range and he hurled himself sideways, slithering through puddles of rain and heaps of stable muck to thump against a bale of straw. The gate was open now, but the moustached gunman did not run, instead he carefully levelled the carbine at Sharpe. He was holding the gun one-handed. There was a pause of a heartbeat, then he smiled and pulled the trigger.

Nothing happened. For a second the man just gaped at Sharpe then, suddenly scared, he hurled the carbine like a club, then took off through the gate after his companion.

Sharpe was climbing to his feet, but had to drop flat again as the gun flew over his head. He stood again, slipped as he began running, found his balance, then clung to the gatepost when he saw that the two men had disappeared into a crowded alley. He swore.

He closed the gate, brushed the horse manure off his jacket and breeches, picked up the thief's carbine and went back to the kitchen. 'Stop your noise, woman!' he snapped at the cook, then stared up to where Harper had appeared at the top of the back stairs. 'What's the matter with you?'

'God save Ireland.' Harper came slowly down the stairs. He had gone pale as paper, and had a hand clapped to the side of his head. Blood showed between his fingers. 'Bugger shot me!' Harper staggered against the wall, but managed to keep his balance. 'I went through the whole damned French wars, so I did, and never once did I take a bullet, and now a damned thief in a damned town at the end of the damned world hits me! Jesus sweet Christ!' He took his hand away and blood oozed from his sandy hair to trickle down his neck. 'I'm feeling dizzy, so I am.'

Sharpe helped Harper to a chair, sat him down, then probed the blood-soaked hair. The damage was slight. The bullet had seared across the scalp, breaking the skin, but not doing any other damage. 'The bullet just grazed you,' Sharpe said in relief.

'Grazed, indeed! I was hit, so I was!'

'Barely broke the skin.'

'Lucky to be alive, I am. Sweet mother of God, but I could have been dead by now.'

'Luckily you've got a skull like a bloody ox.' Sharpe rapped Harper's temple. 'It would take a twelve pounder to dent that skull.'

'Would you listen to him! As near to death as a goose at Christmas, so I am, and all he can do is tap my skull!'

Sharpe went to the big water vat by the back door, soaked a piece of cloth, and tossed it to Harper. 'Hold that against your head. It'll bring you back to life. I'm going to see what the bastards took.'

Apart from their weapons and the chest with Louisa's gold, all of which had been locked in Blair's strongroom, the thieves appeared to have taken everything. Sharpe, disconsolate, went downstairs to where Harper was dabbing his bloody skull with the wet rag. 'The lot,' Sharpe said bitterly. 'Your bag, my bags, our clothes, boots, razors. The lot.'

'The Emperor's thimble?' Harper asked in disbelief.

'Everything,' Sharpe said. 'Bonaparte's portrait, and some stuff of Blair's as well. I can't tell what, but the candlesticks are gone and those small pictures that were on the shelf. Bastards!'

'What about your locket?'

'Round my neck.'

'The guns?'

Sharpe shook his head. 'The strongroom padlock wasn't touched.' He picked up the thief's weapon. 'The bastard tried to shoot me twice. It wouldn't fire.'

'He forgot to prime it?'

Sharpe opened the pan and saw a sludge of wet powder there, then saw that the trigger was loose. He scraped the priming out of the pan and tapped the gun's butt on the floor. His guess was that the carbine's mainspring had jammed because the wood of the stock had swollen in the damp weather. It was a common enough problem with cheap guns. He tapped harder and this time the trapped spring jarred itself free and the flint snapped down on the emptied pan.

'Swollen wood?' Harper asked.

'Saved my life, too. Bugger had me lined up at five paces.' He peered at the lockplate and saw the mark of the Cadiz Armoury, which made this a Spanish army gun. There was nothing sinister in that. The world was awash with old army weapons, even Sharpe and Harper carried rifles with the British Government's Tower Armoury mark on their plates.

Sharpe turned to the whimpering cook and accused her of letting the two thieves into the house, but the woman protested her innocence, claiming that the two men must have climbed across the church roof and jumped from there onto the half-roof at the side of Blair's house. 'It has happened before, *señor*,' she said resignedly, 'which is why the master has his strongroom.'

'What do we do now?' Harper still held the rag against his head.

'I'll make a formal complaint,' Sharpe said. 'It won't help, but I'll make it anyway.' He went back to the Citadel where, in the guardroom, a surly clerk took down a list of the stolen property. Sharpe, as he dictated the missing items, knew that he wasted his time.

'You wasted your time,' Blair said when he came home.

'Place is full of bloody thieves. That clerk will already have thrown your list away. You'll have to buy more clothes tomorrow.'

'Or look for the bloody thieves,' Harper, his head sore and bandaged, growled threateningly.

'You'll never find them,' Blair said. 'They brand some of them on the forehead with a big "L", but it doesn't do any good.' Sharpe guessed the 'L' stood for *ladron* – thief. 'That's why I have a strongroom,' Blair went on. 'It would take more than a couple of cut-throats to break in there.' He had fetched a bottle of gin back from HMS *Charybdis* and in consequence was a happy man. By nightfall he was also a drunken man who once again offered Sharpe and Harper the run of his servants. 'None of them are poxed. They'd better not be, God help them, or I'll have the skin off their backs.'

'I'll manage without,' Sharpe said.

'Your loss, Sharpe, your loss.'

That night the clouds rolled back from the coastal plain so that the dawn brought a wondrous clean sky and a sharp bright sun that rose to silhouette the jagged peaks of the Andes. There was something almost springlike in the air; something so cleansing and cheerful that Sharpe, waking, felt almost glad to be in Chile. Then he suddenly remembered the events of the previous day, and knew that he must spoil this bright clean day by buying a new greatcoat, new breeches, a coat, shirts, small clothes, and a razor. At least, he thought grimly, he had been wearing his good kerseymere coat for his abortive visit to Bautista, which had served to save the coat from the thieves and to save Sharpe from Lucille's wrath. She was forever telling him he should dress more stylishly, and the dark green kerseymere coat had been the first success in her long and difficult campaign. The coat had become somewhat soiled with horse manure when Sharpe rolled in the stableyard, but he supposed that would brush out.

He pulled on shirt, breeches and boots, then carried the coat downstairs so that one of Blair's servants could attack it with a brush. Blair was already up, drinking bitter coffee in the parlour and with him, to Sharpe's utter surprise, was Captain Marquinez. The Captain had a gold-edged shako tucked under one arm. The shako had a tall white plume that shivered as Marquinez offered Sharpe a low bow. 'Good morning, Colonel!'

'Got our travel permits, have you?' was Sharpe's surly greeting.

'What a lovely morning!' Marquinez smiled with delight. 'Mister Blair has offered me coffee, but I cannot accept for we are summoned to the Captain-General's audience.'

'Summoned?' Sharpe asked. Blair clearly thought Sharpe's hostility was inappropriate for he was making urgent signals that Sharpe should behave more gently.

Marquinez smiled. 'Summoned indeed, Colonel.'

Sharpe poured himself coffee. 'I'm an Englishman, Captain. You don't summon me.'

'What Colonel Sharpe means . . .' Blair began.

'Colonel Sharpe reproves me, and quite rightly.' The plume nodded as Marquinez bowed again. 'It would give Captain-General Bautista the most exquisite delight, Colonel, if you and Mister Harper would favour him with your attendance at this morning's audience.'

'Bloody hell,' Sharpe said. And wondered just what sort of man he would find when he at last met Vivar's enemy.

CHAPTER 3

Bautista's audience hall was a palatial room dominated by a carved and painted royal coat of arms that hung above the fireplace. Incongruously, for it was not cold, a small fire burned in a grate that was dwarfed by the huge stone hearth. The windows at either end of the hall were open; those at the east, where the early sun now dazzled, looked onto the Angel Tower and its execution yard, while the western windows offered a view across the defences to the swirling waters of the Valdivia River. The whole room, with its blackened beams, lime-washed walls, bright escutcheon and stone pillars, was intended as a projection of Spanish royal power; a grandiose echo of the Escorial.

The room's real power, though, lay not in the monarch's coat of arms, nor in the royal portraits that hung on the high walls, but in the energetic figure that paced up and down, up and down, behind a long table that was set before the fireplace and at which four aides-de-camp sat and took dictation. Watching the pacing man, and listening to his every word, was an audience of seventy or eighty officers. This was evidently how Captain-General Bautista chose to do his business; openly, efficiently, crisply.

Miguel Bautista was a tall, thin man with black hair which was oiled and brushed back so that it clung like a sleek cap to his narrow skull. His face was thin and pale, dominated by a long nose and the dark eyes of a predator. There was, Sharpe thought, a glint of quick intelligence in those eyes, but there was something else too, a carelessness, as though this young man had seen much of the world's wickedness and was amused by it. He wore a uniform that was new to Sharpe. It was an elegantly cut cavalry tunic of plain black cloth, but with no symbols of rank except for two modest epaulettes of silver chain. His breeches were black, as were his cavalry boots and even the cloth covering of his scabbard. It was a simple uniform, but one which stood in stark contrast to the colourful uniforms of the other officers in the room.

Some of those officers had evidently come as petitioners, others because they had information that Bautista needed, and yet more because they were on the Captain-General's staff. All were necessary to complete what Sharpe realized was a piece of theatre. This was Bautista's demonstration, held at a deliberately inconvenient early hour, to show that he was the enthusiastic master of every detail that mattered in his royal province. He paced incessantly, casting off the matters of business one after the other with a swift efficiency. A Lieutenant of Cavalry was given permission to marry, while a Major of Artillery was refused leave to travel home to Spain. 'Does Major Rodriguez think that no other officer ever had a dying mother?' There was laughter from the audience at that sally, and Sharpe saw Colonel Ruiz, the bombastic artilleryman who had sailed on the *Espiritu Santo*, laughing with the rest.

Bautista called various officers to make their reports. A tall, grey-haired Captain detailed the ammunition reserves in the Perrunque arsenal, then a Medical Officer reported on the number of men who had fallen sick in the previous month. Bautista listened keenly, noting that the Puerto Crucero garrison had shown a marked increase in fever cases. 'Is there a contagion there?'

'We're not sure, your Excellency.'

'Then find out!' Bautista's voice was high and sharp. 'Are the townspeople affected? Or just the garrison. Surely someone has thought to ask that simple question, have they not?'

'I don't know, your Excellency,' the hapless Medical Officer replied.

'Then find out! I want answers! Answers! Is it the food? The garrison's water supply? The air? Or just morale?' He stabbed a finger at the Medical Officer. 'Answers! Get me answers!'

It was an impressive display, yet still Sharpe felt unconvinced by it. It was almost as if Bautista was going through the motions of government merely so that no one could accuse him of dereliction when his province vanished from the maps of the Spanish Empire. He was, Sharpe thought, a young man full of self-importance, but so far Sharpe could see no evidence of anything worse; of, say, the cruelty that made Bautista's name so feared. The Captain-General had resumed pacing up and down before the small and redundant fire, stabbing more questions into his audience as he paced. How many cattle were in Valdivia's slaughteryards? Had the supply ships arrived from Spain? Was there any news of Ruiz's regiment? None? How many more weeks must they wait for those extra guns? Had the Puerto Crucero garrison test-fired their heated shot, and if so, what was their rate of fire? How long had it taken to heat the furnace from cold to operational heat? General Bautista suddenly whirled on Sharpe and pointed his finger, just as if Sharpe was one of the subservient officers who responded so meekly to each of Bautista's demands. 'You were at Waterloo?' The question was rapped out in the same tone that the General had used to ask about the monthly sick returns.

'Yes, sir.'

'Why did Napoleon lose there?'

The question took Sharpe somewhat by surprise, despite Marquinez having warned him that the Captain-General was fascinated by Napoleon and his battles. Did

Bautista see himself as a new Napoleon, Sharpe wondered? It was possible. The Captain-General was still a young man and, like his hero, an artillery officer.

'Well?' Bautista chivvied Sharpe.

'He underestimated the British infantry,' Sharpe said.

'And you, of course, were a British infantryman?' Bautista asked in a sarcastic tone, provoking more sycophantic laughter from his audience. Bautista cut the laughter short with a swift chop of his hand. 'I heard that he lost the battle because he waited too long before beginning to fight?'

'If he'd started earlier,' Sharpe said, 'we'd have beaten him sooner.' That was not true. If Bonaparte had opened the battle at dawn he would have ridden victorious into Brussels at dusk, but Sharpe would be damned before he gave Bautista the satisfaction of agreeing with him.

The Captain-General had walked close to Sharpe and was staring at the Englishman with what seemed a genuine curiosity. Sharpe was a tall man, but even so he had to look up to meet the dark eyes of the Captain-General. 'What was it like?' Bautista asked.

'Waterloo?' Sharpe felt tongue-tied.

'Yes! Of course. What was it like to be there?'

'Jesus,' Sharpe said helplessly. He did not know if he could describe such a day, certainly he had never done so to anyone except those, like Harper, who had shared the experience and who could therefore see beyond the tale's incoherence. Sharpe's fiercest memory of the day was simply one of terror; the terror of standing under the massive concussion of the French bombardment that, hour by hour, had ground down the British line till there were no reserves left. The remainder of the day had faded into unimportance. The opening of the battle had been full of excitement and motion, yet it was not those heart-stirring moments that Sharpe remembered when he woke sweating in the night, but rather that inhuman mincing-machine of the French artillery: the lurid flickering of its massive cannon flames in the smoke bank, the pathetic cries of the dying, the thunder of the roundshots in the over-heated air, the violence of the soil spewed up by the striking shots, and the stomach-emptying terror of standing under the unending cannonade that had punched and crashed and pounded down the bravest man's endurance. Even the battle's ending, that astonishing triumph in which tired and seemingly beaten men had risen from the mud to rout the finest troops of France, had paled in Sharpe's memory beside the nightmarish flicker of those guns. 'It was bad,' Sharpe said at last.

'Bad!' Bautista laughed. 'Is that all you can say?'

It was all Sharpe had said to the Emperor on St Helena, but Napoleon had not needed to hear more. Bonaparte had given Sharpe a look of such quick sympathy that Sharpe had been forced to laugh, and the Emperor had laughed with him. 'It was supposed to be bad!' Bonaparte had said indignantly. 'But it was evidently not bad enough, eh?' But now, because Sharpe spoke to a man who did not know how the heart shuddered with terror every time a shot punched the air with pressure, flame, and death, he could only offer the inadequate explanation. 'It was frightening. The guns, I mean.'

'The guns?' Bautista asked with a sudden intensity.

'The French had a lot of artillery,' Sharpe explained lamely, 'and it was well handled.'

'It was frightening?' Bautista wanted Sharpe's earlier assertion confirmed.

'Very.'

'Frightening.' Bautista repeated the word meaningfully, letting it hang in the air as he walked back to his long table. 'You hear that?' He shouted the question loudly, rounding on the startled audience. 'Frightening! And that is how we will finish this rebellion. Not by marching men into the wilderness, but with guns, with guns, with guns, with guns!' With each repetition of the word he pounded his right fist into his left palm. 'Guns! Where are your guns, Ruiz?'

'They're coming, your Excellency,' Ruiz said soothingly.

'I've told Madrid,' Bautista went on, 'time and again to send me guns! We'll break this rebellion by enticing its forces to attack our strongpoints. Here! In Valdivia! We shall let O'Higgins bring his armies and Cochrane his ships into the range of our guns and then we shall destroy them! With guns! With guns! With guns! But if Madrid doesn't send me guns, how can we win?' He was rehearsing the arguments that would explain the loss of Chile. He would blame it on Madrid for not sending enough guns, yet guns, as any real soldier knew, could not win the war.

Because relying on guns and forts was a recipe for doing nothing. It was generalship by defence. Bautista did not want to risk marching an army into the field and suffering a horrific defeat, so instead he was justifying his inaction by pretending it was a strategy. Let Madrid send enough guns, Bautista claimed, and the enemy would be destroyed when they attacked the royalist strongholds, yet even the dullest enemy would eventually realize it was both cheaper and more effective to starve a fortress into submission rather than drown it in blood. Bautista's strategy was designed solely to transfer the blame of defeat onto other men's shoulders, while he became rich enough to challenge those men when he returned to Madrid. No wonder, Sharpe thought, Blas Vivar had hated this man. He was betraying his soldiers as well as his country.

'Why have you come here, Mister Sharpe?' Bautista had suddenly turned on Sharpe again.

Sharpe, noting that he had not been accorded the honorific of his rank, decided not to make an issue of it. 'I'm here at the behest of the Countess of Mouromorto to carry her husband's remains home to Spain.'

'She is evidently an extravagant woman. Why did she not simply ask me to send her husband home?'

Sharpe did not want to explain that Louisa had not heard of her husband's death or burial when he left, so he just shrugged. 'I can't say, sir.'

'You can't say. Well, it seems a small enough request. I shall consider my decision, though I must say that so far as most of us are concerned the sooner General Vivar is out of Chile, the better.' The quip provoked another outburst of laughter which this time Bautista allowed to continue. 'You knew General Vivar?' he asked Sharpe when the sycophancy had subsided.

'We fought together in '09, at Santiago de Compostela.'

Blas Vivar's fight at Santiago de Compostela had been one of the great events of the Spanish war, a miraculous victory which had proved to many Spaniards that the French were not invincible, and Sharpe's mention of the battle made many of the officers in the audience look at him with a new interest and respect, but to General Bautista the battle was mere history. 'Vivar was like many veterans of the French wars,' Bautista said sarcastically, 'in his belief that the experience of fighting against Bonaparte's armies prepared him for suppressing a rebellion in a country like Chile. But they are not the same kind of fighting! Would you say they were the same kind of fighting, Mister Sharpe?'

'No, sir,' Sharpe replied in all honesty, but even so he felt that he was somehow betraying his dead friend by so agreeing.

Bautista, pleased to have elicited the agreement from Sharpe, smiled, then glanced at Harper's bandaged head. 'I hear you were sadly inconvenienced yesterday?'

Again Sharpe was surprised by the suddenness of the question, but he managed to nod. 'Yes, sir.'

The smile grew broader as Bautista snapped his fingers. 'I would not like you to return to England with an unhappy memory of Chile, or convinced that my administration is incompetent to police Valdivia's alleys. So I am delighted to tell you, Mister Sharpe, that the thieves were apprehended and your effects recovered.' The click of his fingers had summoned two orderlies who each carried a bag into the room. The bags were placed on the table. 'Come!' Bautista ordered. 'Come and examine them! I wish to be assured that everything has been recovered. Please!'

Astonished, Sharpe and Harper walked to the table and, in front of the audience, unpacked the bags. Everything seemed to be there, but not in the same condition. Their clothes, which had been soiled and crumpled from the long sea voyage, had all been laundered and pressed. Their boots had been polished, and Sharpe did not doubt that their razors had been stropped to a murderous edge. 'It's all here,' he said, and, thinking he had not been gracious enough, he made a clumsy half bow to Bautista. 'Thank you, your Excellency.'

'Everything is there?' Bautista demanded. 'Nothing is missing?'

It was then Sharpe realized that one thing was missing: the portrait of Napoleon. Harper's small silver thimble, duly polished, was in one of the bags, but not the silver framed portrait of the Emperor. Sharpe opened his mouth to report the loss, then abruptly closed it as he considered that the portrait's absence could be a trap. Bautista was evidently obsessed with Napoleon, which made it very likely that the Captain-General had himself purloined the signed portrait. Nor, Sharpe decided, was the loss of the portrait important. It was a mere *souvenir*, as the French said, and Lieutenant Colonel Charles could always write and request another such keepsake. Sharpe also had a strong suspicion that if he mentioned the missing picture then Bautista might refuse to issue the travel permits and so, without considering the matter further, Sharpe shook his head. 'Nothing is missing, your Excellency.'

Bautista smiled as though Sharpe had said the right thing, then, still smiling, he clicked his fingers again; this time summoning a squad of infantrymen who escorted two prisoners. The prisoners, in drab brown clothes, had their wrists and ankles manacled. The chains scraped and jangled as the two men were forced to the room's centre. 'These are the thieves,' Bautista announced.

Sharpe stared at the two men. They were both black-haired, both had moustaches, and both were terrified. Sharpe tried to remember the face of the man who had aimed the carbine at him, and in his memory that man had sported a much bigger moustache than either of these prisoners, but Sharpe could not be certain.

'What would you do,' Bautista asked, 'with thieves in your country?'

'Imprison them,' Sharpe said, 'or maybe transport them to Australia.'

'How merciful! No wonder you still have thieves. In Chile we have better ways to deter scum.' Bautista turned to the fire, drew a big handkerchief from his uniform pocket, then wrapped the handkerchief round the metal handle of what Sharpe had supposed to be a long poker jammed into the basket grate. It was not a poker, but rather a branding iron. Bautista jerked it free of the coals and Sharpe saw the letter 'L', for *ladron*, glowing at its tip.

'No! *Señor*! No!' The nearest thief twisted back, but two soldiers gripped him hard by the arms, and a third stood behind the man to hold his head steady.

'The punishment for a first offence is a branding. For the second offence it is death,' Bautista said, then he held the brand high and close to the thief's forehead, close enough for the man to feel its radiant heat. Bautista hesitated, smiling, and it seemed to Sharpe that the whole room held its breath. Colonel Ruiz turned away. The elegant Marquinez went pale.

'No!' The man screamed, then Bautista pushed the brand forward and the scream soared high and terrible. There was a sizzling sound, a flash of flame as the man's greasy hair briefly flared with fire, then the big room filled with the smell of burning flesh. Bautista held the brand on the man's skin even as the thief collapsed.

The iron was pushed back into the coals as the second man was hauled forward. That second man looked at Sharpe. '*Señor*, I beg you! It was not us! Not us!'

'Your Excellency!' Sharpe called.

'If I was in England,' Bautista jiggled the iron in the fire, 'would you think it proper for me to interfere with English justice? This is Chile, Mister Sharpe, not England. Justice here is what I say it is, and I treat thieves with the certain cure of pain. Exquisite pain!' He pulled the brand free, turned and aimed the bright letter at the second man.

'God save Ireland,' Harper said softly beside Sharpe. Most of the audience looked shocked. One uniformed man had gone to a window and was leaning across the wide stone sill. Bautista, though, was enjoying himself. Sharpe could see it in the dark eyes. The second man screamed, and again there was the hiss of burning skin and the stink of flesh cooking, and then the second man, like the first, had the big burned 'L' branded forever on his forehead.

'Take them away.' Bautista tossed the branding iron into the fireplace, then turned and stared defiantly at Sharpe. The Captain-General looked tired, as though all the joy of his morning had suddenly evaporated. 'Your request to travel to Puerto Crucero and recover the body of Don Blas Vivar is granted. Captain Marquinez will issue you with the necessary permits, and you will leave Valdivia tomorrow. That finishes today's business. Good day.' The Captain-General, his morning display of efficiency and cruelty complete, turned on his heels and walked away.

* * *

'Who were they?' Sharpe challenged Marquinez.

'They?'

'Those two men.'

'They were the thieves, of course.'

'I don't believe it,' Sharpe claimed angrily. 'I didn't recognize either man.'

'If they were not the thieves,' Marquinez said very calmly, 'then how do you explain their possession of your property?' He smiled as he waited for Sharpe's answer and, when none came, he opened a drawer of his desk and took out a sheaf of documents. 'Your travel permits, Colonel. You will note they specify you must leave Valdivia tomorrow.' He dealt the documents onto the desk one by one, as though they were playing cards. 'Mister Harper's travel pass, which bears the same date restrictions as your own. This is your fortress pass, which gives you entry to the citadel at Puerto Crucero, and finally a letter from His Excellency giving you permission to exhume the body of General Vivar.' Marquinez smiled. 'Everything you wish!'

Sharpe, after his flash of anger, felt churlish. The papers were indeed everything he needed, even down to the letter authorizing the exhumation. 'What about the church's permission?'

'I think you will find that no churchman will countermand the wishes of Captain-General Bautista,' Marquinez said.

Sharpe picked up the papers. 'You've been very helpful, Captain.'

'It is our pleasure to be helpful.'

'And at least we'll have fine weather for our voyage,' Harper put in cheerfully.

'Your voyage?' Marquinez asked in evident puzzlement, then understood Harper's meaning. 'Ah! You are assuming that you will be travelling on board the *Espiritu Santo*. Alas, she has no spare passenger cabins, at least not till she has dropped those passengers travelling to Puerto Crucero. Which means that you must travel overland. Which is good news, gentlemen! It will offer you a chance to see some of our lovely countryside.'

'But if we don't have to catch the ship,' Sharpe asked, 'why do we have to leave tomorrow?'

'You surely want to have your business in Puerto Crucero finished by the time the *Espiritu Santo* arrives there, do you not? Else how will you be able to travel back to Europe in her? Besides, we always specify the dates for travel, Colonel, otherwise how do we know the permits have been properly used?'

'But I need a tin-lined coffin made!' Sharpe insisted. 'And I can't do that and buy horses all in one day!'

Marquinez brushed the objections aside. 'The armourers at Puerto Crucero will be pleased to make a coffin for you. And I'm sure Mister Blair will be happy to help you buy horses and saddles, as well as supplies for the journey.'

Sharpe still protested at the arrangement. 'Why can't we sleep on the *Espiritu Santo*'s deck? We don't need cabins.'

Marquinez tried to soothe Sharpe. 'The fault is entirely ours. We insisted that Captain Ardiles carry reinforcements for the Puerto Crucero garrison, and he claims he cannot cram another soul on board his ship. Alas.' Marquinez sounded genuinely sympathetic. 'But even if you could change Ardiles's mind, then you would still need new travel permits because these, as you can plainly see, are good only for land travel and do not give you permission to journey by sea. It is the regulations, you understand.' Marquinez offered Sharpe one of his dazzling white smiles. 'But perhaps, Colonel, you will do me the honour of letting me escort you for the first few miles? I could bring some company!' Marquinez raised his eyebrows to indicate that the company would be enjoyable. 'And perhaps you will do me the favour of allowing me to provide you with luncheon? It would provide me with an opportunity to show you some scenery that is truly spectacular. I beg you! Please!' Marquinez waited for Sharpe's assent, then sensed the Englishman's suspicions. 'My dear Colonel,' Marquinez hastened to reassure Sharpe, 'bring Mister Blair if that will make you easier!'

It seemed churlish to refuse. So far Marquinez had exacted neither payment nor bribe for the travel permits, indeed he had produced everything Sharpe had wanted, and the elegant young Captain seemed genuinely enthusiastic about showing Sharpe and Harper some of Chile's most beautiful countryside, and so Sharpe accepted the invitation, and then, with the permits safe in his pocket, he went to seek Blair's urgent help in buying horses and supplies.

Because they had just one day before they rode south to rendezvous with a corpse.

*　　*　　*

It was, Harper said, a countryside so lovely and so fertile that it seemed only fitting that he rode it on a horse of gold.

In truth the horse was nothing special, but the beast had cost more money than either Harper or Sharpe had ever paid for a horse, and Sharpe's horse had cost just as much, yet Blair had been at pains to convince them that the animals had been purchased at something close to a bargain price. 'Horses are expensive here!' the Consul had pleaded, 'and when you leave Chile you should be able to sell them at a profit. Or something close to a profit.'

'At a loss, you mean?' Sharpe asked.

'You need horses!' Blair insisted, and so they had paid for the two most expensive lumps of horseflesh ever bred. Harper's was a big mare, grey with a wall left eye and a hard bruising gait. She was not pretty, but she was stubborn and strong enough to cope with Harper's weight. Sharpe's horse was also a mare, a chestnut with a docked tail and gaunt ribs. 'All she needs is a bit of feeding,' Blair had said, then negotiated the price of a mule that was to carry their luggage as well as the box which, taken from Blair's strongroom, was now even more depleted of its precious gold.

What was left in the box was still a small fortune, and one that seemed increasingly unnecessary. So far, to Sharpe's astonishment, everything had proved remarkably easy. 'It must be your reputation,' Blair had said. The Consul claimed to be too busy to accept Marquinez's invitation, but had assured Sharpe there could be no danger in Marquinez's company. 'Or perhaps Bautista thinks you've got a deal of influence back in Spain. You're a lucky man.'

The lucky man now rode south under a sky so pale and blue that it seemed to have been rinsed by the recent winds and rains. Sharpe and Harper rode with the exquisitely uniformed Captain Marquinez ahead of an ebullient pack of young officers and their ladyfriends. The girls rode side-saddle, what they called 'English-style', provoking laughter in their companions by their loud cries of alarm whenever the road was particularly steep or treacherous. At those moments the officers vied in their attentions to hold the ladies steady. 'The girls are not used to riding,' Marquinez confided to Sharpe. 'They come from an establishment behind the church. You understand?' There was an odd tone of disapproval in Marquinez's voice. Occasionally, when a girl's laughter was particularly loud, Marquinez would wince with embarrassment, but on the whole he seemed happy to be free of Valdivia and riding into such lovely country. A dozen officers' servants brought up the rear of the convoy, carrying food and wine for an outdoor luncheon.

They rode through wide vineyards and past rich villas and through white painted villages, yet always, beyond the vines or the orchards or the tobacco fields, or behind the churches with their twin towers and high peaked roofs, there were the great sharp-edged mountains, deep swooping valleys and rushing white streams that cut like knives down from the peaks, above which, staining the otherwise clear sky, the smoke of two volcanoes smeared the blue with their grey brown plumes. At other times, staring to their right, Sharpe and Harper could see ragged fingers of rocky land jutting and clawing out to an island-wracked sea. A ship, her white sails bright in the sun, was racing southwards from Valdivia.

Luncheon was served beside a waterfall. Hummingbirds darted into a bank of wild flowers. The wine was heady. One of the girls, a dark-skinned *mestiza*, waded in the waterfall's pool, urged by her friends ever further into the deepening water until her skirt was hitched high about her thighs and the young officers cheered their glimpse of dark tantalizing skin. Marquinez, sitting beside Sharpe, was more interested in a patrol of a dozen cavalrymen that idled southwards on small wiry horses. Marquinez raised a languid hand to acknowledge the patrol's presence, then looked back to Sharpe. 'What did you think of the Captain-General?'

A dangerous question, and one that Sharpe parried easily. 'He seemed very efficient.'

'He's a man of genius,' Marquinez said enthusiastically.

'Genius?' Sharpe could not hide his scepticism.

'Customs dues have increased threefold under his rule, so have tax revenues. We have firm government at last!' Sharpe glanced at his companion's handsome face, expecting to see cynicism there, but Marquinez clearly meant every word he said. 'And once we have all the guns we need,' Marquinez went on, 'we'll reconquer the northern regions.'

'You'd best be asking Madrid for some good infantry,' Sharpe said.

Marquinez shook his head. 'You don't understand Chile, Colonel. The rebels think they're invincible, so sooner or later they will come to our fortresses, and they will be slaughtered, and everyone will recognize the Captain-General's genius.' Marquinez tossed pebbles into the pool. Sharpe was watching the *mestiza* girl who, her thighs and skirts soaking, climbed onto the bank. 'You find her pretty?' Marquinez suddenly asked.

'Yes. Who wouldn't?'

'They're pretty when they're young. By the time they're twenty and have two children they look like cavalry mules.' Marquinez fished a watch from his waistcoat pocket. 'We must be leaving you, Colonel. You know your way from here?'

'Indeed.' Sharpe had been well-coached by Blair in the route he must take. He and Harper would climb into the hills where their travel permit dictated that they must spend the night at a high fortress. Tomorrow they would ride down into the wilder country that sprawled across the border of the southern province. It was in that unsettled country, close to the hell-dark forests where embittered Indian tribes lived, that Blas Vivar had died. Blair and Marquinez had both assured Sharpe that the border country had been tamed since Vivar's death, and that the highway could be used in perfect safety. 'There have been no rebels there since Blas Vivar died,' Marquinez said. 'There have been some highway robberies, but nothing, I think, that should worry either you or Mister Harper.'

'They're welcome to try, so they are,' Harper had said, and indeed he and Sharpe fairly bristled with weapons.

Sharpe wore his big butcher's blade of a sword; the sword with which he had fought through Portugal, Spain and France, and then to the field of Waterloo. It was no ordinary infantry officer's sword, but instead the killing blade of a trooper from Britain's heavy cavalry. Soldiers armed with just such big swords had carved a Corps of veteran French infantry into bloody ruin at Waterloo, capturing two Eagles as they did it. The sword was reckoned a bad weapon by experts; unbalanced, ugly and too long in its blade, but Sharpe had used it to lethal effect often enough, and by now he had a sentimental attachment to the sword. He also had a loaded Baker rifle slung on one shoulder, and had two pistols in his belt.

Harper was even more fiercely armed. He too carried a rifle and two pistols, and had a sabre at his waist, yet the Irishman also carried his own favourite weapon; a seven-barrelled gun, made for Britain's navy, yet too powerful for any but the biggest and most robust men to fire. The navy, which had wanted a weapon that could be fired like an overweight shotgun from the rigging onto an enemy's deck, had abandoned the weapon because of its propensity to shatter the shoulders of the men pulling its trigger, but in Patrick Harper the seven-barrelled gun had found a soldier capable of taming its brute ferocity. The gun was a cluster of seven half inch barrels which were fired by a single lock, and was, in its effect, like a small cannon loaded with grapeshot. Sharpe was hoping that any highway robber, seeing the weapon, let alone the swords, rifles and pistols, would think twice before trying to steal the strongbox.

'Bloody odd, when you think about it.' Harper broke their companionable silence an hour after they had parted from Marquinez.

'What's odd?'

'That there wasn't any room on the frigate. It was a bloody big boat.' Harper frowned. 'You don't think the buggers want us on this road so they can do us some mischief, do you?'

Sharpe had been wondering the same thing, but, unaware how best to prepare for such trouble, he had not thought to perturb Harper by talking about it. Yet there was something altogether too convenient about the ease with which Marquinez had given them all the necessary permits, but then denied them the chance to travel on the *Espiritu Santo*, something which suggested that maybe Sharpe and Harper were not intended to reach Puerto Crucero after all. 'But I think we're safe today,' Sharpe said.

'Too many people about, eh?' Harper suggested.

'Exactly.' They were riding through a plump and popu- lated countryside on a road that was intermittently busy with other travellers; a friar walking barefoot, a farmer driving a wagon of tobacco leaves to Valdivia, a herdsman with a score of small bony cattle. This was not the place to commit murder and theft; that would come tomorrow in the wilder southern hills.

'So what do we do tomorrow?' Harper asked.

'We ride very carefully,' Sharpe answered laconically. He was not as sanguine as he sounded, but he did not know how else to plan against a mere possibility of ambush and he was unwilling to think of just turning back. He had come to Chile to find Blas Vivar and, even if his old friend was dead, he would still do his best to carry him home.

That night, in obedience to their travel permits, they stopped at a timber-walled fort that had been built so high above the surrounding land that it had been nicknamed the Celestial Fort. Its simple log ramparts stared east to the mountains and west to the sea. To the north of the Celestial Fort, at the foot of the steep ridge that gave the fort its commanding height, was a small ragged village that was inhabited by natives who worked a nearby tobacco plantation while, to the south, like a sullen warning of the dangers to come, were line after line of dark wooded ridges. 'I trust you brought your own food?' the fort's commander, a cavalry Captain named Morillo, greeted Sharpe and Harper.

'Yes.'

'I'd like to feed you, but rations are scarce.' Morillo gave Sharpe back the travel permits while his men eyed the newcomers warily. Morillo was a tall young man with a weathered face. His eyes were cautious and watchful, the eyes of a soldier. His job was to lead his cavalrymen on long aggressive patrols down the highway, deterring any rebels who might think of ambushing its traffic. 'Not that we have rebels here now,' Morillo said. 'The last Captain-General swept these valleys clean. He was a cavalryman, so he knew how to attack.' There was an unspoken criticism in the words, suggesting that the new Captain-General knew only how to defend.

'I knew Vivar well,' Sharpe said. 'I rode with him in Spain. At Santiago de Compostela.'

Morillo stared at Sharpe with momentary disbelief. 'You were at Santiago when the French attacked the Cathedral?'

'I was in the Cathedral when they broke the truce.'

'I was a child then, but I remember the stories. My God, but what times they were.' Morillo frowned in thought for a few seconds, then abruptly twisted to stare across the fort's parade ground that was an expanse of smoothly trampled earth. 'Do you know Sergeant Dregara?'

'Dregara? No.'

'He rode in an hour ago, with a half troop. He was asking about you.'

'About me? I don't know him,' Sharpe said.

'He knows you, and your companion. They're across the parade ground, round an open fire. Dregara's got a striped blanket over his shoulders.'

Sharpe half turned and surreptitiously stared across the fort to where the group of cavalry troopers squatted about their open fire. Sharpe suspected, but could not be sure, that it was the same patrol that had saluted Marquinez at lunchtime.

Morillo drew Sharpe away from the ears of his own men. 'Sergeant Dregara tells me he proposes to escort you tomorrow.'

'I don't need an escort.'

'Maybe what you need and what you will receive are very different, Colonel Sharpe. Things often are in Chile. Do I need to explain more?'

Sharpe had walked with the tall Spanish Captain through the open gate of the fort where both men stopped and stared towards the distant sea that, from this eyrie, looked like a wrinkled sheet of hammered silver. 'I assume, Captain,' Sharpe said, 'that you regret the death of Don Blas?'

Morillo was tense as he skirted the betrayal of the present Captain-General with his admiration of the last. 'Yes, sir, I do.'

'It happened not far from here, am I right?'

'A half day's journey south, sir.' Morillo turned and pointed across the misted valleys of the wild country. 'It wasn't on the main road, but off to the east.'

'Strange, isn't it,' Sharpe said, 'that Don Blas cleared the rebels out of this region, yet was ambushed here by those same rebels?'

'Things are often strange in Chile, sir.' Morillo spoke very warily.

'Perhaps,' Sharpe said pointedly, 'you could patrol southwards tomorrow? Along the main road?'

Morillo, understanding exactly what Sharpe was suggesting, shook his head. 'Sergeant Dregara brought me orders. I'm to ride to Valdivia tomorrow. I'm to leave a dozen men on post here, and the rest are to go to the

Citadel with me. We're to report to Captain Marquinez before two o'clock in the afternoon.'

'Meaning an early start,' Sharpe said, 'that will leave my friend and me alone with Sergeant Dregara?'

'Yes, sir.' Morillo stooped to light a cigar. The wind whipped the smoke northwards. He snapped shut the glowing tinderbox and pushed it into his sabretache. 'The orders are signed by Captain-General Bautista. I've never received orders direct from a General before.' Morillo drew on his cigar and Sharpe felt a chill creep up his spine. 'You should also understand, sir,' Morillo spoke with an admirable understatement, 'that General Bautista is not kind to men who disobey his orders.'

'I do understand that, Captain.'

'I'd like to help you, sir, truly I would. General Vivar was a good man.' Morillo shook his head ruefully. 'When he was in command we had a score of forts like this one. We were training native cavalry. We were aggressive! Now?' He shrugged. 'Now the only patrols are to keep this road open. We don't really know what's happening fifty miles east.'

Sharpe turned to look back into the fort. 'These aren't built for defence.'

'No, sir. They're just refuges where tired men can spend a few nights in comparative safety. General Vivar deliberately made them uncomfortable so that we wouldn't be tempted to live in them permanently. He believed our place was out there.' Morillo waved towards the darkening hills.

The temporary nature of the fort's accommodation was suggesting an idea to Sharpe. There was only one walled and roofed structure; a log cabin which Sharpe guessed was the officer's perquisite, while the other cavalrymen were sheltered beneath the overhang of the firestep. Essentially the fort was nothing more than a walled bivouac; there was not even a water supply inside the walls. The horses had to be watered at the stream at the ridge's foot, and any other drinking water had to be lugged up from the same place. Sharpe gestured at the log cabin. 'Your quarters, Captain?'

'Yes, sir.'

'Maybe Mister Harper and I can share them with you?'

Morillo frowned, not quite understanding the request, but he nodded anyway. 'We'll be cramped, but you're welcome.'

'What time do you rouse the men?' Sharpe asked.

'Usually at six. We'd expect to leave at seven.'

'Could you leave earlier? While it was dark?'

Morillo nodded cautiously. 'I could.'

Sharpe smiled. 'I'm thinking, Captain, that if Sergeant Dregara is convinced Mister Harper and I are still asleep, he won't disturb us. He may even wait till mid-morning before he ventures to knock on the door of your quarters.'

Morillo understood the ruse, but looked doubtful. 'He'll surely see your horses are gone.'

'He might not notice if the horses are missing. After all, his horses and a dozen of yours will still be here. But he'll notice if the mule is gone, so I'll just have to leave it here, won't I?'

Morillo drew on his cigar, then blew a stream of smoke towards the distant sea. 'Captain-General Bautista's orders are addressed to me. They say nothing about you, sir, and if you choose to leave at three in the morning, then I can't stop you, can I?'

'No, Captain, you can't. And thank you.'

But Morillo was not finished. 'I'd still be unhappy about you using the main road, sir. Even if you get a six-hour start on Dregara, you'll be travelling slowly, while he knows the short cuts.' Morillo smiled. 'I'll give you Ferdinand.'

'Ferdinand?'

'You'll meet him in the morning.' Morillo seemed amused, but would not say more.

The two men went back into the fort where the cooking fires crackled and smoked. Sentries paced the firestep as darkness seeped up from the valleys to engulf the sky and the mountains. Sulphurous yellow clouds shredded off the Andean peaks to spill towards the seaward plains, patterning the stars and shadowing the moon. An hour after sundown Sharpe and Harper accompanied Captain Morillo as he went round the cooking fires to announce that his Valdivia patrol would be leaving three hours before dawn. Men groaned at the news, but Sharpe heard the humour behind their reaction and knew that at least these men still had confidence in their cause. Not all Vivar's work had gone to waste.

'And you, *señor*?' Sergeant Dregara, who had been sitting at the fire with Morillo's sergeants, looked slyly up at Sharpe. 'You will go early, too?'

'Good Lord, no!' Sharpe yawned. 'I'm an English gentleman, Sergeant, and English gentlemen don't stir till at least an hour after dawn.'

'And the Irish not for another hour after that,' Harper put in happily.

Dregara was a middle-aged runt of a man with yellow teeth, a lined face, a scarred forehead, and the eyes of a killer. He was holding a half-empty bottle of clear Chilean brandy that he now gestured towards Sharpe. 'Maybe we can ride south together, *señor*? There is sometimes safety in numbers.'

'Good idea,' Sharpe said in his best approximation of the braying voice some British officers liked to use. 'And one of your men can bring us hot shaving water at, say, ten o'clock? Just tell the fellow to knock on the door and leave the bowl on the step.'

'Shaving water?' Dregara clearly hated being treated as a servant.

'Shaving water, Sergeant. Very hot. I can't bear shaving in tepid water.'

Dregara managed to suppress his resentment. '*Si, señor.* At ten.'

The troopers wrapped themselves in blankets and lay down under the meagre shelter of the fort's firestep. The sentries paced overhead. Somewhere beyond the wall, in the forests that lapped against the ridge, a beast screamed. Sharpe, sleepless on the floor of Morillo's quarters, listened to Harper's snores. If Dregara was supposed to kill them, Sharpe thought, how would Bautista react when he heard they still lived? And why would Bautista kill them? It made no sense. Maybe Dregara meant no harm, but why would Morillo be ordered back to Valdivia? The questions flickered through Sharpe's mind, but no answers came. It made sense, he supposed, that Bautista should resent Doña Louisa's interest in her husband's fate, for that interest could cause Madrid to scrutinize this far, doomed colony, but was killing Louisa's emissaries the way to avert such interest?

He slept at last, but it seemed he was woken almost immediately. Captain Morillo was shaking his shoulder. 'You should go now, before the others stir. My sergeant will open the gate. Wake up, sir!'

Sharpe groaned, turned over, groaned again. There had been a time when he could live on no sleep, but he felt too old for such tricks now. There was a pain in his back, and an ache in his right leg where a bullet had once lodged. 'Oh, Jesus.'

'Dregara's bound to be awake when my men leave, and he mustn't see you,' Morillo hissed.

Sharpe and Harper pulled on their boots, strapped on their sword belts, slung their weapons, then carried their saddles, bags and the strongbox to the fort's gate where a sergeant let them out into the chill night. A moment later Morillo, together with a much smaller man, brought their horses. The mule was left behind in the fort to lull any suspicions Dregara might have.

Morillo introduced the small man. 'This is Ferdinand, he's your guide. He'll take you across the hills and cut a good ten hours off your journey. He's a *picunche*. He speaks no Spanish, I'm afraid, nor any other Christian language, but he knows what to do.'

'*Picunche*?' Sharpe asked.

He was given his answer as a cloud slid from the moon to reveal that Ferdinand, named after the King of Spain, was an Indian. He was a small, thin man, with a flat mask of a face, and dressed in a tatter of a cast-off cavalry uniform decorated with bright feathers stuck into its loops and buttonholes. He wore no shoes and carried no weapon.

'*Picunche* is a kind of tribal name.' Morillo was helping to saddle Harper's horse. 'We use the Indians as scouts and guides. There aren't many savages who are friendly to us. Don Blas wanted to recruit more, but that idea died with him.'

'Doesn't Ferdinand have a horse?' Harper asked.

Morillo laughed. 'He'll outrun your horses over a day's marching. He'll also give you a fighting chance to stay well ahead of Sergeant Dregara.' Morillo tightened a girth strap, then stepped away. 'Ferdinand will find his way back to me when he's finished with you. Good luck, Colonel.'

Sharpe thanked the cavalry Captain. 'How can we repay you?'

'Mention my name to Vivar's widow. Say I was a true man to her husband.' Morillo was hoping that Doña Louisa would still have some influence in Spain; influence that would help his career when he was posted home again.

'I shall tell her you deserve whatever is in her gift,' Sharpe promised, then he pulled himself into the saddle and took the great strongbox onto his lap. 'Good luck, Captain.'

'God bless you, *señor*. Trust Ferdinand!'

The Indian reached up and took hold of both horses' bridles. The moon was flying in and out of ragged clouds, offering a bare light to the dark slope down to where the trees closed over their heads. The main road went eastwards, detouring about the thickly wooded country into which Ferdinand unerringly led them just as a bugle called its reveille up in the Celestial Fort. Sharpe laughed, pulled his hat over his eyes to protect them from the twigs, and followed a savage to the south.

*   *   *

At dawn they rode through the forests of morning, hung with mists, spangled with a million beads of dew that were given light by the lancing, slanting rays of the rising sun. Drifts of vapour softened the great tree trunks amongst which a myriad of bright birds flew. The clouds had cleared, gone back to the mountains or blown out to the endless oceans. Ferdinand had relinquished the horses' bridles and was content simply to lead the way through the towering trees. 'I wonder where the hell we are,' Harper said.

'Ferdinand knows,' Sharpe replied, and the mention of his royal name made the small Indian turn and smile with file-sharpened teeth.

'We could have done with a few hundred of him at Waterloo,' Harper said. 'They'd have frightened the buggers to death by just grinning at them.'

They rode on. At times, when the path was especially steep or slippery, they dismounted and led the horses. Once they circled a hill on a narrow path above a chasm of pearl-bright mist. Strange birds screeched at them. The worst moment of the morning came when Ferdinand brought them to a great canyon that was crossed by a perilously fragile bridge made of leather, rope and green wood. The green wood slats were held in place by the twisted leather straps and the whole precarious roadway was suspended from the rope cables. Ferdinand made gestures at Sharpe and Harper, grunting the while in a strange language.

'I think,' Harper said, 'he wants us to cross one at a time. God save Ireland, but I think I'd rather not cross at all.'

It was a terrifying crossing. Sharpe went first and the whole structure shivered and swayed with every step he took. Ferdinand followed Sharpe, leading his blindfolded horse. Despite its blindfold the horse was nervous and trembling. Once, when the mare missed her footing and plunged a hoof through the slats, she began to panic, but Ferdinand soothed and calmed the beast. Far beneath Sharpe the mist shredded to reveal a white thread which was a quick-flowing stream deep in the canyon's jungle.

Harper was white with terror when he finished the crossing. 'I'd rather face the Imperial bloody Guard than do that again.'

They remounted and rode on, taking it in turns to balance the great box of golden guineas on their saddles' pommels. Ferdinand loped tirelessly ahead. Harper, chewing a lump of hard bread, had begun to think of Bautista. 'Why does that long-nosed bastard want to kill us?'

'God knows. I've been trying to make sense of it, and I can't.'

Harper shook his head. 'I mean if the man wants to be rid of us, then why the hell doesn't he just let us take Don Blas's body and be away? Why send those fellows to kill us?'

'If he did send them.' As the morning unfolded into sun-drenched innocence, Sharpe had again begun to doubt the fears that had crowded in on him during the night.

'He sent them, right enough,' Harper said. 'He's an evil bastard, that Bautista. You only had to look in his eye. If a man like that comes into the tavern I throw him out. I won't have him drinking my ale!'

'I don't know if he's evil,' Sharpe said, 'but he's certainly frightened.'

'Bautista? Frightened?' Harper was scornful.

'He's like a man playing drumhead.' Drumhead was a card game that had been popular in the army. It was a simple game, needing only a pack of cards, as many players as wanted to risk their money, and a playing surface like a drumhead. Each player nominated a card and another man dealt the cards face up onto the drumhead. The man whose card appeared last won the game.

'Drumhead?' Harper was still unconvinced.

'Bautista's playing for very big stakes, Patrick. He's cheating left, right and centre and he knows if he's caught that he'll face court martial, disgrace, maybe even imprisonment. But if he wins, then he wins very big indeed. He's watching the cards turn over and he's dreading that he'll lose. But he can't stop playing because the winnings are so huge.'

'Then why the hell doesn't he fight the war properly?' Harper grunted as he settled the strongbox more comfortably on his pommel.

'Because he knows the war is lost,' Sharpe said. 'It would take an extraordinary soldier to win this war, and Bautista isn't an extraordinary soldier. Don Blas might have won it, but only if Madrid had sent him the ships to beat Cochrane, which they didn't. So Bautista knows he's going to lose, and that means he has to do two things. First he needs to blame someone else for losing the war, and second he has to grab as much of Chile's wealth as possible. Then he can go home rich and blameless, and he can use the money to gain power in Madrid.'

'But why kill us? We're bugger all to do with his problems.'

'We're the enemy,' Sharpe said. 'The closest Bautista came to losing was when Don Blas was here. Don Blas knew something that would destroy Bautista, and he was on the point of confronting Bautista when he died. We're on Don Blas's side, so we're enemies.' It was the only answer that made sense to Sharpe, and though it was an answer full of gaps, it helped to explain the Captain-General's enmity.

'So he'll kill us?' Harper asked indignantly.

Sharpe nodded. 'But not in public. If we can reach Puerto Crucero, we're safe. Bautista needs to blame our disappearance on the rebels. He won't dare attack us in a public place.'

'I pray to God you're right,' Harper said feelingly. 'I mean there's no point in dying here, is there now?'

Sharpe felt a pang of guilt for having invited his friend. 'You shouldn't have come.'

'That's what Isabella said. But, goddamn it, a man gets tired of children after a time. I'm glad to be away for a wee while, so I am.' Harper had left four children in Dublin: Richard, Liam, Sean and the baby, Michael, whose real name was in a Gaelic form that Sharpe could not pronounce. 'But I wouldn't want never to see the nippers again,' Harper went on, 'would I now?'

'There's not much to do now,' Sharpe tried to reassure him. 'We just have to dig up Don Blas, seal him in a tin coffin, then take him home.'

'I still think you should put him in brandy,' Harper said, his fears forgotten.

'Whatever's quickest,' Sharpe allowed, then he forgot that small problem for Ferdinand had led them out from the trees and onto what had to be the main road from Valdivia to Puerto Crucero. The road stretched empty and inviting in either direction, and with no sign of any vengeful pursuers. Ferdinand was grinning, then said something in his own language.

'I think he means he's leaving us here,' Harper said before pointing vigorously to the south.

Ferdinand nodded eagerly, intimating that they should indeed ride in that direction.

Sharpe opened the box, took out a guinea, and gave it to the Indian. Ferdinand tucked the coin into a pocket of his filthy uniform, offered a sharp-toothed grin of thanks, then turned back into the forest. Sharpe and Harper, brought safe to the road and far ahead of their pursuers, were out of danger. Ahead lay Puerto Crucero and a friend's grave, behind was a thwarted enemy, and Sharpe, almost for the first time since he had reached the New World, felt his hopes rise.

CHAPTER 4

That evening, just before sunset, they reined their tired horses on the rocky crest above the natural harbour of Puerto Crucero. Sharpe, weary to his very bones, turned in his aching saddle and saw no sign of any pursuit. Dregara had been cheated. Sharpe and Harper, thanks to Captain Morillo and his Indian guide, had come safe to their haven where, like a sorcerer's castle perched on a crag, stood the citadel of Puerto Crucero.

At the heart of the citadel, and brilliant white in the day's last sunlight, stood the garrison church where Blas Vivar lay buried. Beside the church was a castle keep over which, streaming stiff in the sea's hard wind, the great royal banner of Spain flew colourful and proud. The dark, wild country where murder might have been committed was behind them and in front were witnesses and light. There was also the harbour from which, by God's grace, they would sail home with the body of a dead hero.

The harbour was not a massive refuge like Valdivia's magnificent haven, but instead lay within a wide hook of low rocky land that stopped the surge of the Pacific swells, but allowed the insistent southern winds to tug and fret at the anchorage. Even now the harbour was flecked with white by the wind that streamed the royal banner at the fort's summit.

The town was built where an inner harbour had been made with a stone breakwater. The town itself was a huddle of warehouses, fishing shacks and small houses. Nothing could move in the town or harbour without being observed from the great high fortress. The road to the fort zig-zagged up the rock hill to disappear into a tunnel that pierced a wide stone wall studded with cannon embrasures. 'A bastard of a fort to take,' Harper said.

'Then thank God we don't need to.' Sharpe flourished the pass which gave them entry to the citadel.

The pass, signed and sealed by Miguel Bautista, worked its charm. Sharpe and Harper were saluted at every guardpost, escorted through the fortress's entrance tunnel, and greeted effusively by the officer of the day, a Major Suarez, who seemed somewhat astonished by the pass. In all likelihood, Sharpe suspected, Suarez had never seen such a document, for Sharpe suspected it had been issued only to lull him into a false sense of security, but now, even if unintentionally, Bautista's signature was working a wonderful magic.

'You'll accept our hospitality?' Major Suarez was standing behind his desk, eager to show Sharpe and Harper a due respect. 'There is an inn beside the harbour, but I can't recommend it. You'll permit me to have two officers' rooms made ready for you?'

'And a meal?' Harper suggested.

'Of course!' Suarez, assuming that Bautista was their patron, could not do enough to help. 'Perhaps you will wait in my quarters while the room and the food are made ready?'

'I'd rather see the church,' Sharpe said.

'I'll send for you as soon as things are ready.' Suarez snapped his fingers, summoning ostlers to take care of the tired horses, and orderlies to carry the travellers' bags for safekeeping into the officers' quarters. Sharpe and Harper kept only the strongbox that they carried between them into the welcome coolness of the garrison church which proved to be a building of stern beauty. The walls were painted white while the heavily beamed ceiling was of a shining wood that had been oiled almost to blackness. On the walls were marble slabs that commemorated officers who had died in this far colony. Some had been killed in skirmishes, some had drowned off the coast, some had died in earthquakes, a few, very few, had died of old age. Other marble plaques remembered the officers' families: women who had died in childbirth, children who had been killed or captured by Indians, and babies who had died of strange diseases and whose souls were now commended to God.

Sharpe and Harper put the strongbox down in the nave, then walked slowly through the choir to climb the steps to the altar which was a magnificent confection of gold and silver. Crucifixes, candleholders and ewers graced the niches and shelves of the intricate altar screen on which painted panels depicted the torture and death of Christ.

Many of the flagstones close to the altar were grave-stones. Some had ornate coats of arms carved above the names, and most of the inscriptions were in Latin which meant Sharpe could not read them, yet even without Latin he could see that none of the stones bore the name of his friend. But then Harper moved aside a small rush mat that had covered a paving slab to the right of the altar and thus discovered Don Blas's grave. 'Here,' Harper said softly, then crossed himself. The stone bore two simple letters chiselled into its surface. BV.

'Poor bastard,' Sharpe said gently. There were times when he found his lack of any religion a handicap. He supposed he should say a prayer, but the sight of his old friend's grave left him feeling inadequate. Don Blas himself would have known what to say, for he had always possessed a graceful sureness of touch, but Sharpe felt awkward in the hushed church.

'You want to start digging?' Harper asked.

'Now?' Sharpe sounded surprised.

'Why not?' Harper had spotted some tools in a side chapel where workmen had evidently been repairing a wall. He fetched a crowbar that he worked down beside the slab. 'At least we can see what's under the stone.'

Sharpe expected to find a vault under the gravestone, but instead they levered up the heavy slab to find a patch of flattened yellow shingle.

'Christ only knows how deep he is,' Harper said, then drove the crowbar hard into the gravel. Sharpe went to the side chapel and came back with a trowel that he used to scrape aside the stones and sand that Harper had loosened. 'We'll probably have to go down six feet,' Harper grumbled, 'and it'll take us bloody hours.'

'I reckon Major Suarez will give us a work party tomorrow,' Sharpe said, then moved aside to let Harper thrust down with the bar again.

Harper slammed the crowbar down. It crashed through the shingle, thumped on something hollow, then abruptly burst through into a space beneath.

'Jesus!' Harper could not resist the imprecation.

Sharpe twisted aside, a hand to his mouth. The crowbar had pierced a coffin that had been buried scarcely a foot beneath the floor, and now the shallow grave was giving off a stink so noxious that Sharpe could not help gagging. He stepped backwards, out of range of the effluvia. Harper was gasping for clean air. 'God save Ireland, but you'd think they'd bury the poor man a few feet further down. Jesus!'

It was the smell of death; a sickly, clogging, strangely sweet, and never forgotten stench of rotting flesh. Sharpe had smelt such decay innumerable times, yet not lately, not in these last happy years in Normandy, but the first slight hint of the smell brought back a tidal wave of memories. There had been a time in his life, and in Harper's life, when a man slept and woke and ate and lived with that reek of mortality. Sharpe had known places, like Waterloo, where even after the dead had all been buried the stench persisted, souring every tree and blade of grass and breath of air with its insinuating foulness. It was the smell that traced a soldier's passing, the grave-smell, and now it soured the church where a friend was buried.

'Christ, but you're right about needing an airtight box to hold him.' Harper had retreated to the edge of the choir. 'We'll drink the brandy, and he can have the box.'

Sharpe crept closer to the grave. The stench was appalling, much worse than he remembered it from the wars. He held his breath and scraped with his trowel at the hole Harper had made, but all he could see was a splinter of yellow wood in the gravel.

'I think we should wait and let a work party do this,' Harper said fervently.

Sharpe scuttled back a few feet before taking a deep breath. 'I think you're right.' He shuddered at the thought of the body's corruption, and tried to imagine his own death and decay. Where would he be buried? Somewhere in Normandy, he supposed, and beside Lucille, he hoped, perhaps under apple trees so the blossoms would drift like snow across their graves every spring.

Then the door at the back of the church crashed open, breaking Sharpe's gloomy reverie, and suddenly a rush of heavy boots trampled on the nave's flagstones. Sharpe turned, half dazzled by the sunlight which lanced low across the world's rim to slice clean through the church's door. He could not see much in the eye of that great brilliance, but he could see enough to understand that armed men were swarming into the church.

'Sweet Jesus,' Harper swore.

'Stop where you are!' A voice shouted above the tramp and crash of boot nails.

It was Sergeant Dregara, his dark face furious, who led the rush. Behind him was Major Suarez carrying a cocked pistol and with a disappointed look on his face as though Sharpe and Harper had abused his friendly welcome. Dregara, like his travel-stained men, was carrying a cavalry carbine that he now raised so that its barrel gaped into Sharpe's face.

'No!' Suarez said.

'Easiest thing,' Dregara said softly.

'No!' Major Suarez insisted. There were a score of infantrymen in the church who waited, appalled, for Dregara to blow Sharpe's brains across the altar. 'They're under arrest,' Suarez insisted nervously.

Dregara, plainly deciding that he could not get away with murder in the presence of so many witnesses, reluctantly lowered the carbine. He looked tired, and Sharpe guessed that he and his cavalrymen must have ridden like madmen in their vain pursuit. Now Dregara stared malevolently into the Englishman's face before turning away and striding back down the church's nave. 'Lock them up.' He snapped the order, even though he was a Sergeant and Suarez a Major. 'Bring me their weapons, and that!' He gestured at the strongbox and two of his men, hurrying to obey, lifted the treasure.

Major Suarez climbed to the altar. 'You're under arrest,' he said nervously.

'For what?' Sharpe asked.

'General Bautista's orders,' Suarez said, and he had gone quite pale, as though he could feel the cold threat of the Captain-General's displeasure reaching down from Valdivia. Dregara was plainly Bautista's man, known and feared as such. 'You're under arrest,' Suarez again said helplessly, then waved his men forward.

And Sharpe and Harper were marched away.

* * *

They were taken to a room high in the fortress; a room which looked across the harbour entrance to where the vast Pacific rollers pounded at the outer rocks to explode in great gouts of white water.

Sharpe leaned through the bars of the high window and

stared straight down to see that their prison room lay directly above a flight of rock-cut steps which led to the citadel's wharf. To the north of the wharf was a shingle beach where a handful of small fishing boats lay canted on their sides.

The window bars were each an inch thick and deeply rusted, but, when Harper tried to loosen them, they proved stubbornly solid. 'Even if you managed to escape,' Sharpe said in a voice made acid by frustration, 'and survived the eighty-foot drop to the quay, just where the hell do you think you'd go?'

'Somewhere they serve decent ale, of course,' Harper gave the bars a last massive but impotent tug, 'or maybe to that Jonathon out there.' He pointed to a brigantine which had just anchored in the outer harbour. The boat was flying an outsize American flag, a splash of bright colour in the twilight gloom. Sharpe assumed the flag was intentionally massive so that, should the dreaded Lord Cochrane make a raid on Puerto Crucero, he could not mistake the American ship for a Spanish merchantman.

Sharpe wished Cochrane would make a raid, for he could see no other route out of their predicament. He had tried hammering on their prison door, demanding to be given paper and ink so that he could send a message to George Blair, the Consul in Valdivia, but his shouting was ignored. 'Damn them,' Sharpe growled, 'damn them and damn them!'

'They won't dare punish us.' Harper was either trying to console Sharpe, or else to convince himself. 'They're scared wicked of our Navy, aren't they? Besides, if they meant us harm they wouldn't have put us in here. This isn't such a bad wee place.' Harper looked round their prison. 'I've been in worse.'

The room was not, indeed, a bad wee place. The wall beside the window had been grievously cracked at some point, Sharpe assumed by one of the famous earthquakes that racked this coast, but otherwise the room was in fine repair and comfortably enough furnished. There were two straw-filled mattresses on the floor, a stool, a table and a lidded bucket. Such comforts suggested that Major Suarez, or his superiors, would deal very gingerly with two British citizens.

It was also plain to Sharpe that the Puerto Crucero authorities were waiting for instructions from Valdivia, for, once incarcerated, they were left alone for six days. No one interrogated them, no one brought them news, no one informed them of any charges. The only visitors to the high prison room were the orderlies who brought food and emptied the bucket. The food was good, and plentiful enough even for Harper's appetite. Each morning a barber came with a pile of hot towels, a bowl and a bucket of steaming water. The barber shook his head whenever Sharpe tried to persuade the man to bring paper, ink and a pen. 'I am a barber, I know nothing of writing. Please to tilt your head back, *señor*.'

'I want to write to my consul in Valdivia. He'll reward you if you bring me paper and ink.'

'Please don't speak, *señor*, when I am shaving your neck.'

On the fifth morning, under a sullen sky from which a sour rain spat, the *Espiritu Santo* appeared beyond the northern headland and, making hard work of the last few hundred yards, beat her way into the outer harbour where, with a great splash and a gigantic clanking of chain, she let go her two forward anchors. Captain Ardiles's frigate, like the American brigantine which still lay to her anchors in the roadstead, drew too much water to be safe in the shallow inner harbour, and so she was forced to fret and tug at her twin cables while, from the shore, a succession of lighters and longboats ferried goods and people back and forth.

Next morning, under the same drab sky, the *Espiritu Santo* raised her anchors and, very cautiously, approached the stone wharf which lay at the foot of the citadel's crag. It was clear to Sharpe that the big frigate could only lie alongside the wharf at the very top of the high tide, and that as a result Captain Ardiles was creeping his way in with extreme caution. The frigate was being towed by longboats, and had men casting lead lines from her bows. She finally nestled alongside the wharf and Harper, leaning as far out as the bars would allow him, described how the contents of a cart were being unloaded by soldiers and carried on board the frigate. 'It's the gold!' Harper said excitedly. 'They must be loading the gold! My God, there's enough gold there to buy a Pope!'

The frigate only stayed at the wharf long enough to take on board the boxes from the cart before she raised a foresail and slipped away from the dangerously shallow water to return to her deeper anchorage. 'Lucky bastards,' Harper said as the rattle of the anchor chains echoed across the harbour. 'They'll be going home soon, won't they? Back to Europe, eh? She could take us to Cadiz, we'd have a week in a good tavern, then I'd catch a sherry boat north to Dublin. Christ, what wouldn't I give to be on board her?' He watched as a longboat pulled away from the frigate and was rowed back towards the citadel's steps, then he sighed. 'One way or another we've made a mess of this job, haven't we?'

Sharpe, lying on one of the mattresses and staring at the cracks in the plastered ceiling, smiled. 'Peace isn't like war. In wartime things were simpler.' He turned his head towards the metal-studded door beyond which footsteps sounded loud in the passageway. 'Bit early for food, isn't it?'

The door opened, but instead of the usual two servants carrying the midday trays, Major Suarez and a file of infantrymen now stood in the stone passageway. 'Come,' Suarez ordered. 'Downstairs. The Captain-General wants you.'

'Who?' Sharpe swung his legs off the cot.

'General Bautista is here. He came on the frigate.' The terror in Suarez was palpable. 'Please, hurry!'

They were taken downstairs to a long hall which had huge arched windows facing onto the harbour. The ceiling was painted white, and decorated with an iron chandelier under which a throng of uniformed men awaited Sharpe's arrival. The crowd of officers reminded Sharpe of the audience that had watched Bautista attending to his duties in the Citadel at Valdivia.

Bautista, attended by Marquinez and his other aides, was again offering a display of public diligence. He was working at papers spread on a table on which rested Sharpe's sword and Harper's seven-barrel gun. The strongbox was also there. The sight of the weapons gave Sharpe a pulse of hope that perhaps they were to be released, even maybe allowed to travel home on the *Espiritu Santo*, for Captain Ardiles was among the nervously silent audience. Sharpe nodded at the frigate's Captain, but Ardiles turned frostily away, revealing, to Sharpe's astonishment, George Blair, the British Consul. Sharpe tried to cross the hall to speak with Blair, but a soldier pulled him back. 'Blair!' Sharpe shouted. 'I want to talk to you!'

Blair made urgent hushing motions as though Sharpe disturbed a sacred assembly. Captain Marquinez, as beautifully uniformed as a palace guard, frowned at Sharpe's temerity, though Bautista, at last looking up from his paperwork, seemed merely amused by Sharpe's loud voice. 'Ah, Mister Sharpe! We meet again. I trust you have not been discommoded? You're comfortable here? You find the food adequate?'

Sharpe, suspicious of Bautista's affability, said nothing. The Captain-General, plainly enjoying himself, put down his quill pen and stood up. 'This is yours?' Bautista put his hand on the strongbox.

Sharpe still said nothing, while the audience, relishing the contest that was about to begin, seemed to tense itself.

'I asked you a question, Mister Sharpe.'

'It belongs to the Countess of Mouromorto.'

'A rich woman! But why does she send her money on voyages round the world?'

'You know why,' Sharpe said.

'Do I?' Bautista opened the strongbox's lid. 'One thousand, six hundred and four guineas. Is that correct?'

'Yes,' Sharpe said defiantly, and there was a murmur of astonishment from Bautista's audience as they translated the figure into Spanish dollars. A man could live comfortably for a whole lifetime on six and a half thousand dollars.

'Why were you carrying such a sum in gold?' Bautista demanded.

Sharpe saw the trap just in time. If he had admitted that the money had been given to him for use as bribes, then the Captain-General would accuse him of attempting to corrupt Chilean officials. Sharpe shrugged. 'We didn't know what expenses we might have,' he answered vaguely.

'Expenses?' Bautista sneered. 'What expenses are involved in digging up a dead man? Shovels are so expensive in Europe?' The audience murmured with laughter, and Sharpe sensed a relief in the assembled officers. They were like men who had come to a bullfight and they wanted to see their champion draw blood from the bull, and the swift jest about the price of shovels had pleased them. Now Bautista took one of the coins from the strongbox, picked up a riding crop from the table, and walked towards Sharpe. 'Tell me, Mister Sharpe, why you came to Chile?'

'To collect the body of Don Blas,' Sharpe said, 'as you well know.'

'I heard you were grovelling in General Vivar's grave like a dog,' Bautista said. 'But why carry so much gold?'

'I told you, expenses.'

'Expenses.' Bautista sneered the word, then tossed the coin to Sharpe.

Sharpe, taken by surprise, just managed to snatch the guinea coin out of the air.

'Look at it!' Bautista said. 'Tell me what you see.'

'A guinea,' Sharpe said.

'The Cavalry of St George.' Bautista still sneered. 'Do you see that, Mister Sharpe?'

Sharpe said nothing. The guinea coin had the head of the King on one side, and on its obverse bore the mounted figure of St George thrusting his lance into the dragon's flank. The nickname for such coins was the Cavalry of St George which, during the French wars and in the form of lavish subsidies to foreign nations, had been sent to do battle against Bonaparte.

'The British Government uses such golden cavalry to foment trouble, isn't that so, Mister Sharpe?'

Again Sharpe said nothing, though he glanced towards Blair to see if the Consul planned any protest, but Blair was clearly cowed by the company and seemed oblivious of Bautista's jeering.

'Afraid to send their own men to fight wars,' Bautista sneered, 'the British pay others to do their fighting. How else did they beat Napoleon?'

He let the question hang. The audience smiled. Sharpe waited.

Bautista came close to Sharpe. 'Why are you in Chile, Mister Sharpe?'

'I told you, to collect General Vivar's body.'

'Nonsense! Nonsense! Why would the Countess of Mouromorto send a lackey to collect her husband's body? All she needed to do was ask the army headquarters in Madrid! They would have been happy to arrange an exhumation.'

'Doña Louisa did not know her husband was dead,'

Sharpe said, though it sounded horribly lame even as he said it.

'What kind of fool do you take me for?' Bautista stepped even closer to Sharpe, the riding crop twitching in his hand. His aides, not daring to move, stood frozen behind the table, while the audience watched wide-eyed. 'I know why you came here,' Bautista said softly.

'Tell me.'

'To communicate with the rebels, of course. Who else was the money for? All the world knows that the English want to see Spain defeated here.'

Sharpe sighed. 'Why would I bring money to the rebels in a royal ship?'

'Why indeed? So no one would suspect your intentions?' Bautista was enjoying tearing Sharpe's protests to shreds. 'Who sent you, Sharpe? Your English merchant friends who think they can make more profit out of Chile if it's ruled by a rebel government?'

'The Countess of Mouromorto sent me,' Sharpe insisted.

'She's English, is she not?' Bautista responded swiftly. 'Do you find it noble to fight for trade, Sharpe? For cargoes of hide and for barrels of tallow? For the profits of men like Mister Blair?' He threw a scornful hand towards the Consul who, seemingly pleased at being noticed, bobbed his head in acknowledgement.

'I fought alongside Don Blas,' Sharpe said, 'and I fight for the same things he wanted.'

'Oh, do tell me! Please!' Bautista urged in a caustic voice.

'He hated corruption,' Sharpe said.

'Don't we all?' Bautista said with wonderfully feigned innocence.

'Don Blas believed men could live in freedom under fair government.' It was an inadequate statement of Vivar's creed, but the best Sharpe could manage.

'You mean Vivar fought for liberty!' Bautista was delighted with Sharpe's answer. 'Any fool can claim liberty as his cause. Look!' Bautista pointed at the hugely-flagged American brigantine in the outer harbour. 'The Captain of that ship is waiting for whalers to rendezvous with him so he can take home their sperm oil and whalebone. He comes every year, and every year he brings copies of his country's declaration of independence, and he hands them out as though they're the word of God! He tells the *mestizos* and the *criollos* that they must fight for their liberty! Then, when he's got his cargo, he sails home and who do you think empties that cargo on his precious land of liberty? Slaves do! Slaves! So much for his vaunted liberty!' Bautista paused to let a rustle of agreement sound in his audience. 'Of course Vivar believed in liberty!' Bautista interrupted the murmuring. 'Vivar believed in every impracticality! He wanted God to rule the world! He believed in truth and love and pigs with wings.' The audience laughed delightedly. Captain Marquinez, and one or two others, even clapped at their Captain-General's wit, while Bautista, delighted with himself, smiled at Sharpe. 'And you share Vivar's beliefs, Mister Sharpe?'

'I'm a soldier,' Sharpe said stubbornly, as though that excused him from holding beliefs.

'A plain, bluff man, eh? Then so am I, so I will tell you very plainly that I believe you are telling lies. I believe you came to Chile to bring money and a message to the rebels.'

'So you believe in pigs with wings too?'

Bautista ignored the sneer, striding instead to the table where he opened a writing box and took out an object which he tossed to Sharpe. 'What is that?'

'Bloody hell,' Harper murmured, for the object which Bautista had scornfully shied at Sharpe was the signed portrait of Napoleon which had been stolen in Valdivia.

'This was stolen from me,' Sharpe said, 'in Valdivia.'

'At the time,' Bautista jeered from the window, 'you denied anything more was missing. Were you ashamed of carrying a message from Napoleon to a mercenary rebel?'

'It isn't a message!' Sharpe said scornfully. 'It was a gift.'

'Oh, Mister Sharpe!' Bautista's voice was full of disappointment, as though Sharpe was not proving a worthy opponent. 'A man carries a gift to a rebel? How did you expect to deliver this gift if you were not to be in communication with the rebels? Tell me!'

Sharpe said nothing.

Bautista smiled pitifully. 'What a bad conspirator you are, Mister Sharpe. And such a bad liar, too. Turn the portrait over. Go on! Do it!' Bautista waited till Sharpe had dutifully turned the picture over, then pointed with his riding crop. 'That backing board comes off. Pull it.'

Sharpe saw that the stiffening board behind the printed etching had been levered out of the frame. The board had been replaced, but now he prised it out again and thus revealed a piece of paper which had been folded to fit the exact space behind the board.

'Open it! Go on!' Bautista was enjoying the moment.

At first glance the folded paper might have been taken for a thickening sheet which merely served to stop the glass rattling in the metal frame, but when Sharpe unfolded the sheet he saw that it bore a coded message. 'Oh, Christ,' Sharpe said softly when he realized what it was. The ink-written code was a jumble of letters and numerals and meant nothing to Sharpe, but it was clearly a message from Bonaparte to the mysterious Lieutenant-Colonel Charles, and any such message could only mean trouble.

'You are pretending you did not know the message was there?' Bautista challenged Sharpe.

'Of course I didn't.'

'Who wrote it? Napoleon? Or your English masters?'

The question revealed that Bautista's men had not succeeded in breaking the code. 'Napoleon,' Sharpe said, then tried to construct a feeble defence of the coded message. 'It's nothing important. Charles is an admirer of the Emperor's.'

'You expect me to believe that an unimportant letter would be written in code?' Bautista asked mockingly, then he calmly walked to Sharpe and held out his hand for the message. Sharpe paused a second, then surrendered the message and the framed portrait. Bautista glanced at the code. 'I believe it is a message from your English masters, which you inserted into the portrait. What does the message say?'

'I don't know.' Sharpe, conscious of all the eyes that watched him, straightened his back. 'How could I know? You probably concocted that message yourself.' Sharpe believed no such thing. The moment he had seen the folded and coded message he had known that he had been duped into being Napoleon's messenger boy, but he dared not surrender the initiative wholly to Bautista.

But Sharpe's counter accusation was a clumsy riposte and Bautista scoffed at it. 'If I planned to incriminate you by concocting a message, Mister Sharpe, I would hardly invent one that no one could read.' His audience laughed at the easy parry, and Bautista, like a matador who had just made an elegant pass at his prey, smiled, then walked to one of the high arched windows which, unglazed, offered a view across the harbour and out to the Pacific. Bautista turned in the window and beckoned to his prisoners. 'Come here! Both of you!'

Sharpe and Harper obediently walked to the window which looked down onto a wide stone terrace that formed a gun battery. The guns were thirty-six-pound naval cannons that had been removed from their ship trolleys and placed on heavy garrison mounts. There were twelve of the massive guns, each capable of plunging a vicious fire down onto any ship which dared attack Puerto Crucero's harbour.

Yet Bautista had not invited Sharpe and Harper to see the guns, but rather the man who was shackled to a wooden post at the very edge of one of the embrasures. That man was Ferdinand, the Indian guide who had brought them through the misted mountains ahead of Dregara's pursuit. Now, stripped of his tattered uniform, and dressed only in a short brown kilt, Ferdinand was manacled just seven or eight feet from the muzzle of one of the giant cannons. Dregara, who was clearly an intimate of Bautista's, stood holding a smoking linstock beside the loaded gun. Sharpe, understanding what he was about to see, turned in horror on Bautista. 'What in Christ's name are you doing?'

'This is an execution,' Bautista said in a tone of voice he might use to explain something to a small child, 'a means of imposing order on an imperfect world.'

'You can't do this!' Sharpe protested so strongly that one of the infantrymen stepped in front of him with a musket and bayonet.

'Of course I can do this!' Bautista mocked. 'I am the King's plenipotentiary. I can have men killed, I can have them imprisoned, I can even have them broken down to the ranks, like Private Morillo who is being sent to the mines to learn the virtues of loyalty.'

'What has this man done?' Sharpe gestured at Ferdinand.

'He has displeased me, Mister Sharpe,' Bautista said, then he beckoned the other men in the room forward so they could watch the execution from the other windows. Bautista's eyes were greedy. 'Are you watching?' Bautista asked Sharpe.

'You bastard,' Sharpe said.

'Why? This is a quick and painless death, though admittedly messy. You have to understand that the savages believe their souls will not reach paradise unless their whole body is intact for the funeral rites. They consequently have a morbid fear of dismemberment, which is why I devised this punishment as a means of discouraging rebellion among the Indian slaves. It works remarkably well.'

'But this man has done nothing! Morillo did nothing!'

'They displeased me.' Bautista hissed the words, then he looked down to the gun battery and held up a hand.

Ferdinand, his lips drawn back from his filed teeth, seemed to be praying. His eyes were closed. 'God bless you!' Sharpe shouted, though the Indian showed no signs of hearing.

'You think God cares about scum?' Bautista chuckled, then dropped his hand.

Dregara reached forward and the linstock touched the firing hole. The sound of the cannon was tremendous; loud enough to rattle the iron chandelier and hurt the eardrums of the men crowded at the windows. Harper crossed himself. Bautista licked his lips, and Ferdinand died in a maelstrom of smoke, fire and blood. Sharpe glimpsed the Indian's shattered trunk whirling blood as it was blasted away from the parapet, then the smoke drew apart to reveal a splintered stake, a pair of bloody legs, and lumps and spatters of blood and flesh smeared across the cannon's embrasure. The rest of Ferdinand's body had been scattered into the outer harbour where screaming gulls, excited by this sudden largesse, dived and tore and fought for shreds of his flesh. Far out to sea, beyond the rocky spit of land, the cannonball crashed into the swell with a sudden white plume, while, in the nearer waters, scraps of flesh and splinters of bone and drops of blood rained down to the frenzied gulls. Men had rushed to the rail of the American brigantine, fearful what the gunfire meant, and now they stared in puzzlement at the blood-flecked water. Bautista sighed with pleasure, then turned away as the white-faced gun crew heaved the dead man's legs over the parapet.

There was a stunned silence in the hall. The stench of powder smoke and fresh blood was keen in the air as Bautista, half smiling, turned to his audience. 'Mister Blair?'

'Your Excellency?' George Blair ducked an eager and frightened pace forward.

'You have heard my questions to Mister Sharpe today?'

'Indeed, your Excellency.'

'Do you confirm that I have treated the prisoners fairly? And with consideration?'

Blair smirked and nodded. 'Indeed, your Excellency.'

Bautista went to the table and held up the signed portrait of Napoleon and the folded message. 'You heard the prisoner's assertion that Napoleon wrote this message?'

'I did, your Excellency, indeed I did.'

'And you see it is addressed to a notorious rebel?'

'I do, your Excellency, indeed I do.'

Bautista's face twitched with amusement. 'Tell me, Blair, how your government will respond to the news that Mister Sharpe was acting as an errand boy for Bonaparte?'

'They will doubtless regard any such message as treasonable correspondence, your Excellency.' Blair bobbed obsequiously.

Bautista smiled, and no wonder, for Sharpe's possession of the Emperor's message was enough to condemn Sharpe, not just with the Spanish, but with the British too. The British might possess the greatest Navy and the strongest economy in the world, yet they were terrified of the small fat man cooped up in St Helena's Longwood, and maybe they were terrified enough to allow Bautista to tie two British subjects to wooden stakes and blow their souls into eternity at the mouths of loaded cannon. Sharpe, suddenly feeling very abandoned, also felt frightened.

Bautista sensed the fear and smiled. He had won now.

He turned again to Blair. 'Either Mister Sharpe was carrying a message from Napoleon, which makes him an enemy of his own country, or else this is a message from the British merchants who are my country's enemies, but either way, Mister Sharpe's possession of the message calls for punishment. Might I assume, Blair, that your government would not approve if I were to execute Mister Sharpe?'

Blair beamed as though Bautista had made a fine jest. 'My government would be displeased, your Excellency.'

'But you do accept that Mister Sharpe deserves punishment?'

'Alas, your Excellency, it appears so.' Blair nodded obsequiously at the Captain-General, then snatched a sideways glance at Sharpe who wondered just how much of Doña Louisa's money the Consul was taking as a bribe.

Bautista strolled back to the table where he picked up Sharpe's heavy sword. 'This was carried at Waterloo?' Sharpe said nothing, but Bautista did not need an answer. 'I shall keep it as a trophy! Perhaps I shall have a plaque made for it. "Taken from an English soldier who at last met his match"!'

'Fight for it now, you bastard,' Sharpe called.

'I don't fight against lice, I just smoke them out.' Bautista dropped the sword onto the table, then adopted a portentous tone of voice. 'I declare your possessions are forfeited to the Spanish crown, and that the two of you are unwelcome in Chile. You are therefore expelled from these territories, and will embark on the next ship to leave this harbour.' Bautista had already prepared the expulsion papers which now, with a theatrical flourish, he offered to Captain Ardiles of the *Espiritu Santo*. 'That would be your frigate, Captain. You have no objections to carrying the prisoners home?'

'None,' Ardiles, ready for the request, said flatly.

'Put them to work. No comforts! Sign them onto your crew and make them sweat.'

'Indeed, your Excellency.' Ardiles took the papers and pushed them into the tail pocket of his uniform.

Bautista came close to Sharpe. 'I would have preferred to put you to work in the mines, Englishman, so think yourself lucky.'

'Frightened of the Royal Navy?' Sharpe taunted him.

'Be careful, Englishman,' Bautista said softly.

'You're a thief,' Sharpe said just as quietly. 'And Vivar knew it, which is why you killed him.'

At first Bautista looked astonished at the accusation, then it made him laugh. He clapped with delight at his amusement, then waved at Major Suarez. 'Take them away! Now!' The audience, in ludicrous sycophancy, began to applaud wildly as the infantrymen who had escorted Sharpe and Harper from their prison now chivvied the two men through an archway and onto a flight of wide stone steps that ran down beside the bloody gun battery. The steps, which were very steep and cut from the crag on which the citadel stood, led down to the fortress quay where a longboat from the *Espiritu Santo* waited.

Ardiles followed, his scabbard's metal tip clattering on the stone steps. 'Into the boat!' he ordered Sharpe and Harper when they reached the quay.

'Make them sweat!' Bautista shouted from the gun battery's parapet. 'Put them at the oars now! You hear me, Ardiles! Put them at the oars! I want to see them sweat!'

Ardiles nodded to the bosun who made space for Sharpe and Harper on the bow thwarts. The other oarsmen grinned. Captain Ardiles, cloaked against the cold south wind, sat in the sternsheets where, it seemed to Sharpe, he carefully avoided his two captives' eyes. 'Push off!' He ordered.

'Oars!' the bosun shouted. From the high arched

windows above the battery of heavy guns a row of faces stared down at Sharpe's humiliation.

'Stroke!' the bosun shouted, and Sharpe momentarily thought of rebelling, but knew that such mutiny would lead nowhere. Instead, like Harper, he pulled clumsily. Their oarblades splashed and clattered on the other oars as they dragged the heavy boat away through the blood-flecked water. A gull, disturbed by the longboat's proximity, flapped up from the water with a length of Ferdinand's intestines in its beak. Other gulls screamed as they fought for the delicacy.

'Pull!' the bosun shouted, and Sharpe felt a pang of impotent anger. The rage was not directed at his tormentors, but at himself. He had been in the Americas little more than a week, yet now he would have to crawl back to Europe, confess his failure, and try to return Louisa her money. Which effort, he much feared, would mean bankruptcy. Except he knew that Louisa would forgive him, and that clemency hurt almost as much as bankruptcy. Goddamn and goddamn and goddamn! He had been rooked like a child wandering into a cutpurse's tavern! It was that knowledge which really hurt, that he had been treated like a fool, and deservedly so. And to have lost his sword! The sword was only a cheap Heavy Cavalry blade, ugly and ill-balanced, but it had been a gift from Harper and it had kept Sharpe alive in some grim battles. Now it would be a trophy on Bautista's wall. Christ! Sharpe stared at the fortress where Bautista ruled, and he felt the horrid impotence of failure, and the horrid certainty that he would never have his revenge. He was being taken away, across a world and back to ignominy, and he was helpless.

He was helpless, he was penniless, and he had just come ten thousand bloody miles for nothing.

*　　*　　*

The frigate, with its cargo of gold, sailed on that evening's tide. Sharpe and Harper were put to work on a capstan that raised one of the anchors, then sent down to the gundeck where they helped to stack nine- and twelve-pounder shots in the ready racks about the frigate's three masts. They worked till their muscles were sore and sweat was stinging their eyes, but they had no other choice. The dice had rolled badly, there was no other explanation, and the two men must knuckle under. Which did not mean they had to be subservient. A huge scarred beast of a man, a one-eyed seaman who was an evident leader of the forecastle, came to look them over, and such was the man's power that the bosun's mates quietly edged back into the shadows when he gestured them away.

'My name's Balin,' the huge man said, 'and you're English.'

'I'm English,' Sharpe said, 'he's Irish.'

Balin jerked his head to order Harper aside. 'I've no quarrel with the Irish,' he said, 'but I've no love for Englishmen. Though mind you –' he took a step forward, ducking under the deck beams '– I like English clothes. That's a fine coat, Englishman. I'll take it.' He held out a broad hand. Two score of seamen made a ring to hide what happened from any officers who might come down to the deck. 'Come on!' Balin insisted.

'I don't want trouble,' Sharpe spoke very humbly. 'I just want to get home safe.'

'Give me your coat,' Balin said, 'and there's no trouble.'

Sharpe glanced left and right at the unfriendly faces in the gundeck's gloom. Night had fallen, and the only lights were a few glass-shielded lanterns that hung above the guns, and the flickering flames made the seamen's faces even more grim than usual. 'If I give you the coat,' Sharpe asked, 'you'll keep me from trouble?'

'I'll cuddle you to sleep, diddums,' Balin said, and the men laughed.

Sharpe nodded. He took off the fine green coat and held it out to the massive man. 'I don't want trouble. My friend and I just want to get home. We didn't ask to be here, we don't want to be here, and we don't want to make enemies.'

'Of course you don't,' Balin said scornfully, reaching for the good kerseymere coat, and the moment his hand took hold of the material Sharpe brought up his right boot, hard and straight, the kick hidden by the coat until the instant it slammed into Balin's groin. The big man grunted, mouth open, and Sharpe rammed his head forward, hearing and feeling the teeth break under his forehead's blow. He had his hands in Balin's crotch now, squeezing, and Balin began to scream. Sharpe let go with one hand and used that hand like an axe on the big man's neck. Once, twice, harder a third time, and finally Balin went down, bleeding and senseless. Sharpe kicked him, breaking a rib, then slammed the heel of his right boot into the one-eyed face, thus breaking Balin's nose. The seaman's hand fluttered on the deck so, for good measure, Sharpe stamped on the fingers, shattering them. Then he stooped, plucked a good bone-handled knife from Balin's belt, picked his coat up from the deck and looked around. 'Does anyone else want an English coat?'

Harper had stunned a man who tried to intervene, and now stooped and took that man's knife for himself. The other seamen backed away. Balin groaned horribly, and Sharpe felt a good deal better as well as a good deal safer. From now on, he knew, he and Harper would be treated with respect. They might have made enemies, but those enemies would be exceedingly cautious from now on.

That night, as the frigate's bows slathered into the great rollers and exploded spray past the galley and down to the guns in the ship's waist, Sharpe and Harper sat by the beakhead and watched the clouds shred past the stars.

'Do you think that shithead Bautista invented the letter?' Harper asked.

'No.'

'So it was Boney who wrote it?' Harper sounded disappointed.

'It had to be.' Sharpe was fiddling with the locket of Napoleon's hair that still hung around his neck. 'Strange.'

'Being in code, you mean?'

Sharpe nodded. It probably made sense for Bautista to assume that the message had come from London, and had merely been hidden inside the Emperor's portrait, but Sharpe knew better. That coded message had come from Longwood, from the Emperor himself. Napoleon had claimed that Lieutenant-Colonel Charles was a stranger, a mere admirer, but no one replied to such a man in code. The letter suggested a long-standing and sinister intrigue, but Sharpe could make no other sense of it. 'Unless this Colonel Charles is supposed to organize a rescue?' he guessed.

And why not? Napoleon was a young man, scarce fifty, and could expect to campaign for at least another twenty years. Twenty more years of battle and blood, of glory and horror. 'God spare us,' Sharpe murmured as he realized that the coded letter might mean that the Emperor would be loose again, rampaging about Europe. What had Bonaparte said? That all over the world there were embers, men like Charles, and Cochrane, even General Calvet in Louisiana, who only needed to be gathered together to cause a great searing blaze of heat and light. Was that what the coded message had been intended to achieve? Then maybe, Sharpe thought, it was just as well that Bautista had intercepted the hidden letter. 'But why use us as messengers?' he wondered aloud.

'Boney can't meet that many people on their way to Chile,' Harper observed sagely. 'He'd have to use anyone he could find! Mind you, if I was him, I wouldn't rely on just one messenger getting through. I'd send as many copies of the letter as I could.'

Dear God, Sharpe thought, but that could mean Charles already had his message and the escape could already be under way. He groaned at the thought of all that nonsense being repeated. The last time Bonaparte had escaped from an island it had driven Sharpe and Lucille from their Norman home. Their return had been difficult, for they had to live beside families whose sons and husbands had died at Waterloo, yet Sharpe had gone back and he had won his neighbours' trust again. He could not bear to think that the whole horrid business would have to be endured a second time.

Except that now, in a ship which was being swallowed in the immensity of the Pacific under a sky of strange southern stars, there was nothing Sharpe could do. The Emperor's plot would unfold without Sharpe, Don Blas would rot in his stinking grave, and Sharpe, pressed as a seaman, would go home.

Part Two

COCHRANE

CHAPTER 5

The *Espiritu Santo*'s crew, like their Captain, were eager to
meet Lord Cochrane. They called him a devil, and crossed
themselves when they spoke of him, yet they reckoned they
could match this devil gun for gun and cutlass for cutlass
and still beat him hollow. The crew might grumble when
they were woken to an unexpected gun practice, or to
rehearse repelling boarders, but they also boasted of what
their hardened skills would do to the devilish Cochrane if
he dared attack the *Espiritu Santo*. They also boasted of the
prize money they would win. Cochrane had captured his
fifty-gun flagship, now called the *O'Higgins*, from the
Spanish navy which, stung by the defeat, had promised
a fortune to whichever ship recaptured the lost vessel.
Ardiles's men wanted that prize, and were willing to sweat
as they practised for it. Sharpe and Harper, deemed to be
unskilled men, were allocated pikes and told that their job
would be to stand on deck and be prepared to kill any man
foolhardy enough to board the frigate. 'Though perhaps it
would be better if you did not carry weapons at all?' Captain Ardiles suggested when he heard that Sharpe and
Harper were expected to be among the pikemen.

Ardiles, who was so reluctant to show himself to his
passengers, proved to be a frequent visitor to the lower
decks. He liked to inspect the guns and to smell the powder
smoke which soured the ship with its stench after every
practice session. He liked to talk with his men who
returned his interest with a genuine loyalty and devotion.
Ardiles, the crew told Sharpe and Harper, was a

proper seaman, not some gold-arsed officer too high and mighty to duck his head under the beams of the lowest decks.

Ardiles, on one of his very first tours of inspection of the voyage, had taken Sharpe and Harper aside. 'I hear you made your mark?' he asked drily.

'You mean Balin?' Sharpe asked.

'I do indeed, so watch your backs in a fight.' Ardiles did not seem in the least upset that one of his prime seamen had been hammered, but he warned Sharpe and Harper that others on board might not be so sanguine. 'Balin's a popular man, and he may have put a price on your heads.' It was just after delivering that warning that Ardiles had wondered aloud whether Sharpe and Harper could be trusted to carry weapons in any fight against Lord Cochrane.

Sharpe ignored the question and Ardiles, who seemed amused at Sharpe's silent equivocation, perched himself on one of the tables which folded down between the guns. 'Not that it's very likely that your loyalty will be put to the test,' Ardiles went on. 'Cochrane doesn't usually sail this far south, so every hour makes it less likely that we'll meet him. Nevertheless, there's hope. We've assiduously spread rumours about gold, hoping to attract his attention.'

'You mean there isn't gold on board?' Sharpe asked in astonishment.

'Sir,' Ardiles chided Sharpe softly. So far the Spanish Captain had allowed Sharpe to treat him with scant respect, but now he suddenly insisted on being addressed properly. Sharpe, prickly with hurt pride, did not instantly respond and Ardiles shrugged, as though the use of the honorific did not really matter to him personally, even though he was going to insist on it. 'You've been a commanding officer, Sharpe.' Ardiles spoke softly so that only Sharpe and Harper could hear him. 'And you would have demanded the respect of your men, even those who were reluctant to be under your authority, and I demand the same. You may be a Lieutenant-Colonel on land, but here you're an unskilled seaman and I can have respect thrashed into you at a rope's end. Unlike General Bautista I'm not fond of witnessing punishment, so I'd rather you volunteered the word.'

'Sir,' Sharpe said.

Ardiles nodded acknowledgement of the reluctant courtesy. 'No, there isn't gold on board. Any gold that we might have been taking home has probably been stolen by Bautista, but we went through the routine of loading boxes filled with rock from the citadel's wharf. I just hope that charade, and the rumours it undoubtedly encouraged, are sufficient to persuade Cochrane that we are stuffed with riches, for then he might come south and fight us. We hear that the rebel government owes him money. Much money! So perhaps he'll try to collect it from me. I'd like that. We'd all like that, wouldn't we?' Ardiles turned and asked the question of his crewmen who, hanging back in the gundeck's gloom, now cheered their Captain.

Ardiles, pleased with their enthusiasm, slid his rump off the table, then went back to his earlier question. 'So can you be trusted, Sharpe?'

'What I was hoping for, sir,' Sharpe did not reply directly, 'was that you might put me aboard a fishing boat?' The *Espiritu Santo* had passed a score of boats that had come far out to sea to search for big tunny fish, and Sharpe had concocted the idea that perhaps one of the boats might carry him back to Chile where, in alliance with the rebels, he might yet retrieve Doña Louisa's money, exhume Blas Vivar's body, and restore his own pride.

'No,' Ardiles said calmly. 'I won't. I have orders to take you back to Europe, and I am a man who obeys orders.

But are you? Whose side will you be on if we meet Cochrane?'

This time Sharpe did not hesitate. 'Cochrane's side.' He paused. 'Sir.'

Ardiles was immediately and understandably hostile. 'Then you must take the consequences if there's a fight, mustn't you?' He stalked away.

'What does that mean?' Harper said.

'It means that if we sight Lord Cochrane then he'll send Balin and his cronies to slit our throats.'

Next day there were no more fishing boats, just an empty ocean and a succession of thrashing squalls. Sharpe, under the immense vacancy of sea and sky, felt all hope slide away. He had lost his uniform and sword; things of no value except to himself, but their loss galled him. He had lost Louisa's money. He had been humiliated and there was nothing he could do about it. He had been fleeced, then ignominiously kicked out of a country with only the clothes on his back. He felt heartsick. He was not used to failure.

But at least he was accustomed to hardship, and had no fears about surviving on board the *Espiritu Santo*. The hard bread, salted meat, dried fish and rancid wine that were the seamen's rations would have been counted luxuries in Sharpe's army. The worst part of the life, apart from the damp which permeated every stitch of clothing and bedding, were the bosun's mates who, knowing that Sharpe had been a senior army officer, seemed to take a particular pleasure in finding him the dirtiest and most menial jobs on board; Sharpe and Harper mucked out the sheep and pigs that would be slaughtered for fresh meat during the voyage, they scrubbed the poop deck each morning, they ground the rust off the blades of the boarding pikes that were racked on deck, and each afternoon they collected the latrine buckets from the passenger cabins and scoured them clean. Among the score of passengers aboard the frigate were seven Spanish army officers, two of whom were sailing with their families, and those army officers, knowing Sharpe's history, stared at him with frank curiosity. It was, Sharpe thought, going to be a long voyage home.

Yet, like most ordeals, it abated swiftly. The humiliated Balin might bear a grudge, but Harper inevitably discovered a score of fellow Irishmen aboard the *Espiritu Santo*, all of them exiles from British justice, and all of them eager to hear Harper's news of home. Sharpe, given temporary and flattering status as an honorary Irishman, felt a good deal safer from the Balin faction. One of the bosun's mates was from Donegal and his presence took much of the sting out of Sharpe's treatment. A week into the voyage and Sharpe was even beginning to enjoy the experience.

The next dawn brought proof that the sea could throw up hardships far worse than anything yet inflicted on Sharpe and Harper. They were scrubbing the poop deck when the forward lookout hailed the quarterdeck with a cry that a boat was in sight. Ardiles ran on deck and seized the watch officer's telescope, while the First Lieutenant, Otero, who remembered Sharpe and Harper well from the outward voyage, and who was excruciatingly embarrassed by their change of fortune, climbed to the lookout's post on the foremast from where he trained his own telescope forward.

'What is she?' Ardiles called.

'A wreck, sir! A dismasted whaler, by the look of her.'

'Goddamn.' Ardiles had been hoping it would prove to be the *O'Higgins*. 'Change course to take a look at her, then call me when we're closer!' Ardiles muttered the instruction to the officer on watch, then, before taking refuge in his cabin, he glowered at the handful of passengers who had come on deck to see what had caused the sudden alarm.

Among the spectators were the two army officers' wives who were standing at the weather rail to stare at the stricken whaler. Their excited children ran from one side of the deck to the other, playing an involved game of tag. One of the small girls slipped on the wet patch left by Sharpe's holystone. 'Move back! Give the ladies room!' the bosun ordered Sharpe and Harper. 'Just wait forrard! Wait till the passengers have gone below.'

Sharpe and Harper went to the beakhead where, concealed by the forecastle, they could hide from authority and thus stretch their temporary unemployment. They joined a small group of curious men who gazed at the wrecked whaler. She was a small ship, scarce a third the size of the *Espiritu Santo*, with an ugly squared-off stern and, even uglier, three splintered stumps where her masts had stood. A spar, perhaps a yardarm, had been erected in place of the foremast, and a small sail lashed to that makeshift mast. Despite the jury rig she seemed to be unmanned, but then, in answer to a hail from the Spanish frigate's masthead, two survivors appeared on the whaler's deck and began waving frantically towards the *Espiritu Santo*. One of the two unfolded a flag that he held aloft to the wind. 'She's an American,' the First Lieutenant shouted down to the forecastle where a midshipman was deputed to carry the news back to the Captain's cabin.

Ardiles, though, was not in his cabin, but had instead come forward. He had avoided the inquisitive passengers by using a lower deck, but now he suddenly appeared out of the low door which led to the beakhead. He nodded affably to the men who were perched on the ship's lavatory bench, then trained his telescope on the whaler.

'She isn't too badly damaged.' Ardiles spoke to himself, but as Sharpe and Harper were the closest men, they grunted an acknowledgement of his words. 'Hardly damaged at all!' Ardiles continued his assessment of the beleaguered American whaler.

'She looks buggered to me, sir,' Sharpe said.

'She's floating upright,' Ardiles pointed out, 'so, as they say in the Cadiz boatyards, her hull must be as watertight as a duck's backside. Mind you, the hulls of whaling ships are as strong as anything afloat.' He paused as he stared through the glass. 'They've lost their rudder, by the look of it. They're using a steering oar instead.'

'What could have happened to her, sir?' Harper asked.

'A storm? Perhaps she rolled over? That can snap the sticks out of a boat as quick as you like. And she's lost all her whale boats, so I suspect her topsides were swept clean when she rolled. That would explain the rudder, too. And I'll warrant she lost a few souls drowned too, God rest them.' Ardiles crossed himself.

Three men were now visible on the whaler's deck. Lieutenant Otero, still high on the foremast, read the whaler's name through his telescope and shouted it down to Captain Ardiles. 'She's called the *Mary Starbuck*!'

'Probably the owner's wife,' Ardiles guessed. 'I hope the poor man has got insurance, or else Mary Starbuck will be making do with last year's frocks.'

Lieutenant Otero, now that the *Espiritu Santo* was nearing the hulk, slid down the ratlines to leave tar smeared on his white trousers. 'Do we rig a towing bridle?' he asked Ardiles.

Ardiles shook his head. 'We haven't time to take them in tow. But prepare to heave to. And fetch me a speaking trumpet from the quarterdeck.' Ardiles still stared at the whaler, his fingers drumming on the beakhead's low rail. 'Perhaps, Sharpe, you'll find out what the Americans need? I doubt they want us to rescue them. Their hull isn't broached, and under that jury rig they could sail from here to the Californias.'

The speaking trumpet was brought to the bows. Ten minutes later the frigate heaved to, backing her square sails so that she rolled and wallowed in the great swells.

Sharpe, standing beside one of the long-barrelled nine-pounder bow guns that were the frigate's pursuit weapons, could clearly read the whaler's name that was painted in gold letters on a black quarterboard across her stern. Beneath that name was written her hailing port, Nantucket. 'Tell them who we are,' Ardiles ordered, 'then ask them what they want.'

Sharpe raised the trumpet to his mouth. 'This is the Spanish frigate *Espiritu Santo*,' he shouted. 'What do you want?'

'Water, mister!' One of the Americans cupped his hands. 'We lost all our fresh water barrels!'

'Ask what happened.' Ardiles, who spoke reasonable English, had not needed to have the American's request for water translated.

'What happened?' Sharpe shouted.

'She rolled over! We were close to the ice when a berg broke off!'

Sharpe translated as best he could, for the answer made little sense to him, but Ardiles both understood and explained. 'The fools take any risk to chase whales. They got caught by an iceberg calving off the ice-mass. The sea churns like a tidal wave when that happens. Still, they're good seamen to have brought their boat this far. Ask where they're heading.'

'Valdivia!' came the reply. The whaler was close now, close enough for Sharpe and Ardiles to see how gaunt and bearded were the faces of the three survivors.

'Ask how many there are on board,' Ardiles commanded.

'Four of us, mister! The rest drowned!'

'Tell them to keep away.' Ardiles was worried that the heavily built whaler might stove in the *Espiritu Santo*'s ribs. 'And tell them I'll float a couple of water barrels to them.' Ardiles saw Sharpe's puzzlement, and explained. 'Barrels of fresh water float in salt water.'

Sharpe leaned over the rail. 'Keep away from our side! We're going to float water barrels to you!'

'We hear you, mister!' One of the Americans dutifully leaned on the makeshift steering oar, though his efforts seemed to have little effect for the clumsy whaler kept heaving herself ever closer to the frigate.

Ardiles had ordered two barrels of water brought onto deck and a sling rove to heave them overboard. Now, while he waited for the barrels to arrive, he frowned at the *Mary Starbuck*'s wallowing hulk. 'Ask them where Nantucket is,' he ordered suddenly.

Sharpe obeyed. 'Off Cape Cod, mister!' came back the answer.

Ardiles nodded, but some instinct was still troubling him. 'Tell them to sheer away!' he snapped, then, perhaps not trusting Sharpe to deliver the order with sufficient force, he seized the speaking trumpet. 'Keep clear! Keep clear!' he shouted in English.

'We're trying, mister! We're trying!' The man on the steering oar was desperately pushing against the whaler's weight.

'Trying?' Ardiles repeated the word, then, still in English, he swore. 'The devil! They didn't lose their tryworks when they rolled!' He turned to shout towards the quarter-deck, but already events were accelerating to combat pace and Ardiles's warning shout was lost in the sudden chaos.

For just as Ardiles turned, so a massive wave lifted the whaler's square stern and an officer on the *Espiritu Santo*'s quarterdeck saw that the *Mary Starbuck*'s rudder was not shorn away after all, but was in place and being steered from a tiller concealed beneath the whaler's deck. The rudder was bringing the heavy boat towards the Spanish frigate, which meant the steering oar was faked, which meant the shipwreck was faked. This was a fact that Ardiles had simultaneously guessed when he saw that the whaler's tryworks, a brick furnace built amidships in which the whale blubber was rendered down into the precious oil, had survived the apparent rolling of a ship that had destroyed three solid masts.

The Spaniards were shouting in warning, but the *Mary Starbuck* was already within ten feet of the frigate. A man aboard the whaler suddenly cut free the American flag and, in its place, unfurled a red, white and blue flag which was unfamiliar to Sharpe, but all too familiar to Ardiles. It was the flag of the Chilean rebel government. 'Beat to quarters!' Ardiles shouted, and as he called the order aloud, so the hatch covers on the whaler's deck were thrust aside and Sharpe, astonished, saw that a huge gun was mounted in the hold. It was a carronade: a squat, wide-mouthed, short-range killer designed to shred men rather than smash the timbers or rigging of a ship. Sharpe also saw, before he and Harper dropped for cover behind the nine-pounder cannon, that a mass of men were seething up onto the whaler's deck. The men were armed with muskets, pikes, cutlasses, pistols and grapnels.

'Fire!' The order was shouted on board the *Mary Starbuck*, and the carronade belched a bellyful of iron scraps and links of rusted chain up at the *Espiritu Santo*'s waist. Most of the missiles struck the starboard gunwale, but a few Spanish crewmen, helping to lower the first water barrel over the side, were thrown back in a sudden spray of blood. The barrel, holed in a hundred places, sprayed drinking water into the bloody scuppers.

Grapnels came soaring across the narrowing gap of water. The metal hooks snagged on rigging or thumped into the decks. The *Espiritu Santo*'s crew, trained to just such an emergency, reacted fast. Some men started slashing at the ropes attached to the grapnels, while others ran to seize pikes or muskets. 'Gun crews! Gun crews!' Ardiles had left the frigate's bows and was striding back to the quarterdeck where the children were screaming in terror.

'Passengers down to the orlop deck!' Ardiles was astonishingly calm. 'Quick now! Below!'

Musket balls whiplashed up from the whaler which suddenly struck hard against the frigate's side, so hard that some of the *Espiritu Santo*'s crew were knocked down by the force of the collision. The first boarders were already swarming up their ropes. Sharpe, snatching a glance from the beakhead, saw two of the invaders fall back as their rope was cut free. Another, gaining the gunwale, screamed as a pike slammed into his face to blind him and hurl him back to the *Mary Starbuck*'s crowded deck. The attackers, jostling at the ropes, were screaming a war cry that at first sounded jumbled and indistinct to Sharpe, but which now became clear. 'Cochrane! Cochrane!' Ardiles, it seemed, was having his dearest wish granted.

A grapnel soared high over the *Espiritu Santo*'s bows to fall and catch on the beakhead. For the moment Sharpe and Harper were alone on the small hidden platform of the beakhead, and neither man moved to cut free the rope. 'We're joining the fight then, are we?' Harper asked.

'I like Ardiles,' Sharpe said, 'but I'm damned if I'll fight for a man on the same side as Bautista.'

'Ah, well. Back to the wars.' Harper grinned, then instinctively ducked as another carronade fired, this one from the forecastle above them. The *Espiritu Santo*'s forecastle carronade, unable to depress its muzzle sufficiently, had not done great damage to the attackers, but its noise alone seemed to encourage the Spaniards who now began to shout their own war cry, '*Espiritu Santo! Espiritu Santo!*'

'So what do we do?' Harper asked.

'We start with that big bugger up there.' Sharpe jerked his chin up towards the forecastle carronade. He had to shout, for more big guns were firing, these new ones from down below on the gundeck where the Spanish were evidently firing straight into the *Mary Starbuck*'s upper deck. Sharpe could hear the screams of men being disembowelled and flensed by the close-range horror of the big guns. Sharpe jumped, caught the edge of the forecastle's deck, and hauled himself up to where three men were serving the carronade. One of them, the gun captain, snapped at Sharpe to fetch some quoins so that the breech of the carronade could be elevated.

'I'm not on your side!' Sharpe yelled at the man. Behind Sharpe, Harper was struggling to haul his huge weight up the sheer face of the forecastle which, though only eight feet high, was too much for a man as heavy as Harper which meant that Sharpe, for the moment, was alone. He grabbed one of the carronade's heavy spikes, a six-foot shaft of hardwood tipped with an iron point. The spike was used to aim the heavy gun by levering its trail around, and the wooden deck under the carronade's tail was pitted with holes left by the sharp iron point. Sharpe now lunged with the spike as though it was a bayonet. He did not want to kill, for his attack was unexpected and unfair, but the gun's captain suddenly pulled a pistol from under his coat and Sharpe had no choice but to ram the spike forward with sudden and savage force so that the iron point punctured the man's belly. The gun captain dropped his pistol to grip the spike's shaft. He was moaning sadly. Sharpe, still lunging forward, slammed the wounded man against the rail and, still pushing, heaved him overboard. Sharpe let go the spike so that the gun captain, blood cartwheeling away from his wound, fell to the sea with the spike's shaft still rammed into his belly.

Sharpe turned. He ducked to retrieve the gun captain's pistol and the carronade's rammer, swung with terrible force by one of the two remaining crewmen, slashed just above his head. Sharpe's right hand closed on the pistol just as he charged forward to ram his left shoulder into the Spaniard's belly. He heard the man's breath gasp out, then he brought the heavy pistol up and hammered it onto his attacker's skull. The third crew member had backed to the inboard edge of the forecastle where he was uselessly shouting for help. Harper, abandoning his attempt to climb the forward face of the forecastle, had ducked through the galley and was now climbing the companionway steps which led from the main deck. The third crew member, thinking that help was at last arriving, leaned down to give Harper a helping hand. Harper grabbed the offered hand, tugged, and the crewman tumbled down into the churning mass of men who fought in the ship's waist.

That larger fight was a gutter brawl of close-quarter horror. Cochrane's invaders had succeeded in capturing a third of the *Espiritu Santo*'s main deck, but were now faced by a disciplined and spirited crew that fiercely defended their ship. Cochrane's men, screaming like demons, had achieved an initial surprise, but Ardiles's hours of practice were beginning to pay dividends as his men forced the invaders back.

Sharpe, seeing his very first sea fight, was horrified by it. The killing was done in the confining space of a ship's deck which gave neither side room to retreat. On land, when faced by a determined bayonet attack, most soldiers gave ground, but here there was no ground to give, and so the dead and dying were trampled underfoot. The heaving ocean added a horrid air of chance to death. A man might parry a thrust efficiently and be on the point of killing his opponent when a wave surge might unsteady him and, as he flailed for balance, his belly would be exposed to a steel thrust. One of the bosun's mates who had made Sharpe's first days aboard such misery had been so wounded and was now dying in the scuppers. The man writhed in brief spasms, his hands fluttering and clawing at the broken sword blade that was embedded in his belly. A midshipman was bleeding to death, calling for his mother, which pathetic cry swelled into a shriek of terror as a rebel stepped back on the boy's sliced belly. That rebel then died with a pistol bullet in his brain, hurled back in a spray of bright blood to slide down beside the bosun's mate.

'God save Ireland,' Harper muttered.

'Is the gun loaded?' Sharpe slapped the carronade, then ducked as a stray musket bullet passed over his head.

'Looks like it!'

Sharpe found another spike which he used to lever the gun's trail round so that the carronade faced straight down the *Espiritu Santo*'s length to menace the quarterdeck where Ardiles was assembling a group of seamen. Those seamen were undoubtedly intended to be the counter-attack which would finish off Cochrane's assault. Sharpe hammered a quoin out from under the carronade's breech, thus raising the muzzle so that the dreadful weapon was pointing straight at the quarterdeck. The carronade was a pot of a gun, not a long, elegant and accurate cannon, but a squat cauldron to be charged with powder and metal scraps that flayed out like buckshot. A carronade's range was short, but inside that brief range it was foully lethal.

The whole ship quivered as another broadside slammed from the frigate's gundeck to shatter the heavy timbers of the whaler. Most of Cochrane's men were off the whaler now and crammed onto the Spaniard's deck where they were hemmed in by bloody pikes and bayonets. Ardiles, preparing his reserves to slam into the left flank of the invaders, was making things worse for Cochrane by destroying his only chance of escape by pounding the whaler into matchwood. Smoke was sifting from the open hold of the *Mary Starbuck*. Presumably some of the wadding from one of the *Espiritu Santo*'s cannon had set fire to a splintered timber inside the attacking ship.

Harper cocked the flintlock that was soldered onto the carronade's touch-hole. Naval guns did not use linstocks, for the spluttering sparks of an open match were too dangerous on board a wooden ship crammed with gunpowder. Instead, just like a musket, the gun was fired by a spring-tensioned flint that was released by a lanyard. 'Are you ready?' Sharpe gripped the lanyard and scuttled to one side of the gun to escape its recoil.

'Get down!' Harper shouted. Ardiles's men on the quarterdeck had at last seen the threat of the forecastle carronade and a dozen muskets were levelled. Sharpe dropped just as the volley fired. The sound of a musket volley, so achingly familiar, crackled about the ship as the balls whipsawed overhead. Sharpe answered the volley by yanking the carronade's lanyard.

The world hammered apart in thunder, in an explosion so close and hot and violent that Sharpe thought he was surely dead as the frigate shivered and dust spurted out of the cracks between her deck planks. Sharpe's second and more realistic thought was that the barrel of the carronade had burst, but then he saw that the gun, recoiling on its huge carriage, was undamaged.

The explosion had been aboard the *Mary Starbuck*. A store of gunpowder in the whaler's hull had ignited and ripped the boat apart in a moment's blinding horror, tearing her deck into shards and exploding the wounded into the sea. Now what remained of the whaler was ablaze. The dark red flames leaped voraciously from her oil-soaked planks to flare as high as the *Espiritu Santo*'s topmasts.

'Mary, Mother of God,' Harper said in awe, not at the incandescent whaler, but rather because the *Espiritu Santo*'s mainmast was toppling. The explosion had ripped out the frigate's chainplates and now the great mast swayed. Some men, recovering their wits from the concussion of the explosion, shouted in warning, while others, from both sides of the fight, were desperately slashing at the remaining grapnels so that the roaring blaze on the whaler would not leap across to destroy the frigate. Beyond that chaos Sharpe could see a red horror on the poop and quarterdecks where the blast of his carronade had taken a terrible toll among Ardiles's men.

A rebel officer shouted a piercing warning. The swaying mainmast splintered and cracked. Canvas billowed down onto the deck and into the sea. The collapsing mast dragged in its wake the fore topmast and a nightmarish tangle of yards, halyards, lines and sails.

'Come on, Patrick!' Sharpe cocked the pistol and jumped down from the forecastle. A Spanish sailor, groggy from the explosion, tried to stand in Sharpe's way so he thumped the man on the side of his head with the pistol's heavy barrel. A Spanish army officer lunged at Sharpe with a long narrow sword. Sharpe turned, straightened his right arm and pulled the trigger. The officer seemed to be snatched backwards with a halo of exploding blood about his face. Smoke from the burning whaler whirled thick and black and choking across the deck. Sharpe hurled the pistol away and snatched up a fallen cutlass. 'Cochrane!' he shouted. 'Cochrane!' A mass of Cochrane's men were swarming towards the frigate's stern. The explosion and the subsequent fall of the mast had torn the heart out of the frigate's defenders, though a stubborn rearguard, under an unwounded Ardiles, gathered for a last stand on the quarterdeck.

To Sharpe's left was a tall man with red hair who carried a long and heavy-bladed sword. 'To me! To me!' The red-haired man was wearing a green naval coat with two gold epaulettes and was the man the rebels were looking to for orders and inspiration. The man had to be Lord Cochrane. Then Sharpe turned away as a swarm of Spanish fighters came streaming up from the gundeck below. These new attackers were the frigate's guncrews who, their target destroyed, had come to recapture their main deck.

Sharpe fought hand to hand, without room to swing a blade, only to stab it forward in short, hard strokes. He was close enough to see the fear in the eyes of the men he killed, or to smell the garlic and tobacco on their breath. He knew some of the men, but he felt no compunction about their killing. He had declared his allegiance to Ardiles, and Ardiles could have no complaint that Sharpe had changed sides without warning. Nor could Sharpe complain if, this fight lost, he was hanged from whatever yardarm was left to the Spanish frigate. Which made it important not to lose, but instead to beat the Spaniards back in blood and terror.

Harper climbed the fallen trunk of the mainmast. He carried a boarding pike that he swung in a huge and terrifying arc. One of the Irish crew members, having decided to change sides, was fighting alongside Harper. Both men were screaming in Gaelic, inviting their enemies to come and be killed. A musket crashed near Sharpe, who flinched aside from its flame. He ripped the cutlass blade up to throw back an enemy. The cutlass was a clumsy weapon, but sea fighting was hardly a fine art. It was more like a gutter brawl, and Sharpe had grown up with such fighting. He slipped, fell hard on his right knee, then clawed himself up to ram the blade forward again. Blood whipped across a fallen sail. A sailor trapped beneath a fallen yard shrieked as a wave surge shifted the timber baulk across his crushed ribs. Balin, his face and hand still bandaged, lay dead in the portside scuppers that ran with the blood from his crushed skull. A group of rebels had found room to use their pikes. They lunged forward, hooking men with the crooked blade on the pike's reverse, then pulling their victims out of the *Espiritu Santo*'s ranks so that another pikeman, using the weapon's broad axe-head, could slash down hard. The pikemen were driving the frigate's guncrews back to the poop deck where a rearguard waited with Ardiles and Lieutenant Otero.

The ship lurched on the swell, staggering Sharpe sideways. A bleeding man screamed and fell into the sea. It seemed that the *Espiritu Santo* must have taken on water for she did not come fully upright, but stayed listed to starboard. A volley of musket fire from Ardiles's group on the quarterdeck punched a hole in the rebels' ranks, but Cochrane, seeing the danger, had led a rampaging attack up to the poop deck and now his men clawed and scrabbled up the last companionway to attack Ardiles and his men on the quarterdeck.

Royalist Captain faced rebel Admiral. Their two swords clashed and scraped. More rebels were running past their leader, swarming up to the quarterdeck where a final, fanatic group of Spaniards, including most of the army officers, stood to protect their royal ensign.

A few despairing men still fought on the main deck. Sharpe kicked a man in the ankle, then hammered down the cutlass hilt as the man fell. Two men slashed at him, but Sharpe stepped back from their clumsy blades, then sliced his own forward. A rebel joined him, stabbing forward with a bayonet, and suddenly the portside steps to the poop deck were open. Sharpe ran up. Above him on the quarterdeck, Ardiles was pressed back by the man Sharpe supposed was Cochrane. Ardiles was no mean swordsman, but he was no match for the red-haired rebel who was taller, heavier and quicker. Ardiles lunged, missed, retreated and was toppled over the railing by a sudden thrust of his opponent's sword. The Spanish Captain fell onto the poop deck at Sharpe's feet. Sharpe stooped and took his sword.

'You,' Ardiles said bleakly.

'I'm sorry,' Sharpe said.

'Who the hell are you?' the red-haired man asked from above Sharpe.

'A friend! Are you Cochrane?'

'I am, friend, indeed I am.' Cochrane sketched a salute with his sword, then turned to lead the attack on the desperate group that waited to defend their flag. On the poop and main decks the victorious rebels disarmed Spaniards, but about the great gaudy ensign a terrible battle still waged. Pistols flared, muskets crashed smoke. A rebel squirmed in awful pain in the scuppers. Other rebels, trying to fire down at the stubborn sternguard, climbed the mizzen rigging, but Lieutenant Otero, seeing the danger, ordered a group of the frigate's marines to fire upwards. One of the rebels screamed as a bullet thudded into his belly. For a second he hung from the ratlines, his blood spraying bright across the driver-sail, then he fell to crash down into the sea. Another rebel, losing his nerve, leaped after his dying colleague. The horror was not all visited on the attackers. One of the *Espiritu Santo*'s midshipmen, no more than eleven years old, was clutching his groin from which blood seeped to spread along a seam between two scrubbed planks of the quarterdeck. The boy was weeping and on his face was a look of utter astonishment. The *Mary Starbuck*, her fire roaring like a blast furnace, had drifted away from the frigate. The sea between the two ships was littered with wreckage and dead and drowning men.

Lieutenant Otero ordered a final quixotic charge, perhaps hoping to kill Lord Cochrane, but his men would not obey. A rebel officer shouted at the sternguard to surrender. Sharpe, the handle of his cutlass slippery with blood, climbed to thicken the ranks of the rebels who now made a threatening semi-circle about the frigate's last defenders.

'Surrender, sir!' Lord Cochrane called. 'You've done well! I salute you! Now, I beg you, no more killing!'

Lieutenant Otero crossed himself, then, bitterly, threw down his sword. There was a clatter of falling guns and blades as his men followed his example. An army officer, disgusted, hurled his own sword overboard so he would not have to surrender it to rebels. A ship's boy wept, not because he was wounded, but because of the shame of losing the fight. A rebel slashed at the ensign's halyard and the bright flag of Spain fluttered down.

'Where are the pumps?' Cochrane shouted in urgent and execrable Spanish. It seemed an odd way to celebrate victory, but then the frigate lurched, and Sharpe, to his horror, realized the *Espiritu Santo*, just like the burning *Mary Starbuck*, was sinking. 'The pumps!' Cochrane shouted.

'This way!' Sharpe jumped down to the poop, then down to the waist. From there he slithered down a rope to the gundeck where the main pumps were situated. He saw that the explosion of the *Mary Starbuck* had made a terrible slaughter on the gundeck. Until the moment the whaler blew up, the frigate's gunners had been firing point-blank through open hatches into the wooden hull that had been grinding against the Spanish warship, but the explosion had speared flame and debris through the open gun hatches to fan slaughter through the low-beamed deck. Two of the frigate's guns had been blown clean off their carriages. One dismounted gun was lying atop a dying, screaming man. Cochrane killed the man with an efficient slice of his sword, then shouted at his men to start the pumps working.

'Chippy! Find me the chippy!' Cochrane roared. The carpenter was fetched and ordered to discover the extent of the damage to the frigate's hull, then to start immediate repairs. The wounded Spanish gunners moaned. The frigate was already listing so far over that roundshot was rolling across her deck. 'Can't talk now, bloody boat's sinking,' Cochrane said to Sharpe. 'We'll all be dead if we don't watch it. Pump, you bastards! Pump! Put the prisoners to work! Pump! Well done, Jorge! Well fought, Liam! But start pumping or we'll all be sucking the devil's tits before this day's done!' Cochrane, ducking under the gundeck's beams, scattered praise and humour among his victorious men. He set the rear pump working and peered down into the orlop deck where the women and children cowered. 'Not flooded yet. Good! Maybe there's hope.

Christ, but that bugger should never have exploded. Are you Spanish?' This last question was addressed to Sharpe, shouted as Cochrane climbed nimbly back up to the bloody and wreckage-strewn main deck.

'English.'

'Are you now?' Cochrane brushed ineffectively at the powder stains on his green uniform coat. 'I suppose I've got to take the proper surrender from their poor bastard of a captain. Rotten luck for him. He fought well. Ardiles, isn't it?'

'Yes,' Sharpe said. 'He's a good man.' Then he took a pace backwards as Captain Ardiles, his face stricken, walked with fragile dignity towards Lord Cochrane. The Spanish Captain had retrieved his sword, but only so that he could offer it in surrender to his victor. Ardiles held the sword hilt forward, the gesture of surrender, but he could not bring himself to speak the proper words.

Cochrane touched the hilt – his gesture of acceptance – then pushed the weapon back to Ardiles. 'Keep it, Captain. Your men fought well, damned well.' His Spanish was enthusiastic, but clumsy. 'I also need your help if we're to save the ship. I've sent a carpenter down to the bilge, but your man will know the timbers better than him. The pumps are going. That damned explosion must have sprung some of the timbers! Would you fetch your ladies up? They'll not be harmed, I give you my word. And where's the gold?'

'There is no gold,' Ardiles said very stiffly.

Cochrane, who had been speaking and moving with a frenetic energy, now stopped still as a statue and stared open-mouthed at Ardiles. Then, a second later, looked quizzically at Sharpe who confirmed the bad news with a nod. 'Goddamn!' Cochrane said, though without any real bitterness. 'No gold? You mean I just blunted a sword for nothing!' He gave a great billow of laughter, that turned into a whoop of alarm as the *Espiritu Santo* gave another creaking jolt to starboard. A cutlass slid down the canted deck to clash into the scuppers. 'Help me!' Cochrane said to Ardiles, and suddenly the two men disappeared, lost in technical discussion, while beneath Sharpe's feet the pumps clattered to pulse puny jets of water over the side.

Somehow they stopped the ship from sinking, though it took the best part of that day to do it. Cochrane's men salvaged the mainsail that had fallen overboard when the mainmast fell and from it cut great squares of canvas. They sewed the squares together to make a huge pad that was then dragged under the ship by means of cables which were first looped under the frigate's bows, then dragged back under her hull till the huge pad of material was fothered up against the sprung timbers. The explosion on board the whaler had driven in a section of the frigate's hull, but once the canvas fother was in place the pumps at last could begin to win the battle. Behind them, on an ocean scattered with the flotsam of battle, the *Mary Starbuck* gave a last hiss of steam as she sank.

On board the captured *Espiritu Santo* the wounded were treated. The surgeon worked on deck, tossing the amputated limbs overboard. A step behind the surgeon was the *Espiritu Santo*'s chaplain who gave the final unction to dying seamen. To those who were dying in too much pain the chaplain gave a quietus with a narrow blade. Once dead the shriven sailors were sewn into hammocks weighted with roundshot. The last stitch, by custom, was forced through the corpse's nose to make certain he was truly dead. None of the corpses twitched in protest. Instead, after a muttered prayer, they were all slid down to the sea's bed.

'What a resurrection there'll be on the Day of Judgment!' Cochrane, his emergency work done, had asked Sharpe and Harper to join him on the frigate's quarterdeck from where they watched the miserable procession of dead splashing over the side. 'Just think of Judgment Day,'

Cochrane said exuberantly, 'when the sea gives up its dead and all those sailormen pop out of the waves and start hollering for a tot of rum and a heavenly whore.' His Lordship had protuberant eyes, a strong nose, full lips and an excited, energetic manner. 'Christ —' he hit Sharpe on the back, '— but that was a close thing! They're the best fighters I've ever seen on a Spanish ship!'

'Ardiles's great ambition was to fight you,' Sharpe explained. 'He trained his men for years. All he wanted to do was to fight and beat you.'

'Poor bastard. I sneak up on him like a rat, and he was dreaming of an honest broadside to broadside battle, eh?' Cochrane seemed genuinely sympathetic. 'But a broadside pounding match was exactly what I wanted to avoid! I thought that sneaking up like a rat would do less damage to this ship. Now look at it! No mainmast and half a bottom blown away!' He sounded remarkably cheerful despite the appalling damage. 'You didn't give me the honour of your name, sir,' he said to Sharpe, whereas the truth was that he had not given Sharpe a moment of time to make any kind of introduction.

'Lieutenant Colonel Richard Sharpe.' Sharpe decided to go full fig with his introduction. 'And this is my particular friend, Regimental Sergeant Major Patrick Harper.'

Cochrane stared at both men with a moment's disbelief, that vanished as he decided Sharpe must be telling the truth. 'Are you, by God?' Cochrane, flatteringly, had evidently heard of the Riflemen. 'You are?'

'Yes, my Lord, I am.'

'And I'm Thomas, Tommy, or Cochrane, and not "my Lord". I was once a Knight Commander of the Order of the Bath, till the buggers couldn't stand my company so they turfed me out. I also had the honour of being held prisoner in the Fleet prison, and I was once a member of Parliament, and let me tell you, Sharpe, that the company in prison is a damned sight more rewarding than that available in His Fat Majesty's House of Commons which is packed full of farting lawyers. I also once had the honour of being a Rear Admiral in His Fat Majesty's Navy, but they didn't like my opinions any more than the Order of the Bath liked my company, so they threw me out of the Navy too, so now I have the signal honour to be Supreme Admiral, Great Lord, and chief troublemaker of the Navy of the Independent Republic of Chile.' He gave Sharpe and Harper an elaborate bow. 'Pity about the *Mary Starbuck*. I bought her off a couple of Nantucket Yankees with the very last cash I possessed. I thought I'd get my money back by capturing the Holy Spirit. Awful damned name for a ship. Why do the dagoes choose such names? You might as well call a ship *Angel-Fart*. They should give their boats real names, like *Revenge* or *Arse-Kicker* or *Victory*. Are you really Richard Sharpe?'

'I truly am,' Sharpe confessed.

'Then just what the hell are the two of you doing on this ship?'

'We were thrown out of Chile. By a man called Bautista.'

'Oh, well done!' Cochrane said happily. 'First class! Well done! You must be on the side of the angels if that piece of half-digested gristle doesn't like you. But what about that snivelling turd Blair? Didn't he try to protect you?'

'He seemed to be on Bautista's side.'

'Blair's a greedy bastard,' Cochrane observed gloomily. 'If we ever get off this ship alive you should look him up and give him a damned good thrashing.' His Lordship's gloom seemed justified for, despite the fothering and the pumping, the condition of the damaged frigate seemed to be suddenly worsening. The wind was rising and the seas were steeper, conditions that made the damaged hull pound ever harder into the waves. 'The fother's shifting,' Cochrane guessed. He had turned the *Espiritu Santo* northwards and the captured frigate was running before the wind and current, yet even so her progress was painfully slow because of the damaged hull and because of the amount of wreckage that still trailed overboard.

Cochrane's sailing master, an elderly and lugubrious Scot called Fraser, threw a trailing-log overboard. The log was attached to a long piece of twine which was knotted at regular intervals. Fraser let the twine run through his hands and counted the knots as they whipped past his fingers, timing them all the while on a big pocket watch. He finally snapped the watch shut and began hauling the log back. 'Three knots, my Lord, that's all.'

'Christ help us,' Cochrane said. He frowned at the sea, then at the rigging. 'But we'll speed up as we get the damage cleared. Eight days, say?'

'Ten,' the sailing master said doubtfully, 'maybe twelve, but more probably never, my Lord, because she's taking water like a colander.'

'Five guineas says we'll make it in eight days,' Cochrane said cheerfully.

'Eight days to what?' Sharpe asked.

'To Valdivia, of course!' Cochrane exclaimed.

'Valdivia?' Sharpe was astonished that Cochrane was trying to reach an enemy haven. 'You mean there isn't a harbour closer than that?'

'There are hundreds of closer harbours,' Cochrane said blithely, 'thousands of harbours. Millions! There are some of the best natural harbours in the world on this coast, Sharpe, and they're all closer than Valdivia. The damned coast is thick with harbours. There are more harbours here than a man could wish for in a thousand storms! Isn't that so, Fraser?'

'Aye, it is, my Lord.'

'Then why go to an enemy harbour?' Sharpe asked.

'To capture it, of course, why else?' Cochrane looked at Sharpe as though the Rifleman was mad. 'We've got a ship, we've got men, we've got weapons, so what the hell else should we be doing?'

'But the ship's sinking!'

'Then the bloody ship might as well do something useful before it vanishes.' Cochrane, delighted with having surprised Sharpe, whooped with laughter. 'Enjoy yourself, Sharpe. If we take Valdivia all Chile is ours! We're launched for death or victory, we're sailing for glory, and may the Devil take the hindmost!' He rattled off the old clichés of the French wars in a mocking tone, but there was a genuine enthusiasm on his face as he spoke. Here was a man, Sharpe thought, who had never tired of battle, but revelled in it, and perhaps only felt truly alive when the powder was stinking and the swords were clashing. 'We're sailing for glory!' Cochrane whooped again, and Sharpe knew he was under the command of a genial maniac who planned to capture a whole country with nothing but a broken ship and a wounded crew.

Sharpe had met Spain's devil, and his name was Cochrane.

CHAPTER 6

The wind rose next day. It shrieked in the broken rigging so that the torn shrouds and halliards streamed horizontally ahead of the labouring frigate as she thumped in slow agony through the big green seas. Both rebel and royalist seamen manned the pumps continually, and even the officers took their turns at the blistering handles. Sharpe and Harper, restored to grace as passengers, nevertheless worked the sodden handles for three muscle-torturing hours during the night. Besides the women and children, only Cochrane and Captain Ardiles were spared the agony of the endless pumps. Ardiles, suffering the pangs of defeat, had closeted himself in his old cabin that Cochrane, with a generosity that seemed typical of the man, had surrendered to his beaten opponent.

In the grey morning, when the wind was whistling to blow the wavetops ragged, Lord Cochrane edged the broken frigate nearer to land so that, at times, a dark sliver on the eastern horizon betrayed high ground. He had not wanted to close the coast, for fear that the captured *Espiritu Santo* might be seen by a Spanish pinnace or fishing boat that could warn Valdivia of his approach, but now he sacrificed that caution for the security of land. 'If the worst comes to the worst,' he explained, 'then perhaps we might be able to beach this wreck in the channels. Though God knows if we'd survive them.'

'Channels?' Sharpe asked.

Cochrane showed Sharpe a chart which revealed that the Chilean coast, so far as it was known, was a nightmare tangle of islands and hidden seaways. 'There are thousands of natural harbours if you can get into the channels,' Cochrane explained, 'but the channel entrances are as wicked as any in the world. As dreadful as the western coast of Scotland! There are cliffs on this coast that are as tall as mountains! And God only knows what's waiting inside the channels. This is unexplored country. The old maps said that monsters lived here, and maybe they do, for no one's ever explored this coast. Except the savages, of course, and they don't count. Still, maybe the *O'Higgins* will find us first.'

'Is she close?'

'Christ only knows where she is, though she's supposed to rendezvous with us off Valdivia. I've left a good man in charge of her, so perhaps he'll have the wits to come south and look for us if we're late, and if he does, and finds us sinking, then he can take us off.' He stared bleakly at the chart which he had draped over the *Espiritu Santo*'s shot-torn binnacle. 'It's a devil of a long way to Valdivia,' he said under his breath.

Sharpe heard a sigh of despair in Cochrane's voice. 'You're not serious about Valdivia, are you?' Sharpe asked.

'Of course I am.'

'You're going to attack with this broken ship?'

'This and the *O'Higgins*.'

'For God's sake,' Sharpe protested, 'Valdivia harbour has more fortresses than London!'

'Aye, I know. The English Fort, Fort San Carlos, Fort Amargos, Corral Castle, Fort Chorocomayo, Fort Niebla, the Manzanera Island batteries and the quay guns.' Cochrane rattled off the list of fortifications with an irritating insouciance, as though such defences were flimsy obstacles that were bound to fall before his reputation. 'Say two thousand defenders in all? Maybe more.'

'Then why, for God's sake?' Sharpe gestured at the

exhausted men who stared dull-eyed at the threatening seas which roared up astern of the damaged frigate, hissed down her flanks, then rushed ahead in great gouts of wind-blown chaos.

'I have to attack Valdivia, Sharpe, because my lords and masters of the independent Chilean government, whom God preserve, have ordered me to attack Valdivia.' Cochrane suddenly sounded glum, but offered Sharpe a rueful grin. 'I know that doesn't make sense, at least not till you understand that the government owes me a pile of money that they desperately don't want to pay me.'

'That still doesn't make sense,' Sharpe said.

'Ah.' Cochrane frowned. 'Try it this way. The government promised me hard cash for every Spanish ship I captured, and I've taken sixteen so far, and the buggers don't want to honour the contract! They don't even want to pay my crews their ordinary wages, let alone the prize money. So instead of paying up they've ordered me to attack Valdivia. Now do you understand?'

'They want you to be killed?' Sharpe could only suppose that with Cochrane's death the debt due to him would be cancelled.

'They probably wouldn't overmuch object to my death,' Cochrane confessed, 'except that it might encourage the damned Spaniards, so I suspect that the reasoning behind their order is slightly more subtle. They don't want to pay me, so they have issued me with an impossible order. Now, if I refuse to obey the order they'll send me packing for disobedience, and refuse to give me my cash as a punishment for that disobedience, but if, on the other hand, I dutifully attack and fail then they'll accuse me of incompetence and punish me by confiscating the money they owe me. Either way they win and I am royally buggered. Unless, of course –' Cochrane paused, and an impudent, wonderful grin crossed his face.

'Unless you win,' Sharpe continued the thought.

'Oh aye, that's the joy of it!' Cochrane slapped the rail of the quarterdeck. 'My God, Sharpe, but that would be something! To win!' He paused, frowning. 'Why was there no gold on this boat?'

'Because its presence was merely a rumour to lure you into making an attack.'

'It damn well worked, too!' Cochrane barked with laughter. 'But think of it, Sharpe! If the gold isn't here, then it has to be in Valdivia! Bautista's as greedy as any Presbyterian! He's been thieving for years, and now he's Captain-General there's been nothing to stop his mischief. Imagine it, Sharpe! The man has chests of money! Pots of gold! Rooms full of silver! Not a piddling little pile of coins, but enough treasure to make a man drool!' Cochrane laughed in relish of such plunder, and Sharpe saw in the Scottish nobleman a wonderful relic of an older, more glorious and more sordid age. Cochrane was a fighting sailor of the Elizabethan breed; a Drake or a Raleigh or a Hawkins, and he would fight like the devil the Spanish thought he was for gold, glory or just plain excitement.

'No wonder they turfed you out of Parliament,' Sharpe said.

Cochrane bowed, acknowledging the compliment, but then qualified his acknowledgement. 'I went into the Commons to achieve something, and it was a cruel shame I failed.'

'What did you want to achieve?'

'Liberty, of course!' The answer was swift, but followed immediately by a deprecating smile. 'Except I've learned there's no such thing.'

'There isn't?'

'You can't have freedom and lawyers, Sharpe, and I've discovered that lawyers are as ubiquitous to human society as rats are to a ship.' Cochrane paused as the frigate thumped her bluff bows into a wave trough. The ship seemed to take a long time to recover from the downward plunge, but gradually, painfully, the bows rose again. 'You build a new ship,' Cochrane went on, 'you smoke out its bilges, you put rat poison down, you know the ship's clean when you launch it, but your first night out you hear the scratch of claws and you know the little bastards are there! And short of sinking the ship they'll stay there for ever.' He scowled savagely. 'That's why I came out here. I dreamed it would be possible to make a new country that was truly free, a country without lawyers, and look what happened! We captured the capital, we drove the Spaniards to Valdivia, and is Santiago filled with happy people celebrating their liberty? No. It's filled with goddamned lawyers making new laws.'

Sharpe recalled Napoleon's similar scorn of lawyers. Were soldiers and lawyers natural enemies, he wondered? Perhaps lawyers were the makers of peace which was why warriors feared them. 'Surely,' he said carefully, 'you can't have peace without laws?'

'Lawyers don't want peace,' Cochrane responded fiercely. 'All they want is to make money enforcing the law. That's what lawyers do. They make laws that no one needs, then make money disagreeing with each other what the damned law means, and the more they disagree the more money they make, but still they go on making laws, and they make them ever more complicated so that they can get paid for arguing ever more intricately with one another! You call that peace? I grant you they're clever buggers, but God, how I hate lawyers.' Cochrane shouted the despairing cry to the cold, ship-breaking wind. 'In all history,' he went on, 'can you name one great deed or one noble achievement ever done by a lawyer? Can you think of any single thing that any lawyer has ever done to increase human happiness by so much as a smile? Can you think of even one lawyer who could stand with the heroes? Who could stand with the great and the daring and the saintly and the imaginative and the wondrous and the good? Of course not! Can a rat fly with eagles?' Cochrane had talked himself into a bitter mood. 'It's the lawyers, of course, who refuse to honour the contract the government made with me. It's the lawyers who ordered me to capture Valdivia, knowing full well that it can't be done. But that doesn't mean we shouldn't try.' He paused again, and looked down at the chart. 'Except I doubt this broken ship will ever sail as far as Valdivia. Perhaps I'll have to console myself by capturing Puerto Crucero instead.'

Sharpe felt his heart give a small leap of hope. 'That's where I want to go,' he said.

'Why in God's name would you want to go to a shit-stinking hole like Puerto Crucero?' Cochrane asked.

'Because Blas Vivar is buried there,' Sharpe said.

Cochrane stared at Sharpe with a sudden and astonishing incredulity. 'He's what?'

'Blas Vivar is buried in the garrison church at Puerto Crucero.'

Cochrane seemed flabbergasted. He opened his mouth to speak, but for once could find nothing to say.

'I've seen his grave,' Sharpe explained. 'That's why I was in Chile, you see.'

'You crossed the world to see a grave?'

'I was a friend of Vivar. And we came here to take his body home to Spain.'

'Good God Almighty,' Cochrane said, then turned to look up at the foremast where a group of his men were retrieving the halliards that had been severed when the mainmast fell. 'Oh, well,' he said in a suddenly uninterested voice, 'I suppose they had to bury the poor fellow somewhere.'

It was Sharpe's turn to be puzzled. Cochrane's first reaction to Don Blas's burial had been an intrigued astonishment, but now his Lordship was feigning an utter carelessness. And suddenly, standing on the same quarterdeck where Captain Ardiles had told him the story, Sharpe remembered how Blas Vivar had been carried north in the *Espiritu Santo* for a secret rendezvous with Lord Cochrane; a story that had seemed utterly fantastic when Sharpe had first heard it, but which now seemed to make more sense. 'I was told that Don Blas once tried to meet you, but was prevented by bad weather. Is that true?' he asked Cochrane.

Cochrane paused for an instant, then shook his head. 'It's nonsense. Why would a man like Vivar want to meet me?'

Sharpe persisted, despite his Lordship's glib denial. 'Ardiles told me this ship carried Vivar north, but that a storm kept him from the rendezvous.'

Cochrane scorned the tale with a hoot of laughter. 'You've been at the wine, Sharpe. Why the hell would Vivar want to meet me? He was the only decent soldier Madrid ever sent here, and he didn't want to talk to the likes of me, he wanted to kill me! Good God, man, we were enemies! Would Wellington have hobnobbed with Napoleon? Does a hound bark with the fox?' Cochrane paused as the frigate wallowed in a trough between two huge waves, then held his breath as she laboured up the slope to where the wind was blowing the crest wild. The pumps clattered below decks to spurt their feeble jets of splashing water overboard. 'You said you were a friend of Blas Vivar?' Cochrane asked, when he was sure that the frigate had endured.

'It was a long time ago,' Sharpe said. 'We met during the Corunna campaign.'

'Did you now?' Cochrane responded blithely, as though he did not really care one way or another how Sharpe and Vivar had met, yet despite the assumed carelessness Sharpe detected something strangely alert in the tall, red-haired man's demeanour. 'I heard something very odd about Vivar,' Cochrane went on, though with a studied tone of indifference. 'Something about his having an elder brother who fought for the French?'

'He did, yes.' Sharpe wondered from where Cochrane had dragged up that ancient story, a story so old that Sharpe himself had half forgotten about it. 'The brother was a passionate supporter of Napoleon, so naturally wanted a French victory in Spain. Don Blas killed him.'

'And the brother had the same name as Don Blas?' Cochrane asked with an interest which, however he tried to disguise it, struck Sharpe as increasingly acute.

'I can't remember what the brother was called,' Sharpe said, then he realized exactly how such a confusion might have arisen. 'Don Blas inherited his brother's title, so in that sense they shared the same name, yes.'

'The brother was the Count of Mouromorto?' Cochrane asked eagerly.

'Yes.'

'And the brother had no children —' Cochrane continued the explanation ' — so Blas Vivar inherited the title. Is that how it happened?'

Sharpe nodded. 'Exactly.'

'Ah!' Cochrane said, as though something which had been puzzling him for a long time abruptly made good sense, but then he deliberately tried to pretend that the new sense did not matter by dismissing it with a flippant comment. 'It's a rum world, eh?'

'Is it?' Sharpe asked, but Cochrane had abruptly lost interest in the coincidence of Blas Vivar and his brother sharing a title and had started to pace his quarterdeck. He touched his hat to one of the two Spanish wives. The other, who had abruptly been translated into a widow the previous day, was in her cabin where her maid was trying to staunch her mistress's grief with unripe Chilean wine while her husband, a waxed thread stitched through his nose, was mouldering at the bottom of the Pacific.

Cochrane suddenly stopped his pacing and turned on Sharpe. 'Did you sail in this ship from Valdivia?'

'No, from Puerto Crucero.'

'So how did you get from Valdivia to Puerto Crucero? By road?'

Sharpe nodded. 'Yes.'

'Ah ha!' Cochrane's enthusiasm was back. 'Is it a road on which troops can march?'

'They can march,' Sharpe said dubiously, 'but they'll never drag cannon all that way, and two companies of infantry could hold an army at bay for a week.'

'You think so, do you?' Cochrane's enthusiasm faded as quickly as it had erupted. Cochrane had clearly been fantasizing about a land attack on Valdivia, but such an attack would be an impossibility without a corps of good infantry and several batteries of artillery, and even then Sharpe would not have wagered on its success. Siege warfare was the cruellest variety of battle, and the most deadly for the attacker.

'Surely,' Sharpe said, 'O'Higgins can't blame you if you fail to capture Valdivia?'

'Bernardo knows which way his breeches button,' Cochrane allowed, 'but you have to understand that he's been seduced by the vision of becoming a respectable, responsible, sensible, reliable, boring, dull and pious national leader. By which I mean that he listens to the bloody lawyers! They've told him he mustn't risk his own reputation by attacking Valdivia, and persuaded him that it's better for me to do the dirty work. Naturally they haven't given me any extra soldiers, because I just might succeed if they had. I'm just supposed to work a miracle!' He glowered unhappily, then folded up the chart. 'No doubt we'll all be at the sea's bottom before the week's out,' he said gloomily. 'Valdivia or Puerto Crucero? We probably won't reach either.' The frigate creaked and rolled, and the pumps spewed their feeble splashes of water over the side. The motion of the stricken *Espiritu Santo* seemed ever more sluggish and ever more threatening. Sharpe, glancing up at the skies which glowered with clouds run ragged by the endless wind, sensed the hopelessness of the struggle, but even when there was no hope, men had to keep on fighting.

And so they did, northwards, towards the great citadels of Spain.

* * *

They pumped. By God, how they pumped. The leather pump hoses, snaking down into the *Espiritu Santo*'s bilges, thrashed and spurted with the efforts of the men on the big oak handles. A man's spell at the handles was cut to just fifteen minutes, not because that was the extent of anyone's endurance, but rather because that was as long as any man could pump at full exertion, and if the pumps slackened by so much as an ounce a minute Cochrane swore the ship would be lost. Cochrane took turns himself now. He stripped to his waist and attacked the pump as though it was a lawyer whose head he pounded in with the big handles. Up and down, grunting and snarling, and the water spilt and slurped feebly over the side and still the frigate seemed to settle lower in the water and wallow ever more sluggishly.

The carpenters sounded the bilges again and reported that the hull timbers had been rotten. The frigate had been the pride of the Spanish navy, yet some of her protective copper must have been lost at sea, and the teredos and gribble worms had attacked her bottom starboard timbers. The wood had been turned into riddled pulp which, compressed by the explosion of the *Mary Starbuck*, had shattered into rotted fragments.

'No one noticed the worm damage?' Cochrane asked, but no one had, for it had been concealed in the darkest, deepest, foulest, rankest depths of the ship, and so the sea had flooded in and now the battle's survivors must pump for their lives. The men who were not pumping formed a bucket chain, desperately scooping water out of the dark flooding bilges. The carronades were jettisoned, then the long chasing nine-pounders, and finally all the other guns on board the frigate were thrown overboard, save only the two stern chasers which, mounted in Ardiles's quarters, were left untouched out of respect for the grieving Spanish Captain. Yet still the *Espiritu Santo* continued to take on water and to settle ever lower into the cold sea. Cochrane surreptitiously ordered the frigate's longboats to be provisioned with water casks and barrels of salt pork. 'There's enough space to save half the ship's people,' Cochrane admitted to Sharpe, 'but only half. The rest of us will drown.' The rats, sensing the disaster that was going to overtake the ship, had long abandoned the bilges to run about the gundeck and to cause screams from the women and children in the passengers' quarters.

On their fifth day, when the ship seemed sure to founder, so low was she riding, Cochrane ordered another fother made, but this he ordered big enough to straddle half the starboard hull. The tired, wet, hungry men heaved the great cloth pad into place. It took hours, but, not long after the job was finished, the carpenter sounded the ship's well and claimed the pumps were maybe holding their own, and a tired cheer went up at such grudging good news.

Some of the men were all in favour of running ashore and risking the channel entrances in hope of finding a safe haven, but Cochrane stubbornly insisted on keeping his northward course. On the sixth day they sighted a great black cliff off to the east, but Cochrane wore ship and stood back out to sea. The squalls crashed about the frigate, streaming from the scuppers that had at last been scoured of their blood.

Cochrane's ebullience was gone, frayed by weariness and hunger. Everyone was hungry. The *Espiritu Santo*'s food had been kept in the bilge and, when it flooded, the seawater destroyed what a legion of rats had been unable to consume. The bread and flour had been reduced to a soggy paste inside their barrels. There was plenty of strongly-salted meat, but finding it in the dark slopping water that still churned about the bilges was increasingly hard. The pigs, chickens and sheep that had been put aboard to provide fresh meat in the mid-Atlantic were slaughtered, their squeals and blood thick in the wet air.

More men died. The sailcloth shroud of one man tore when he was jettisoned overboard and the roundshot, that should have dragged his body to the seabed, fell free. The corpse, in its grey bag, floated behind the ship as a reminder of just how slowly the *Espiritu Santo* was sailing. She was limping north, travelling scarce faster than a half-shrouded body. At dusk the corpse was still there, its face bobbing up and down from the green waves in mocking obeisance, but then, in a churning horror of foam and savagery, a great black and white beast, with fangs like saw blades, erupted out of the deep to carry the corpse away. Sharpe, who did not see the attack, was inclined to dismiss the story as another monstrous invention, but Cochrane confirmed it. 'It was a killer whale,' he told Sharpe with a shudder. 'Nasty things.' Some of Cochrane's men swore the whale's coming was an evil omen, and as the day waned it seemed they must be right for the ship had begun to settle again, ever deeper. The pumps and buckets were losing the battle.

Still they fought, none harder than Cochrane's band of seasoned fighters. They were a strange piratical mixture of *criollos*, *mestizos*, Spaniards, Irish, Scots, Englishmen, Americans, and even a handful of Frenchmen. They reminded Sharpe yet again of Napoleon's observation about the world being filled with troubled men, accustomed to war, who only waited for a leader to bring them together to assault the citadels of respectable property.

Cochrane's seamen, good fighters all, were as savage as their master. 'They fight for money,' Cochrane told Sharpe. 'Some, a few, are here to free their country, but the rest would fight for whichever side paid the largest wages. Which is another reason I need to capture Valdivia. I need its treasury to pay my rascals.'

Yet, next dawn, under a grey sad sky from which a thin spiteful rain leeched like poison, the frigate was lower in the water than it had been all week. The carpenters suggested that more planks had sprung and suggested heading for land. Cochrane gloomily agreed, but then, just as he had given up hope, a strange sail was seen to northwards.

'God help us now,' an Irish sailor said to Harper.

'Why's that?' Harper, seeing the sail, anticipated a rescue.

'Because if that's a Spanish ship then we're all dead men. They don't have a broadside, nor do we, so they'll either stand off and pound us down into lumpy gravy, or else take us all prisoner, and there'll be no mercy shown to us in Valdivia. They'll have a priest bellowing in our ears while the firing squad sends us all to Abraham's bosom. That's if they don't just hang us from their yardarms first to save the cost of the powder and balls. Jesus, but I should have stayed in Borris, so I should.'

Cochrane ran to the foremast and climbed to the crosstrees where he settled himself with a telescope. There was a long, agonizing wait, then his Lordship sent a cheer rippling down the deck. 'It's the *O'Higgins*, my boys! It's the *O'Higgins*!' The relief was as palpable as if a flight of rescuing angels had descended from heaven.

Cochrane's flagship had come south to search for its Admiral, and the men on the *Espiritu Santo* were saved. To fight again.

* * *

Captain Ardiles, with the *Espiritu Santo*'s crew and passengers, was ferried across to the Chilean flagship. The transfers were made in longboats that crashed hard against the *Espiritu Santo*'s side as the prisoners climbed down precarious scrambling nets. The women and children, terrified of the nets, were lowered into the longboats with ropes.

For every prisoner or passenger carried to the *O'Higgins*, a seaman came back. The *O'Higgins* also sent food, water and two portable pumps that were lowered into the *Espiritu Santo*'s bilges. Fresh strong arms took over the pumping and suddenly the tired and leaking ship was filled with a new life and hope.

Cochrane, so closely snatched from shipwreck, was ebullient again. He welcomed the reinforcements aboard the *Espiritu Santo*, hurrahed as their new pumps began spewing water overboard, and insisted on sending obscenely cheerful messages to his own flagship. When he became bored with that occupation he paced the quarterdeck with a bottle of wine in one hand and a cigar in the other. 'You never told me, Sharpe –' he hospitably offered a drink from the bottle '– just why Bautista threw you out of Chile. Surely not because you wanted to filch Vivar's corpse?'

'It was because I was carrying a message for a rebel.'

'Who?'

'A man called Charles. Do you know him?'

'Of course I know him. He's my friend. My God, he's the only man in Santiago I can really trust. What did the message say?'

'I don't know. It was in code.'

Cochrane's face had gone pale. 'So who was it from?' He asked the question in a voice that suggested he was afraid of hearing the answer.

'Napoleon.'

'Oh, dear God.' Cochrane paused. 'And Bautista has the message now?'

'Yes.'

Cochrane swore. 'How in hell's name did you become Boney's messenger?'

'He tricked me into carrying it.' Sharpe explained as best he could, though the explanation sounded lame.

Cochrane, who had seemed appalled when he first heard of the intercepted message, now appeared more interested in the Emperor. 'How was he?' he asked eagerly.

'He was bored,' Sharpe said. 'Bored and fat.'

'But alert? Energetic? Quick?' The one-word questions were fierce.

'No. He looked terrible.'

'Ill?' Cochrane asked.

'He's out of condition. He's fat and pale.'

'But he made sense to you?' Cochrane asked urgently. 'His brain is still working? He's not lunatic?'

'Christ, no! He made perfect sense!'

Cochrane paused, drawing on his cigar. 'You liked him?'

'Yes, I did.'

'Funny, isn't it? You fight a man most of your life and end up liking the bugger.'

'You met him?' Sharpe asked.

Cochrane shook his head. 'I wanted to. When I was on my way here I wanted to call at St Helena, but the winds were wrong and we were already late.' Cochrane had crossed to the rail where he stopped to gaze at the *O'Higgins*. She was a handsome ship, a fifty-gun battleship that had once sailed in the Spanish navy and had been renamed by her captors. Her solidity looked wonderfully reassuring compared to the fragility of the half-sinking *Espiritu Santo*. 'They should have killed Bonaparte,' Cochrane said suddenly. 'They should have stood him against a wall and shot him.'

'You surprise me,' Sharpe said.

'I do?' Cochrane blew a plume of cigar smoke towards his flagship. 'Why?'

'You don't seem a vengeful man, that's why.'

'I don't want vengeance.' Cochrane paused, his eyes resting again on the *O'Higgins* which rocked her tall masts against the darkening sky. 'I feel sorry for Bonaparte. He's only a young man. It's unfair to lock up a man like that. He set the world on fire, and now he's rotting away. It would have been kinder to have killed him. They should have given him a last salute, a flourish of trumpets, a blaze of glory, and a bullet in his heart. That's how I'd like to go. I don't want to make old bones.' He drank from his bottle. 'How old is Bonaparte?'

'Fifty,' Sharpe said. Just seven years older than himself, he thought.

'I'm forty-five,' Cochrane said, 'and I can't imagine being cooped up on an island for ever. My God, Bonaparte could fight a hundred battles yet!'

'That's exactly why they've cooped him up,' Sharpe said.

'I can't help feeling for the man, that's all. And you say he's unwell? But not badly ill?'

'He suffers from nothing that a day's freedom and the smell of a battlefield wouldn't cure.'

'Splendid! Splendid!' Cochrane said delightedly.

Sharpe frowned. 'What I don't understand is why Napoleon would be writing in code to your friend Charles.'

'You don't?' Cochrane asked, as if such a lack of understanding was extraordinary. 'It's simple, really. Charles is a curious fellow; always writing to famous people to seek their versions of history. He doubtless asked the Emperor about Austerlitz or Waterloo or whatever. Nothing to it, Sharpe, nothing at all.'

'And he wrote in code?' Sharpe asked in disbelief.

'How the hell would I know? You must ask Charles or the Emperor, not me.' Cochrane dismissed the matter testily, then leaned over the gunwale to shout a rude greeting at the last longboats to bring men from the *O'Higgins*.

Those last reinforcements were a group of Chilean marines under the command of Major Miller, a portly Englishman who, resplendent in a blue uniform coat, had a tarred moustache with upturned tips. 'Proud to meet you, Sharpe, proud indeed.' Miller clicked his heels in formal greeting. 'I was with the Buffs at Oporto - you will doubtless recall that great day? I was wounded there, recovered for Albuera, and what a bastard of a fight that was, got wounded again, was patched up for that bloody business in the Roncesvalles Pass, got shot again and was invalided out of the service with a gammy leg. So now I'm fighting for Cochrane. The money's better if we ever get paid, and I haven't been shot once. This old ship's a bit buggered, isn't she?'

The *Espiritu Santo* was indeed buggered, so much so that, despite the influx of fresh muscle and the extra pumps, Cochrane reluctantly accepted that the captured frigate could never sail as far as Valdivia without repairs. 'It'll have to be Puerto Crucero,' he told Major Miller, who bristled with confidence at the news and alleged that capturing the smaller harbour would entail less work and smaller risk than a night spent in a Santiago whorehouse. 'My chaps will make short work of Puerto Crucero. Mark my words, Sharpe, these are villains!' Miller's villains numbered exactly fifty, of whom only forty-five actually carried weapons. The remaining five marines were musicians: two drummers and three flautists. 'I used to have a bagpiper,' Miller said wistfully. 'A splendid fellow! He couldn't play to save his life, but the noise he made was simply magnificent! Bloody dagoes shot him in a nasty little fight when we captured one of their frigates. One squelch of a dying chord, and that was the end of the poor bugger. Shame. They shot the bagpipes too. I tried to mend them, but they were beyond hope. We buried them, of course. Full military honours!'

Sharpe diffidently wondered whether abandoning ten

per cent of his muskets to music was wise, but Miller dismissed Sharpe's implied objections. 'Music's the key to victory, Sharpe. Always has been and always will be. One thing I noted in the Frog wars was that our chaps always won when we had music. Stirs up the blood. Makes a chap think he's invincible. No, my dear fellow, my forty-five chaps fight like tigers so long as the music's chirruping, but if a flute stops to take a breath they wilt into milksops. If I could find the instruments I'd have half the bastards playing music and only half fighting. Nothing would stop me then! I'd march from here to Toronto and kill every-thing in between!' Miller looked extraordinarily pleased at such a prospect. 'So, my dear fellow, you've been to Puerto Crucero, have you? Much in the way of defences there?'

Sharpe had already described the defences to Lord Cochrane, but now, and as soberly as he could, he described the formidable fortress that dominated Puerto Crucero's harbour. From the landward side, Sharpe averred, it was impregnable. The seaward defences were probably more attainable, but only if the cannon on the wide firesteps could be dismounted or otherwise destroyed. 'How many guns?' Miller asked.

'I saw twelve. There must be others, but I didn't see them.'

'Calibre?'

'Thirty-six pounders. They've also got the capacity to heat shot.'

Miller sniffed, as if to suggest that such defences were negligible, but Sharpe noted that the belligerent Major seemed somewhat crestfallen, and so he should have been, for a dozen thirty-six-pounder cannon were a considerable obstacle to any attack. Not only were such guns heavier than anything on board Cochrane's ships, but they were also mounted high on the fortress and could thus fire down onto the decks of the two frigates. Such huge roundshot, slamming into the decks and crashing on through the hull to thump through a boat's bilges, could sink a ship in minutes. Indeed, the fragile *Espiritu Santo* would hardly need one such heavy shot to send her to the bottom.

Worse still, the thirty-six-pound iron shots could be heated to a red heat. Then, if such a ball lodged in a ship's timber, a fire could start in seconds and Sharpe had already seen, in the *Mary Starbuck*, just how vulnerable wooden ships were to fire. From the moment the two ships entered the outer harbour until the moment they touched against the quay, they would be under a constant hammering fire. Captain-General Bautista was a man of limited military imagination, but his one certainty was that artillery won wars, and by trying to sail the *Espiritu Santo* and the *O'Higgins* into Puerto Crucero's harbour, Cochrane was playing right into Bautista's unimaginative trap. The red hot thirty-six-pound cannonballs, with whatever other guns the defenders could bring to bear, would pound the two warships into embers of bloody matchwood long before they reached the quay, and even if, by some miracle, one of the ships did limp through the hail of roundshot and managed to land an attacking force on the quay, there would still be plenty of Spanish infantry ready to defend the steep open stairway with musket fire and bayonets. Miller's two drummers and three flautists would be helpless against such flailing and punishing fire.

Yet Cochrane insisted it could be done. 'Trust me, Sharpe! Trust me!'

'I've told you, my Lord, you are doing precisely what the Spaniards want you to do!'

'Trust me! Trust me!'

The Spanish fortress guns were not the only obstacles to Cochrane's blithe optimism. Even the tide pattern suggested the attack could not succeed. The waterlogged *Espiritu Santo*, which Cochrane insisted would be the assault ship, could only get alongside the fortress quay at the very top of the high tide. If the attack was just one hour late the water would have dropped far enough to prevent the frigate reaching the quayside. That narrow tidal opportunity dictated that the attack would have to be mounted at dawn, and the approach to the harbour made in a misty half-darkness, for the next morning's suitable high tide fell just as the sun would be rising. Sharpe, not given easily to despair, suspected the whole assault was doomed, yet Cochrane still insisted it could be done. 'It would be more sensible to use the *O'Higgins* to carry the assault troops, of course,' Cochrane allowed. 'She's got guns and is undamaged, but if anything went wrong, I'd lose her, so I might as well stay in the *Espiritu Santo*. Of course, Sharpe, if you're scared of the proceedings, then I'll quite understand if you'd rather watch from the deck of the *O'Higgins*.'

Sharpe was almost tempted to accept the offer. This was not his fight, and he had no particular taste for Cochrane's elaborate suicide mission, but he was unwilling to admit to Cochrane or to Major Miller that he was frightened, and besides, he had business of his own in Puerto Crucero, and a grudge against the man who had expelled him, so he did have a reason to fight, even if the fight was hopeless. 'I'll stay with the ship,' he said.

'Even though you think it's suicide?' Cochrane teased Sharpe.

'I wish I could think otherwise,' Sharpe said.

'You forget,' Cochrane said, 'what the Spaniards say of me. I'm their devil. I work black magic. And in tomorrow's dawn, Sharpe, you'll see just how devilish I can be.' His Lordship laughed, while his ship, pumps clattering, limped towards battle.

CHAPTER 7

Major Miller possessed a large watch that was made, he touchingly claimed, of East Indian gold, yet it was a gold stranger than any Sharpe had ever seen, for the outside of the watchcase was rusted orange and its insides tarnished black. The watch itself was famously erratic, causing Miller to be forever shaking it or tapping it or even dropping it experimentally on what he described as the 'softer' portions of the deck. Once it was ticking, however, he declared the watch to be the most accurate and reliable of all timepieces.

'One hour to high tide,' he now confidently declared, then held the watch to his ear before adding, somewhat ominously, 'or maybe less.'

Sharpe hoped it was more, much more, for the stricken *Espiritu Santo* still seemed a long way from the rocky headland which protected Puerto Crucero's harbour, and if the frigate was to be successfully sailed right alongside the fortress quay then the manoeuvre would need to be completed by the last moments of the rising tide. There would be sufficient water to make a landing possible for a whole hour after the high tide, but both Cochrane and his sailing master doubted that the attack could succeed after the tide had turned. The captured frigate's hull was so fouled by damage and by fothering, and her upperworks poorly rigged, that the ship would probably be pushed backwards by the opposition of even the most feeble ebbing current.

'But we'll make it!' Major Miller was imbued with an

unconquerable optimism. 'Tommy's too clever to make silly mistakes with the tide!'

'Tommy' was Lord Cochrane, and Miller's hero. Miller shook the watch dubiously, then, realizing that his gesture might suggest to an onlooker that the precious timepiece was not working to its vaunted perfection, he stuffed it back into a pocket of his waistcoat. 'You and Mister Harper will do me the honour of attacking in our company? 'Pon my soul, Sharpe, but I never thought I'd live to see the day when I'd swing a sword in your company.'

'The honour will all be mine,' Sharpe said gallantly, then turned as one of the two remaining cannon on board the *Espiritu Santo* banged its flat, hard sound across the water.

The success of the attack depended entirely on a ruse devised by Lord Cochrane, but a ruse so brilliantly conceived that Sharpe was convinced it must succeed in deceiving the enemy. The deception was a piece of theatre which had been suggested to his Lordship by the *Espiritu Santo*'s woeful condition. The Spanish frigate was, even to the most untutored eye, a ship on the very edge of disaster, a ship battered and sinking, a ship partially dismasted, a ship canted and stricken, a wounded ship that had been outfought and near sunk, a ship at the very end of her life. And if, Lord Cochrane reasoned, such a beaten vessel was to be seen limping into Puerto Crucero's harbour, and if, moreover, the broken vessel was seen to be under attack by the dreaded *O'Higgins*, then the fort's defenders must assume that the *Espiritu Santo* was still fighting for Spain, and those defenders, instead of firing at the limping ship, would actually seek to protect her from the pursuing rebel flagship.

The *O'Higgins*, in order to make the illusion complete, had changed her own appearance. The main and mizzen topmasts had been unshipped and slung down to the deck to make it seem that she had suffered damage in what Puerto Crucero's defenders must be convinced had been a long running fight at sea. Old sails had been left draped on the *O'Higgins*'s decks to suggest that not enough men remained alive to clear her battle damage. Then, to add verisimilitude to the deception, the *O'Higgins* had been firing at the *Espiritu Santo* since dawn, but the shots were deliberately sporadic, as though the rebel gunners were tired to the point of despair.

Thus, if the ruse succeeded, the watchers in Puerto Crucero would see a shattered Spanish warship fighting her way into the refuge of their harbour, desperately needing the fort's assistance to drive away her battered and wounded pursuer. The ruse, Sharpe did not doubt, would succeed in bringing the *Espiritu Santo* safe to the defenders' quay, but it would not guarantee that Cochrane's handful of men would then succeed in climbing from that quay to capture the towering citadel. Cochrane's devilment had, if the tide permitted, guaranteed success for the first part of the assault, but Sharpe did not know what magic would then take over to waft Miller's marines up the steep stone stairs.

Not that Major Miller had any doubts. 'I just hope,' he declared again and again to Sharpe, 'that General Bautista is still in the fortress. It would give me great pleasure to capture him! My God, Sharpe, but I'll teach him to insult an Englishman!' Miller, who seemed to forget sometimes that he officially fought for the Chilean Republic now, touched the stiff tarred tips of his moustache. 'How many defenders are there in the fort, d'you think?' Miller suddenly asked.

It seemed a little late to be asking such a question. 'Three hundred?' Sharpe guessed, but having been inside the citadel, he was fairly sure of his guess. He estimated that the Spanish had three understrength companies of infantry, say two hundred men, supported by sixty or seventy gunners and a group of cooks, clerks and quartermaster's staff. 'Three hundred,' Sharpe said again, but more firmly.

'And we have one hundred in the attacking party,' Miller said, not with despair, but rather with a kind of pride that the imminent victory would be gained by such an outnumbered band. Half the attackers were Miller's marines, the other half Cochrane's seamen; a vagabond band of fearsome men carrying butchers' weapons and double-shotted muskets.

Ahead of the *Espiritu Santo* now the sun was rising above the far mountains so that the world's edge seemed to be a jagged black silhouette lined with fire. Torn clouds of gold and scarlet flew above the sun's ascent. In the nearer valleys, still hugged by darkness, a mist silvered the threatening shadows. A shimmer of smoke showed above the black headland to betray where Puerto Crucero's kitchen fires were lit. Above that headland was the grim outline of the waiting fortress high on its crag. Closer yet was a handful of fishing boats which, terrified of stray shots from the pair of fighting warships, were trying to reach the safety of the harbour.

The gunfire crashed again as the *O'Higgins* turned to fire a pretend broadside. Some of the Chilean flagship's guns were properly loaded with roundshot, for Cochrane insisted that the sound of a blank gun was utterly different to the full-throated explosion of a barrel charged with lethal roundshot. Besides, the huge splashes of water exploding close to the *Espiritu Santo* as the roundshot ploughed into the sea only added to the verisimilitude of Cochrane's deception. That deception was furthered by the huge, shot-torn banner of Spain that he had ordered hoisted at the *Espiritu Santo*'s stern.

'They'll have seen us by now!' Miller declared in a voice so loud and confident that Sharpe knew the jaunty marine was nervous. Men's voices always seemed louder in the moments before battle; the moments when they had nothing to say, but spoke anyway just to prove that fear was not making their hearts flabby and bellies sour.

'They'll have heard us an hour ago,' Sharpe said. He imagined the defenders high on the fortress ramparts staring through long brass telescopes at the sea battle. He imagined, too, the iron roundshot being heated in the roaring furnaces beneath the bastions. The thirty-six pounders were probably already loaded, perhaps double-shotted, with cold missiles, but their second and third salvos could leave traces of smoke as the red-hot shots seared above the cold morning sea.

'Hide yourselves, gentlemen! Hide yourselves!' Lord Cochrane, gripping the quarterdeck rail above Sharpe's head, spoke softly, yet Sharpe could hear the excitement in the rebel Admiral's voice. Cochrane, Sharpe thought, was febrile with anticipation. If Cochrane was nervous, it did not show, and somehow his confidence communicated itself to the attack force which now dutifully concealed itself deep in the shadows under the break of the poop. They would stay under the concealing quarterdeck until the frigate actually touched the stone of the fortress quay. Then, screaming their battle cry, they would erupt onto the astonished defenders. By which time, if Cochrane was right, the *Espiritu Santo* would be too close to the citadel for the gunners in their high batteries to be able to depress their cannons' barrels. It was possible, Cochrane allowed, that there might be cannons on the quay, cannons which could wreak a terrible slaughter from the moment the Spanish ensign was dropped and the Chilean run up, so the first of Cochrane's men ashore were under orders to assault any such close and inconvenient guns. Major Miller, following hard on the heels of those first desperate men, would then lead his marines in their attack up the rock-built stairs that led initially to the big thirty-six pounders on their wide bastion, and afterwards into the very heart of the citadel.

'Not long now, boys, not long now!' Cochrane called softly.

The wind felt cold. Sharpe shivered. He was thinking of that long open stairway that ran so steeply up the wind-fretted crag. It would only take one company of Spanish infantry to hold those stairs through all eternity. He looked sideways at Harper and saw a strained look on his friend's broad face. Harper, catching Sharpe's glance, grimaced as if to suggest that he realized how mad they were to be taking a part in this foolery. One of Miller's two drummers gave his instrument an experimental tap. A man coughed horribly, then spat relievedly. Behind the waiting men, in the *Espiritu Santo*'s lavish stern cabins, the long-barrelled nine pounders fired. Sharpe imagined the splash of the skipping shots as they whipped past the pursuing *O'Higgins*. Footsteps sounded loud on the quarterdeck above. Sharpe and Miller, peering out from under the poop, saw that the frigate had passed the outer headland and was now limping towards the fort that lay only a half mile away. The American brigantine, with her flamboyantly huge ensign, still lay at her twin anchors in the outer roadstead.

'Heads down, my lads!' Cochrane called from the quarterdeck. Besides Cochrane himself, only a dozen men were on deck, all of them Spanish speakers. One of those men was waiting with the furled rebel ensign because, under the rules of war, not a shot could be fired against the enemy till the *Espiritu Santo* displayed her true colours.

The fort's defenders, doubtless recognizing the *Espiritu Santo* as one of their own ships, would be watching the *O'Higgins* now, measuring their distance, waiting for her hull to clear the headland and thus expose herself to their dreadful fire. Sailors were lining the rails of the American brigantine, drawn there by the great percussive explosions of gunfire that had startled this Chilean dawn. Gulls screamed in the frigate's broken rigging. Sharpe could smell shellfish and seaweed. He could also smell the smoke from the cooking fires in the fishing hovels beyond the beach, and he thought how different the land smelt from the sea, then he obsessively drew the sword he had borrowed from Lord Cochrane an inch free from its scabbard to make sure that the blade was not stuck. In battle he had known men killed because their swords had rusted into their scabbards. The pumps clattered on the lower deck to spurt discoloured bilge water into the silver-grey harbour. One of Miller's flautists blew three fast and plaintive notes as if checking that his instrument still worked. 'Not yet, boys,' Miller said, 'not yet! And when we do attack, boys, I want to hear *Heart of Oak!*' He beat time to a tune heard only in his head, then explained to Sharpe that two of his flautists were Chilean and therefore unfamiliar with patriotic British songs. 'But I taught 'em, Sharpe, 'pon my soul I taught 'em.' Unable to restrain himself the Major burst into song:

'Come, cheer up, my lads! 'tis to glory we steer,
To add something more to this wonderful year;
To honour we call you, not press you like slaves,
For who are so free as the sons of the waves?
Heart of oak are our ships!
Heart of oak are our men!
We always are ready! Steady, boys, steady . . .'

'Stop that bloody caterwauling down below!' came a bellow from the quarterdeck.

'A thousand apologies, my Lord!' Miller was mortified to have earned a reproof from his beloved Cochrane.

'Save your dreadful music for the enemy, Miller!' Cochrane was clearly amused by Miller's singing.

'Whatever you say, my Lord. And I'm much obliged for your Lordship's advice!'

'And cheer up, lads!' Cochrane called down to all the hidden men who were nervously waiting for the attack to begin. 'There are whores with tits of purest gold ashore! One more hour and we'll all be drunk, rich and rogered witless!'

Major Miller smiled confidingly at Sharpe. 'A great man, our Tommy, a great man! A hero, Sharpe, like yourself. Cut from the old cloth, poured from an antique mould, sprung from ancient seed, clean hewn from solid oak!' Miller, moved by this elaborate encomium, sniffed. 'He may be a Scotsman, but at heart there's English oak there, Sharpe, pure English oak! I'm proud to know him, I am, proud indeed.' Miller looked as if he needed to cuff a tear from his eyes, but his emotional outpouring of loyalty was cut short by an appalling crash of gunfire from the castle ramparts. Heavy roundshot screamed overhead, slashing above the *Espiritu Santo*'s truncated masts to blast fountains of water close to the pursuing *O'Higgins*. The Chilean flagship immediately answered with a deafening full broadside.

'God save Ireland,' Harper said, 'but I never thought to be in a battle again.'

The Chilean shots cracked against the castle crag, splintering shards of stone, but otherwise doing no damage. Other guns were firing now, lighter guns, cracking their missiles down from the citadel's highest ramparts. Sharpe imagined the roundshot smashing through the *O'Higgins*'s hull timbers. God help them, he thought, God help them. So far, at least, the deception had worked and no Spanish guns were firing at the *Espiritu Santo*; all the dreadful gunnery was aimed at the *O'Higgins*.

A strange voice called in a lull between the gun shots, and Sharpe, with an apprehensive leap of his heart, realized that the voice must have been calling from somewhere ashore. They were close, so close. A wisp of mist drifted across the wreckage which Cochrane had artistically strewn on the *Espiritu Santo*'s maindeck. The voice called again, and this time a man shouted in answer from the frigate's bows, explaining that the *Espiritu Santo* had been in a running fight with the devil Cochrane these last six days, and that the frigate was filled with wounded, but praise God and St James they had slaughtered and wounded scores of their enemies and might even have killed that devil Cochrane with their gunnery.

Another terrible crash of gunfire was followed by a horribly familiar rending sound as the great cannonballs ripped the sky apart. Sharpe, looking up through the *Espiritu Santo*'s tattered rigging, saw the smoke trails of heated shot. 'God help the *O'Higgins*,' he said softly.

'God help us all,' Harper responded. A marine crossed himself. Miller was singing again, though under his breath for fear of offending Cochrane. The men at the pumps faltered for a second, then began their desperate pumping again. Footsteps paced slow and comforting on the quarterdeck above.

'Not long now, lads,' Cochrane's voice called softly. 'Think of the waiting whores. Think of the gold! Think of the plunder we'll take! Not long now!'

The man on the frigate's beakhead was calling more news ashore. Captain Ardiles was dead, he said, and the First Lieutenant dying. 'We have women and children on board!' he called ashore.

'Twenty paces, no more!' Cochrane warned his attackers.

'I pray there's water under our keel!' Miller said in sudden fear. 'God, give us water!' and Sharpe had a sudden image of the frigate stranded fifteen paces from land and being pulverized by cannonfire.

'Fifteen paces! Stay hidden now!' Cochrane said.

A marine nervously scraped a sharpening stone down his fixed bayonet. Another felt the edge of his cutlass with his thumb; Sharpe had seen the man do the same thing at least a dozen times in the last minute. Miller took a huge deep breath, then spat onto the snakeskin handle of his sword. A gust of wind reflected off the citadel's crag to flog the edge of a sail and spray dew thick as rain down onto the frigate's deck.

'Ensign!' Cochrane called sharply. 'Hoist our colours!'

The Spanish flag rippled down, to be replaced immediately with the new Chilean flag. At the very same moment there was a crash as the frigate's starboard quarter slammed into the quay.

'Come on!' Cochrane roared. 'Come on!'

The assault force was still staggering from the impact of the frigate's crashing arrival against the quay, but now they pushed themselves upright and, screaming like devils, scrambled into the dawn's wan light.

Cochrane was already poised on the ship's rail. The frigate had struck the quay, and was now rebounding. The gap was two paces, three, then Cochrane leaped. Other men were jumping ashore with berthing lines.

'Come on, lads! Music!' Miller's sword was high in the air.

A seaman had slung a prow ashore to act as a gangplank. A few men jostled to use it, but most men simply leaped to the quay from the frigate's starboard rail. A flute screeched. A drummer, safe ashore, gave a ripple of sound. A man screamed as he missed his footing and fell into the water.

A cannon fired from the quay's far end and a ball slashed harmlessly across the quarterdeck, bounced, and ripped out a section of the port gunwale. Sharpe was at the rail now. Christ, but the gap looked huge and beneath him was a churning mass of dirty white water, but men were shouting at him to make way, and so he jumped. The first men ashore were screaming defiance as they ran towards the small battery at the quay's end where the gunners were desperately trying to slew their guns round to face the sudden enemy. Cannon smoke was blowing across the harbour. The *O'Higgins* had cleverly taken shelter behind the American brigantine and the Spanish gunners, fearful of bombarding a neutral ship, and unable to depress their heavy cannon sufficiently to fire down onto the *Espiritu Santo*, had temporarily ceased fire.

Harper jumped and sprawled on the quay beside Sharpe. He picked himself up and ran towards the stone stairs. Major Miller was already on the steps, climbing as fast as his short legs would carry him. Behind him a mass of men flooded onto the stairway. Fear gave the attack a desperate impetus. A last cannon fired from the quay battery and Sharpe saw one of Miller's marines torn bloody by the ball's terrible strike.

Then a musket banged from the citadel high above and the ball flattened itself on the quay. The quay battery was finished, its gunners were either bayonetted, shot, or had jumped into the water. Lord Cochrane, that task successfully completed, was running to the stairs, trying to catch up with Miller's frantic assault. Sharpe ran with Cochrane, easily outpacing the fat Harper who was struggling behind. 'Jesus Christ, but this is wonderful! Oh God, but this is wonderful! What joy this is!' Cochrane was talking to himself, lost in a heaven of weltering blood and banging gunfire. 'Christ, but what a way to live! Isn't this wonderful? 'Pon my soul, what a morning!' His Lordship elbowed his way through Miller's rear ranks so he could lead the attack.

The stairs led first to the terrace where the Indian, Ferdinand, had been murdered by the big thirty-six-pounder gun. Three of those guns fired as Sharpe neared the terrace and their muzzle flashes seemed to fill the whole sky with one searing and percussive explosion. The gunners had not fired at any particular target, but had merely emptied their barrels before abandoning the huge weapons. Major Miller and his marines were on the bastion now, but the Spanish gunners were in full flight, leaping off the battery's far wall to scramble away across the bare rock slope. The iron door of the shot-heating furnace had been left open so that the air above the brick structure shimmered with a dreadful heat.

'Leave them be!' Cochrane roared at the handful of

marines who seemed intent on chasing the gunners. 'Miller! Up the stairs! Follow me!'

The main battery was captured, but the citadel itself was still in Spanish hands and the hardest part of the attack was yet to be completed. Cochrane, knowing that he had to exploit the surprise he had achieved, was leading a madcap charge up the wider flight of stairs that led into the very heart of the fortress. Once those stairs were climbed the fort must inevitably fall, but Cochrane knew only too well that he needed to reach the summit before the Spaniards recovered from the shock of the attack. The staircase was foully steep and offered an attacker no shelter, so that a handful of determined defenders could hold the stairs for eternity. 'Follow! Follow! Follow!' Cochrane, knowing he had only seconds to capture the citadel, roared the word.

'Cochrane!' his men responded, but faintly, for they were out of breath. They had spent too long on board ship and their legs seemed weak. The assault was slowing down as burning muscles and cramp took their toll.

Then, appallingly, a rank of muskets crashed and flamed from high above the breathless attackers. One of Miller's marines toppled backwards, his mouth full of blood. A seaman screamed, then cartwheeled down the steps to carry two more men away in his helpless tumble. Sharpe saw musket smoke spurting out of the arched windows from where he had watched Ferdinand's grisly death, then he saw a mighty billow of smoke erupt from the arch at the top of the stairway and he knew that the Spanish had succeeded in posting a company of infantry at the top of the rock-cut stairs, and if those infantrymen were only half good then the Spanish must win.

The infantry was good enough. Their first two volleys were followed by another within just fifteen seconds. Two more marines fell backwards. A dozen men had collapsed on the steps; some were dead, some wounded. A drummer was screaming in pain, his hand fluttering on the drumskin to make a grotesque dying music. Cochrane's gamble, that had depended on reaching the top of the stairs before the Spanish defenders barred the archway, had failed.

'Fire!' Miller shouted, and his men hammered a feeble volley at the musket smoke, but the volley was almost immediately answered by another cracking smack of musket fire. The balls sliced and lashed past Sharpe's ears. A corporal was vomiting blood and slipping back down the slope. Miller fired a useless pistol at the defenders, then screamed defiance, but the Spaniards had the best of this fight. Not only were there more of them, but they had the advantage of the high ground. They were well trained, too. The company was rotating its ranks. As soon as the front rank had poured its musketry down into the rebel attack, it stepped back to be replaced by the second rank which, its guns reloaded and ready, added its fire before the third rank stepped forward. They were firing like British infantry had used to fire. They had established a murderous rhythm of volleys that would keep firing till the attackers were reduced to twitching, bloody carcasses on the steps. It was volley fire like this which had defeated Napoleon at Waterloo and which now was throwing back Cochrane at Puerto Crucero.

'Down!' Cochrane shouted. 'Get down!' The man had the devil's own luck, for, despite being in the front rank, he was unscathed, but his assault was in horrid confusion.

Sharpe had a pistol that he fired at one of the arched windows that lay high to his right. He saw a chip of stone fly off the windowledge. Harper dropped beside Sharpe. 'Christ save Ireland,' Harper panted, 'but this is desperate!' He levelled his borrowed musket and fired up into the smoke. 'I told the wife I'd be doing nothing dangerous. Not a thing, I told her, except the sea voyage, and that never worries her because she's a great believer in Saint Brendan's protection, so she is.' All this while Harper was reloading the musket with a skill that betrayed his years of soldiering. 'Jesus, but the money that woman wastes on candles! Christ, I could have lit my way to the shit hole of hell and back with all the bloody candles she's given to the holy saints, but I wish she'd lit a bloody candle to keep me safe in a fight.' He aimed up the steps in the general direction of the smoke cloud and pulled the trigger. 'God help us.' He began reloading. 'I mean there's no way out of here, is there? The bloody boat will be hard aground in a minute or two.'

Sharpe saw a man leaning out of a window to fire at the attackers cowering on the steps. He aimed the reloaded pistol and fired, and saw a spurt of blood vivid in the grey morning as the man toppled down the crag's face. 'Got one,' he said happily.

'Good for you.' Harper raised himself and fired over the prone bodies of the marines higher up the steps. A volley smacked down, blasting a chip of stone from the stair beside Sharpe.

'This can't last!' Sharpe shouted at Harper. He needed to shout for the musketry was almost continuous now, suggesting that the Spaniards had concentrated even more muskets at the top of the steps. For the defenders this was like shooting rats in a barrel. They would be grinning as they fired, knowing that this day they were defeating the dreaded Lord Cochrane and that all Spain would rejoice when that news reached home. Another volley banged, and the dead bodies which made a protective breastwork for Sharpe and Harper twitched under the flail of lead. 'On, my good boys, on!' Miller called, but no one obeyed, for there could be no chance of surviving an uphill attack into that rending, flickering, crashing and unending fire. Any man who tried to climb the stairs would be cut down in seconds, then thrown back to the quay that was already piled with the blood-spattered dead who had rolled down the steps. 'Stay down!' Cochrane countermanded Miller's hopeless order. 'Stay low! It's all going to be well! I've a trick or two yet, boys.'

'Jesus, but he needs a bloody trick now,' Harper said, then raised the musket blindly over the parapet of the dead bodies to pull its trigger. 'God save Ireland, but we're dead men unless he can get us out of here.'

Miller shouted at his musicians to play louder, as though their feeble and ragged music could somehow turn back the surging tide of disaster. Some of Miller's experienced marines, realizing how hopeless was their plight, began to edge backwards. There had been a chance of capturing the fortress, even a good chance, but only if the surprise attack had reached the head of the staircase before the defenders had rallied. But the attackers had failed by yards, and now the Spaniards were grinding Cochrane's men into blood and bones. More attackers began slipping down the steps. They were looking for possible escape routes round the harbour's edge.

'Stay there!' Cochrane shouted. 'It's all right, lads! Stay where you are! Wait for it! I promise everything will be well! Heads down now! Heads down! Keep your . . .' Cochrane's voice was swamped as the whole world suddenly exploded in noise and stone fragments.

'Christ!' Harper screeched as the citadel's foundations seemed to shudder with the impact of gunfire.

The *O'Higgins*, now that the citadel's main thirty-six-pound battery had been silenced, had sailed out from the unwitting protection offered by the American ship and had anchored with her starboard broadside facing the fortress. She had just fired that full broadside at the defenders bunched at the top of the broad flight of stairs. The volley of cannonfire had been shockingly dangerous to the attackers, but magnificent shooting all the same. At a range of almost half a mile the flagship's guns were firing just feet over the heads of Cochrane's attackers. At least one cannonball fell short, for Sharpe saw a marine virtually disintegrate just five steps above him. At one moment the man was aiming his musket, the next there was just a gory mess on the stairs and a crack of murderous intensity as the ball ricocheted on up towards the Spaniards.

'Heads down!' Cochrane called again, and once again the broadside thundered from the Chilean warship. Stone shards, struck from the battlements, sang viciously over Sharpe's head. This, he remembered from the tales of survivors, was precisely how Wellington had captured San Sebastian. That great fortress, the last French bastion in Spain, had resisted every British attack until, at the very last moment of the very last assault, when the helpless attackers were dying in the great breach as the French garrison poured a murderous fire into the redcoated ranks, Wellington had ordered his siege guns to fire just above the attackers' heads. The unexpected cannonade, catching the French defenders out of their entrenchments and exposed behind the breach's makeshift barricades, had turned a glorious French victory into a butcher's nightmare. The huge roundshot had destroyed the French defenders, blowing them ragged, and a British defeat had turned into sudden triumph. Now Cochrane was trying the exact same trick.

'Heads down!' Cochrane called again. He had clearly anticipated that the defenders might block the head of the stairs, and had thus arranged with the *O'Higgins* for this drastic solution that had caught the Spaniards bunched at the stairhead. 'One more broadside, lads, then we'll fillet the bastards!'

The third broadside slammed into the citadel above Sharpe. The defenders' musket fire, that a moment before had been so overwhelming, had now vanished, blown into whimpering carnage by the shocking violence of the naval gunnery.

'Charge!' Cochrane was shouting even as the brutal echo of the third broadside reverberated around the harbour. 'Now charge!'

They charged. They were men who wanted to revenge a near defeat, and the sound of their vengeance as they scrambled up the shot-mangled steps was bloodcurdling. Somewhere ahead of Sharpe steel scraped on steel and a man screamed. The top of the stairs was a slaughteryard of broken stone, blood and mangled flesh. A Spanish drummer boy, scarce ten years old, was curled at the side of the archway, his hands contracting into claws as he died. Sharpe, reaching the stair's head, found himself shrouded in a fog of dust and smoke. Screams sounded ahead of him, then a Spanish soldier, his face a mask of blood, came charging from Sharpe's right. The man lunged his bayonet at Sharpe who, with a practised reflex, stepped back, tripped the man, then hacked down once with the sword. The borrowed blade seemed horribly light and seemed to do so little damage. Harper, a pace behind Sharpe, killed the man with a thrust of his bayonet. A volley of muskets sounded through the smoke, but no bullets came near Sharpe or Harper, suggesting that the volley was a rebel salvo fired at the retreating defenders. 'This way!' Miller's voice shouted. His remaining drummer was beating the charge while the flautists were playing an almost recognizable version of *Heart of Oak*.

The marines ran to the left, charging down a stone tunnel that led to the parade ground. Sharpe and Harper went the other way. They pushed through a half open door, stepped over the mangled body of a Spanish soldier, and found themselves in the great audience hall where Bautista had so effortlessly humiliated Sharpe just days before. Now, in the smoky dust which hung in slanting beams of morning sunlight, they found the hall deserted of all but the dead. Sharpe stepped over a fallen bench and edged past a headless Spanish officer. One of the *O'Higgins*'s cannonballs had struck the huge iron chandelier which, grotesquely bent and ripped from its chains, was now canted against the far wall. The defenders, who had been firing down from the great arched windows, had fled, leaving a litter of torn cartridge papers behind them. A dozen cannonballs lay on the stone floor. The places where they had struck the wall opposite the big arched windows were marked by plate-sized craters. One of the roundshot must have taken off the head of the Spanish officer, for the hall's dusty floor was decorated with a monstrous fan of freshly sprayed blood.

Sharpe pushed open a door at the hall's far end to emerge onto the big parade ground. The Spaniards, in sheer terror, were abandoning the citadel's defences, running towards the gate at the far side of the citadel. A nearby battery of nine-pounder cannons was deserted, the gunner's linstocks still smoking, the dirty sponge water in the buckets still rippling. Sharpe sheathed his sword and walked to the ramparts that had been smeared black with powderstains from the nine-pounders' discharge and leaned over the citadel's high edge to draw in a great breath of clean cold air. Somewhere in the fortress a dog howled and a child screamed.

'One of ours,' Harper said.

'What's one of ours?' Sharpe asked.

'The gun!' Harper slapped the hot breech of the closest nine-pounder cannon and Sharpe saw there the cipher of King George III. The gun was presumably one of the thousands that the British government had given to the Spanish during the French wars. Sharpe touched the raised cipher and suddenly felt homesick; not for England and King George, but for Lucille and for her kitchen in Normandy and for the smell of dried herbs hanging from the beams, and for the rime of frost in the orchard and cat ice in the dairy yard, and for the sound of his children's laughter. Then, like a warm rush, the knowledge flooded through Sharpe that his job in Chile was done, that there were no obstacles now to his taking Vivar's body, except the minor one of finding a ship to carry the corpse home to Europe and Sharpe supposed Cochrane would help him over that difficulty.

Beneath Sharpe, her job well done, the *Espiritu Santo* was hard aground beside the wharf and beginning to list as she took the ground on the falling tide. Skeins of cannon smoke thinned and drifted across the outer harbour where long-boats, crammed with reinforcements from the *O'Higgins*, were being rowed ashore. The sailors on the American brig-antine were cheering the passing boats because, so far as they were concerned, Cochrane's rebels fought for liberty.

Cochrane's rebels thought they were fighting for Coch-rane, for whores and for gold, while the Spaniards, their cause lost, were fleeing. Sharpe and Harper, walking unmolested around the citadel's inner ramparts, watched scores of defeated soldiers running pell-mell down the hair-pin bends of the approach road. A few, presumably officers, had horses and were galloping towards the high road which led north to Valdivia. Some townsfolk, aston-ished by what this dawn had brought, stared in astonish-ment as the citadel's defeated garrison fled. 'God, but they broke fast,' Harper said in wonderment.

'They did,' Sharpe agreed. He had seen soldiers run before, but never so easily as this. At Waterloo the French had run, but only after they had fought all day with snarling courage, yet these Spanish defenders, after firing a handful of volleys, had simply collapsed. Sharpe, given the citadel to defend, would have sheltered his men as soon as the frigate fired her first broadside, then counter-attacked the moment the cannonade lifted, but the Spanish defences and the morale of the garrison had proved as brittle as eggshells. The royal forces had been on the very edge of victory, but no one on the Spanish side had realized it or had known how to capitalize on it. 'They've rotted away,' Sharpe said in the tone of a man suddenly understanding a truth. 'Maybe all the Spaniards here are rotten.' He was suddenly assailed by a fantastic vision of Cochrane, with his diminishing band of heroes, capturing fortress after fortress, and more and more Spaniards running pell-mell for safety until, at the end, there was nowhere to run and Chile would be united under its rebel government.

A cheer turned Sharpe round. From the top ramparts of the citadel's main tower, above the great audience chamber, a marine tossed a roll of plundered cloth that cascaded and rippled to hang like a monstrous banner from the battlements. Another marine cut the halliard which held the Spanish flag.

'So what now?' Harper asked.

'We dig up Blas Vivar and take him home.' Sharpe was wiping the blade of Cochrane's spare sword clean. It was a good sword, nicely balanced and with a wickedly sharp edge, but it lacked the ugly killing weight of his old Heavy Cavalry blade.

'Do you think that bugger Bautista might still be here?' Harper was watching a small group of Spanish officers walk under guard from the large tower towards the barrack rooms.

'Bautista will have buggered off days ago.' Sharpe scrubbed at the sticky blood with the corner of his coat, then grinned because he could almost hear Lucille's exasperated complaint, for he suddenly realized that this coat was none other than his good dark green kerseymere that Lucille liked so much and which was such a trouble to clean. 'I'm going to be in the doghouse when I get home,' he told Harper, 'for fighting in my best coat.'

'Women don't understand these things, nor do they.'

Somewhere in the citadel a child cried. Sharpe supposed that most of the men in the Spanish garrison would have taken themselves wives, and now those women would be finding new protectors. Major Miller, his tarred moustache looking more perky than ever, was protecting two such girls, one on each arm. 'Did you enjoy yourself?' he called up to Sharpe.

'I did, thank you.'

'I can offer you a fruit of victory, perhaps?' Miller gestured at the girls.

'Keep them, Major.' Sharpe smiled, then turned to stare from the rampart far across the hills to where the ragged Andean peaks tore at the sky. The smoke of volcanoes was a brown smear in the new morning's sunlight. 'Thank God,' he said quietly.

'What for?' Harper asked.

'Because it's over, Patrick.' Sharpe was still overwhelmed by the sense of relief. 'Honour is even. Cochrane rescued us from the *Espiritu Santo*, and we've helped him capture this place, and we don't need to do anything more. We can go home. It's a pity to have lost my sword, but I'll not be needing it again, not in this life, and I don't give a bugger about the next. As for Louisa's money, well, she wanted it spent on finding her husband, and we've found him, so it's over. We've fought our last fight.'

Harper smiled. 'Maybe we have at that.'

Sharpe turned and looked down at the garrison church where Vivar lay buried. He saw rebels carrying gold out of the church, and he guessed that they had ripped apart the ornate altar screen. A cheer from the tower suggested that yet more treasure had been discovered. 'If you want to join in?' Sharpe invited Harper.

'I'm all right, so I am. Just glad to be in one piece.' The Irishman yawned hugely. 'But I'm tired, so I am.'

'We can sleep today. All day.' Sharpe pushed himself away from the wall. 'But first we've got to lift a gravestone.'

Because they had come to journey's end, to the grave of a friend, and this time there was no one to stop them retrieving Vivar's body from its cold tomb. The citadel had fallen, Cochrane was victorious, and Sharpe could go home.

CHAPTER 8

The paving slab which bore Blas Vivar's initials had been replaced, but the stoneworkers' tools were still in the side chapel and, with Harper's help, Sharpe inserted the crowbar beside the big sandstone slab. 'Ready?' Sharpe asked. 'Heave.'

Nothing happened. 'Bloody hell!' Harper said. Behind them, in the nave of the church, a man screamed. The *O'Higgins*'s surgeon, a maudlin Irishman named MacAuley, had ordered the wounded of both sides to be brought into the church where, on a trestle table, he sliced at mangled flesh and sawed at shattered bones. A Dominican monk, who had been a surgeon in the citadel's sick bay, was helping the Irish doctor, as were two orderlies from the Chilean flagship.

'I hate listening to surgeons working,' Harper said, then gave Vivar's gravestone a kick. 'Bugger doesn't want to move.' The big Irishman spat on both hands, gripped the crowbar firmly and, with his feet solidly planted either side of the slab, heaved back until the veins stood out on his forehead and sweat dripped down his cheeks, yet all he succeeded in doing was bending the crowbar's shaft. 'Jesus Christ!' he swore as he let go of the crowbar. 'They've cemented the bugger in place, haven't they?' He went to the side chapel and came back with a sledgehammer. 'Stand back.' Sharpe sensibly stepped back as the Irishman swung, then drove the head of the sledgehammer hard down onto the gravestone. The noise of the impact was like the strike of a cannonball, cracking the gravestone clean across. Harper swung the hammer again and again, grunting as he crazed the obstinate stone into a score of jagged-edged chunks. He finally dropped the hammer when the stone was reduced to rubble. 'That's taught the bugger a lesson.'

Lord Cochrane, who had come into the church while Harper was feverishly annihilating the stone, now took out his watch, snapped open its lid, and showed the face to Sharpe. 'Thirteen minutes and forty-three seconds.'

'My Lord?' Sharpe enquired politely.

'Thirteen minutes and forty-three seconds! See!'

'Has everyone gone mad round here?' Sharpe asked.

'Thirteen minutes and forty-three seconds is precisely how long it took us to capture the citadel! This watch measures elapsed time, do you see? You press this trigger to start it and this to stop it. I pressed the trigger as our bows touched the wharf, and stopped it when the last defender abandoned the ramparts. In fact I was a bit late, so we probably took less time, but even thirteen minutes and forty-three seconds is rather good for the capture of a citadel this size, don't you think?' His Lordship, who was in an excitedly triumphant mood, snapped the watch lid shut. 'I must thank you. Both of you.' He graciously bowed to both Sharpe and Harper.

'We didn't do anything,' Sharpe said modestly.

'Not a great deal,' Harper amended Sharpe's modesty.

'Numbers count for so much,' his Lordship said happily. 'If I'd attacked with just thirty men then there would have been no hope of victory, but I've discovered that in this kind of war success is gained by small increments. Besides, your presence was worth more than you think. Half of my men fought in the French wars, and they know full well who you are, both of you! And they feel more confident when they know that famous soldiers such as yourselves are fighting beside them.'

Sharpe tried to brush the compliment aside, but

Cochrane would have none of his coyness. 'They feel precisely the same about my presence in a scrap. They fight
better when I'm in command because they believe in me.
And because they believe in my luck!'

'And Mister Sharpe's always been lucky in a fight,'
Harper added.

'There you are!' Cochrane beamed. 'Napoleon always
claimed he'd rather have lucky soldiers than clever ones,
though I pride myself on being both.'

Sharpe laughed at his Lordship's immodesty. 'Why
didn't you tell us you'd arranged to have the *O'Higgins* fire
just over our heads if the attack faltered?'

'Because if men know you've got an ace hidden up your
sleeve they expect you to play it whether it's needed or not.
I didn't want to run the risk of using the broadside unless I
really had to, but if the men had known the broadside might
be used they would have held back in the knowledge that
the gunners would do some of the hard work for them.'

'It was a brilliant stroke,' Sharpe said.

'How truly you speak, my dear Sharpe.' Cochrane at
last seemed to notice the destruction wrought by Harper's
sledgehammer. 'What are you doing, Mister Harper?'

'Blas Vivar.' Harper explained. 'He's under here. We're
digging him up, only since we were last here the buggers
have cemented him in place.'

'The devil they have.' Cochrane peered at the mess
Harper had made of the slab as though expecting to see
Vivar's decayed flesh. 'Do you know why people are
buried close to altars?' he asked Sharpe airily.

'No,' Sharpe answered in the tone of a man who did not
much care about the answer.

'Because very large numbers of Catholic churches have
relics of saints secreted within their altars, of course.'
Cochrane smiled, as if he had done Sharpe a great favour
by revealing the answer.

The Dominican surgeon, his white gown streaked and

spattered with bright new blood, had come to the altar to protest to Lord Cochrane about the spoilage being wrought by Harper, but Cochrane turned on the man and brusquely told him to shut up. 'And why,' Cochrane continued blithely to Sharpe, 'do you think the relics in the altar are important to the dead?'

'I really don't know,' Sharpe said.

'Because, my dear Sharpe, of what will happen on the Day of Judgment.'

Harper had fetched a spade with which he chipped away the fragments of limestone. 'They have used bloody cement!' he said in exasperation. 'Goddamn the buggers. Why did they do that? It was just shingle when we tried to pull him out before!'

'They used cement,' Cochrane said, 'because they don't want you to dig him up.'

'The Day of Judgment?' Sharpe, interested at last, asked Cochrane.

His Lordship, who had been examining the mangled remains of the altar screen, turned round. 'Because, my dear Sharpe, common sense tells our papist brethren that, at the sound of the last trump when the dead rise incorruptible, the saints will rise faster than us mere sinners. The rate of resurrection, so the doctrine claims, will depend on the holiness of the man or woman being raised from the dead, and naturally the saints will rise first and travel fastest to heaven. Thus the wise papist, leaving nothing to chance, is buried close to the altar because it contains a saint's relic which, on the Day of Judgment, will go speedily to heaven, creating a draught of wind which will catch up those close to the altar and drag them up to heaven with it.'

'He'll be dragged up in a bloody barrowload of cement and shingle if he tries to fly out of this bloody grave,' Harper grumbled.

Cochrane, who seemed to Sharpe to be taking an inordinate interest in the exhumation, peered down at the mangled grave. 'Why don't I have some prisoners do the digging for you?'

Harper tossed the spade down in acceptance of the offer and Cochrane, having shouted for some prisoners to be fetched, stirred the cemented shingle with his toe. 'Why on earth do you want to take Vivar's body back to Spain?'

'Because that's where his widow wants him,' Sharpe said.

'Ah, a woman's whim! I hope my wife would not wish the same. I can't imagine being slopped home in a vat of brandy like poor Nelson, though I suppose if one must face eternity, then one might as well slip into it drunk.' Cochrane, who had been pacing about the church choir, suddenly stopped, placed one foot dramatically ahead of the other, clasped a left hand across his breast, and declaimed in a mighty voice that momentarily stilled even the moaning of the wounded. ' "Not a drum was heard, not a funeral note, As his corse to the rampart we hurried!" ' His Lordship applauded his own rendering of the lines. 'Who wrote that?'

'An Irishman!' MacAuley shouted from the nave of the church.

'Was it now?' Cochrane enquired sceptically, then whirled on Sharpe. 'You know the poem, Sharpe?'

'No, my Lord.'

'You don't!' Cochrane sounded astonished, then again assumed his declamatory pose. ' "But he lay like a warrior taking his rest, With his martial cloak around him." The verses, you understand, refer to the burial of Sir John Moore. Did you know Moore?'

'I met him,' Sharpe said laconically, recalling a hurried conversation on a snow-bright hillside in Galicia. French dragoons had been leading their horses down an icy road on the far side of a wide valley towards a shivering Greenjacket rearguard, and Lieutenant General Sir John Moore, shaking with the cold, had courteously enquired of Lieutenant Richard Sharpe whether the enemy horsemen had been more bothersome than usual that morning. That distracted conversation, Sharpe now remembered, must have been held only days before he had met Major Blas Vivar of the Cazadores.

'So you will remember that Moore was buried on the battlefield of Corunna,' Cochrane continued, 'and without any nonsense of being carried home to his ever-loving wife. Soldiers normally lie where they fall, so why would this wife want General Vivar taken home? Why does she not leave him in peace?'

'Because the family has a particular connection with the cathedral in Santiago de Compostela.' Sharpe offered the best explanation he could.

'Ah! There are more powerful relics in a cathedral, you see.' Cochrane sounded gloomy. 'In Spain he'll be buried next to Saint James himself, not some snivelling little Chilean holy man. He'll be in heaven before the rest of us will have had a chance to pick our resurrected noses or scratch our resurrected arses.'

'You won't need a wind to carry you, my Lord,' the Irish doctor called. 'You'll just roll downhill to perdition with the rest of us miserable bastards.'

'You note the respect in which I am held.' Cochrane, who clearly relished the comradeship, smiled at Sharpe, then changed into his lamentable Spanish to order the newly-arrived prisoners to start digging. Major Suarez, the Spanish officer who had been so cordial to Sharpe when he had first arrived at Puerto Crucero, and who had suffered the misfortune of being captured by Cochrane's men, had insisted on accompanying the three prisoners to protest about their being employed for manual labour, but he calmed down when he recognized Sharpe and when he saw that the digging was hardly of a martial nature. He calmed down even more when Cochrane, ever courteous, invited him to share in the breakfast he had ordered to be brought to the church. 'Most of your fellow officers escaped capture by running away,' Cochrane observed, 'so I can only congratulate you on having the courage to stay and fight.'

'Alas, *señor*, I was asleep,' Suarez confessed, then crossed himself as he looked at Vivar's grave.

'You were here, *señor*, when the Captain-General was buried?' Cochrane asked politely.

Suarez nodded. 'It was at night. Very late.'

Cochrane could not resist the invitation. '"We buried him darkly at dead of night, The sods with our bayonets turning." How dead was the night?' Cochrane asked Suarez suddenly in Spanish and, when the Major just gaped at him, Cochrane condescended to make the question more intelligible. 'What time was Blas Vivar buried?'

'Past midnight.' Suarez gazed at the grave which was now deepening perceptibly. 'Father Josef said the mass and whoever was still awake attended.'

Sharpe, remembering his conversation with Blair, the British Consul in Valdivia, frowned. 'I thought a lot of people were invited here for the funeral?'

'No, *señor*, that was for a requiem mass a week later. But Captain-General Vivar was buried by then.'

'Who filled the grave with cement?' Sharpe asked.

'The Captain-General ordered it done, after you had left the fortress. I don't know why.' Suarez hunched back onto the stone bench that edged the choir. Above him a marble slab recalled the exemplary life of a Colonel's wife who, with all her children, had drowned off Puerto Crucero in 1711. Beside that slab was another, commemorating her husband, who had been killed by the heathen savages in 1713. The garrison church was full of such memorials, reminders of how long the Spanish had ruled this harsh coast.

Cochrane watched the cement being chipped out of the hole, then turned accusingly on the mild Major Suarez. 'So what do they say about Vivar's death?'

'I'm sorry, *señor*, I don't understand.'

'Did the rebels kill him? Or Bautista?'

Suarez licked his lips. 'I don't know, *señor*.' He reddened, suggesting that gossip in the citadel pointed to Bautista's guilt, but Suarez's continuing fear of the man was quite sufficient to impose tact on him. 'All I do know –' he tried to divert Cochrane with another morsel of gossip '– is that there was much consternation when Captain-General Vivar's body could not be found. I heard that Madrid was asking questions. Many of us were sent to search for the body. I and my company were sent twice to the valley, but –' Suarez shrugged to show that his men twice failed to find Vivar's corpse.

'So who did find it?' Sharpe asked.

'One of General Bautista's men from Valdivia, *señor*. A captain called Marquinez.'

'That greasy bastard,' Sharpe said feelingly.

'The General was much relieved when the body was discovered,' Suarez added.

'And no wonder,' Cochrane laughed raucously. 'Bloody careless to lose the supremo's body!'

'This is a church!' The Dominican surgeon, goaded by Cochrane's laughter, snapped the reproof in English.

'MacAuley?' Cochrane called to his own surgeon. 'If yon tonsured barber speaks out of turn again, you will fillet the turdhead with your bluntest scalpel, then feed him to the crabs. You hear me?'

'I hear you, my Lord.'

'Goddamn holy bastards.' Cochrane spat the insult towards the monk, then let his temper be triggered by irritation. 'You know who crucified Our Lord?' This was shouted at the Dominican. 'Bloody priests and bloody lawyers! That's who! Not the soldiers! The soldiers were just obeying orders, because that's what soldiers are paid to do, but who gave the orders? Priests and lawyers, that's who! And you're still making your mess on God's earth. Jesus Christ, but I should revenge my Saviour by slicing your rancid head off your useless body, you foul poxed son of a whore!'

MacAuley was plainly enjoying the tirade. The Domini-can, whose piety had stirred up the whirlwind, tried to ignore it. Suarez looked scared, while Harper, who had no love of priests, laughed aloud.

'Christ on his cross!' Cochrane's anger was ebbing. 'I'd rather roast in hell with a battalion of damned soldiers than sip nectar in heaven alongside a thieving lawyer or a poison-filled priest.'

'You sound like Napoleon,' Sharpe said.

Cochrane's head snapped up as though Sharpe had struck him, except the Scotsman's face betrayed nothing but pleasure. 'If only I was indeed like him,' he said warmly, then strode to the deepening grave where one of the soldiers had evidently reached the coffin for the nauseating stench that had so repelled Sharpe and Harper when they had excavated the grave before now filled the church choir again. The Spanish soldier who had broken through the grave's crust turned away retching. Suarez was gasping for breath, and only Cochrane seemed unmoved. 'Get on with it!' he snapped at the prisoners.

The three Spanish prisoners could not finish the job. Terror, superstition, or just the rank stink of the decaying body was making them shudder uncontrollably. Coch-rane, impatient of such niceties, and oblivious of the foul stench, leapt into the excavation and, with vigorous sweeps of the shovel, cleared the coffin of its last layer of coagulated shingle.

Sharpe steeled himself to endure the nauseous odour and to stand at the edge of the grave to look at the simple wooden casket that served as Blas Vivar's coffin. The lid of the casket, made from some yellow timber, had cracked, and the wood itself had been badly stained by the cement, but some words which had been inscribed on the box in black paint were still visible; 'Blas Vivar', the simple epitaph read, '*Requiescat in Pace*'.

'Shall I open it?' Cochrane, who seemed more intent

than Sharpe on finding Vivar's body, volunteered.

'I'll do it.' Sharpe took one of the discarded spades and rammed its blade under the thin yellow planks. The grave was so shallow that he had no trouble in levering up the lid by wrenching out the horseshoe nails which had held the crude coffin together. Cochrane helped by pulling the planks free, then tossing them onto the piles of broken concrete.

The smell grew worse, filling the church with its nauseous bite. MacAuley, unable to suppress his interest, had temporarily abandoned a patient to come and gape into the open coffin.

Vivar was draped in a shroud of blue cloth that looked like matted velvet. Sharpe worked the edge of the spade under the cloth and, dreading the fresh wave of smells he would provoke, jerked it upwards. For a second or two the material clung to the rotting flesh beneath, then it pulled free to billow a fresh gust of effluvial stench into the church. Sharpe swept the cloth aside and let it fall, with the spade, beside the grave.

'Oh, Christ Almighty.' MacAuley made the sign of the cross on his blood-soaked chest.

'Oh, good God,' Sharpe whispered.

Major Suarez could not speak, but just sank to his knees.

'Mary, Mother of God.' Harper crossed himself, then looked with horror at Sharpe.

' "Few and short were the prayers we said." ' Lord Cochrane reverted to poetry. ' "And we spoke not a word of sorrow, But we steadfastly gazed on the face that was dead, And we bitterly thought of the morrow." ' Then his Lordship began to laugh, and his laugh swelled to fill the whole church, for in the coffin, that had been partly weighted with stones, was the foully rotted corpse of a dog; a yellow dog, a wormy and half-liquefied dog that had been buried by an altar so that on Judgment Day it would fly to its creator with the speed of a saint's resurrection. 'Oh, woof, woof,' Cochrane said. 'Woof, woof,' and Sharpe wondered just what in hell's name he was supposed to do next.

* * *

'No wonder Bautista didn't want us to get at the grave,' Harper said. 'Jesus! Why did he bury a dog?'

'Because Madrid was pestering him to find Don Blas,' Sharpe guessed. 'Because Louisa's enquiries were more effective than she knew. Because he knew that if he didn't find a body then the questions would get more persistent and the enquiries more urgent.'

'But a dog?' Harper asked. 'Jesus, it isn't as if he couldn't find a dead man. They're ten a penny in this damned country.'

'Bautista hated Vivar. So maybe using the dog was his idea of a joke? Besides, he didn't think anyone would open the coffin, and why should they? Because by the time he needed to produce a body Don Blas had been dead three months, so all Bautista needed to do was produce a coffin that stank and he sent off his trusted Marquinez to concoct the wretched thing. And it worked, at least till we turned up.' Sharpe said the words bitterly, a despairing cry to the cold wind that whipped up from the mysterious Chilean southlands. He and Harper were walking round the citadel's ramparts over which, just moments before, the decomposed remains of the yellow dog had been tossed away.

'So maybe the bastard faked that message in Boney's picture just to have a reason to throw us out!' Harper said. 'But Doña Louisa would have sent another request for the body! The thing wouldn't have ended with us, nor would it.'

'And Bautista would have provided her with a body, or rather a skeleton so rotted down that no one could ever tell who it had been, but he would have needed time to prepare it. He'd probably have had a lavish coffin made, with a silver plate on it, and he'd have found an unrecognizably decayed body to put inside, dressed in a gilded uniform, and he couldn't arrange all that with us sniffing round Puerto Crucero.'

Harper stopped at an embrasure and stared at the far mountains. 'So where's Blas Vivar?'

'Still out there.' Sharpe nodded at the broken countryside to the north, at the retreating ridges and dark valleys where, he knew, he must now search for a friend's body. He did not want to make the search. He had been so sure that he would find the body under the garrison church's flagstones, and now he faced yet more time in this country that was so bitterly far from everything he loved. 'We'll need two horses. Unless, of course, you've had enough?'

'Are you sure we need to stay?' Harper asked unhappily.

Sharpe's face was equally miserable. 'We haven't found Vivar, so I don't think I can go home yet.'

Harper shook his head. 'And we'll not find him! You heard what Major Suarez said. He's looked twice and found nothing. Christ! Bautista probably had a thousand men looking!'

'I know. But I can't go back to Louisa and tell her I couldn't be bothered to search the place where Don Blas died. We have to take a look, Patrick. I do, anyway.' Sharpe added the last three words hurriedly.

'I'll stay,' Harper said robustly. 'Jesus, if I get home I'll only have the bloody children screaming and the wife telling me I should drink less.'

Sharpe smiled. 'So she does think you're too fat?'

'She's a woman, what the hell does she know?' Harper tried to pull in his gut, and failed.

'You're thinner than you were,' Sharpe said truthfully.

Harper patted his belly. 'She won't know me when I get home. I'm dwindling. I'll be a wraith. If I'm alive at all.'

'Two weeks.' Sharpe heard the gloom in his friend's voice, and tried to alleviate it with a promise. 'We'll stay two weeks more, and if we can't find Don Blas in a fortnight, then we'll give up the search, I promise. Just two weeks.'

It was a promise that looked increasingly fragile as the days passed. Sharpe needed to search the valley where Don Blas had disappeared, but refugees from the countryside spoke of horrors that made travel unsafe. The Spaniards, retreating towards the guns of Valdivia, were pillaging farms and settlements, while the savages, scenting their enemy's weakness, were hunting down the refugees from Puerto Crucero's defeated garrison. The whole province was churning with bitterness, and Cochrane insisted that Sharpe and Harper could not risk travelling through the murderous chaos. 'The damned Indians don't know you're English! They see a white skin and suddenly you're the evening's main dish: white meat served with fig sauce. Come to think of it, that's probably what happened to your friend Vivar. He was turned into a fricassee and three belches.'

'Are the savages cannibals?' Sharpe asked.

'God knows. I can't make head or tail of them,' Cochrane grumbled. He wanted Sharpe to forget Vivar, and instead enrol for the assault on Valdivia. 'Half the bloody Spanish army searched that valley,' Cochrane protested, 'and they found nothing! Why do you think you can do better?'

'Because I'm not the Spanish army.'

The two men were standing on the highest seaward rampart of the captured fortress. Above them the flag of the Chilean Republic snapped in the cold southern wind, while beneath them, in the inner harbour, the *Espiritu Santo* lay grounded on a sandy shoal that was only flooded at the very highest tides. A stout line had been attached to the *Espiritu Santo*'s mainmast, then run ashore to where a team of draught horses, helped by fifty men, had taken the strain, pulling the frigate over, so that now she lay careened on her port side and with her wounded flank facing the sky.

Carpenters from the town, and from Cochrane's flagship, were busy patching the damage done by the exploding *Mary Starbuck*. The *Espiritu Santo* was now called the *Kitty*, named in honour of Cochrane's wife. Her old crew had been divided; Captain Ardiles, with his officers and those seamen who had not volunteered to join the ranks of the rebels, were locked in the prison wing of the citadel, while the other seamen, about fifty in all, had volunteered to join Cochrane's ranks. Those fifty would all be part of the crew which would take the *Kitty* north to attack Valdivia.

Among the plunder captured in Puerto Crucero had been a Spanish pinnace, with six small guns, which Cochrane had sent north with news of his victory. The pinnace, a fast and handy sailor, had orders to avoid all strange sails, but just to reach the closest rebel-held port and from there to send the news of Puerto Crucero's fall to Santiago. Cochrane had also written to Bernardo O'Higgins requesting that more men be sent to help him assault Valdivia. If O'Higgins would give him just one battalion of troops, Cochrane promised success. 'I won't get the battalion,' Cochrane gloomily told Sharpe, 'but I have to ask.'

'They won't give you troops?' Sharpe asked in surprise.

'They'll send a few, a token few. But they won't send enough to guarantee victory. They don't want victory, remember. They either want me to refuse to obey their orders or to make a hash out of obedience. They want rid of me, but with your help, Sharpe, I might yet . . .'

'I'm riding north,' Sharpe interrupted, 'to look for Don Blas.'

'Look for him after you've helped me capture Valdivia!' Cochrane suggested brightly. 'Think of the glory we'll win! My God, Sharpe, men will talk about us forever! Cochrane and Sharpe, conquerors of the Pacific!'

'It isn't my battle,' Sharpe said, 'and besides, you're going to lose it.'

'You didn't believe I'd capture this place.' Cochrane

swept a victor's arm around the vista of the citadel's ramparts.

'True,' Sharpe allowed, 'but only because you used a trick to get your attackers in close, and that trick won't work twice.'

'Maybe it will.' Cochrane smiled. For a few seconds the Scotsman was silent, then his desire to reveal his plans overcame his instinct for caution. 'You remember telling me about those artillery officers who crossed the Atlantic with you?'

Sharpe nodded. He had described to Lord Cochrane how Colonel Ruiz and his officers had sailed ahead of their men, which meant, Cochrane now said, that the two slow transports carrying the men and the regiments' guns were probably still lumbering across the Atlantic. 'And I'll wager a wee fortune that if I disguise the *Kitty* and the *O'Higgins* I can get right inside Valdivia harbour by pretending to be those two transports.' His voice, eager and excited, had been filled with amusement at the thought of again deceiving the Spaniards. 'You saw how the garrison collapsed here! You think morale is any better in Valdivia?'

'Probably not,' Sharpe admitted.

'So join me! I promised you a share of the prize money. That bastard Bautista took almost everything of value out of here, so it must all be in Valdivia, and that includes your money, Sharpe. Are you going to let the bastard just take it?'

'I'm going to look for Don Blas,' Sharpe said doggedly, 'then go home.'

'You won't fight for money?' Cochrane sounded astonished. 'Not that I blame you. I tell myself I fight for more than money, but that's the only thing these rogues want.' He nodded down at his men who were scattered about the citadel. 'So, for their sakes, I'll fight for money and pay them their wages, and the lawyers in Santiago can whistle at the wind for all I care.' The thought of lawyers plunged the mercurial Scotsman into instant unhappiness. 'Have you ever seen a lawyer apologize? I haven't, and I don't suppose anyone else has. It must be like watching a snake eat its own vomit. You won't help me force a lawyer to apologize?'

'I have to . . .'

'. . . find Blas Vivar.' Cochrane sourly finished the sentence.

A week after the citadel's capture the reports of atrocities and ambush began to decline. A few refugees were still arriving from the distant parts of the province, and even a handful of the fort's defeated garrison had come back rather than face the vengeful savages, but it seemed to Sharpe that the countryside north of Puerto Crucero was settling back into a wary silence. The savages had gone back to their forests, the settlers were creeping out of hiding to see what was left of their farms and the Spaniards were licking their wounds in Valdivia.

Sharpe decided it was safe to ride north. He assembled what he needed for his journey: guns, blankets, salted fish and dried meat, and earmarked two horses captured in the citadel's stables and two good saddles from among the captured booty. He persuaded Major Suarez to describe the valley where Don Blas had ridden into mystery, and Suarez even drew a map, telling Sharpe what parts of the valley had been most thoroughly searched for Blas Vivar's body. Cochrane made one last feeble effort to persuade Sharpe to stay, then wished him luck. 'When will you leave?'

'At dawn,' Sharpe said. But then, as night fell red across the ocean to touch the sentinels' weapons with a scarlet sheen, everything changed again.

Because Don Blas was not dead after all. But living.

*   *   *

His name was Marcos. Just Marcos. He was a thin young man with the face of a starveling and the eyes of a cutthroat. He had been an infantryman in the Puerto Crucero garrison, one of the men who had poured such a disciplined fire at Cochrane's attack, but who, after the citadel's fall, had fled northwards, only to be driven back by his fear of rampaging Indians. Major Miller had interrogated Marcos, and Miller now fetched Marcos to Sharpe. They spoke around a brazier on Puerto Crucero's ramparts, and Marcos, in the strangely-accented Spanish of the native Chileans, told his story of how Don Blas Vivar, Count of Mouromorto, and erstwhile Captain-General of Chile, still lived. Marcos told the tale nervously, his eyes flicking from Sharpe to Miller, from Miller to Harper, then from Harper to Cochrane who, summoned by Miller, had come to hear Marcos's story.

Marcos had been stationed in Valdivia's citadel when Blas Vivar disappeared. He knew some of the cavalrymen who had formed part of the escort which had accompanied Captain-General Vivar on his southern tour of inspection. That escort had been commanded by a Captain Lerrana, who was now Colonel Lerrana and one of Captain-General Bautista's closest friends. Marcos accompanied this revelation with a meaningful wink, then paused to scratch vigorously at his crotch. An interval of silence followed, during which he pursued and caught a particularly troublesome louse that he squashed bloodily between his thumb and fingernail before hitching the rent in his breeches roughly closed.

'Hurry now! Don't keep the Colonel waiting!' Miller barked.

Marcos flinched as if he expected to be hit, then reminded Sharpe that Captain-General Vivar had been riding on a tour of inspection that was supposed to end at the citadel in Puerto Crucero. 'From there, señor, he would go back to Valdivia by ship. But no one came back! Neither the Captain-General, nor Captain Lerrana. No one. Not even the troopers! No one came back till after we heard the Captain-

General had vanished, then General Bautista arrived from Puerto Crucero, and Captain Lerrana came with him, but by then he was a Colonel and in a new uniform.' Marcos clearly felt that the detail of Lerrana's new uniform was exceedingly telling. He described it in detail, how it had thickly-cushioned epaulettes from which hung gold chains, and how it had gold-coloured lace on the coat, and high boots that were new and shining.

'Tell him about the prisoner!' Miller interrupted the admiring description of the uniform.

'Ah, yes!' Marcos snatched another bite from his sausage. 'General Bautista was the senior officer in the province, so he came to take over the Captain-General's duties. He came by ship, you understand, and his men came by boat up the river to the citadel in Valdivia. They came by day, and we made an honour guard for the General. But one boat came at night. In it, *señor*, was a prisoner who had come from Puerto Crucero, a prisoner so secret that no one even knew his name! The prisoner was hurried into the Angel Tower in the citadel. You have to understand, *señor*, that the Angel Tower is very old, very mysterious! It used to be a terrible prison! They say the ghosts of all the dead cling to its stones. Once a man was put in there he only came out as a corpse or an angel.' Marcos superstitiously crossed himself. 'They stopped using the tower as a prison in my grandfather's time, and now no one will step inside for fear of the spirits, but that is where the Captain-General's prisoner was taken and, so far as I know, *señor*, he is still there. Or he was when I left.' Marcos ended the tale in a rush, then looked eagerly at Miller as though seeking praise for his telling of it.

'And you think Captain-General Vivar is that prisoner?' Sharpe asked Marcos.

Marcos nodded energetically. 'I saw his face, *señor*. I was on duty at the inner gate, and they brought him past me to the door of the tower. I was ordered to turn round and not look, but I was in shadow and they did not see me. It was the Captain-General, I swear it.'

'God save Ireland,' Harper said under his breath.

Sharpe leaned back. 'I wish I could believe him,' he said in English, to no one in particular.

'Of course you can believe him!' Cochrane said stoutly. 'Who the hell else do you think Bautista's got in there? The Virgin Mary?'

Marcos greedily bit into a hunk of bread, then looked alarmed as Sharpe leaned forward again.

'Did you ever see your cavalry friends from the Captain-General's escort again?' Sharpe spoke Spanish once more.

'Yes, *señor.*'

'What do they say happened to General Vivar?'

Marcos swallowed a half-chewed lump of bread, scratched his crotch, looked sideways at Miller, then shrugged. 'They say that the Captain-General disappeared in a valley. There was a road which went down the valley's side like this —' Marcos made a zig-zag motion with his right hand '— and the Captain-General ordered them to wait at the top of the road while he went down into the valley. And that was it!'

'No gunfire?' Sharpe asked.

'No, *señor.*'

Sharpe turned to stare at the dark ocean. The sea's roar came from the outer rocks. 'I don't know if I trust this man.'

Cochrane responded in Spanish, loud enough for Marcos to hear. 'If the dog lies, we shall cut off his balls with a blunt razor. Are you telling lies, Marcos?'

'No, *señor*! I promise!'

'It still doesn't make sense,' Sharpe said softly.

'Why not?' Cochrane stood beside him.

'Why would Vivar ride into the valley without an escort?'

'Because he didn't want anyone to see who he was going to meet?' Cochrane suggested.

'Meaning?'

Cochrane drew Sharpe away from the others, escorting him down the ramparts. His Lordship drew on a cigar, its smoke whirling away in the southern wind. 'I think he was meeting Bautista. This man's story –' Cochrane jerked his cigar towards Marcos '– confirms other things I've been hearing. Your friend Vivar had learned something about Bautista, something that would break Bautista's career. He was going to offer Bautista a choice: either a public humiliation, or a private escape. I believe he went into the valley to meet Bautista, not knowing that Bautista would take neither choice, but planned a coup d'état. That's what we're talking about, Sharpe! A coup d'état! And it worked brilliantly!'

'Then why didn't Bautista kill Vivar?'

Cochrane shrugged. 'How do I know? Perhaps he was frightened? If everything went wrong, and Vivar's supporters rallied and opposed Bautista, he could still release Vivar and plead it was all a misunderstanding. That way, whatever other punishment he faced, Bautista would not have the iron collar round his neck, eh?' Cochrane grimaced in grotesque imitation of a man being garotted.

'But Don Blas must be dead by now!' Sharpe insisted. He had spoken in Spanish and loud enough for Marcos to hear.

'*Señor?*' Marcos's frightened face was lit from beneath by the lurid glow of the brazier's coals. 'I think he was alive six weeks ago. That was when I left Valdivia, and I think General Vivar was alive then.'

'How can you tell?' Sharpe asked scornfully.

The infantryman paused, then spoke low so that his voice scarcely carried along the battlements. 'I can tell, *señor*, because the new Captain-General likes to visit the Angel Tower. He goes alone, after dark. He has a key. The tower has only one door, you understand, and they say there is only one key, and General Bautista has that key. I have seen

235

him go there. Sometimes he takes an aide with him, a Captain Marquinez, but usually he goes alone.'

'Oh, sweet Jesus.' Sharpe rested his hands on the parapet and raised his face to the sea wind. The detail of Marquinez had convinced him. Dear God, he thought, but let this man be lying, for it would be better for Don Blas if he were dead.

'What are you thinking?' Cochrane asked softly.

'I'm frightened this man Marcos is telling the truth.'

Cochrane listened for a few seconds to the sound of the sea, then he spoke gently. 'He is telling the truth. We're dealing with hatred. With madness. With cruelty on a monumental scale. Vivar and Bautista were enemies, that much we know. Vivar would have treated his enemy with honour, but Bautista does not deal with honour. I hear Bautista likes to see men suffer, so think how much he would like to watch his greatest enemy suffer! I think he goes to the Angel Tower at night to watch Vivar's misery, to remind Vivar of his defeat and to see Vivar's humiliation.'

'Oh, Christ,' Sharpe said wearily.

'We know now why Vivar's body was never found,' Cochrane said, 'because plainly there is no body, and never was. Bautista had to pretend to make a search, for he dared not let anyone suspect Vivar was alive, but he must have been laughing every time he sent out another search party. And there's something else,' Cochrane added with relish.

'Which is?'

'The Angel Tower is in Valdivia!' Cochrane chuckled. 'So perhaps you had better come with me after all?'

'Oh, shit,' Sharpe said, for he had lost his taste for battle, and could find no relish for the kind of suicidal horror that Cochrane risked at Valdivia.

But Valdivia it would have to be, for Sharpe's word was given, and so a last battle must be fought. To pluck a friend from madness.

Part Three
VIVAR

CHAPTER 9

The embers were gathering.

Reinforcements arrived from the northern provinces. They were not many, and none was officially despatched by the republic's government in Santiago, yet still they came. A few owed Lord Cochrane for past favours, but most were adventurers who smelt plunder in Chile. They arrived at Puerto Crucero in small groups, the largest brought back on Cochrane's pinnace, but others came by land, daring the forests and the savages as they skirted the Spanish-held territory to gather at Puerto Crucero. After two weeks the newcomers had added just over two hundred volunteers to Cochrane's meagre forces, but Cochrane was convinced that his war would be won by just such small increments. At least half of the newcomers had fought in the European wars, and more than a few recognized Sharpe and hoped he would remember them. 'I was in the breach at Badajoz with you,' a Welshman told Sharpe. 'Bloody terrible, that was. But I'm glad you're here, sir. It means we're going to win again, does it not?'

Sharpe did not have the heart to tell the Welshman that he believed the attack on Valdivia to be suicidal. Instead he asked what had brought the man to this backside of the world. 'Money, sir, money! What else?' The Welshman was confident that the royalists, having been defeated in Peru, Chile, and in the wide grasslands beyond the Andes, must have carried the spoils of all that empire back to Valdivia.

'It's their last great stronghold in South America!' the Welshman said confidently. 'So if we capture it, sir, we'll all be rich. I shall buy a house and a farm in the border country, and I'll find a fat wife, and I shall never want for a thing again. All it takes is money, sir, and all we need for money is this battle. Life is not for the weak or timid, sir, but for the brave!'

The Spaniards were making no effort to recapture Puerto Crucero. Instead they had pulled all their forces back into the Valdivia region, abandoning a score of towns and outlying forts. Cochrane's volunteers arrived at Puerto Crucero with tales of burning stockades, deserted customs posts and empty guard houses. 'Maybe,' Sharpe suggested, 'they're planning a complete withdrawal?'

'Back to Spain, you mean?' Cochrane scorned the suggestion. 'They're waiting for reinforcements. Madrid won't abandon Chile. They believe God gave them this empire as a reward for slaughtering all those Muslims in the fifteenth century, and what God gives, kings keep. No, they're not withdrawing, Sharpe, they're just planning more wickedness. They know we're going to attack them, so they're drawing in their horns and getting their guns ready.' He rubbed his hands with glee. 'All those guns and men in one place, just waiting to be captured!'

'That's just what Bautista wants,' Sharpe warned Cochrane. 'He believes his guns will pound you into mincemeat.'

Cochrane spat. 'The man's useless. His guns couldn't kill a spavined chicken. Besides, we'll be taking him by surprise.'

The surprise depended entirely on the Spaniards being deceived by the two disguised warships. The *O'Higgins*, brought into the inner harbour, was being disguised with tar so that her gunports were indistinguishable from any distance. She looked, by the time Cochrane's men had done with her, as drab and ugly a ship as had ever sailed the ocean. The fine giltwork at her bows and stern had been ruthlessly stripped away so that she resembled some unloved transport ship. The *Kitty*, the erstwhile *Espiritu Santo*, was being similarly disfigured. She was also being made seaworthy, and Cochrane chivvied his carpenters unmercifully because every day that the *Kitty* spent careened on the sand shoal was a day lost, a day in which Lord Cochrane worried that the two real Spanish transport ships might reach Valdivia, or a day in which he worried that some Spanish spy might report back to Valdivia just what preparations the rebels were making.

Even a half-witted spy, Cochrane grumbled, could have guessed his plans by just looking at the work being done on the two warships. In essence Cochrane was repeating the trick that had won him Puerto Crucero. That trick had enabled the Scotsman to take his men to the very edge of the defences before their presence was detected, yet if the Spaniards had been alerted to the trick and had opened fire on the *Espiritu Santo* as soon as she had shown at the harbour mouth, then blood would have poured thick from the frigate's scuppers and Cochrane would have earned his first defeat.

The Spaniards could easily inflict that first defeat in the massive harbour at Valdivia. Valdivia's six forts contained far more guns than Puerto Crucero's one fortress, and Valdivia's guns were spread out so that a surprise assault on one bastion could only serve to alert the others. It was that dispersion of enemy guns that worried Sharpe. Five of Valdivia's forts were on the harbour's western shore, while the sixth, Fort Niebla, was on the eastern bank and guarded the entrance to the River Valdivia. Cochrane, if he was to capture the town with its citadel and reputed treasure, had to capture Fort Niebla, for with the river mouth in his hands he could prevent the garrisons of the remaining fortresses from reinforcing the town's defenders.

Cochrane's plan to capture Fort Niebla was unveiled at

a council of war that he held in the high arched room of Puerto Crucero's citadel. He spread a map on a table and weighted its corners with bottles of Chilean brandy, then, in a calm voice, spoke of sailing the disguised ships past the silent guns of the Spanish forts. Sharpe, like the other dozen officers in the room, listened to Cochrane's confident voice, but saw on the map the terrible dangers that the Scotsman so blithely discounted. Most of the forts had been built high on the hills which surrounded the harbour; so high that, while they could plunge a lethal fire down into Cochrane's ships, his own cannon could never elevate enough to return the fire. 'But no one will open fire if they believe us to be the long awaited transports with Colonel Ruiz's guns and men!' Cochrane said confidently. He would keep his false ensigns flying until his two ships actually reached the quays in the river's mouth. There, sheltered from all the western fortresses, as well as from the guns on Manzanera Island, he would launch a sudden landward assault against Fort Niebla. 'And when Niebla falls, the whole thing collapses!' Cochrane said again. 'Niebla controls the river! The river controls the town! The town controls what's left of Spanish Chile!'

'Brilliant! Genius! Superb!' Major Miller's eyes glowed with admiration for his hero's cleverness. 'Superb, my Lord! Quite magnificent! Worthy of Wellington! I applaud you, 'pon my soul, I do!'

'I believe Major Miller trusts our plan!' Cochrane said happily.

'I don't,' Sharpe said.

'You don't believe it will work?' Cochrane asked sarcastically.

'I believe it will work, my Lord, just so long as not one Spanish soldier can tell the difference between a transport ship and a warship. It will work so long as the real transport ships haven't arrived yet. It will work so long as those real transport ships weren't supplied with a password we

242

don't know. It will work so long as not one single officer of Colonel Ruiz's regiment isn't carried out to the arriving ships to check their cargoes. Good Lord! You think the Spaniards won't be suspicious of every ship that comes into sight? They know how you captured this fortress, my Lord, so they'll surely suspect that you'll try the same trick again! How do we know that the Spanish aren't inspecting every ship before it's allowed to enter harbour?' Sharpe spoke in English so that his pessimism would not be obvious to every man in the room, but his tone was more than enough. Even those who did not understand his words could look at the map and imagine the hell of being caught in the harbour, at the centre of a ring of heavy guns that would be splintering the ships into floating charnel houses.

'If we attack at night –' Miller was surreptitiously trying to coax his precious watch into life '– the Spaniards will be asleep!'

No one responded. Miller tapped the watch on the table and was rewarded with a ticking sound.

'How many defenders will there be?' The question was put by Captain Simms, who had skippered the *O'Higgins* during Cochrane's absence.

'Two thousand?' Cochrane suggested airily.

Someone at the table took a deep loud breath. 'We have three hundred men?' the man asked.

'Close to.' Cochrane smiled, then, in Spanish, he challenged anyone to suggest a better scheme for capturing the harbour. 'You, Sharpe? Can you think of a way? My God, man, I'm not rigid! I'll listen to anyone's ideas!'

Sharpe, given a choice, would not have attacked at all. Three hundred men against two thousand were not good odds, and the odds worsened appreciably when the two thousand defenders were safely ensconced behind ditches, palisades, walls, embrasures, and the wickedest array of cannonfire assembled in all South America. But it was no use expressing such defeatism to Lord Cochrane, and so

Sharpe tried to find some other weakness in the Spanish defences. 'When I sailed into Valdivia I seem to remember there was a beach here.' He leaned over the map and pointed to the very tip of the headland round which the attackers would have to sail.

'The Aguada del Ingles,' Fraser, Cochrane's elderly sailing-master, offered the name of the beach. *Aguada* meant a watering place, and the old Scotsman explained that Bartholomew Sharp, a seventeenth-century English pirate, had landed on that same beach, right under the Spanish defences, to fill his barrels from a freshwater spring.

'There's an omen, eh, Sharpe?' Miller said happily. 'Your namesake, eh?'

'It rather depends on whether he got away with it,' Sharpe said.

'Aye, he did,' Fraser said. 'They called him a devil in his time, too.'

'Why don't we land there ourselves,' Sharpe suggested, 'and attack the forts one by one? These forts aren't designed to defend themselves against a landward attack, and if we take the English fort, then the very sight of the defeat may demoralize the other garrisons.'

There was a few seconds' silence as the men about the table stared at the map. Part of Sharpe's solution made sense. Most of the westernmost forts had not been built to defend against a landward attack, but merely to threaten any ship foolish enough to sail unwanted into Valdivia's harbour, but Corral Castle and Fort Niebla were both proper fortresses, built to resist ships, artillery and infantry, and even if Cochrane's men could tumble the defenders out of the English Fort and Fort San Carlos and Fort Amargos, they would still need to capture the far more formidable Corral Castle before they marched round the southern side of the harbour to lay siege to Fort Niebla.

Cochrane rejected Sharpe's half-hearted ideas. 'Good

God, man, but think of the time you're taking! An hour to land our men, that's if we can land them at all, which we can't if the surf's high, then another half hour to form up, and what are the Spaniards going to be doing? You think they'll sit waiting for us? Christ, no! They'll meet us on the beach with a Hail Mary of musket balls. We'll be lucky if ten men survive! No. We'll risk the gunfire, hoist the ensigns, and run straight for the defence's heart!'

'If we make a land attack at night,' Sharpe persisted in his less risky plan, 'then the Spanish will be confused.'

'Have you ever tried landing men on an exposed beach at night?' Cochrane demanded. 'We'll all be drowned! No, Sharpe! To the devil with caution. We'll go for their heart!' He spoke enthusiastically, but detected that others, besides Sharpe, doubted that the thing could be done. 'Don't you understand,' Cochrane cried passionately, 'that the only reason we'll succeed is because the Spanish know this can't be done? They know Valdivia is impregnable, so they don't expect anyone to be mad enough to attack. Our very chance of victory comes from their strength, because their strength is so great that they believe themselves to be unbeatable! And that belief is lulling them to sleep. Gentlemen! We shall lance their pride and bring their great forts down to dust!' He picked up one of the bottles of brandy and eased out its cork. 'I give you Valdivia, gentlemen, and victory!'

Men raised the bottles and drank to the toast, but Sharpe, alone, could not bring himself to respond to Cochrane's toast. He was thinking of three hundred men ranged against the greatest fortress complex on the Pacific coast. The result would be slaughter.

'There was a time –' Harper had seen Sharpe's reluctance and now spoke very softly '– when you would have done the impossible, because nothing else would have worked.'

Sharpe heard the reproof, accepted it, and reached for

245

a bottle. He pulled the cork and, like Harper, drank to the impossible victory. 'Valdivia,' he said, 'and triumph.'

*　　*　　*

Fraser, Cochrane's sailing master, opined that the repaired *Kitty* might stay afloat long enough to reach Valdivia, but he did not sound optimistic. 'Not that it matters,' the old Scotsman told Cochrane, 'for you'll all be dead bones once the dagoes start their guns on you.'

The two ships, both clumsily disguised as unloved transport hulks, had sailed four days after Cochrane's council of war. Cochrane had left just thirty men in Puerto Crucero, most of them walking wounded, and barely sufficient to guard the prisoners and hold the fort against a possible Spanish patrol. Every other man sailed on board the *Kitty* and the *O'Higgins*. The two warships stood well out to sea, travelling far from land so that no stray Spanish vessel might spot them.

The *Kitty*'s pumps clattered ceaselessly. She was repaired, but the new wood in her hull had yet to swell and close her seams, and so, from the moment the frigate was refloated, the pumps had been manned. Despite her repairs she was proving a desperately slow ship. Some of the men in Cochrane's expedition had declared her an unlucky ship and had been reluctant to sail in her, a superstition that Cochrane had lanced by choosing to sail in the fragile *Kitty* himself. Sharpe and Harper also sailed on the erstwhile *Espiritu Santo*, while Miller and his marines were on the *O'Higgins*. 'I'll salute as you sink,' had been Miller's cheerful farewell to Sharpe.

'If we don't sink, we'll die under the guns,' Fraser opined, and the nearer the two ships came to Valdivia, the gloomier the old man became, though his gloom was always shot through with an affectionate admiration for Cochrane. 'If any man can do the impossible, it's Cochrane,' Fraser told Sharpe and Harper. They were five nights out of Puerto

Crucero, on the last night before they reached Valdivia, and the ships were sailing without lights, except for one shielded lantern that burned on the faster *O'Higgins*'s stern. If the *O'Higgins* looked like going too far ahead in the darkness a signal gun would be fired from one of the *Kitty*'s two stern guns which were still the only heavy armament that the frigate possessed. 'I was with Cochrane when he took the *Gamo*,' Fraser, who was steering the *Kitty,* said proudly. 'Did you ever hear how he did that?'

'No.'

'It was in '01, off Barcelona. His Lordship had a brig, called the *Speedy*. The smallest seagoing thing in the Royal Navy, she was, with just fifty-two men aboard and four-teen guns; seven guns a side and none of them more than four pounders, and the mad devil used her to capture the *Gamo*. She was a Spanish frigate of thirty-two guns and three hundred men. You'd have said it couldn't be done, but he did it. He disguised us with an American flag, ran in close under her side, then held her up against the frigate as he blasted his seven popguns up through her decks. He held her there for an hour and a half, then boarded her. She surrendered.' Fraser shrugged. 'The trouble with Cochrane is that every time he does something insane, he gets away with it. One day he'll lose, and that'll be the end of him. Mind you, whenever he tangles with the lawyers, he loses. His enemies accused him of defrauding the stock exchange, which he didn't do, but they hired the best lawyers in London and his Lordship was so sure of his own innocence that he didn't even bother to turn up in court, which made it much easier for the bastards to find him guilty and put him into prison.'

'And they hurled me out of the most noble Order of the Bath,' Cochrane himself had crept up behind them and now intervened in his own story. 'Do you know what they do when they expel a man from the Order of the Bath, Sharpe?'

'No, my Lord.'

Cochrane, who clearly relished the story, chuckled. 'The ceremony happens at dead of night in Westminster Abbey! In the chapel of Henry VII. It's dark! At first you hear nothing but the rustle of robes and the scratching of shoes. It sounds like a convocation of rats, but it's merely the lawyers and lords and pimps and bumsuckers gathering together. Then, on the stroke of midnight, they tear the disgraced man's banner from above the choir stalls, and afterwards they take a nameless man, who stands in for the villain, and they strap a pair of spurs on his heels and then, with an axe, they chop the spurs off! At night! In the Abbey! And all the rats and pimps applaud as they kick the man and the spurs and the banner down the steps, and down the choir, and down the nave, and out into the darkness of Westminster!' Cochrane laughed. 'They did that to me! Can you believe it? We're in the nineteenth century, yet still the bastards are playing children's games at midnight. But one day, by Christ, I'll go back to England and I'll sail up the Thames and I'll make those bastards wish their mothers had never given birth. I'll hang those dry bastards from the roofbeams of the Abbey, then play pell-mell with their balls in the nave.'

'They're lawyers, Cochrane,' Fraser said sourly. 'They don't have balls.'

Cochrane chuckled then cocked his face to the night. 'The wind's piping up, Fraser. We'll have a blow before tomorrow night.'

'Aye, we will.'

'So do you still think we're doomed, Sharpe?' Cochrane demanded fiercely.

'I think, my Lord, that tomorrow we shall need a miracle.'

'It'll be easy!' Cochrane said dismissively. 'We'll arrive an hour before nightfall, at the very moment when the garrisons will be wanting to go off duty and put their feet up. They'll think we're transports, they'll ignore us, and as soon as it's dark we'll be swarming up the ramparts of Fort Niebla. By this time tomorrow night, Sharpe, you and I will have our feet under the commandant's table, drinking his wine, eating his supper, and choosing between his whores. And the day after that we'll go downriver and take Valdivia. Two days, Sharpe, just two days, and all Chile is ours. We will have won.'

It all sounded so easy. Two days, six forts, two hundred guns, two thousand men, and all Chile as the prize.

In the darkness a glimmer of light showed from the stern lantern of the *O'Higgins*. The sea hissed and roared, lifting the sluggish hull of the *Kitty*, then dropping her down into the cold heart of the wave troughs. Beyond the one small glimmer of light there was no other sign of life in all the universe: neither a star nor moon nor landward light. The ships were in an immensity of darkness, commanded by a devil, sailing under a night sky of thick cloud, and travelling towards death.

*   *   *

They sighted land an hour after dawn. By midday they could see the signal tower that stood atop Fort Chorocomayo, the highest strongpoint in Valdivia's defences. The signal tower held a vast semaphore mast that reported the presence of the two strange ships, then fell into stillness.

Three hours before sunset Sharpe could see the Spanish flag atop the English fort and he could hear the surf crashing on the rocks beside the English beach. No ships had come from the harbour to enquire their business. 'You see,' Cochrane crowed, 'they're fools!'

Two hours later, in the light of the dying sun, the *O'Higgins* and the *Kitty* trimmed their sails as they turned east about the rocky peninsula that protected Valdivia's harbour. They had arrived at the killing place.

The great clouds had gone, torn ragged by a morning gale that had gentled throughout the day until, in this evening of battle, the wind blew steady and firm, but without malice. The wind might have gentled, but the sea was still ferocious. The huge Pacific rollers, completing their great journey across an ocean, heaved the *Kitty* up and down in a giant swooping motion, while to Sharpe's right the great waves shattered in shredding explosions of foam off the black rocks. 'You would not, I think, want to make a landing on the English beach in these conditions.' Cochrane was searching the shore with his telescope and suddenly stiffened. 'There!'

'My Lord?' Sharpe asked.

'See for yourself, Sharpe!'

Sharpe took the glass. Dim in the gauzy light and through the shredding plumes of foam that obscured the sea's edge like a fog he could just see the first of the harbour's forts. 'That's Fort Ingles!' Cochrane said. 'The beach is just below it.'

Sharpe moved the glass down to where the massive waves thundered up the English beach. He edged the glass back to the fortress which looked much as he remembered it from his earlier visit; a makeshift defence work with an earthen ditch and bank, wooden palisades, and embrasures for cannon. 'They're signalling us!' he said to Cochrane as a string of flags suddenly broke above the fort's silhouette.

'Reply, Mister Almante!' Cochrane snapped, and a Chilean midshipman ran a string of flags up to the *Kitty*'s mizzen yard. The flags which Cochrane was showing formed no coherent message, but were instead a nonsense combination. 'In the first place,' Cochrane explained, 'the sun's behind us, so they can't see the flags well, and even if they could see the flags they'd assume we're using a new Spanish code which hasn't reached them yet. It'll make the buggers nervous, and that, after all, is a good way to begin a battle.' At the *Kitty*'s stern the Spanish ensign rippled in the wind, while below her decks the pumps sucked and spat, sucked and spat.

The gaunt arms of the telegraph atop the English fort began to rise and fall. 'They're telling the other forts where we are,' Cochrane said. He glanced down at the waist of the ship where a crowd of men lined the starboard gunwale. Cochrane had permitted such sightseeing, reckoning that if the *Kitty* were indeed a Spanish transport ship then the men would be allowed on deck to catch this first glimpse of their new station. Also on deck were four ninepounder field guns that had been manhandled on board from Puerto Crucero's citadel. The guns were not there for their firepower, but rather to make it look as if the *Kitty* was indeed carrying artillery from Spain. Cochrane, unable to hide his excitement, beat a swift tattoo on the quarterdeck rail with his hands. 'How long?' He snapped the question to Fraser.

'We'll make the entrance in one more hour.' Fraser spoke from the helm. 'And an hour after that we'll have moonlight.'

'The tide?' Cochrane asked.

'We're on the flood, my Lord, otherwise we'd never make her past the harbour entrance. Say two and a half hours?'

'Two and a half hours to what?' Sharpe asked.

'One hour to clear the point,' Cochrane explained, 'and another hour to work our way south across the harbour, then half an hour to beat in against the river's current. It'll be dark when we reach Fort Niebla, so I'll have to use a lantern to illuminate our ensign. A night attack, eh!' He rubbed his big hands in anticipation. 'Ladders by moonlight! It sounds like an elopement!' Below the *Kitty*'s decks was a score of newly-made ladders which would be taken ashore and used to assault Niebla's walls.

'There's a new signal, my Lord!' The midshipman called aloud in English, the language commonly used on the quarterdeck of Cochrane's ship.

'In Spanish from now on, Mister Almante, in Spanish!' If the Spaniards did send a guard ship then Cochrane wanted no one using English by mistake. 'Reply with a signal that urgently requests a whore for the Captain.' Cochrane gave the order in his execrable Spanish. 'Then draw attention to the signal with a gun.'

The grinning Midshipman Almante began plucking signal flags from the locker. The new message, gaudily spelt out in a string of fluttering flags, ran quickly to the *Kitty*'s mizzen yard and, just a second later, one of the stern guns crashed a blank charge to echo across the sea.

'We are spreading confusion!' Cochrane happily explained to Sharpe. 'We're pretending to be annoyed because they're not responding to our signal!'

'Another shot, my Lord?' Midshipman Almante, who was not a day over thirteen, asked eagerly.

'We must not over-egg the pudding, Mister Almante. Let the enemy worry for a few moments.'

The smoke from the stern gun drifted across the wildly heaving swell. The two ships were close to land now, close enough for great drifting mats of rust-brown weed to be thick in the water. Gulls screamed about the rigging. Two horsemen suddenly appeared on the headland's skyline, evidently galloping to get a closer look at the two approaching boats.

'Nelson was always seasick until battle was imminent,' Cochrane said suddenly.

'You knew Nelson?' Sharpe asked.

'I met him several times. In the Mediterranean.' Cochrane paused to train his telescope on the two riders. 'They're worried about us, but they can't be seeing much. The sun's almost dead behind us. A strange little man.'

'Nelson?'

'"Go for them," he told me, "just go for them! Damn the niceties, Cochrane, just go and fight!" And he was right! It always works. Oh, damn.'

The curse, spoken mildly, was provoked by the appearance of a small boat that was sailing out of the harbour and was clearly intending to intercept the *Kitty* and *O'Higgins*. Cochrane had half expected such a guard boat, but clearly his disguise would have been easier to preserve if no such boat had been despatched. 'They are nervous, aren't they?' he said to no one in particular, then walked to the quarter-deck's rail and picked up a speaking trumpet. 'No one is to speak in any language but Spanish. You will not shout a greeting to the guard boat. You may wave at them, but that is all!' He turned sharply. 'Spanish naval dress, gentlemen!'

Blue coats, cocked hats and long swords were fetched up from Cochrane's cabin and issued to every man on the quarterdeck. Harper, pleased to have a coat with epau-lettes, strutted up and down. Fraser, dwarfed by his naval coat, scowled at the helm while Cochrane, his cocked hat looking oddly piratical, lit a cigar and pretended to feel no qualms about the imminent confrontation. The Third Lieutenant, a man called Cabral who, though a fierce Chilean patriot, had been born in Spain, was deputed to be the *Kitty*'s spokesman. 'Though remember, Lieuten-ant,' Cochrane admonished him, 'we're called the *Niño*, and the *O'Higgins* is now the *Cristoforo*.' Cochrane glowered at the approaching boat which, under a bellying red sail, contained a dozen uniformed men. 'We'll all be buggered,' he muttered to Sharpe in his first betrayal of nerves, 'if those two transport ships arrived last week.'

The guard boat hove to under the *Kitty*'s quarter, pre-sumably because she was the ship showing the signal flags, and was therefore deemed to be the ship in command of the small convoy. A man with a speaking trumpet demanded to know the *Kitty*'s identity.

'We're the *Niño* and *Cristoforo* out of Cadiz!' Cabral called back. 'We're bringing Colonel Ruiz's guns and men.'

'Where's your escort?'

'What escort?' Cochrane asked under his breath, then, almost at once, he hissed an answer to Cabral. 'Parted company off Cape Horn.'

'We lost them off Cape Horn!'

'What ship was escorting you?'

'Christ Almighty!' Cochrane blasphemed. 'The *San Isidro*.' He plucked the name at random.

'The *San Isidro, señor*.' Cabral obediently parroted the answer.

'Did you meet the *Espiritu Santo*?' the guard boat asked.

'No!'

The interrogating officer, a black-bearded man in a naval captain's uniform, stared at the sullen faces which lined the *Niño*'s rails. The man was clearly unhappy, but also nervous. 'I'm coming aboard!' he shouted.

'We've got sickness!' Cabral, prepared for the demand, had his answer ready and, as if on cue, Midshipman Almante hoisted the yellow fever flag.

'Then you're ordered to anchor off the harbour entrance!' the bearded man shouted up. 'We'll send doctors to you in the morning! You understand?'

'Tell them we don't trust the holding here, we want to anchor inside the harbour!' Cochrane hissed.

Cabral repeated the demand, but the bearded man shook his head. 'You've got your orders! The holding's good enough for this wind. Anchor a half mile off the beach, use two anchors on fifteen fathom of chain apiece, and sleep well! We'll have doctors on board at first light!' He signalled to his helmsman who bore away from the *Kitty*'s side and turned towards the harbour.

'Goddamn it!' Cochrane said.

'Why don't you just ignore the bugger?' Sharpe asked.

'Because if we try to run the entrance without permission they'll open fire.'

'So we wait for dark?' Sharpe, who until now had been dead set against any such attack, was now the one trying to force Cochrane past the obstacle.

'There'll be a gibbous moon,' Fraser said pessimistically, 'and that will serve to light their gunners' aim as well as broad sunlight.'

'Damn. Damn. Damn.' Cochrane, usually so voluble, was suddenly enervated. He stared at the retreating guard boat and seemed bereft of ideas. Fraser and the other officers waited for his orders, but Cochrane had none to give. Sharpe felt a sudden pang of sympathy for the tall Scotsman. All plans were nothing but predictions, and like all predictions they were likely to be transformed by their first collision with reality, but the art of war was to prepare for such collisions and have a second or a third or a fourth option ready. Cochrane suddenly had no such options to hand. He had pinned his hopes on the Spanish supinely accepting his ruse then feebly collapsing before his attack. Was this how Napoleon had been on the day of Waterloo? Sharpe wondered. He watched Cochrane and saw a man in emptiness, a clever man drained of invention who seemed helpless to stop the tide of disaster flooding across him.

'We've two hours of fair water, my Lord.' Fraser, recognizing the moment of crisis, had adopted a respectful formality.

Cochrane did not respond. He was staring towards the harbour entrance. Was he thinking of making a dash for it? But how could two slow ships dash? Their speed, even with the tide's help, was scarcely above that of a man walking.

'We'll not get through, my Lord.' Fraser growled the warning, reading his Lordship's mind.

'No,' Cochrane said, but said nothing more.

Fraser shot a beseeching look at Sharpe. Sharpe, more than any other man in the expedition, had counselled against this attack, and now, Fraser's look seemed to be saying, was the time for Sharpe to urge withdrawal. There was just one chance of avoiding disaster, and that was for the two ships to turn and slip away southward.

Sharpe said nothing.

Fraser, desperate to end the indecision, challenged Sharpe directly. 'So what would you do, Sharpe?'

Cochrane frowned at Sharpe, but did not countermand Fraser's invitation.

'Well?' Fraser insisted. The ship was still creeping towards the harbour mouth. In another half mile she would open the entrance and be under the guns of Fort San Carlos.

Cochrane was a devil, Sharpe thought, and suddenly he felt a smaller imp rise in himself. Goddamn it, but a man did not come this far just to be challenged by a toy boat and then turn back! 'If we anchor off the beach,' Sharpe said, 'they'll think we're obeying their orders. We wait till it's dark, then we send a boat or two ashore. We can say we're looking for fresh water if anyone questions us. Then we'll attack the nearest fort. We may only capture a few kegs of powder, but at least we'll have let the bastards know that we're still dangerous.'

'Magnificent!' Cochrane, released from his torpor, shouted the word. He slapped Sharpe's back. 'Goddamn it, man, but magnificent! I like it! Mister Almante! A signal to the *O'Higgins*, if you please, ordering them to ready anchors!' Cochrane was suddenly seething with energy and enthusiasm. 'But bugger snatching a few kegs of powder! Let's go for the whole pot! We'll capture the western forts then use their guns to bombard Niebla while our ships work their way inside. That'll be at dawn, Mister Fraser, so perhaps you will work out the time of the morning's flood tide for me? I don't know why I didn't think to do it this way from the very start! Mister Cabral? Order a meal served below decks. Tell the men they've got two hours' rest before we begin landing troops.'

'Now you've done it,' Fraser grumbled to Sharpe.

'You spoke, Mister Fraser?' Cochrane demanded.

'Nothing, my Lord.'

'As soon as we're at anchor,' Cochrane went on, 'you'll lower boats, but do it on the side facing away from the land! We don't want the enemy to see we're launching boats, do we?'

'A hole in each end, my Lord?' Fraser asked.

'Then suck the damned egg dry!' Cochrane, knowing he had given Fraser an unnecessary order, gave a brief guffaw of laughter.

Behind the *Kitty* the sky was a glorious blaze of gold touched scarlet, in which a few ragged clouds floated silver grey. The sea had turned molten, slashed with shivering bands of black. The great Spanish ensign, given an even richer colour by the sun's flaming gold, slapped and floated in the fitful wind.

The two ships crept towards the shore. Sharpe could hear the breakers now and see where they foamed white as they hissed and roared towards the sand. Then, just when it seemed that the *Kitty* must inevitably be caught up in that rush of foam and be swept inexorably to her doom, Fraser ordered both anchors let go. A seaman swung a sledgehammer, knocking a peg loose from the cathead, and the starboard anchor crashed down through the golden sea. The port anchor followed a second after, the twin chains rattling loud in the dusk. Then, with a jerk, the *Kitty* rounded up and lay with her bows pointing towards the setting sun and her stern towards the mainland. The headland, on which the English fort stood, was now on her port side.

The *O'Higgins* anchored a hundred yards further out. Both ships jerked and snubbed angrily, but Fraser reported that the anchors were holding. 'Not that it will help us,' he added to Sharpe, 'for the boats will never land on that beach.' He jerked an unshaven chin towards the Aguada del Ingles where, in the last slanting light, the foam was shredding spray like smoke. Cochrane might believe a landing to be possible, but Sharpe suspected that

257

Fraser was right and that any boat which tried to land through that boiling surf would be swamped.

Cochrane stared up to where his topmen were efficiently gathering in the *Kitty*'s sails. 'The wind's backing, Fraser?'

'Aye, my Lord, it is.'

Cochrane fidgeted a second. 'We might leave the spanker rigged for mending, Mister Fraser. It will hide your boats as they're launched.'

Fraser did not like the idea. 'The wind could veer, my Lord.'

'Let's do it! Hurry now!'

The orders were given. Fraser offered Sharpe an explanation. The wind, he said, had been southerly all day, but had now gone into the west. By leaving the aftermost sail half hoisted he turned the ship into a giant weather vane. The wind would then keep the ship parallel to the beach, leaving the starboard side safely hidden from the fort. Cochrane could then launch his boats in the last of the daylight, safe from enemy gaze.

'Why not rig the sail full?' Sharpe asked. The sail was only half raised.

'Because that would look unnatural when you're at anchor. But half rig is how you'd hoist her for mending, and a half-collapsed sail hides the far side of the quarter-deck a deal better than a fully hoisted sail. Not that I suppose anyone up there understands seamanship.'

Fraser had jerked a derisive thumb towards the English fort above the beach. From Sharpe's position on the quarterdeck the fort's ramparts formed the skyline, clearly showing six embrasures in its grim silhouette. The guns were less than half a mile from the *Kitty*. If the Spanish did suddenly discover that the two anchored ships were hostile, then the guns would wreak havoc in the crowded lower decks. Sharpe shuddered and turned away. Harper, seeing the shudder, surreptitiously crossed himself.

The sun was now a bloated ball of fire on the horizon.

Ashore, the shadows were lengthening and coalescing into a grey darkness. On the *Kitty*'s quarterdeck, behind the concealing folds of heavy canvas, the ship's four longboats and two jolly boats were being lowered overboard. The Captain's barge was the last boat to be launched. Each boat held a single seaman whose job was to keep his craft from being crushed as the frigate heaved up and down on the swells. 'Another hour,' Cochrane spoke to Sharpe and Harper, 'and it'll be dark enough to land troops. Why don't you get something to eat?'

Harper brightened at the thought and went below to the gundeck where the cooks were serving a stew of goat meat to the waiting men. Sharpe wanted to stay on deck. 'Bring me something,' he called as Harper swung off the quarterdeck.

Sharpe, left alone, leaned on the rail and gazed at the fort. A sudden gust of wind came off the land, ruffling the sea and forcing Sharpe to snatch at his old-fashioned tricorne hat. The wind gust billowed the loosely rigged spanker, driving the canvas across the deck and occasioning a shout of alarm from Lieutenant Cabral who was almost thrown overboard by the gusting sail. 'Stow that sail now!' Fraser ordered. The longboats were safe overboard and the spanker no longer hid any suspicious activity.

A dozen topmen scrambled up the ratlines and edged out on the mizzen yard to haul in the spanker. The wind was still pushing the sail, driving the stern of the *Kitty* away from the beach.

The wind gusted again, sighing in the rigging and making the boat lean seawards. Some of the men in the longboats feared being trapped under the hull and pushed off from the threatening *Kitty* with their long oars. The boats were all tethered to the frigate with lines, but now, as the heavy warship with its clanking pumps continued to blow towards them, the boat-minders pushed themselves as far from her tarred hull as their tethers would allow.

The *Kitty* kept turning so that her bows were pointing almost directly at the English fort. Fraser knew that the fort's garrison must be able to see the longboats and even the dullest Spanish officer would realize what such a sight portended. Innocent ships waiting for medical attention did not launch a fleet of longboats. 'Close up, damn you, close up!' Fraser shouted at the boat-minders. The topmen had furled the sail and the *Kitty* was swinging back again.

Cochrane came running up from his cabin where he had been eating an early supper. 'What the hell is happening?'

'Wind veered.' Fraser decently did not add that he had warned of just such a danger. 'It drove us round.'

'Sweet Jesus!' Cochrane, a leg of chicken in his hand, stared at the fort. The longboats were hidden again. 'Did they see?' He asked the question of no one, merely articulating a worry.

The fort's silhouette betrayed nothing. No one moved there, no one waved from the ramparts. The gaunt semaphore gallows stayed unmoving.

Cochrane bit into the chicken. 'Buggers are asleep.'

'Thank God for that,' Fraser said.

'Thank God indeed,' Cochrane said fervently, for the only thing that had kept the *Kitty* safe from a murderous bombardment was the Spaniards' inattention. Cochrane bit the last meat off the chicken leg. 'No harm done, eh? The silly buggers are all dozing!' He hurled the chicken bone towards the high fortress as a derisory gesture.

And the fortress replied.

For the sentries on the ramparts of the English fort had seen the longboats after all. The garrison had not been dozing, and now the gunners opened fire. Sharpe saw the smoke, heard the scream of a cannonball, then felt the shuddering crashes as the first two shots slammed into the *Kitty*'s weakened hull.

For the Spaniards had been ready, and Cochrane's men were trapped.

CHAPTER 10

Screams sounded from the gundeck. The Spanish shots had hit with a wicked exactness, slicing through the *Kitty*'s disguised gunports and into the crowded deck where Cochrane's assault force had been snatching its hasty meal.

Two more guns fired. One cannonball smacked into the sea then bounced up into the frigate. The other slammed into the hull, lodging in a main timber.

'The boats! Into the boats!' Cochrane was shouting. 'Assault force! Into the boats!' The sun was a flattened bar of melting light on the horizon, the moon a pale semicircle in the cloud-ridden sky above. Powder smoke drifted from the fort with the land wind. A signal rocket suddenly flared up from the fort's ramparts, its feather of flame shivering up into the darkling sky before a white light burst to drown the first pale stars.

'Into the boats! We're going to attack! Into the boats!'

More shots, more screams. Sharpe leapt off the quarterdeck just as a cannonball screeched across the poopdeck, gouging a splintered trench in the scrubbed wood. He twisted aside from the roundshot's impact, scrambled for the officers' companionway where, disdaining to use the ladder with its rope handles, he slithered down to the gundeck. 'Patrick! Patrick!'

It was dark below. The lanterns had been extinguished as soon as the first shots struck the *Kitty* and the only illumination was the day's dying light that seeped into the carnage through the ragged holes ripped by the incoming roundshot. Those roundshot had ripped across the deck, flinging men aside like bloody rags. The wounded screamed, while the living trampled over the bodies in their desperate attempts to reach the open air.

'Patrick!'

Another roundshot banged into the deck. It cannoned off a ship's timber to slash slantwise through the struggling men. Splinters felled three men close to where the shot struck, while the shot itself sliced down a half dozen more. A spray of blood drops fogged the light for a foul instant, then the terrible screams began. Another ball cracked into the tier below. The pumps had stopped, and Sharpe could hear the gurgle of water slopping into the bilges. 'Patrick!'

'I'm here!' the voice shouted from the deck's far end.

'I'll see you ashore!' There was no chance of struggling through the demented pack of panicking men. Harper and Sharpe must get themselves ashore as best they could and hope that in the sudden chaos they would meet on land.

Sharpe turned and hauled himself up to the poopdeck. Men were scrambling down the starboard side into the longboats. The *O'Higgins* was returning the fort's fire, but Sharpe could see the warship's roundshot was falling short. Gouts of black earth were erupting from the slope in front of the English fort, and though some of the balls were ricocheting up towards the defenders, Sharpe doubted that the naval gunnery was doing the slightest good. The *O'Higgins* herself was wreathed in cannon smoke so that, in the day's death light, she looked like a set of black spidery masts protruding from a yellow-white, red-tinged bank of churning smoke. The fort had turned two guns onto the *O'Higgins*. A great splash of water showed where a shot fell short inside the bank of smoke, then Sharpe was at the rail, rope in hands and he shimmied desperately down to a longboat already crammed with sailors. The sailors had cutlasses, muskets, swords, pikes and clubs. 'Bastards,' one man said again and again, as if, somehow, the Spanish defenders had broken a rule of war by opening fire on the two anchored ships.

'Fast as you can! Fast as you can!' Cochrane was in another longboat and shouting at his oarsmen to make the journey to land as swiftly as possible. For the moment, shielded by the great bulk of the *Kitty*, the longboats were safe from the fort's gunfire, but the moment they appeared on the open sea the cannon would surely change their aim.

'Let go!' Lieutenant Cabral had taken charge of Sharpe's boat. 'Row!' The oarsmen strained at the long oars. Sharpe could see Harper in another boat. A cannon-ball whipped overhead, making a sizzling noise as it slanted down to slam into a green wave.

'Row!' Cabral shouted, and the longboat shot out from behind the *Kitty*'s protection. The coxswain turned the rudder so the boat was aimed for the shore. 'Row!' Cabral screamed again, and the men bent the long oar shafts in their desperate urgency to close on the beach. A shot slapped the sea ten yards to the left, bounced once, then hammered into the *Kitty*'s stern where it sprang a six-foot splinter of bright wood. Sharpe glanced back at the frigate to see a bloody body, dripping intestines, heaved out of a half-opened gunport. Gulls screamed and slashed down to feed. Then Sharpe looked back to the beach because a new sound had caught his ear.

Muskets.

The Spaniards had sent a company of infantry down to the beach where the blue-coated soldiers were now drawn up at the high-tide line. Sharpe saw the ramrods flicker, then the muskets came up into the company's shoulders, and he instinctively ducked. The splintering sound of the volley came clear above the greater sounds of guns and booming surf. Sharpe saw a flicker of small splashes on the face of a wave and knew that the volley had gone wide.

'Row!' Cabral shouted, but the port-side oars had become entangled in a mat of floating weed and the boat broached. Behind Sharpe the *O'Higgins* fired a broadside and one of the balls whipped through the Spanish company, slinging two men aside and fountaining blood and sand up from the beach behind the company. Sharpe stood, his balance precarious as he aimed his pistol. He fired. Muskets flamed bright from the beach. He heard the whistle of a ball near his head as he sat down hard.

'Row, row, row!' Cabral, standing beside Sharpe in the sternsheets, shouted at his oarsmen. 'Row!' The oars were free of the weed again. There were a dozen men rowing and a score of men crouching between the thwarts. The oarsmen, their backs to the land and the muskets and the surf and the cannon, had wide, frightened eyes. One man was gabbling a prayer as he tugged at his oar.

'Bayonets!' Sharpe shouted at the men crouched on the bottom-boards. 'Fix bayonets!' He said it again in Spanish and watched as a dozen men twisted their blades onto their muskets. 'When we land,' he called to the crouching men, 'we don't wait to give the bastards a volley, we just charge!'

Off to the left were a dozen other longboats. Some had come from the *O'Higgins* and were carrying marines. The attacking boats were scattered across the sea. Sharpe flinched as he saw a great gout of exploding water betray where a cannonball had slapped home beside one of the labouring longboats, and he was certain that the roundshot's strike had been close enough to swamp the fragile-looking boat but when the spray fell away he saw the boat was still afloat and its oarsmen still rowing.

The Spanish infantrymen fired again, but, just like the fort's gunners, their own powder smoke was now obscuring their aim. Nor were they being intelligently led, for their officer was telling the men just to fire at any of the boats. If they had concentrated their fire on one boat at a time they could have reduced each longboat into a screaming horror of blood and splinters, but instead their musketry was flying wild and wide. Yet the Spaniards held the advantage, for the longboats still had to negotiate the murderous tumbling of the breaking surf. If a boat broached in the breaking waves and spilt its cargo, then the waiting infantrymen would be presented with a bout of twilight bayonet practice.

The sun was gone, but there was still light in the sky. Sharpe crouched in the sternsheets and made sure his borrowed sword was loose in its scabbard. A broadside from the *O'Higgins* crashed overhead, twitching a skein of powder smoke as it slammed above the Spanish infantry to shatter the further slope into gouts of soil and grass. A gull screeched in protest. Another signal rocket whooshed into the sky to splinter into a fountain of light. It was too dark to use the semaphore arms, so the English fort's defenders were rousing Valdivia harbour's garrisons with the bright rockets.

'Row!' Cabral shouted, and the oarsmen grunted as they laid their full weight into the oars, but another great mat of floating weed impeded the boat, slewing it round. A man in the bows leaned overboard and hacked at the weed with a cutlass. 'Back your oars!' Cabral screamed. 'Back!'

A bullet smacked into the gunwale, while another shattered an oar blade. Cochrane was shouting off to Sharpe's left, screaming at his men to be the first ashore. Cabral beat at the side of the boat in his frustration. One of the oarsmen shouted that it was too dangerous, that they would all drown in the surf, and Cabral drew his sword and threatened to skewer the man's guts if he did not row, and row hard! Then the longboat was again free of the clinging weed and the oars could pull again. One or two of the rowers looked nervous, but any thoughts of mutiny were quelled by the sight of Cabral's drawn sword. 'Row!' he shouted and the crest of a wave lifted the boat, driving it fast, and one of the rowers jerked forward and collapsed, as blood slopped out of his mouth.

'Overboard!' Cabral shouted. 'Heave him over! Juan, take his place! Row!' They rowed. Another wave took them, hissing them forward, driving them up to its white crest. Then the wave was past and they slid down into a scummy, weedy trough, and the oarsmen pulled again, and the sky echoed with the thunder of guns and the crackle of musketry. The beach was close now, close enough for Sharpe to hear the sucking roar as the waves slid back towards the foam, then another breaker plucked them, bubbled them about with surf and hurled them fast towards the beach, and suddenly Sharpe could see the whole expanse of sand and the dark, smoke-fogged shapes of the waiting Spaniards at the top of the beach. Those dark shapes blossomed with pink flames as the muskets flared, but the strike of the musket balls was drowned in the sound and fury of the shattering surf's maelstrom that was now all around the shivering boat. Cabral was screaming orders, and somehow the coxswain was holding the bows straight on to the beach as the oarsmen gave a last desperate pull. Then the bows dropped, bounced on sand, drove on up and Cabral was shouting at the men to jump out and kill the bastard sons of poxed whores, yet still the longboat was sliding up the beach, driven by the wave, while ten yards to the left another boat had turned sideways and rolled so that the welter of white water was littered with men, weapons and oars. Cabral's boat jarred to a halt. Sharpe leaped off the gunwale and found himself up to his knees in freezing water and churning sand.

He drew the borrowed sword. 'Charge!' He knew he must not give these enemy infantrymen a chance. The Spaniards, if they did but know it, could have calmly shot each landing boat to hell, then advanced in good order with outstretched bayonets to finish off the poor wet devils at the sea's edge, but Sharpe guessed the infantrymen were scared witless. The devil Cochrane was coming from the sea to kill them, and now was the time to add blood to their fears. 'Charge!' he shouted. His boots were full of water and heavy with sand. He floundered up the beach, screaming at the men to follow him.

The rest of Cochrane's assault force scrambled ashore. The boats landed within seconds of each other and the men shook themselves free of the sucking breakers to charge the enemy in the maddened rush of men who wanted to revenge themselves for the terrors of the recent moments. The last of the light gleamed dully on the steel of swords and cutlasses and bayonets and boarding pikes. One man carried a great axe that was designed to cut away the wreckage of fallen rigging, but which now, like some ancient Viking berserker, he whirled over his head as he ran towards the Spanish company.

Which company, seeing Cochrane's devils erupt from the sea like avenging fiends, turned and fled. God, Sharpe thought, but this was how pirates had assaulted the Spanish dominions for centuries: desperate men, armed with steel and stripped of scruples, erupting from small ships to shatter the perilous crust of civilized discipline that Madrid had imposed on the New World's golden lands.

'Form here! Form here!' Cochrane, tall and huge in the dusk, stood at the edge of the sand dunes behind the beach. 'Let them go! Let them go!' Sharpe would have kept pursuing the fleeing Spaniards, but Cochrane wanted to make order out of the chaos. 'Form here! Major Miller! You'll make the left of the line if you please!' As if in answer one of Miller's drummers gave a rattle, then a flute sounded feebly in the twilight. Harper, safely ashore and carrying a cutlass, ran behind the attackers to join Sharpe. 'This is a rare business, so it is!' But the big Irishman seemed pleased, as though all the uncertainties of the last few weeks had dropped away.

Cannons roared from the fortress above them. Sharpe saw the flames stab pale across the sandy slope, then writhe and shrivel away inside the smoke. The roundshot crashed past Cochrane's men to spew sand up from the beach. The abandoned longboats and their clumsy oars rolled and jerked at the surf's edge, while out to sea the skeleton crews left aboard the two warships had abandoned the boats' anchors and, with just their foresails set, were taking the two boats out of range of the fort's guns.

'Down!' Cochrane would shelter his men behind the dunes while he organized his assault. 'Get down!' He paced along the front of his ragged attackers. 'Did anyone bring ladders? Did anyone bring ladders?'

No one had brought ladders. Three hundred wet and frightened men clung to a beach beneath a fort and all they had to fight with were their hand weapons: muskets, pistols, swords, pikes and cutlasses.

'Did you bring a ladder?' Cochrane asked Sharpe.

'No.'

Cochrane slashed his sword at dune grass. 'We're rather buggered. Damn!'

The gunfire from the fort changed sound. Instead of the short percussive crack that denoted roundshot, there was suddenly the more muffled sound which betrayed that the defenders were loaded with canister or grape. Now each of the fort's cannon was like a giant shotgun, spraying a lethal and expanding fan of musket balls towards the attackers. Cochrane, as the rain of shot whistled overhead, ducked down. 'Shit!' He peered over the sand dune. Even through the smoke, and in the last of the daylight, it was plain that the earthen and wooden facade of the English fort could not be assaulted without ladders, and even with ladders it would be suicidal for men to rise and walk into that gale of grapeshot. 'Shit!' Cochrane said again, even more angrily.

'They'll only have guns on this face of the fort!' Sharpe shouted.

Cochrane nodded confirmation. 'Facing the sea, yes!'

'We'll flank them! Give me some men!'

'Take the starboard Kittys,' Cochrane ordered. The 'Kittys' were the men from the *Kitty* who were divided into two companies, port and starboard.

'Keep them busy here!' Sharpe told Cochrane. 'Fire at them, make a noise, let them see you here. And when I shout for you, charge like hell!'

Sharpe called for the starboard Kittys, then ran right, along the beach, under cover of the dunes. Fifty men followed him. Harper was there, Lieutenant Cabral was there. The rest of Cochrane's attackers fired a volley up towards the fort as Sharpe, safely out of the cannon's line of fire, turned uphill. The moon was bright on the sand, bleaching it to look like heaped snow. The sea was crashing loud behind.

'Jesus, we're mad,' Harper said.

Sharpe saved his breath. The hillside was steep and the tough grass stems slippery. He was working his way to his right, trying to stay well out of sight of the fort's defenders. With any luck the Spaniards would be mesmerized by the shrieking crowd of men crammed with Cochrane on the beach. Why had the Spaniards not charged down with more infantry? That question made Sharpe wonder whether the signal rockets were intended to summon infantry from the other forts. Behind him the defenders' cannon crashed their loads of canister and the attackers' muskets crackled a feeble reply. More muskets fired from the fort and Sharpe tried to gauge how many infantrymen were defending its ramparts from the noise of those muskets. He reckoned two hundred men, say three thin companies? That was more than enough to finish Cochrane's two hundred and fifty invaders, many of whom had damp powder and whose muskets were therefore useless for anything except clubbing men to death. One good bayonet charge by three companies of Spanish infantry would finish Cochrane. The whole affair could be over in fifteen minutes, and the Chilean rebels would be bereft of their Admiral, and probably of their navy. Valdivia would be safe, Cochrane could be carried back to Madrid for a humiliating trial and a public execution, the Royalist provinces in Chile could be reinforced, the Spanish navy would blockade the northern ports to starve out O'Higgins, and in two years, maybe less, the whole of Chile, and probably Peru as well, would be Spanish again. For Captain-General Bautista it would be total triumph, a vindication of all his theories of defensive warfare, and for Blas Vivar, if indeed he still lived and was a prisoner in the Angel Tower, it would mean death, for no one in Madrid would dare punish Bautista for a mere murder if, in exchange, he gave them back their God-given empire. And all it would take for all those things to happen – for Vivar to die, for Bautista to triumph, for Cochrane to be humiliated, for Spain to win this war, and for the whole history of the world to be nudged into a new course – was three companies of infantry. Just three! And surely, Sharpe thought, those three companies, and more, were being assembled for the charge at this very minute.

'Jesus, look at that!' Harper, panting beside Sharpe, was staring at a wooden fence that had been built across the headland and which now lay between Sharpe's small force and the English fort. The fence was as tall as a man and made of split palings that formed a solid barrier, but what purpose such a fence served Sharpe could not understand. It hardly seemed defensive, for he could see no loopholes and no embrasures.

'Come on!' Sharpe said. There was nothing to be gained by gaping at the fence. It had to be approached, and a reconnaissance made of the ground beyond.

The strange fence lay on the far side of a crude ditch. It seemed to have been built to stop a flanking attack like the one Sharpe was making, but as no defenders manned the fence it had been a waste of effort constructing it. Sharpe's men rested at the bottom of the ditch while he peered through a chink between two palings. The fort lay two hundred yards away across open ground. There were no cannon embrasures on this western wall of the fort, though there was a deep ditch and the wall itself was steep enough to require ladders. A sentry was clear in the moonlight, standing on the wall's flat top.

Sharpe slid down to the ditch's bottom and stared up at the fence. It seemed to have been prefabricated in sections twenty feet long which had been fastened to thick posts sunk into the turf. Each section of fence would make, if not a ladder, at least a ramp. 'Patrick? When I give the word I want you to knock out two sections of fence. They'll be our assault ladders.' Sharpe was speaking in Spanish, loud enough for all the fifty men to hear him. 'There's just one sentry on this side, everyone else is looking at the beach. The Spanish are scared. They're terrified of Cochrane and terrified of you because you're Cochrane's men. They think you're demons from hell! If we attack them hard and fast, they're going to crumple! They're going to run! We can take this fort! Your war cry is Cochrane! Cochrane! Now get your breath, make sure your guns are loaded, and be ready.'

The men whose powder had been soaked when their boats overturned at the sea's edge were denoted to carry the fence sections. Those men would lead the charge. The rest would follow behind and, once the twin makeshift bridges were in place, stream across to bring terror to the fort. It would be a desperate throw, but better than being trapped on the beach by three companies of infantry. And, despite Cochrane's avowed intention to carry every fort tonight, Sharpe knew that just this single strongpoint would save the expedition. If Cochrane possessed just one fort then he would have guns and walls with which to defeat a Spanish counter-attack, and so make a stand till the men left on the ships could arrange a rescue. Lord Cochrane might yet live, if this one fort could fall.

* * *

The fence sections had been nailed to their posts, and each nail needed nothing more than a strong wrench with a bayonet to be wrested free. Sharpe experimented on a couple of nails, then, satisfied, he slid down into the ditch's bottom where he reloaded the pistol he had fired from the boat. He checked that his other pistol was primed, then nodded at the men standing by the posts. 'Go!' he said.

The men ripped the fence nails free. There was a splintering sound, the wavering of two great sections of wood, then the fence was falling. 'Take hold of it!' Harper shouted. 'Together now! Lift it, turn! Now go!'

'Charge!' Sharpe shouted, and he stumbled up the ditch side into the moonlight. Behind him the sea was a flicker of silver and black, while ahead of him the fortress walls were shadowed dark. The two pistols were in his belt, the sword in his hand. 'Cochrane!' he shouted. 'Cochrane!'

The men carrying the fence sections were lumbering across the tangle of ferns and grasses. The charge was slow, much slower than Sharpe had anticipated, made so by the weight of the cumbersome timber ramps. The carrying parties were advancing at scarcely more than a walking pace, but without the ramps the attack must fail, and so Sharpe knew he must hold his patience.

The single sentry on the fort's western wall gaped for a second, unslung his musket, decided that there were too many attackers for his single cartridge to destroy, and so turned to shout for help. His cry was drowned as the cannons cracked the night apart, slitting the moonlit darkness with their sharp stabs of flame. The wind carried the smoke towards Cochrane, away from Sharpe. The sentry shouted again, and this time he was heard.

'Cochrane!' Sharpe shouted. 'Cochrane!' And suddenly

men began to appear at the wall ahead. 'Spread out!' Sharpe called. The first stabs of flame showed dark red on the ramparts. A ball fluttered near Sharpe, another flicked through the grass, a third cracked off one of the fence sections. The men carrying the makeshift ramps were running faster now, but the other men, unencumbered with the heavy burdens, were outstripping them, sprinting across the headland as though there would be security in the deep black shadows of the fort's ditch.

Sharpe ran with them. There were just fifty yards to go. The muskets crashed from the wall ahead. A man fell cursing to Sharpe's left, his hands clutching at his thigh. Sharpe could smell blood in the night; blood and powder smoke, the old and too familiar smells. Thirty yards, twenty, and another volley whipped overhead. The Spanish were firing high; the error of all inexperienced troops. The first of Sharpe's men were at the ditch. 'Take aim!' Sharpe shouted at them. 'Aim for their bellies!'

He put his sword into his left hand as he dragged one of his two pistols free. He cocked it, dropped to one knee beside the ditch, and took aim. The defenders were silhouetted against the moonlit sky while the attackers were dark shapes against the darker ground. Sharpe found a target, lowered the muzzle to the man's belly, fired. Sparks jetted bright and the recoil jarred up Sharpe's arm. The smoke blossomed, but when it was snatched away by the wind the man was gone, plucked off the fort's ramparts. Those ramparts were ten feet above Sharpe and twelve feet away. Then the first of the fence sections arrived and Harper was yelling at the men to plant its leading edge at the side of the ditch, then to lever the whole thing up and over, like a giant trapdoor that swung in the night to crash sickeningly against the sloping earth wall. The makeshift ramp lodged some three feet below the parapet, but that was close enough. 'Come on!' Sharpe shouted. 'Follow me!'

He ran across the makeshift bridge. The wooden palings

bounced under Sharpe's boots. A musket flamed ahead. There were men either side of him, then he leaped for the rampart's top and the Spaniards were backing away, terrified of this sudden assault. Sharpe was screaming like a wild thing, his sword chopping down hard, and a defender was at his feet, squirming and screaming. Harper swung his cutlass like a bullock-killer, almost decapitating a man. The second bridge thumped into place and yet more men swarmed up its palings. Sharpe was leading the assault towards the cannon. An infantryman lunged with his bayonet. Sharpe knocked it aside and rammed the hilt of his sword into the man's face. The rest of the defenders, terrified by this horror that had sprung from their flank, were running away, leaving the ramparts open for Sharpe and his assault party to reach the fort's northern bastions where the guns faced out to sea.

'Cochrane! Cochrane!' the attackers shouted, and to Sharpe their ragged chorus of voices sounded desperately thin, but they were enough to terrify the gunners who turned and bolted from their embrasures. The defending infantry, swept off the wall's top, were milling uncertainly in the courtyard beneath, and now the gunners added to the panic. Sharpe dragged his second pistol free, aimed it down into the melee, and pulled the trigger.

'Cochrane!' He turned and bellowed the name into the darkness, down towards the white-fretted beach where the abandoned longboats still rolled and crashed in the tumbling surf. 'Cochrane!'

'Sharpe?' Cochrane's voice sounded from the dark dunes.

'It's ours! Come on!' Christ, Sharpe thought, but they had done it! They had done it! His men were flooding into the first embrasure, hitting the captured gun with their cutlasses so that its barrel rang like a bell. 'Come on, Cochrane! We've won!'

'Reload!' Harper was bellowing. 'Reload!' He jumped down into the gunpit beside Sharpe. 'Those bastards will counter-attack.' He nodded towards the fort's courtyard.

'Let's go for the bastards!' Sharpe said.

Behind him the slope was suddenly swarming with Cochrane's men. Sharpe did not wait for them to reach the fort, but instead shouted at his men to attack the panicked Spaniards in the fort's courtyard. An officer was trying to rally the fugitives, and if that man succeeded, and if the gunners recaptured their weapons, then Cochrane's men would be cut down in swathes. Sharpe had fewer than fifty men, and there were at least two hundred in the courtyard, but the latter were demoralized and they must not be allowed to recover their wits. 'Come on!' Sharpe screamed. 'Finish them off!' He charged.

Harper and a flood of maddened men came with him. Cutlasses chopped down, swords stabbed, pikes ripped at frightened men, but suddenly the enemy was melting away, running, because the panicked Spaniards had thrown open the fort's gate and were fleeing across the moonlit heath of the headland. They had left the Spanish flag flying on its staff beside the semaphore gallows, had abandoned their guns and were now running towards another fort that was visible from the ramparts of the captured English fort.

'After them!' Sharpe screamed. 'After them!'

This was an added madness. One fort had fallen, and one captured fort was enough to guarantee Cochrane's survival. A hundred determined men could hold this fort by manhandling the guns to the land-facing ramparts and blasting away the Spanish counter-attacks while Cochrane ferried his men off the beach to the waiting frigates, but suddenly Sharpe saw a chance to capture a second fortress and so he took it.

He took the mad chance because he remembered a horror from long ago, a horror he had witnessed in Spain when, riding with German horsemen, he had seen a French square broken.

The survivors of that broken square had fled towards a second square which, opening its ranks to let in their fellow Frenchmen, had also opened itself to the crazed horses and blood-spattered swords of the King's German Legion. The big horsemen had been riding among the fugitives and had broken that second square. The survivors of the second square, together with the few men who still lived from the first, had run for a third square which, rather than let itself be turned into a slaughterhouse, had opened fire on its own men. All of them had still gone down, ridden into hell by big horses and screaming cavalrymen.

Now Sharpe reckoned he could work a similar effect. The demoralized men from the English fort were running towards Fort San Carlos which, not more than four hundred yards away, was opening its gates to receive them. In the moonlight, and in the confusion, he reckoned his men would be indistinguishable from the fleeing Spaniards. 'On!' he shouted at his fifty men. 'On!'

They ran with him. A broad beaten track led from the English fort to Fort San Carlos which, unlike the north-facing English fort, looked east across the neck of the harbour. Sharpe pushed a running Spaniard in the back, driving the man down into a ditch beside the road. He was among the Spaniards now, but they took no notice of him, nor of any of the other panting seamen who had infiltrated their ranks. The Spanish infantrymen cared only about reaching the safety of Fort San Carlos. The defenders of that second fort were standing on their ramparts, staring into the moonlight and trying to make sense of the confusion that had erupted on the headland's tip.

Some of the fugitive Spaniards at last understood their danger. An officer shouted and lashed his sword at a seaman who calmly rammed his pike into the man's ribs. Some of the running infantrymen broke off the road, running south towards the headland's further fortresses. Cochrane had reached the first fort and, understanding what was happening, had already launched his men along the path behind Sharpe. The defenders of the San Carlos Fort, seeing that second wave of attackers, assumed them to be their only threat. Muskets stabbed flame into the gathering darkness and the balls whipped over the heads of Sharpe's men.

Sharpe reached the bridge over the ditch of the San Carlos Fort. The gateway was crammed with desperate men. Some, trying to escape their pursuers, clambered up the sides of the ramparts and Sharpe joined them, pulling himself up the steep earth slope. The defences facing inland were negligible, designed to deter rather than hold off any real assault, perhaps because the fort's builders had never really expected an enemy to attack from the land. These forts were designed to pour a destructive cannonade down onto attacking ships, not to repel a madcap assault from the land. Corral Castle, the southernmost fort on the headland, had been built to resist such an assault, and Fort Chorocomayo, high on the headland's spine, was equipped with field artillery designed to keep a land attack from reaching the headland's neck, but no one had expected a landing on the English beach and then a crazy shrieking assault in the blood-sodden darkness.

Sharpe's boots flailed for a grip on the earth slope, and a Spanish defender, assuming him to be a refugee from the English fort, reached down to help. Sharpe let the man pull him to the summit, thanked him, then tipped him down into the ditch. He swung his sword back, slicing at another man who wriggled desperately away. Two sailors from the *Kitty* ran past Sharpe, driving forward with fixed bayonets, but the Spanish defenders did not wait for the challenge, but just fled. 'Cochrane!' Sharpe shouted. 'Cochrane!' He drove his attackers towards the men firing at the English fort who, nervous of being trapped, were already abandoning the ramparts and edging backwards. Harper was in the gate, slashing and screaming at the men who blocked the entrance.

Then, with a suddenness that came from their desperately fragile morale, the defenders of Fort San Carlos shattered just as the garrison of the English fort had broken. The gunners, who were in their embrasures overlooking the moonwashed waters of the harbour, turned to see a churning mass of fighting men silhouetted against their western ramparts. They saw more men scramble onto the walls and they feared that the flood of men would wash down to swamp the courtyard and bring bayonets to the gunpits, and so the gunners fled. They leaped from their embrasures, scrambled up the ditch's far side and ran south towards the third fort, Amargos, that lay a half mile away and which, like San Carlos, faced east onto the harbour.

The Spanish infantry, seeing the gunners go and realizing that there was nothing left to defend, broke as well. Sharpe, still on the western ramparts, cupped his hands and screamed towards Cochrane's men. 'They're running! Go south! South!' He shouted in English. 'Do you hear me, Cochrane?'

'I hear you!' the voice came back.

'They're running for the next fort!'

'Tally-ho! Tally-ho!' And Cochrane, throwing all caution to the wind, turned his men off the track to charge south towards the Amargos Fort. The headland echoed with the yelps and cheers of the hunting rebels. Miller's drummers were trying to beat a quick tattoo, but the pace of the advance was too swift for such formal encouragement. The defenders of the San Carlos Fort, denied the use of their gate, spilled over their earth walls to flee towards safety. Now two sets of men were running for the Amargos Fort which, thinking they were both loyal Spanish forces, opened its wooden gates to receive them.

Sharpe, his men disorganized and blown by their attacks on the first two forts, did not join the assault on Fort Amargos. Instead he jumped down to the courtyard and crossed to the flagpole that was nothing but a thin tree trunk skinned of its bark. He sawed with his sword till the flag fluttered free. Lieutenant Cabral, foraging through the fort's buildings, found a thin horse shivering in a stable. He offered to ride after Cochrane and bring back news of the night, an offer Sharpe gratefully accepted. Then, when picquets had been set on the captured ramparts and search parties sent to find the wounded, Sharpe sheathed his sword and walked to the gun embrasures.

Harper joined him. Most of the *Kitty*'s sailors were ransacking the fort, hurling bedding out of the log huts and hunting for coins in abandoned valises and rucksacks. A midshipman, deputed by Sharpe to bring a butcher's bill, reported that he had found just three dead Spaniards and one dead rebel.

'God save Ireland,' Harper said in amazement, 'but that wasn't a battle, it was more like herding cattle!'

'They think we're devils,' the midshipman said. 'I spoke to a wounded man and he said their bullets can't kill us. We're charmed, you see. We're protected by magic.'

'No wonder the poor sods ran.' Harper made the sign of the cross, then yawned hugely.

Sharpe sent the midshipman to find Cochrane's surgeon, MacAuley. There were six men badly wounded, all Spaniards. Some of the *Kitty*'s men had sword cuts, and one had a bullet in his thigh, but otherwise the injuries were paltry. Sharpe had never known a victory come so cheap. 'Cochrane was right,' he said to Harper. Or perhaps it had been the Spaniards who had defeated themselves, for men who believe in demons can be defeated easily.

Sharpe leaned on a gun embrasure and stared at the moon-glossed water of Valdivia harbour. A score of ships, their cabin lights like cottage windows bright in the night, lay in the great bay, while across the water, perhaps a thousand yards away, a blaze of torches showed in the Niebla Fort. Beside the fort was the entrance to the River

Valdivia, leading to the town where Blas Vivar was supposedly a prisoner.

'We could give those bastards a shot or two?' Harper nodded towards the lights of Fort Niebla.

'They're out of musket range,' Sharpe said idly.

'Not with muskets. With these buggers!' Harper slapped the nearest cannon. It was a massive thirty-six pounder, a ship-killing lump of artillery that had a depressed barrel in expectation of enemy ships coming through the harbour's entrance channel. The gun's roundshot would be held in place by a rope ring rammed against the ball to stop it rolling down the inclined barrel. A quill filled with a finely mealed powder stuck from the cannon's touchhole, and a portfire smoked and fizzed inside a protective barrel at the back of the gunpit. All the gun needed was to be re-aimed, then fired.

'Why not?' Sharpe said, then turned the cannon's elevating screw until it pointed to a spot just above the far Niebla Fort. Harper had already levered the trail round. Sharpe plucked the portfire from its barrel and blew on its burning tip till the fuse glowed a brilliant red. 'Would you like to do the honours?'

'You do this one,' Harper said, 'and I'll do the next.'

Sharpe stood to one side, reached over, and touched the glowing match to the quill in the touch-hole. The fire flashed down to the charge, the gun crashed back on its carriage and a cloud of smoke billowed to hide the harbour. Men cheered as the ball screamed away across the water. Burning scraps of wad floated down the hillside and started small fires in the grass.

Harper fired the next gun, and so they went down the embrasures, sending the heavy shots towards the distant fort. Sharpe doubted that the cannonfire would do any damage, for he had no training in aiming such big guns, yet the shots were an expression of relief, even of joy. Fort

Niebla, doubtless confused by the noises and alarms of the night, did not fire back.

As the sound of the last shot echoed round the confining hills of the harbour, Sharpe looked south and saw that Cochrane's men were swarming across the ramparts of Fort Amargos. The fort's Spanish defenders were a fleeing rabble, the gate gaped open, and its flag was captured. Others of Cochrane's men, diverted from the newly-captured Fort Amargos, were scrambling up the headland's central ridge to attack the gun emplacements of Fort Chorocomayo. Musket fire splintered the night as the attackers climbed. Cheers sounded from the ridge, a bugle called, while out in the harbour the nervous crews of neutral ships displayed bright lanterns in their rigging, advertising to any attackers that they had no part in this night's fighting.

That fighting was ending. High on the ridge, under the bright sparks of the stars, musket flashes and cannon flames showed where Fort Chorocomayo briefly resisted Cochrane's assault, but Chorocomayo had been constructed to stop an attack from the south, not the north, and the firing flared for only a few minutes before there was a sudden silence and, through the moonlit mist of powder smoke, Sharpe saw the silhouetted flag drop. Chorocomayo, like Amargos and San Carlos and the English fort, had fallen. Three hundred wet and frightened men, coming from the sea, had ripped Valdivia's outer defences into tatters. 'Bloody amazing, is what it is!' Harper said.

'It surely is,' Sharpe agreed, though he knew the worst was yet to come, for the most formidable of the Spanish defence works, Corral Castle, the Niebla Fort, Manzanera Island, and Valdivia's Citadel, were still in enemy hands, and all those strongholds, save only the gun batteries on Manzanera Island, were stone-walled and properly supplied with glacis, ditches and revetments. Yet those more taxing defences would have to wait for daylight. Lieutenant Cabral, coming back on his horse, confirmed that

Cochrane had called a halt for the night. The attack would continue in the morning, and till then the rebel forces were to stay where they were; to eat, sleep and rejoice.

Sharpe washed his sword blade clean in a trough of water, then joined Harper by a brazier where they ate Spanish sausages and a great loaf of bread, all washed down by a skin of harsh red wine. Harper had also found a basket of apples, and their smell reminded Sharpe of Normandy and, for an instant, the homesickness was acute as a bullet's strike. He shook it away. The smell of the battle, of powder smoke and blood, was already gone, blown southwards by the salt sea wind.

Major Miller, excited and proud, brought a further message from Cochrane. In the morning, Cochrane said, they would bombard the stone forts while the *Kitty* and the *O'Higgins* came into the harbour. Once Fort Niebla had surrendered the rebels would make the fourteen-mile journey up river to attack Valdivia itself. Cochrane clearly had no doubts that the forts would surrender. 'They're rotten!' Miller spoke of the defenders. 'They've no heart, Sharpe, no belly for a fight!'

'They're badly led.' Sharpe felt sorry for the Spaniards. In the French wars he had seen Spaniards fight with fantastic bravery and enviable skill, yet here, with only a corrupted regime to defend, they had collapsed. 'They think we're devils,' Sharpe said, 'and that we can't be touched by bullets or blades. It isn't fair on a man to fight demons.'

Miller laughed and touched the spiky tips of his moustache. 'I always wanted a forked tail. Sleep well, Sharpe. Tomorrow will bring victory!'

'So it will,' Sharpe said, 'so it will,' and he hoped the morrow would bring so much more besides. For tomorrow he would reach Valdivia where his sword and his money and his friend all lay captive. But all that must wait on the morning and on the new day's battle. Until which time, Sharpe slept.

CHAPTER 11

The morning brought cloud and a thin mist through which, in an uncanny silence, Cochrane's two ships ghosted into Valdivia harbour. The wounded *Kitty* was low in the water with a list to starboard and her pumps spitting water. She kept close to the western shore and to the protection of the captured guns of Fort San Carlos, while the *O'Higgins*, larger and more threatening, sailed boldly up the centre of the channel. The *O'Higgins*'s gunports were open, but the Niebla Fort did not respond to the challenge. Cochrane had ordered the fifty-gun ship to hold her fire, daring to hope that the Spanish would thereby be lulled into quiescence, and now, astonishingly, the harbour's remaining defenders simply stared as the enemy ships passed through the lethal entrance. It was almost as though the Spanish, stunned by the night's events, had become mere spectators to their Empire's fall.

It was falling with hardly a shot, collapsing like a rotten tree in a brisk wind. Corral Castle was the first strongpoint to surrender. Cochrane ordered one shot fired from Fort Chorocomayo, and, within seconds of the roundshot thumping harmlessly into the fort's earthen glacis, the gates were dragged open, the flag was hurried down, and an artillery Major rode out under a flag of truce. The castle's commander, the Major told Cochrane, was drunk, the men were mutinous and the castle belonged to the rebellion. The artillery Major surrendered his sword with indecent haste. 'Just send us home to Spain,' he told Cochrane.

With the fall of Corral Castle every gun on the western side of the harbour was aimed at either Fort Niebla or at the batteries on Manzanera Island. The *Kitty* had been run aground to stop her from sinking, while the *O'Higgins* had anchored so that her formidable broadside was aimed at the guns on Manzanera. 'What I plan to do –' Cochrane had summoned Sharpe to Fort Amargos, the stronghold that was closest to Fort Niebla, and where his Lordship was dividing his attention between a tripod-mounted telescope aimed at the enemy fort and Fort Amargos's drunken commander's collection of pornographic etchings '– is demand Niebla's surrender. Do you think it's possible for two women to do that? I wondered if you would be willing to go to Fort Niebla and talk to the commander? Oh, my word. That would give a man backache, would it not? Look at this, Miller! I'll bet your mother never did that with your father!'

Miller, who was shaving from a bowl set on a parapet, chuckled at the picture. 'Very supple, my Lord. Good morning, Sharpe!'

'The commander's name is Herrera,' Cochrane said to Sharpe. 'I'm assuming he has command of Manzanera Island as well, but you'd better check when you see him. That's if you're willing to go.'

'Of course I'll go,' Sharpe said, 'but why me?'

'Because Herrera's a proud man. Good God! I think I'll keep these for the *Kitty*. Herrera hates me, and he'd find it demeaning to surrender to a Chilean, but he'll find nothing dishonourable in receiving an English soldier.' Cochrane reluctantly abandoned the portfolio of pictures to pull an expensive watch from his waistcoat pocket. 'Tell Herrera that his troops must leave their fortifications before nine o'clock this morning. Officers can wear sidearms, but all other weapons must be . . .' His Lordship's voice tailed away to nothing. He was no longer looking at his watch, nor even at the salacious pictures, but was instead staring incredulously across the misted harbour. Then, recovering himself, he managed a feeble blasphemy. 'Good God.'

'Bloody hell,' Sharpe said.

'I don't believe it!' Major Miller, his chin lathered, stared across the water.

'Good God,' Cochrane said again, for the Spaniards, without waiting for an envoy, or for any kind of attack, were simply abandoning their remaining defences. Three boats were rowing hard away from Manzanera Island, while the flag had rippled down over the Niebla Fort and Sharpe could see its garrison marching to the quay where a whole fleet of longboats waited. The Spanish were withdrawing up the river, going the fourteen miles to the Citadel itself. 'Christ on a donkey!' Cochrane blasphemed obscurely. 'But it rather looks like complete victory, does it not?'

'Congratulations, my Lord,' Sharpe said.

'I never thanked you for last night, did I? Allow me to, my dear Sharpe.' Cochrane offered Sharpe a hand, but continued to gape in disbelief at the Spanish evacuation. 'Good God Almighty!'

'We still have to take Valdivia,' Sharpe said cautiously.

'So we do! So we do!' Cochrane turned away. 'Boats! I want boats! We're in a rowing race, my boys! We don't want those bastards adding their muskets to the town's defences! Let's have some boats here! Mister Almante! Signal the *O'Higgins*! Tell them we need boats! Boats!'

In the first pearly light of dawn Sharpe had seen a Spanish longboat beached beneath the ramparts of Fort San Carlos. He presumed the boat had served to provision the fort from the main Spanish commissary in the Niebla Fort, but now it would help Cochrane complete his victory. Sharpe, knowing it would take time to fetch boats from the *O'Higgins*, ran back to the smaller Fort San Carlos where, shouting at Harper and the seamen to bring their weapons, he scrambled down the steep cliff path which led to a small shingle beach. A dozen startled seals flopped into the water as his hurried progress triggered a score of small avalanches, then his boots grated on the shingle and he began heaving the boat towards the sea.

The first thirty men to reach the shingle gained places in the boat. Sixteen seamen took the oars, the rest crouched between the thwarts. They carried muskets and cutlasses. Sharpe told them their task was to overtake the fleeing Spaniards and stop them from reinforcing Valdivia. Then he encouraged the oarsmen by saying that the fugitives were bound to be carrying Fort Niebla's valuables in their boats.

The boat, fuelled by greed, fairly leaped ahead. Cochrane, still waiting at Fort Amargos for his own boats to come from the *O'Higgins*, bellowed at Sharpe to pick him up, but Sharpe just waved, then urged his oarsmen on.

They passed the *O'Higgins*. What was left of the warship's crew gave a cheer. The coxswain of Sharpe's boat, a grey-haired Spaniard, was muttering that the sequestered Spanish longboat was a pig, with a buckled keelson and sprung planks, and that Cochrane would soon catch them in his superior boats. 'Row, you bastards!' the coxswain shouted at the oarsmen. It was a race now, a race to snatch the plunder from the demoralized enemy.

Far off to Sharpe's right a warship had raised the Royal Navy's white ensign. The name *Charybdis* was inscribed in gold at her stern. A nearby merchant ship flew the Stars and Stripes. The two crews watched the odd race and some waved what Sharpe took to be encouragement. 'Nice to see the Navy here,' Harper shouted from the bows. 'Maybe they can give us a ride home!'

The longboat reached the strait between Manzanera Island and Fort Niebla. The gun barrels that should have kept Valdivia safe now stared emptily from abandoned embrasures. The gates of the Niebla Fort hung open, while the remains of a cooking fire dribbled a trickle of smoke from a hut on Manzanera Island. A small rough-haired dog yelped at the passing boat from the beach beneath the earthworks that protected the island's guns, but there were no other signs of life. The Spanish had deserted a position as strong as any Sharpe had ever seen. A man could have died of old age before he would have needed to yield Niebla or Manzanera, yet the Spanish had vanished into the morning mist without firing a shot.

The oarsmen grunted as the boat slammed into the turgid current of the outflowing Valdivia River. Harper, in the boat's bows, was watching for the fugitives, but Sharpe, in the stern, was looking for Cochrane. Some of the men in Sharpe's boat were baling with their caps. The old boat had gaping seams and was leaking at an alarming rate, but the men were coping and the oarsmen had found a good steady rhythm. Sharpe could see Cochrane's boats striking out from the far shore, but they were still a long way behind.

'What do we do if we catch up with the bastards?' the coxswain asked Sharpe.

'Say boo to them. They'll surrender.'

The coxswain laughed. They were rowing past the quays at the river's mouth. A group of bemused families had come from the fishermen's cottages to stare at the morning's events. Sharpe wondered what difference any of this would make to such pitiably poor people. Bautista's rule could not be easy, but would O'Higgins make life better? Sharpe doubted it. He had talked once with an old man in the village of Seleglise, a man ancient enough to remember the old French King and to remember all the other Paris governments that had come through bloody revolution or coup d'état, and the old man had reckoned that not one of those governments had made the slightest difference to his life. His cows had still needed milking, his vegetables had needed weeding, his corn had needed cutting, his cherries needed picking, his taxes needed paying, the church had needed his money and no one, neither priest, politician, taxman, or prefect, had ever given him a penny or a thank you for any of it. No doubt the Chilean peasantry would feel the same. All this morning's excitement meant was that a different set of politicians would become rich at the country's expense.

The boat was in the river valley now. The hills either side were thick with trees. Two herons flapped lazily down one bank. The oarsmen had slowed down, settling to the long haul. A fisherman, casting a hand net from a small leather boat, abandoned his tackle and paddled furiously for the safety of land as the strange boat full of armed men appeared. Harper had cocked a musket in case the Spaniards had set an ambush beyond the river's first bend.

The coxswain hugged the right hand bank, cutting the corner and risking the shallows to make the bend swiftly. The oars brushed reeds, then the river straightened and Sharpe, standing to get a clear view ahead, felt a pang for there were no boats in sight. For a second he thought the Spaniards must have such superior boats that they had somehow converted a two-mile lead into four or five miles, but then he saw that the Spanish longboats had stopped altogether and were huddled on the southern river bank. There must have been twenty boats there, all crammed with men and none of them moving. 'There!' He pointed for Harper.

Then Sharpe saw horsemen on the river's bank. Cavalry? Had Bautista sent reinforcements up river? For a second Sharpe was tempted to turn the boat and seize Fort Niebla before the Spaniards, realizing how hugely they outnumbered Cochrane's puny forces, made their counter-attack, but Harper suddenly shouted that the dagoes on the river bank were flying a white flag.

'Bloody hell,' Sharpe said, for there was indeed a white flag of truce or surrender.

The oarsmen, sensing Sharpe's momentary indecision, and needing a rest, had stopped rowing and the boat was beginning to drift back downstream. 'A trap?' the coxswain asked.

'God knows,' Sharpe said. Cochrane was forever using flags as a trick to get himself close to the enemy, and were the Spaniards now learning to use the same ruse? 'Put me ashore,' he told the coxswain.

The oars dipped again, took the strain, and drove hard for the southern bank. The bow touched, Sharpe clambered over the thwarts, then jumped up onto tussocky grass. Harper followed him. Sharpe loosened the sword in its scabbard, checked that his pistols were primed, and walked slowly towards the horsemen who were a half mile away.

There were not many horsemen, perhaps twenty, and none was in uniform, suggesting that this was not a cavalry unit. The men carried two flags: one the white flag of truce, and the other a complicated ensign which bore a coat of arms. 'They look like civilians,' Harper commented.

The horsemen were cantering towards Sharpe and Harper. One of the leading riders had a large black hat and a scarlet sash. That man stood in his stirrups and waved, as if to signify that he meant no harm. Sharpe checked that the longboat with its cargo of armed sailors was close enough to offer him support, then waited.

'There's that bastard Blair!' Harper exclaimed.

'Where?'

'White horse, six or seven back.'

'So it is,' Sharpe said grimly. George Blair, the merchant and British Consul, was among the horsemen who, like Blair, were mostly middle-aged and prosperous-looking. Their leader, the man wearing the scarlet sash, slowed as he neared Sharpe.

'Are you Cochrane?' he called in Spanish.

'Admiral Cochrane is following. He'll be here soon,' Sharpe replied.

'We've come to surrender the town to you.' The man reined in his horse, took off his hat, and offered Sharpe a bow. 'My name is Manuel Ferrara, I have the honour to be the *alcalde* of Valdivia, and these gentlemen are senior and respected citizens of our town. We want no trouble, *señor*. We are merely merchants who struggle to make a poor living. As you know, our sympathies have always been with the Republic, and we beg that you will treat us with the respect due to civilians who have taken no part in the fighting.'

'Shut up,' Sharpe said. He pushed past the offended and astonished Mayor to reach Blair. 'You bastard.'

'Mister Sharpe?' Blair touched a nervous hand to his hat.

'You're supposed to look after British interests, you bugger, not suck Bautista's tits because you're frightened of him!'

'Now, Mister Sharpe, be careful what you say!'

'You shit-faced son of a whore.' Sharpe took hold of Blair's right boot and heaved up, chucking the Consul bodily out of his saddle. Blair gave a yelp of astonishment, then collapsed into the mud on the far side of the horse. Sharpe steadied the beast, then mounted it himself. 'You!' he said to the Mayor, who was still protesting his undying loyalty to the ideals of liberty and republicanism.

'Me, *señor*?'

'I told you to shut up. I don't give a fart for your republics. I'm a monarchist. And get off your damned horse. My friend needs it.'

'My horse? But this is a valuable beast, *señor*, and . . .'

'Get off,' Sharpe said, 'or I'll blow you off it.' He drew one of his two pistols and cocked it.

The Mayor hastily slid off his horse. Harper, grinning,

heaved himself into the vacated saddle. 'Where's Bautista?' Sharpe asked the Mayor.

'The Captain-General is in the Citadel. But his men don't want to fight.'

'But Bautista wants to fight?'

'Yes, *señor*. But the men think you are devils. They say you can't be killed!' The Mayor crossed himself, then turned fearfully as a shout from the river announced the arrival of Lord Cochrane and his boats.

'All of you!' Sharpe shouted at the Mayor's nervous deputation. 'Off your horses! All of you! Now!' He kicked his heels to urge Blair's white horse forward. 'What's this flag?' He gestured at the ornate coat of arms.

'The flag of the town of Valdivia, *señor*,' the Mayor answered.

'Hold on to it, Patrick!'

Cochrane jumped ashore, roaring with questions. What was happening? Who were these men? Why had Sharpe tried to race ahead?

'Bautista's holed up in the Citadel,' Sharpe explained. 'Everyone else in Valdivia wants to surrender, but Bautista doesn't. That means he's waiting for your boats and he'll fire on you. But if a small group of us goes ahead on horseback we might just fool them into opening the gates.'

Cochrane seized a horse and shouted for others of his men to find themselves mounts. The remainder of his piratical force was to row upriver as fast as it could. The Mayor tried to make another speech about liberty and the Republic, but Cochrane pushed him aside and dragged himself up into his saddle. He grinned at Sharpe. 'Christ, but this is joy! What would we do for happiness if peace came?' He turned his horse clumsily, rammed his heels back, and whooped as the horse took off. 'Let's go get the whores!'

His men cheered. Hooves thumped mud into the faces of the Mayor's delegation as Sharpe and Harper raced after Cochrane. The rebellion was down to a spearhead of just twenty men, but with a whole country as their prize.

*　　*　　*

They rode hard, following the river road east towards the town. On the horsemen's left the river flowed placidly towards the sea, while to their right was a succession of terraced vineyards, tobacco fields and orchards. There were no military posts, no soldiers, and nothing untoward in the landscape. Bautista had not put any picquets on the harbour road, and had set no ambushes in the trees. Cochrane and his men rode untroubled through two villages and past white-painted churches and plump farmhouses. Cochrane waved at villagers who, terrified of strangers, crouched inside their cottages till the armed horsemen had passed. Cochrane was in understandably high spirits. 'It was impossible, you see! Impossible!'

'What was?' Sharpe asked.

'To capture the harbour with just three hundred men! That's why it worked. They couldn't believe there were so few of us. My God!' Cochrane pounded the pommel of his saddle in his exuberant enthusiasm. 'I'm going to capture the Spanish treasury and those prickless legal bastards in Santiago will have to grovel at my feet to get the money!'

'You have to capture the Citadel first,' Sharpe reminded him.

'Simplicity itself.' In his present mood Cochrane would have attacked the rock of Gibraltar with just a boat's crew. He whooped with delirious joy, making his horse prick its ears back. The horses were tired, breathing hard on the slopes and sweating beneath their saddlecloths, but Cochrane ruthlessly pressed them on. What did it matter if he lost horses, so long as he gained a country?

Then, two hours after they had encountered the Mayor's delegation on the river bank, the road breasted a low ridge and there, hazed with the smoke of its fires and dominated by the great Citadel within the river's bend, lay Valdivia.

Sharpe was about to ask just how Cochrane wanted to approach the Citadel, but his Lordship, seeing the prize so close, had already scraped back his heels and was shouting at Harper to hold the flag high. 'We'll go straight for them! Straight for them! The devil take us if we fail! Go! Go! Go!'

'God save Ireland!' Harper shouted the words like a war cry, then he too raked back his heels.

'Jesus wept,' Sharpe said, and followed. This was not war, it was madness, a race, an idiocy. An admiral, a Dublin publican, an English farmer and sixteen rebels were attacking the biggest fort in Chile, and doing it as though it were a child's game.

Harper, his horse pounding alongside Cochrane, held the flag high so that its fringed symbol streamed in the wind. Cochrane had drawn his sword and Sharpe now struggled to do the same, but pulling a long blade free when trying to stay aboard a galloping horse was not the easiest task. He managed it just as the horsemen funnelled into the town itself, clattering into a narrow street which led to the main square. A woman carrying a tray of bread tripped in her frantic effort to get out of the way. Fresh loaves spilt across the roadway. Sparks chipped off the cobbles from the horses' hooves. A priest shrank into a doorway, a child screamed, then the horsemen were in the main square and Cochrane was shouting at the fortress to open its gates.

'Open! Open!' he shouted in Spanish, and maybe it was the sight of the flag, or perhaps the urgency of the horsemen that suggested they were fugitives from the disasters that were known to have occurred in the harbour, but magically, just as every other Spanish fortress had opened its gates, so this one threw open its entrance.

The horses crashed across the bridge. Cochrane and

Harper were in the lead. Cochrane had a drawn sword, and the sight of the bare blade made the officer in the gateway shout in alarm, but it was too late. Harper dropped the tip of the flag and, at full gallop and with all his huge weight behind the flag's staff, he drove the tip of the pole into the officer's chest. There was an explosion of blood, a crunch of bone, then the officer went down with a shattered chest and a blood-soaked flag impaled in his ribs, while Harper, letting the staff go, was through the archway and into the outer courtyard.

'Surrender! Surrender!' Cochrane was screaming the word in a demented voice, flailing at panicked soldiers with the flat of his drawn sword. 'Drop your muskets! Surrender!'

A musket fired from an upper window and the bullet flattened itself on the cobbles, but no other resistance was offered. The gate to the inner courtyard, hard by the Angel Tower, was closed. All around Sharpe the Spanish soldiers were throwing down their muskets. Cochrane was already out of his saddle, hurling men aside to reach a door into the main buildings where, he supposed, the treasury of a defeated empire would be found. His sailors followed him, abandoning their horses in the yard and screaming their leader's name as a war shout. It was the sound of that name which did the most damage. The Spanish soldiers, hearing that the devil Cochrane was among them, decided to drop to their knees rather than fight.

Sharpe threw himself out of the saddle. He knew the geography of the fort better than Cochrane and, with Harper beside him, he ran into the corridor which led to the inner guardroom. Footsteps thumped on floorboards above as men tried to escape the invaders. A pistol fired somewhere. A woman screamed.

Sharpe pushed open the door which led to the inner courtyard. A nine-pounder cannon stood there, facing the gate, and with it was a crew of four men who clearly had orders to fire the gun as soon as the gate was opened. 'Leave it alone!' Sharpe shouted. The gun's crew turned and Sharpe saw that Captain Marquinez was its commander. Marquinez, as exquisitely uniformed as ever, saw Sharpe, and foolishly yelped that his men should slew the gun round to face Sharpe.

There was no time to complete such a clumsy manoeuvre. Sharpe charged the gun.

A second man turned. It was Dregara. The Sergeant was holding a linstock to fire the cannon, but now dropped the burning match and fumbled to unsling the carbine from his shoulder.

'Stop him!' Marquinez screamed, then fled to the door of the Angel Tower. Sergeant Dregara raised the carbine, but too late, for Sharpe was already on him. The cavalryman backed away, tripped on the gun's trail, and fell. Sharpe slashed down with the sword, driving the carbine aside. Dregara tried to seize the sword blade, but Sharpe whipped the steel hard away, ripping off two of the cavalryman's fingers. Dregara hissed with pain, then lashed up with his boot, trying to kick Sharpe's groin. Sharpe swatted the kick aside with his left hand, then drove the sword with his right. He plunged it into Dregara's belly, then sliced it upwards, using all his strength, so that the blade tore through the muscles and cartilage to pierce into the cavalryman's chest cavity. The ribs stopped the slashing cut so Sharpe rammed the blade down, twisted it, then pulled it free. Dregara gave a weird, almost feminine scream. Blood welled to fill his belly's cavity, then spilt bright onto the cobbles of the yard where so many rebels had been executed. The other two men of the gun's makeshift crew had tried to flee, but Harper had caught them both. He felled one with a fist, the other with a cutlass stroke.

The dying Dregara twitched like a landed fish. Sharpe stepped across the cannon's trail, around the puddling blood, then ran at the door of the Angel Tower.

He hit the door with his shoulder, gasped in pain and bounced off. Marquinez, safe inside the tower, had locked its door.

Behind Sharpe Dregara gave a last gasp, and died. The inner courtyard gate scraped open and Cochrane stood there, red-haired, victorious and triumphant. 'It's ours! They've surrendered!'

'Bautista?'

'God knows where he is! Come and help yourselves to the plunder!'

'We've got business in here.'

Harper had seized a spike and now, with Sharpe's help, he turned the heavy cannon. It was a British gun, decorated with the British royal cipher, evidently one of the many cannon given by Britain to help Spain defeat Napoleon. The trail scraped on the cobbles and the ungreased axle protested, but finally they succeeded in swivelling the gun around until its bronze barrel, which Sharpe suspected was charged with canister, faced directly at the door of the Angel Tower. The door was only ten paces away. According to Marcos, the soldier who had told Vivar's story at Puerto Crucero, this door was the only way into the mysterious Angel Tower which, like a castle turret, was a fortress within a fortress. This ancient stone tower had withstood rebellion, war, earthquake and fire. Now it would meet Sharpe.

He plucked the fallen linstock from beside the disembowelled body of Sergeant Dregara, told Harper to stand aside, then touched the linstock to the quill.

The gun's sound echoed in the courtyard like the clap of doom. The gun had been double shotted. A canister had been rammed down on top of a roundshot, and both projectiles now cracked in smoke and flame from the gun's barrel. The gun recoiled across the yard, crushing Dregara's body before it smacked brutally hard against the guardroom wall.

The door to the Angel Tower, struck by the exploding load of canister, simply vanished. One moment there had been a heavy wooden door reinforced with iron, and the next there were empty hinges and charred splinters of wood. The cannonball whipped through the smoke and wreckage to ricochet round the downstairs chamber of the tower.

When the noise and smoke subsided Sharpe stepped cautiously through the wreckage. He had the bloody sword blade in his hand. He expected to encounter the foetid stench of ancient dungeons and recent death, but there was only the acrid smell of the cannon's smoke inside the tower. The lowest storey of the tower was a single room that was disappointingly commonplace: no barred cells, no racks or whips or manacles, nothing but a round white-washed room that held a table, two chairs and a stone staircase that circled round the wall to disappear through a hole in the ceiling. That ceiling was made of thick timber planks that had been laid across huge crossbeams.

Harper had scooped up Dregara's carbine. He cocked the gun and edged up the stairs, keeping his broad back against the tower's outer wall. No noise came from the upper floors of the tower.

Sharpe drew a pistol and followed. Halfway to the gaping hole in the ceiling he reached out, held Harper back, and stepped past him. 'My bird,' he said softly.

'Careful, now,' Harper whispered unnecessarily.

Sharpe crept up the stair. He carried his sword in his left hand, the heavy pistol in his right. 'Marquinez!' he called.

There was no answer. There was no sound at all from the upper floors.

'Marquinez!' Sharpe called again, but still no answer. Sharpe's boots grated on the stone stairs. Each step took an immense effort of will. The butt of the pistol was cold in his hand. He could hear himself breathing. Every second he expected to see the blaze of a gun from the trapdoor-like hole that gaped at the stair's head.

He took another step, then another. 'Marquinez!'

A gun fired. The sound was huge, like a small cannon. Sharpe swore and ducked. Harper held his breath. Then, slowly, both men realized that no bullet had come near either of them. It was the sound of the gun, huge and echoing, that had stunned them.

'Marquinez!' Sharpe called.

There was a click, like a gun being cocked.

'For God's sake,' Sharpe said, 'there are hundreds of us! You think you can fight us all?'

'Oh, by Jesus, look at that, will you?' Harper was staring at a patch of the timber ceiling not far from the stairway. Blood was oozing between the planks to form bright droplets which coalesced, quivered, then splashed down to the floor beneath.

Sharpe ran up the stairs, no longer caring what noise he made. He pounded through the open trapdoor to find himself in another, slightly smaller, but perfectly circular room that took up all the rest of the space inside the tower. There had once been another floor, but it had long fallen in and its wreckage been removed, and all that was left was a truncated stair which stopped halfway round the wall.

But the rest of the room was an astonishment. It was a sybaritic cell, a celebration of comfort. It was no prison, unless a prison would be warmed with a big stone fireplace and lit by candles that were mounted in a lantern which hung from the apex of the stone roof. The walls, which should have been of cheerless stone, were draped with rugs and scraps of tapestry to make a soft, warm chamber. The wooden floor was scattered with more rugs, some of them fur pelts, while another pelt was draped on the bed which stood in the very centre of the circular room and on which lay the remains of Captain-General Miguel Bautista. Or rather what Sharpe supposed had been Captain-General

Miguel Bautista, for all that was left of him was a headless body dressed in the simple black and white uniform that Sharpe remembered well.

Bautista's head had disappeared. It had been blown away by Harper's seven-barrelled gun with which Bautista had committed suicide. The gun lay on his trunk that had spilt so much blood onto the floorboards. Some blood had matted in the fur of the bed's coverlet, but most had puddled on the floor and run through the cracks between the ancient boards.

All around the room's outer edge were boxes. Plain wooden boxes. Between the boxes was a corridor which led to an open door. Sharpe had been told there was only the one entrance to the tower, but he had found a second. The stone around this second door had a raw, new appearance, as though it had only recently been laid. Sharpe, still holding his weapons, walked between the boxes and through the new doorway, and found himself in Captain Marquinez's quarters: the very same rooms in which the handsome Captain had received them on their first day in Valdivia.

Marquinez was sitting on his bed and was holding a pistol to his head. He was shaking with fear.

'Put the gun down,' Sharpe said quietly.

'He made me promise! He said he couldn't live without me!'

Sharpe opened his mouth, did not know what to say, so closed it again. Harper, who had stepped into the room behind Sharpe, said something under his breath.

'I loved him!' Marquinez wailed the declaration.

'Oh, Jesus,' Sharpe said, then he crossed the room and lifted the pistol from Marquinez's nerveless fingers. 'Where's Blas Vivar?'

'I don't know, *señor*, I don't know.' Marquinez was in tears now. He had begun to shake, then slid down to his knees so that he was at Sharpe's feet where he wrapped his arms round Sharpe's legs like a slave pleading for life. 'I don't know!'

Sharpe reached down and disengaged the arms, then gestured towards the tower. 'What's in the boxes, Marquinez?'

'Gold, plate, pearls, coin. We were going to take it back to Spain. We were going to live in Madrid and be great men.' He was weeping again. 'It was all going to be so wonderful!'

Sharpe gripped Marquinez's black hair and tipped the man's tearful face back. 'Is Blas Vivar here?'

'No, *señor*, I swear it!'

'Did your lover ambush Vivar?'

'No, *señor*!'

'So where is he?'

'We don't know! No one knows!'

Sharpe twisted his grip, tugging Marquinez's hair painfully. 'But you were the one who took the dog to Puerto Crucero and buried it?'

'Yes, *señor*, yes!'

'Why?'

'Because he ordered me to. Because it was embarrassing that we could not find the Captain-General's body. Because Madrid was demanding to know what had happened to General Vivar! We didn't know, but we thought he must be dead, so I found a dead dog and put that in a box instead. At least the box would smell right!' Marquinez paused. 'I don't know where he is! Please! We would have killed him, if we could, because General Vivar had found out about us, and he was threatening to tell the church of our sin, but then he vanished! Miguel said it had to be the rebels, but we never found out! It wasn't our doing! It wasn't!'

Sharpe released Marquinez's hair. 'Bugger,' Sharpe said. He released the flint on his pistol and pushed the weapon back into his belt. 'Bugger!'

'But look, *señor!*' Marquinez had climbed to his feet and, eager as a puppy for approval, edged into the tower room which had been his secret tryst. 'Look, *señor*, gold! And we have your sword, see?' He ran to a box, opened it, and drew out Sharpe's sword. Harper was opening other boxes and whistling with astonishment, though he was not so astonished to forget to fill his pockets with coins. 'Here, *señor.*' Marquinez held out Sharpe's sword.

Sharpe took it, unbuckled the borrowed scabbard, and strapped his own sword in its place. He drew the familiar blade. It looked very dull in the dim lantern light.

'No, *señor!*' Marquinez thought Sharpe was going to kill him.

'I'm not going to kill you, Marquinez. I might kill someone else, but not you. Tell me where Bautista's quarters are.'

Sharpe left Harper in his Aladdin's cave, went through Marquinez's rooms, across a landing, down a long corridor, and so into a stark, severe chamber. The walls were white, the furniture functional, the bed nothing but a campaign cot covered with thin blankets. This was how Bautista wanted the world to see him, while the tower had been his secret and his fantasy. Now Lord Cochrane sat at Bautista's plain table with two pieces of paper in front of him. Three of Cochrane's sailors were searching the room's cupboards, but were evidently finding nothing of great value. Cochrane grinned as Sharpe came through the door. 'You found me! Well done. Any news of Bautista?'

'He's dead. Blew his own head off.'

'Cowardly way out. Found any treasure?'

'A whole room full of it. Top of the tower.'

'Splendid! Go fetch, lads!' Cochrane snapped his fingers and his three men ran out into the corridor.

Sharpe walked to the table and leaned over Cochrane's two pieces of paper. One he had never seen before, but he recognized the other as the coded message that had been concealed in Bonaparte's portrait. Bautista must have kept the coded message, and Cochrane had found it. Sharpe suspected that the message was the most important thing in all the Citadel for Cochrane. The Scotsman talked of whores and gold, but really he had come for this scrap of paper that he was now translating by using the code which was written on the other sheet of paper. 'Is there a Colonel Charles?' Sharpe asked.

'Oh, yes, but it wouldn't have done for anyone to think that Boney was writing to me, would it? So Charles was our go-between.' Cochrane smiled happily, then copied another letter from the code's key.

'Where's Vivar?' Sharpe asked.

'He's safe. He's not a happy man, but he's safe.'

'You made a bloody fool of me, didn't you?'

Cochrane heard the dangerous bite in Sharpe's voice, and leaned back. 'No. I didn't. I don't think anyone could make a fool of you, Sharpe. I deceived you, yes, but I had to. I've deceived most people here. That doesn't make them fools.'

'And Marcos? The soldier who told the story of Vivar being a prisoner in the Angel Tower? You put him up to it?'

Cochrane grinned. 'Yes. Sorry. But it worked! I rather wanted your help during the assault.'

Sharpe turned the coded message round so that it faced him. 'So this was meant for you, then?'

'Yes.'

Cochrane had only unlocked the first sentence of the Emperor's message. The words were in French, but Sharpe translated them into English as he read them aloud. '"I agree to your proposal, and urge haste." What proposal?'

Cochrane stood. An excited Major Miller had come to the door, but Cochrane waved him away. His Lordship lit a cigar, then walked to a window which looked down into the main courtyard where two hundred Spaniards had surrendered to a handful of rebels. 'It was all the Emperor's fault,' Cochrane said. 'He thought Captain-General Vivar was the same Count of Mouromorto who had fought for him at the war's beginning. We didn't know Mouromorto had a brother.'

' "We"?' Sharpe asked.

Cochrane made a dismissive gesture with the cigar. 'A handful of us, Sharpe. Men who believe the world should not be handed over to dull lawyers and avaricious politicians and fat merchants. Men who believe that glory should be undimmed and brilliant!' He smiled. 'Men like you!'

'Just go on.' Sharpe shrugged the compliment away, if it was a compliment.

Cochrane smiled. 'The Emperor doesn't like being cooped up on St Helena. Why should he? He's looking for allies, Sharpe, so he ordered me to arrange a meeting with the Count of Mouromorto, which I did, but the weather was shit-terrible, and Mouromorto couldn't get to Talcahuana. So we made a second rendezvous and, of course, he arrived and he heard me out, and then he told me I was thinking of his brother, not him, and, one way or another, it turned out that I was fumbling up the wrong set of skirts. So, of course, I had to take him prisoner. Which was a pity, because we'd met under a flag of truce.' Cochrane laughed ruefully. 'It would have been easier to kill Vivar, but not under a flag of truce, so I took him to sea, and we stranded him with a score of guards, six pigs and a tribe of goats on one of the Juan Fernandez islands.' Cochrane drew on the cigar and watched its smoke drift out of the window. 'The islands are three hundred and fifty miles off the coast, in the middle of nothing! They're where Robinson Crusoe was marooned, or rather where Alexander Selkirk, who was the original of Crusoe, spent four not uncomfortable years. I last saw Vivar eight weeks ago, and he was well and as comfortable as a man could be. He tried to escape a couple of times in this last year, but it's very hard to get off an island if you're not a seaman.'

Sharpe tried to make sense of all the information. 'What did Napoleon want of Don Blas, for God's sake?'

'Valdivia, of course. But not just Valdivia. Once it was secure we'd have marched north and taken over Chile, but the Emperor insisted that we provide him with a secure fortress before he'd join us, and this place is as fine a stronghold as any in the Americas. The Emperor thought Vivar was his man and would have just handed the fortress over!'

'To Napoleon?'

'Yes,' Cochrane said, as though that was the most normal thing in all the world. 'And why not? You think I fought these last months to watch more goddamned lawyers form a government? For Christ's sake, Sharpe, the world needs Napoleon! It needs a man with his vision!' Cochrane was suddenly enthusiastic, full of the contagious vigour that made him such a formidable leader of men. 'South America is rotten, Sharpe. You've seen that for yourself! It's an old empire, full of decay. But there's gold here, and silver, and iron, and copper, and fields as rich as any in Scotland's lowlands, and orchards and vines, and cattle! There are riches here! If we can make a new country here, a United States of South America, we can make a power like the world has never seen! We just need a place to start! And a genius to make it work. I'm not that genius. I'm a good Admiral, but I don't have the patience for government, but there is a man who does, and that man's willing!' Cochrane strode back to the table and snatched up the coded letter. 'And Bonaparte can make this whole continent into a magical country, a place of gold and liberty and opportunity! All that the Emperor demanded of us was that we provided him with a secure base, and the beginnings of an army.' Cochrane swept an arm round in a lavish gesture that encompassed all of Valdivia's Citadel, its town and its far harbour. 'And this is it. This is the kernel of Napoleon's new empire, and it will be a greater and a better empire than any he has ever had before.'

'You're mad!' Sharpe said without rancour.

'But it's a glorious madness!' Cochrane laughed. 'You want to be dull? You want to live under the rule of pen-pushers? You want the world to lose its fire? You want old jealous men to be cutting off your spurs with a butcher's axe at midnight just because you dare to live? Napoleon's only fifty! He's got twenty years to make this new world great. We'll bring his Guardsmen from Louisiana, and ship volunteers from France! We'll bring together the best fighters of the European wars, from both sides, and we'll give them a cause worth the sharpening of any man's sword.' Cochrane stabbed a finger towards Sharpe. 'Join us, Sharpe! My God, you're the kind of man we need! We're going to fight our way north. Chile first, then Peru, then up to the Portuguese territories, and right up to Mexico, and God knows why we need to stop there! You'll be a General, no! A Marshal! Marshal Richard Sharpe, Duke of Valdivia, whatever you want! Name your reward, take whatever title you want, but join us! If you want your family here, tell me! I'll send a ship for them. My God, Sharpe, it could be such joy! You and I, one on land, one on sea, making a new country, a new world!'

Sharpe let the madness flow round him. 'What about O'Higgins?'

'Bernardo will have to make up his mind.' Cochrane was pacing the room restlessly. 'If he doesn't want to join us, then he'll go down with his precious lawyers. But you, Sharpe? You'll join us?'

'I'm going home,' Sharpe said.

'Home?'

'Normandy. To my woman and children. I've fought long enough, Cochrane. I don't want more.'

Cochrane stared at Sharpe, as though testing the words he had just heard, then he abruptly nodded his acceptance of Sharpe's decision. 'I'm sending the *O'Higgins* for Bonaparte. If you won't join me, then I'll have to keep you from betraying me, at least till he gets here or until I can find you another ship to take you home. I'll bring Vivar here, and you and he can sail back to Europe together. There's nothing you or he can do to stop us now. It's too late! We have our fortress, and we just have to fetch Bonaparte from his prison, then march to glory!'

'You'll never get Bonaparte out of St Helena,' Sharpe said.

'If I can take Valdivia's harbour and Citadel with three hundred men,' Cochrane said, 'I can get Bonaparte off an island. It won't be difficult! Colonel Charles has found a man who looks something like the Emperor. He'll pay a courtesy visit, just like you did, and leave the wrong man inside Longwood. Simple. The simple things always work best.' Lord Cochrane mused for a moment, then barked a joyous yelp of laughter. 'What joy you are going to miss,' he said to Sharpe. 'What joy you will miss.'

For Cochrane was unchaining Bonaparte. The devil, bored with peace, would open the vials of war. The Corsican ogre was to be let loose to make mischief, to conquest and to battle without end. Bonaparte, who had drenched Europe in blood, would now soak the Americas, and Sharpe, who was trapped in Valdivia, could do nothing about it.

Except watch as the horror started all over again.

EPILOGUE

Blas Vivar arrived in Valdivia harbour three weeks after the fall of the Citadel, three weeks after the collapse of Spanish Chile. He refused to step ashore. It was bad enough being on board one of Cochrane's ships, without riding Cochrane's roads or sleeping in Cochrane's citadel or taking Cochrane's hospitality. Sharpe went to the harbour and found his friend full of an understandable bitterness. 'The man broke his word,' Vivar said of Cochrane. 'He betrayed a truce.'

'You called him a devil, remember, so why be surprised when he behaves like one?'

'But he gave his word!' Vivar protested painfully. He had become a pale, grey figure, shrunken from the man Sharpe remembered, beaten down by a year's imprisonment and saddened by his failure. That failure, Vivar now knew, had done more than lose Spain's divinely ordained Empire, it had released the horror of war across a whole continent, perhaps a whole world. 'I thought when Cochrane wanted to meet me that he would talk terms of surrender! I thought I had won. I thought they would offer me the southern half of Chile and plead to keep the north. I was not going to accept, but I wanted to hear their terms. Instead they asked me to surrender Valdivia. For Bonaparte!'

On the eve of their departure Cochrane entertained Sharpe and Harper in the captured Niebla Fort where he laughingly recounted how the government in Santiago was begging him to send Valdivia's captured treasury north, but Cochrane was pleading time to count the coins before he released them. The truth was that he was holding the treasury against the arrival of his new master. 'Bonaparte knows you can't fight wars without cash.'

'How long before he gets here?' Sharpe asked.

'A month? No more than six weeks. Then, my dear Sharpe, we shall set this world ablaze!'

Cochrane had already returned Louisa's money to Vivar, now he insisted on Sharpe and Harper taking a share of the plunder. He filled two sea chests with coins that he ordered carried down to the wharf. It was cold. Snow flurries whirled over the blazing torches that lit the quay and a strip of black water. Cochrane, caped in a naval cloak, shivered. 'Why don't you stay here, Sharpe? March north with me! We'll become rich!'

'I'm a farmer, not a soldier.'

'At least you're not a lawyer.' Cochrane gave Sharpe a bear-hug of farewell. 'No hard feelings?'

'You're a devil, my Lord.'

Cochrane laughed at the compliment. 'Give General Vivar my apologies. I suppose he'll never forgive me?'

'I fear not, my Lord.'

'So be it.' Cochrane hugged Harper. 'Go safe home. Fair winds to you both.'

They sailed in the dawn, beating south against a cold sea and a freezing wind. They were travelling in a brig that was carrying hides to London. She made heavy weather of Cape Horn, but at last began to beat her way north.

Vivar brooded. He was a wise man, yet his understanding could not encompass a man who would break his word. 'Is the world changing so much?' he asked Sharpe.

'Yes,' Sharpe said bleakly. 'The war changed it.'

'So that results justify methods?'

'Yes.'

Vivar, cloaked and scarved against the bitter sea wind,

paced the brig's small poop. 'Then it's not a world I want a part of.'

Sharpe feared his friend was contemplating suicide. 'You have a wife and children!'

Vivar smiled and shook his head. 'Not that, Sharpe. I mean that I shall retire from service. I shall go to Orense and look after my estates. I, at least, shall be honourable. I will read, work, pray, and watch the war from a distance.'

And there would be war, Sharpe was certain of that. Europe would not stand idle while the Ogre ravaged the Americas. Sharpe imagined the troops sailing from Portsmouth and Plymouth, travelling across a world to catch Bonaparte one last time. Only this time, he supposed, they would hang the Emperor, because Bonaparte would have caused one mischief too many.

The weather was becoming warmer as the ship sailed north, but just when Sharpe was beginning to count the days until they reached home, a series of vicious westerly gales beat the brig hard towards the east. She shortened sail, battened her hatches, and clawed against the weather's spitefulness. For six days and nights the gales came, one after the other, until Sharpe began to believe that some malevolent spirit was intentionally keeping him from ever seeing Lucille again.

Then, after a sixth night of storm, the weather gentled and the ship wore onto a new tack. Clothes and bedding were brought up to dry on lines rigged between the masts. The Captain of the brig, an elderly and courteous Chilean, came to Sharpe. 'I don't know if any of you gentlemen are interested, sir, but we'll not be far from St Helena. We don't need to put in there, our supplies are plentiful, but if you want to see the place, sir?'

Sharpe suspected that the Chilean wanted to see St Helena for himself, or rather he wanted to discover whether Lord Cochrane's conspiracy had worked, and so Sharpe sought out Vivar and tentatively suggested the visit. He half expected Vivar to be adamantly opposed to any such exploration, but to Sharpe's surprise Vivar was as eager as the brig's Captain. 'I'd like to know what happened,' Vivar explained his interest. 'The worst thing about being on board a ship is that you never know what's happening in the world. Maybe Cochrane failed? That's something worth praying for.'

'He's not used to failure,' Sharpe observed.

'Maybe no one has prayed hard enough. My God, Sharpe, but I've been praying these past few weeks.'

The brig put into the harbour at Jamestown three days later. It was a hot day. The Captain ordered a boat lowered, then accompanied Vivar, Sharpe and Harper towards the small town that was hardly more than a row of houses above a stone quay. The hills, green and lush, climbed to the cloudy summits. A semaphore station stood with drooping arms at the foot of the road where Sharpe had climbed to meet a defeated Emperor.

The brig's longboat landed them at the water steps where a very young Lieutenant waited to receive them. It was the same young officer who had greeted Sharpe's first arrival on the island. 'It's Colonel Sharpe, isn't it, sir?' The Lieutenant seemed pleased to see Sharpe again.

'Yes.' Sharpe could not remember this boy's name, and he felt guilty. Napoleon never forgot a soldier's name. Soon, no doubt, the Emperor would be welcoming his veterans to Chile by name, but for the life of him, Sharpe could not recall this one soldier's name. 'I'm sorry,' Sharpe said. 'I don't remember your . . .'

'Lieutenant Roland Hardacre, sir. The same name as my father.'

'Of course,' Sharpe said. 'You remember Mister Harper? And this is General Vivar of the Spanish Army.'

'Sir!' Hardacre offered Vivar a smart salute.

'We came here, Lieutenant,' Vivar said, 'to discover what happened when the *O'Higgins* called here.'

'The *O'Higgins*?' Hardacre frowned as he tried to recall the particular ship, then his face cleared. 'Ah, yes! Our first visitor from the Chilean navy! She called here a month ago.' He shrugged, as though he could recall nothing significant in the *O'Higgins*'s visit. 'She reprovisioned, sir, then sailed away. To be honest none of us were very sure why she came this far. There can hardly be any Chilean interests in this part of the world.'

Sharpe felt an immense relief. Hardacre had treated the query very casually, which suggested to Sharpe that nothing important could have occurred during the Chileans' visit. 'So Bonaparte's at Longwood still?' Sharpe asked.

'At Longwood, sir?' Hardacre repeated the question, but very hesitantly, and this time Sharpe knew something was wrong. The Lieutenant blushed, then frowned. 'You haven't heard, sir?'

'Heard? Heard what?'

'The Emperor's dead, sir. He died last month. He's buried in the hills. The grave isn't far from the house. I'm sure if you'd like to visit the grave we can find some mules. Not that there's much to see there. Some people like to visit the house and take a keepsake.'

Sharpe could say nothing. He was not sure he had heard right or, if he had, that such news could be true. Napoleon, dead? He touched the locket about his neck, suddenly glad that he possessed it.

Harper crossed himself.

Vivar, whose prayer had come true, also crossed himself. 'How did he die, Lieutenant?'

'The doctors said it was a cancerous ulcer, sir.'

'It sounds painful,' Vivar said. He gazed up into the hills, to where a mist clung to the high green slopes. 'Poor man. To die so far from home.'

'Would you like to visit the grave, sir?' Hardacre asked.

'I would,' Vivar said.

'And me,' Harper added.

'But not me,' Sharpe said, 'not me.'

Vivar, Harper and the brig's Captain rode mules up into the hills to see the plain grave where an Emperor lay buried. Sharpe waited on the quay. The wind blew fresh from the south and an Emperor was dead, his mischief stilled for ever. Sharpe wanted to laugh, for it had all been for nothing, for absolutely nothing, and nothing had changed despite the banging of guns and the clangour of swords, but even that did not matter, for he was full of happiness, and he was at peace, and he was going home. For good and for ever, he was going home.

HISTORICAL NOTE

Thomas, Lord Cochrane, 10th Earl of Dundonald, was an extraordinary and eccentric figure; a radical politician as well as one of the greatest naval commanders of the early nineteenth century. After a brilliant career in the Royal Navy, and an ignominious one in the House of Commons, he was expelled from both institutions after being convicted of a stock fraud in 1814. There is some evidence that the case against him was rigged, but Cochrane was never a man to behave sensibly when lawyers were arrayed against him, and so he went down to defeat and imprisonment. He escaped from prison (of course) and after a series of adventures, became Admiral of the Chilean Navy in that country's war of independence against Spain. He eventually fell out with Bernardo O'Higgins, but not before he had scoured the Spanish Navy from the Pacific coast of South America, effectively making independence a reality for both Chile and Peru.

Probably the most astonishing victory of the many he gained in that war was his attack on Valdivia, which occurred much as described in these pages. It was a stunning victory which destroyed the last vestige of Spanish power in Chile.

After Valdivia Cochrane took himself off to become an Admiral in the Brazilian Navy's struggle against the Portuguese, before transferring his flag to the Greek Navy in that country's fight for independence against the Turks. Restored to grace in his homeland, he was reinstated in the Royal Navy in the 1830s and was bitterly disappointed not to be given command of a fleet in the Crimean War, by which time he was over eighty years old. *Cochrane* by Donald Thomas (André Deutsch, 1978) is a most readable biography of this extraordinary man, and I am indebted to Donald Thomas's book for the delicious account of how Cochrane was vicariously ejected from the Order of the Bath in a sinister midnight ceremony in Westminster Abbey.

I am also indebted to Donald Thomas for the extraordinary story of how Cochrane plotted to bring Napoleon to Valdivia and thus begin a campaign for a United States of South America. The plot was so far advanced that, following the capture of Valdivia, Cochrane did indeed send a rescue ship to St Helena. When Lieutenant Colonel Charles reached the island he found Napoleon in his last illness, and so abandoned the attempt to free the Emperor. What might have occurred had Bonaparte lived, and had Cochrane rescued him, remains one of the great tantalizations of history.

But Bonaparte was dead, probably poisoned by French Royalists who feared his return to France. He remained in his grave on St Helena until 1840 when his body was returned to France to be interred in the domed church of Les Invalides in Paris. Sharpe also returned to France, and Harper to Ireland, where, so far as I know, they lived happily ever after.